COMMUTERS

COMMUTERS

A Novel

EMILY GRAY TEDROWE

HARPER  PERENNIAL

NEW YORK • LONDON • TORONTO • SYDNEY • NEW DELHI • AUCKLAND

HARPER ● PERENNIAL

FIRST EDITION

Library of Congress Cataloging-in-Publication Data

Tedrowe, Emily Gray.
      Commuters : a novel / Emily Gray Tedrowe.—1st ed.
         p. cm.
      ISBN 978-0-06-185947-2
   1.   Upper   class   families—Fiction. 2.   Older   people—Fiction.
3. Marriage—Fiction. 4. New York (State)—Fiction. I. Title.
   PS3620.E4354C66 2010

---

10 11 12 13 14   OV/RRD   10 9 8 7 6 5 4 3 2 1

To my parents

Part I

One

WINNIE

It was a small-town June wedding, and the bride was seventy-eight.

From the church balcony where she sat alone, Winnie could see how it all looked, without her: rows and rows of dark wood pews, the flutter and ripple of the guests who filled them, twin thumb-sized bursts of yellow and white gladiolas set before the altar. She was supposed to be downstairs, in a small lounge off the vestibule; it was the place young children were rushed to when their fussing threatened to interrupt the service. She should have been admiring herself in the mirror, in this tea-length wedding gown of cream silk; she should have been conserving energy. But her face was as fixed as it would ever be, and she couldn't rest anymore.

It seemed there was something she needed to know, something she could only discover from this vantage point, so Winifred Easton McClelland—soon to be Trevis—had slowly climbed the stone stairs and found her way to a front-row seat, above the place where the ceremony was about to begin.

Sixty years ago, she had stood in the foyer of this same church, in an itchy, off-the-rack suit. It was a modest Wednesday morning wedding; it matched everything about marrying steady, quiet, reliable George, her first husband. Winnie's father had been uncharacteristically distant and preoccupied, on that windy November day, as they waited together for their musical cue. But he had a lot on his mind, as Hartfield's station manager. *Those trains don't run themselves*, he used to say. Or was he worried about what this was costing him? She had tried to find something they could talk about, together in the chilly hall.

"You don't have to," her father had said abruptly, staring at a spot above her head. "A wife doesn't, I mean. Every night. Even if *he* wants to."

Well. Winnie now felt a slow flush of heat rise within her, right there in the First Presbyterian balcony. No one was around to give her such advice now, nor did she need it. She thought of Jerry Trevis, her Jerry, and the way he would touch her—the anticipation was part of the pleasure. She knew enough from their few evenings alone together, to guess how their bodies would join and respond to each other: with a lively ease, with recognition. No, she wasn't at all the same bride that she had been, on the day her father gave his wedding-night counsel.

Is that why she was sitting all the way up here, alone? Winnie wondered what she could discover, given a clear line of sight and a moment's reflection. What was different, what had changed, in the years between that first wedding and today.

The shoes, for one thing—or her ability to choose them. Winnie raised one foot and sighed, studying the compromise heel, which was a good inch and a half lower than that impossibly flimsy pair in which she had teetered for twenty minutes at Nordstrom, even as she knew what her daughter would make her buy instead: something expensive, subdued, sturdy. *Old-lady shoes. On my wedding day.*

Nor did she have illusions about the sentimentality of this occasion, those unnecessary details that probably most of the guests— and some from her own family, even—would see as trivial or self-indulgent. Winnie didn't need all this: the ring, the dress (but oh, she loved how she looked in this dress), the lavish reception to come. She knew how it looked. Winnie's social circle was composed mostly of other long-time widows, and there was a history of light jokes about the phenomenon of two older people coming together late in life. She knew all the usual arrangements, all the wink-and-nudge euphemisms—those "companions" or "special friends." Why bother with anything formal, anything official?

But when a man like Jerry Trevis said he wanted to get married, he meant *married*. He hadn't moved to tiny Hartfield from Chicago for anything else. And there was this; Winnie ran her palm across the smooth surface of her dress. The truth was, she wanted this day too—the pomp and show of it, the public display. She had married once because it was a good match, mostly for her parents and his; that was how things were done, and she hadn't argued with it. But now she found herself about to do something that felt like the first thing she'd ever done on her own. And maybe that called for a lot of witnesses, the gratuitous flowers, a tiered and too-sweet cake.

She was marrying a man for the delicious and wicked and simple reason that she wanted to.

Not that everyone saw it that way. Earlier in the day, Winnie and Jerry had posed together for a photograph on the sloping lawn in front of the church, next to the welcome signboard where their own names were spelled out in white plastic letters, below today's date. (Above that, for the morning wedding, another couple's names were listed, which only slightly ruined the effect.) For the occasion, Winnie had agreed to be interviewed by a reporter from the local paper—she often was, a frequent obligation, part of her role as the daughter of what many considered to be the town's founder, the man who had linked little Hartfield to New York City. Dutifully, she gave her quotes when asked, and had learned not to argue with young people's fascination with the past—especially those awful railroad aficionados. Relentless. But she had hoped for more, this time. She wanted to explain what it was like, meeting Jerry just three months ago. How she had never expected to be in love again, and what it took to upend your placid and settled life: the one you led with dignity, the one people expected of you.

"At times, what I feel is closer to regret than anything else," Winnie had told the reporter. "Maybe that's inevitable. After all, most of my life will have been spent without Jerry, and getting married now keeps bringing that to mind. So then all this happiness actually—"

"Yes," the polite reporter said, nodding. Her pen hovered over the pad, unmoving. "So interesting. Can you tell me exactly how old Mr. Trevis is? And confirm your birth date?"

And so, little by little, there on the soft church lawn, Winnie discovered the reporter's agenda: a fluff piece, a throwaway. Something to warm the heart. She and Jerry were meant to be a symbol—of hope springing eternal, and all that. How could it be otherwise? She and Jerry couldn't be themselves; they had to be much bigger than that. They were the *human interest*.

Below her, most of the guests had been seated by now, although there was the usual waving and rearranging of places as people called to each other and organized themselves. The front of the church, though, by the altar, was still empty. Jerry and the minister would enter from one of the side doors—if she saw that happen, Winnie thought, she'd really have to hustle down there. Still, she sat and watched.

That minister—a nice young man. About thirty-five, maybe forty. Nervous and a little overeager, he'd met with them a few weeks ago to discuss the order of the ceremony: what hymns, in which order, and who would do the readings. At one point, though, she couldn't understand what he was going on about—he was explaining something quite earnestly, with grave import. Finally she gathered that the minister was letting them know that the phrase "promise to obey" was now commonly omitted from the vows, and the various reasons, and so on. He seemed quite intent on the point. And he was a little disconcerted when Winnie couldn't help a short burst of laughter, Jerry's hand in hers. She understood the changing politics that made this seem necessary, to a younger person. But what did this minister think he was protecting her from? She had no qualms about promising to obey Jerry. In any case, so much of marriage was unspoken, was made up of two people striving for kindness and respect, in a countless series of actions and gestures, day in and day out. It was touching, the way the minister wanted to get these mere *words* right. Well, all right, she had told him. If it makes you feel more comfortable.

Footsteps, behind her: green-robed Helen Ryan came in silently and took the cloth cover off the wooden handles of the tower bells. If she was surprised to find the bride up here alone, she didn't show it.

"You've got a few minutes yet," Helen said, clicking on a small light and turning a page of music. "In fact, I believe there's a saying . . ."

Winnie smiled. "They can't start without me."

"Congratulations, by the way." Winnie started to thank her, but Helen went on. "We hear you're moving."

Winnie flinched. She had lived too long in a small town to pretend surprise at the way people heard things, before the ink was dry, almost. She could tell herself that she hadn't said anything to her family yet because of the rush and flurry of this wedding. Plus, it had all happened so fast, what she and Jerry had planned—what they had done, actually, as of yesterday morning. But the truth was that Winnie just hadn't been able to bring herself to explain the house to anyone, especially her daughter, Rachel, who lived in Hartfield too, and whose reaction would be . . . complicated.

As Helen began to send music from the organ pipes lodged in the church stone above, stately chords designed to warn any last-minute lingerers that they'd better hurry, Winnie searched the pews below. She knew she really ought to go downstairs, but she had to find Rachel first. She scanned the crowd, now a blurry mass, with no luck. Where was she? Where could she be? For a moment, not being able to see her daughter cut Winnie's breath short. But then her son-in-law's head gave it away: that thick white scar on his bald head caught the light. And so there was Rachel next to him, in a pale pink dress, her long limbs in their usual restless motion. And there were her girls, Winnie's grandchildren: sitting up straight and serious, those lovely girls. Winnie started to examine the tiny figures across the aisle—most of all, she wanted to catch a glimpse of Jerry's grandson, Avery, as she'd heard plenty: drugs, fights, dropping out of school. But when the guests grew quiet and expectant, she forgot all that. Jerry. He was there now, at the steps in front of the altar, with his dark suit and bristly white hair.

His gaze raked the crowd, and though it was hard to be sure, she thought he might be frowning. Jerry usually frowned when he stood for any length of time, the only outward sign of his chronic spinal pain. In Korea, in one particularly heavy firefight, an explosion had thrown Jerry from the bunker, breaking three vertebrae that never fully healed. But Winnie knew the details only partially; he angrily dismissed any references to his injury. She was sure that the pain was worse than he let on, even today, and this above all made her want to get the ceremony started.

The organ music swelled; the notes were wide open and strong. Winnie put a hand on the pew in front of her, fighting off a surge of exhaustion. It was suddenly unbearable to be this far from him. She watched Jerry and saw his gaze travel up slowly until he seemed to be looking right at her. He put a hand over his eyes, as if to shield them from the light. Winnie raised her own hand. *Yes, it's me. Here I am.*

Even though she was used to the way weakness could now suddenly overtake her, Winnie still hated it, and no more so than now. How would she manage those stairs? But now one lone portly figure was walking purposefully back down the aisle; it was Daniel, her son. She'd been found; she would be rescued. Helen let the hammers fly, their ancient handles rattling in the wood. And though the time had come, Winnie remained where she was, waiting.

Something was growing inside her, a thought should have been taboo to a mother, to anyone who had loved and raised up children—but it was a thought as clear and true as a sharp intake of breath.

Everything begins now.

Yes.

Her son Daniel's voice came from the stairwell; he was calling her name—no, not her name, he was calling for his mother, calling *Mom*. He would be up here any minute, to collect her, to walk her gently down the aisle. It would be her son's job this time, not her father's. Helen must have finished—the knocking of metal on wood was silent now, although one last full bar of music unfolded itself outside, across the June-green lawns of Hartfield's town square. And even though everything within her strained toward Jerry, Winnie held herself still.

Not yet, she thought, and then said it aloud. She wouldn't be given this kind of moment again, Winnie knew. Her life had arrayed itself before her, in offspring and friendships assembled below—in the surrounding hills and houses she'd known since childhood—and now it waited politely for her to reappear and change everything.

Oh, not just yet.

Two
RACHEL

"And now, it gives me great, great pleasure to introduce to you the bride and groom—" But the bandleader was drowned out by the room's sudden outburst of warm applause, and even a few hooting cheers, before he could finish with the phrase Rachel had been most curious to hear aloud: "—Mr. and Mrs. Jerome Trevis." She stood to the side of the Waugatuck Tennis Club's main dining room and watched her mother gaily cross the dance floor on Jerry's arm, a green disco spotlight swirling around them.

"Ladies and gentlemen, their first dance." A respectful hush fell across the crowd as the Moonlight Express Band swung easily into "Night and Day," and Winnie put her hand lightly on Jerry's upper arm, where the fabric of his suit was all bunched up.

Rachel Brigham was having trouble experiencing this moment, in which her nearly eighty-year-old mother danced with her new husband on their wedding day; all she could sense was the pressure of expectation from friends and neighbors throughout their small town, even those not invited. Was she supposed to cry? Smile? Both? Everyone Rachel had talked to, in the weeks leading up to this event, from the caterer's assistant to customers at the store to Lisa, her dental hygienist, had wanted to know *How does it feel?* With an airlock-tight gaze fixed on her, they would ask: What was it like for Rachel to see her mom fall in love again this late in life? Wasn't it unbelievably sweet and hopeful? Wasn't it a testament to the power of . . . something?

Maybe what they wanted was a little dirt. To have her express a fraction of dismay, some sense of loss about her father—dead now twelve years—or even for her to slip quickly into a knowing ridicule. After all, there *was* plenty that was ridiculous about all of this: the band, the arranged flowers, the cake, all produced for a couple whose combined age spanned a century and a half. More than once, Rachel had suffered pangs of embarrassment on her mother's behalf, while helping to plan this wedding that everyone in town had been talking about. Why couldn't Winnie have a small ceremony with Judge Greenberg, and then a lunch at La Finestra, for twenty, maybe thirty people? But one of her mother's best, and most infuriating, qualities was a blithe disregard for what other people would think. Most of the time, Rachel found this admirable, or wanted to.

She watched Winnie step tremulously, lightly, back and forth to the syrupy music, Jerry's big arms held stiffly around her.

Why were the most important things the hardest to say? The friends who wanted a glimpse at Rachel's emotions said nothing— asked nothing—about what had really changed for her. Nothing about the obvious fact of Jerry's money, and the sudden, immense difference between what her mother now had and what she herself did not. How could they, when Winnie and Rachel themselves had addressed it only through the most fleeting, joking comments. For example, what they imagined Jerry's high-powered daughter Annette must think of Hartfield's one hair salon, where men's cuts were still fourteen dollars, and women crowned with tinfoil took amiable turns under the chipped pink metal hood of the one ancient dryer.

Did they want her to admit that it had been a long, long time since a man had held her the way Jerry was holding her mother, out there on the dance floor? Well, she could do that. She'd be the first to do that, say how long it had been. As she stood there watching, Winnie tipped her head down slowly and knocked her forehead ever-so-softly against Jerry's chest; he reached under her chin and lifted her face, all while they kept dancing, so that when their eyes met again, he could say something to her without words: *Yes, I'm here. Yes, this is really happening.* Rachel held herself very, very still.

It had been such a long time.

One person, at least, wasn't struck dumb by the display of love out there on the dance floor. Her husband, Bob, was still talking over the music, straining to be heard by the rest of their table, where Danny, Rachel's brother, and his wife, Yi-Lun, were also seated. Bob's voice, ever since the accident, was louder than he seemed able to recognize without a nudge from Rachel. It was as calm and unflappable as ever, only *louder*.

"The eventual goal would be a book deal, of course, but my writing teacher seems to think that if I place the first chapter as a stand-alone piece in a magazine—"

Her mother laughed at something a friend called out from a nearby table. Rachel willed herself to be in the moment. Like in a yoga class.

"Right, and now I'm bringing in various other angles, like this whole industry of self-help experts that's sprung up in the past few years."

Isn't this writing itself basically a part of that? Rachel thought. Bob had started taking writing classes just after he was out of the hospital. The first one had been designed to reintegrate people into their lives after medical trauma—if Rachel remembered correctly, it had been called something like Writing to Heal. (There was one woman in the class who, week after week, practiced typing her name using the toes of one bare foot.) Rachel and Bob used to joke about some of these programs, like the one that had him solemnly repeat out loud statements like, "I accept that I am different. I accept that things have changed." But Bob had taken to writing with a fervor that surprised Rachel, and now he had joined a long-term workshop, at the local college, called Write Your Life.

"It won't just be about me," Bob went on, speaking to Danny and Yi-Lun. "I mean, the first part is—that's the hook, my experience, what it was like to wake up in the hospital three weeks after it happened."

"I'm holding out for René Russo," Rachel interrupted, with her back still to the table. "You know that actress? She can play me in the movie version."

There was a blessed pause, and a polite murmured response from someone. Rachel could see both her daughters standing on the other side of the room, near one of the Trevis family tables. Melissa, as usual, was chattering intently to Lila, who steadily watched her grandmother. Rachel wished that Winnie had said something, anything, to Lila about having to miss her last diving meet of the year—well, it wasn't a meet, she knew, but an end-of-season celebratory "showcase" in which several teams would display all those twists, flips, and half-turns without pressure of official competition. Lila had simply shrugged when Rachel, apologetically, told her what the date of the wedding would be. And of course you couldn't expect Winnie to rearrange everything based on the Brighton Water League's Saturday schedule. Still, it would have been nice if Winnie had remembered, and said something. It was so unlike her.

Even though the silence behind her continued, Rachel was sure that her husband hadn't finished yet. Shouldn't she interrupt now? Turn and lay a hand on his arm, direct his attention to the way Winnie was twirling carefully to Cole Porter? The bride wasn't even fighting to look demure—no, she grinned up at Jerry with all the subtlety of a moony fifteen-year-old.

"The interesting thing is how the Internet factors in, how it can connect all the different groups, disseminate some of the cutting-edge research so much faster—in fact, I'm guest-blogging this week on this site called Skullcrack dot com—"

"Bob. We're up, I think." Rachel tapped him a little desperately on the arm. "Danny, go cut in and get Mom. Their song's almost over."

"That's great," Danny said, standing up. "Listen, an old buddy of mine from college is doing something at Random House—or maybe it's the other one. Let me know if you want me to shoot him an e-mail, put you two together."

Rachel shot a look at Danny and managed to pull Bob out onto the dance floor.

"All *right*, Ray," Bob said. "I'm coming." They watched Danny smoothly take over from Jerry, who stepped back and stood awkwardly alone on the dance floor. At once, Rachel realized her mistake and dropped Bob's hands.

And then Winnie stopped dancing too. "Oh, why not one more with my new husband," she said lightly, but with a frown at both of her children.

"It's okay, Mom," Rachel said. "Jerry, how clumsy of me. May I have this dance?" The five of them were now standing in an uncertain huddle in the middle of the room. And now someone would have to go sit down again—with everyone watching. Where on earth was Annette, Jerry's daughter? Rachel scanned the tables in vain, as the lead singer built to a croon.

"Bob, you should probably—" But he had already left and was crossing the floor alone, and that slight drag of his left foot, a split-second hitch she rarely noticed anymore, was suddenly much more apparent. Rachel thought he might leave the room altogether—he was heading in the opposite direction from their table—but then she saw him stop in front of their girls, confer for a moment, and lead Lila by the hand onto the dance floor. When they began a father-daughter waltz, Rachel heard murmurs as the room warmed with approval.

"No rest for the weary," Jerry said. "You might have taken pity on an old man." Despite this, he swung her around firmly and precisely, in the style of someone who has put in considerable time at dances. Jerry was not, Rachel realized, one to let a woman lead.

"I wouldn't have missed it," she said, trying to keep up. She and Bob would have been merely swaying back and forth.

"I want you to know that your mother will be very well taken care of," Jerry said.

"Oh," Rachel said, surprised and touched at this stiff and formal speech. "I'm so happy for you both. It's wonderful how much you care for her—I mean," Rachel quickly corrected herself, "How much you love her." *For God's sake*, she told herself. *Quit being so prim.*

"Yes," Jerry said, as if this was beside the point. "The mutual funds are a little flat this year; I'll be making some changes there.

But I've set up two accounts for her at a decent rate. And then this business with the trust—well, I'll be meeting with Jack Moynihan next week, so it all should—"

"That's all fine, Jerry. Really." Rachel glanced around. "Maybe Danny would be the better person to—"

"I've already spoken to your brother. But he lives in San Francisco. You're here."

"That's true," Rachel said. "How does Annette . . ." She trailed off.

"I'll handle Annette," Jerry said. "She'll come around—I know she will. She's just had a tough time at work recently. She and the board—never mind. You just leave that to me, all right?"

"All right," Rachel said, oddly relieved in the face of Jerry's brusque, all-business manner. Sometimes she forgot he *had* been all business, for many years, as the founder of two separate Chicago companies—what were they, something to do with manufacturing—both built from scratch and sold at incredible profit. Now he technically presided over a corporation that had tripled those earlier efforts—TrevisCorp. Annette was apparently CEO—or CFO. Or COO? Rachel had seen but not read the copies of the industry magazines Winnie proudly displayed, where Jerry or his Midwestern empire had been lavishly profiled, accompanied by photos of a glowering, younger Jerry Trevis. But in the three months since he had met and now married her mother—shocking, that three months—her own interactions with this gruff man had consisted of a couple of exhausting meals where everyone tried very hard to make small talk. Now she got a glimpse of how he must have been during those boom years, when he had been her age.

Still, she strained to find Annette, to try to gauge her expression during this interminable song. Wouldn't she like to cut in to dance with her father? There was the head Trevis table, full of relatives she had met yesterday but couldn't keep straight, and no Annette in sight. She couldn't still be at the bar, where Rachel had glimpsed her last. However, there was Annette's son, Avery, sitting right next to Melissa, and he seemed to be nodding politely enough while Mel pointed something or somebody out. Rachel pushed back at Jerry, who was attempting to turn her around. She wanted to keep an eye on this kid Avery, especially with what she'd heard about him from Winnie. Hardly a kid—a young man, tall and wiry and slouching in an expensive-looking jacket and tie. He had that artfully spiky hair all these guys wore, and it was the pure blond color that Annette's must have been before she began all that expensive tinting and frosting. Those sharp good looks—and that calm air of solitude. That was it: Avery didn't seem fidgety or bored or sarcastic—any of those usual, familiar teenage poses. Instead he looked perfectly at ease sitting by himself, scanning the crowd. Trouble. Rachel felt a surge of motherly sympathy for Annette.

"There's something else," Jerry said, and he was so intent on speaking that he continued to steer Rachel through the end of the song and right into the next one. "It's not my place to say, but that's never stopped me before. And I say it's a damn shame what you've been through, with—" Here Jerry tilted his head toward the place where Bob had been dancing.

"Yes, it's been a rough few years." Her standard reply. "But we're lucky, of course."

"No, I wouldn't say so. And I'm not talking about his accident. I'm talking about his job."

Rachel sucked in her breath. "Well. The pace at the firm . . . it got to be too much, afterward. The strain . . ."

"You don't have to explain."

"It's supposed to help, all the writing. It's good for him, I guess. For now, at least, while he's on leave." Rachel was jostled by a couple dancing nearby. The floor was crowded now, though her mother and brother had left.

"He's writing his autobiography? At his age?"

"Well, it's more like . . . a kind of therapy." She petered out, suddenly exhausted. "It's supposed to help him deal with the whole— you know—memory thing."

"In my opinion, a man attends to his family's needs and not to his own literary"—here Jerry waggled his big head back and forth—"whims."

Rachel sighed. She knew she should feel offended, but Jerry's blunt assessment of the situation soothed her. Their own friends mostly danced around the subject.

Jerry went on. "And I think now that he's back on his feet, things should change. When are you moving home?"

"Technically," Rachel said, "we are home."

Jerry snorted. "You know what I mean."

"I sure do," she said, matching his tone note for note, and startling herself. Jerry pulled back to get a better look at her, pleased. For a second, she basked in their sudden shared skepticism, a little secret exchanged in public, right there on the dance floor.

They were still marching in circles to "Strangers in the Night." Rachel saw that most of the tables were beginning to be served their salad, and she hoped Jerry might allow them to sit down soon. She was starving, and of course the dinner would be excellent—

Winnie and she had pored over faxed menus and finally decided on the roast beef and a chicken Kiev, which was Waugatuck's specialty.

"I've asked him plenty of questions about his head," Jerry said, determined to continue. "And he seems all up to snuff."

"Actually the doctors say—"

"I'm no medical expert, but seems to me he's healthy enough, now. Dodged a bullet, is what I'd say."

"Maybe," Rachel said. "But he doesn't remember much, in any case. The accident, the surgeries—nothing. It's all a blank."

"You mean he doesn't know how he—"

"It's just gone, is all," Rachel said. "Or that's what they tell me." Listening to this old man, a near stranger, voice every one of her own doubts was unfolding a surprising, slow warmth inside her, the sense of . . . *finally!*

"Let me get this straight," Jerry said. Rachel noticed his breathing was a bit labored. "Your husband quit his job, for all intents and purposes . . . to write a whole book about a day he can't even remember?"

Rachel stifled a smile. *Not bad*, she thought. There were two tiny medical bandages taped to the side of his head, near his ear. "It's your wedding day," she said. "Let's just enjoy it."

"One last. Thing," huffed Jerry. They had slowed considerably, although the song was now a Motown classic, designed to get the floor jumping. "The house."

"Hmm?" Surely the entrées would be out by now.

"Your mother won't want to do anything substantial. She has a notion it will bother me. But I told her you'd help—you ladies can fix it up all you want. Encourage her. Good for her."

"The house?" Rachel followed Jerry's stiff gait off the dance floor. She waved back—*hi there! Just one second!*—distracted, to several friends who beckoned. "What are you talking about?"

"Scotch and soda," Jerry said, and sat heavily. Not his table, but close enough. "Someone move my drink?"

"Jerry," Rachel said, "What house?" Though a sharp little awareness now bloomed inside her. The time she'd teased her mother about having to clear out closet space, make room for a man's things, in her tidy one-bedroom apartment. The way Winnie, hemming and hawing, avoided her eyes.

"Fifty Greenham, of course," Jerry said. He squinted up at her, annoyed. "Closed yesterday. Is that the waiter?"

She couldn't have.

Rachel stumbled through a conversation with Marilyn French, who'd played the piano during cocktail hour, and excused herself suddenly, rudely. Then she was caught by Sandy Hinton, who fretted lightly in the form of a joke that no one from Hand Me Down, the children's clothes consignment store where Rachel worked, had called her back yet about a double stroller, hardly used. If they weren't interested, surely she could find . . . Rachel promised to pick it up on Monday, and broke away. Her cheeks were burning. *No. She couldn't have—Jerry had it all wrong.* Not that business-mogul Jerry could make a mistake about something this substantial. Not about *that* property—the one everyone in Hartfield talked about, a true 1920s Tudor right on Greenham Avenue, a stately oak-lined street that arched high above the center of town. Rachel shook her head, dumbfounded. A part of her had to admire the sheer craziness of this endeavor. He bought that place? For two eighty-year-olds to live in? It must be falling down, now nothing but the shell of a once-grand property—a structure people slowed down to point out as one of Hartfield's eccentric oddities.

"My God, Mom," Rachel muttered to herself, in the hallway leading to the restrooms. She leaned back against the wall. *Well, we might need a little more room*, she remembered now, was what Winnie had said, that afternoon, turned away and fussing with some grocery bags. Rachel had assumed she meant a two-bedroom condo! So Winnie had known, even then. Why hadn't she said anything?

But Rachel knew why, and she closed her eyes. It was cooler downstairs, quiet. Her heels sank into the thick, salmon-colored carpet, and she could feel the grainy pattern of the metallic toile wallpaper against her bare shoulders. On the one hand, she had sympathy for her mother's position. Rachel's own move, last year, certainly made it hard, if not impossibly awkward, for anyone to raise the subject of Hartfield real estate in her presence.

Melissa called it "the switcheroo," and Winnie had been one of its biggest supporters.

"*Please*." She'd scowled when Rachel once ventured fears about, well, what people would think.

And there certainly hadn't been anything on the market, anything close to what they would need or could afford, without changing the girls' school midyear. Neither Lila nor Mel had protested once the plan was explained to them—though probably this wasn't healthy—and Bob was just relieved, happy to find a solution, a way of accepting that leave of absence . . . and so that left Rachel. She had signed on, full of misgiving, and so they had moved. If you could call it that, when their address, 144 Locust Drive, didn't even change.

Their house's attached two-bedroom rental unit had intimidated Bob when they were first shown the property, that summer before

Lila was born. He hadn't liked the idea of being a landlord, hadn't liked the word itself, and had visions of endless tenant disputes, late-night phone calls about plumbing problems. But both Rachel and their Realtor, Billie, had convinced him otherwise, Rachel so deeply in love with the square-sided painted-white brick house on Locust that she felt she would happily plunge any stopped-up toilet herself, even seven months pregnant. And even Bob would admit that every-thing had gone smoothly. Billie always took care of finding the right people, and the renters had been a series of quiet young couples on the first leg of their exodus from Manhattan, a lot like Rachel and Bob had been. Mostly, they got pregnant and then moved out. Meanwhile, Rachel and Bob—and later Lila and Melissa—paid hardly any attention to that part of the house, or the round pale stones paving a discreet path around to the separate side entrance.

Then, last year, several factors aligned all at once, like tumblers in a lock clicking into place. Once it became clear that Bob was struggling to keep up, the partners at his firm offered a year's leave at half pay—or demanded one. (It was never made clear to Rachel which.) The Copenhavers, who had rented for almost three years, decided to move to Boston and open a health-food store, and gave only one month's notice. And Billie, when Rachel called in a panic, said that she might have one prospect, a single banker who trav-eled a lot . . . but that he wanted something bigger than their unit. Something much bigger.

So the plan was hatched: keep the house, lease the main part, live in the smaller unit. For a while, until Bob got back on his feet. It wasn't *unheard of*, Billie assured them, but this didn't really hold true for Rachel. In a matter of weeks, the Brighams went from four bedrooms to two, from three full baths to one and a half, from the center of their home to its shoved-off-to-the-side appendage. Or at least that's how Rachel felt, especially on the nights where she would lie awake and listen to Vikram Desai, a perfectly pleasant man, a total stranger, move around her kitchen. She'd follow his footsteps across the cream-colored tiles she'd chosen six years ago, up the stairs where the girls posed for Christmas photos, and into what used to be her bedroom. Hers and Bob's, that is.

Here in the Waugatuck hallway, little by little Rachel became aware of a sound—not the music and voices at the reception upstairs, but from behind her. Behind the wall, inside the ladies' room. A high-pitched wail that came and went. Gasps, then a pause. Without thinking, she went to the door and pulled it open.

Annette, slumped on a low overstuffed stool in front of the dressing table mirror, raised her head. Another woman stood nearby, hovering anxiously. She shot a distressed look at Rachel.

"Oh, perfect," Annette said loudly, waving an arm. Her makeup was smeared and her eyes raw. "Un-fucking-believable."

"Excuse me," Rachel said, taken aback by the slap of anger. She turned to leave.

"Don't you run away now! You came to find me, well—here I am. You want to drag me back upstairs to that whole— Can you believe this?" Annette turned to her friend, a shorter woman in a gray silk suit, who was trying to hush her.

The friend nodded to Rachel, as if they shared an understanding, and then toward the door. "She's just a little upset," she said. "Probably it would be better if—"

"What *is* it with you people? Don't you have a single ounce of dignity? Do you really think I'm going to let my father get suckered into losing *everything* at the end of his life? He's worked damn hard for what he's made, and if you think I'm going to just stand around while you and your mother take what you—"

"Annette," the friend groaned. "Don't."

"—please . . . Do you *know* what my lawyer says? You have no idea what you've gotten yourself into."

"Well, I'm sorry you feel this way," Rachel said. "And to tell you the truth—"

She stopped, confused. Though she'd only spoken with Annette briefly, once or twice before, Rachel could tell that Jerry's daughter was none too pleased about this marriage. But she'd had no idea that Annette was this furious. And all along, Rachel had somehow assumed that Annette's objections to the marriage were her own—that everything about this gaudy spectacle, this wedding, was unseemly and unnecessary, a bit tacky and more than a little embarrassing. But now, underneath Annette's wine-soaked vehemence, Rachel heard something else: fear. The kind of sharp, blinding fear that springs from loss.

"It must be hard," she said. "With his moving here. But I think—"

"This all makes me sick," Annette moaned, and she really did look ill—white in the corners of her mouth, and trembling. "Sitting up there, smiling while you all wink at each other and count your lucky stars that my father has decided to act like a fool. Like an *idiot*. I won't let you do this to him. His reputation—what this would have done to my mother—" She choked on a sob.

"Annette," Rachel began. She might have taken a step closer.

"Don't touch me!" Annette shrieked. "I'm sorry—I'm sorry," she said to the friend, suddenly conciliatory. "I'll get it together in a minute. I just won't be *pitied*. Not by her."

Rachel went quickly past them into the next room. As she expected, there was a stack of small plastic cups on a shelf above the sinks. She filled one, hands shaking.

Back in the dressing room, Rachel set the water down in front of Annette and pulled up a stool, close enough to see the dots of mascara beaded along the other woman's lower eyelashes.

"Now you listen to me. That is *my mother* up there, and it's her wedding day, and I won't have you making a drunken scene to ruin even *one minute* of it for her. Do you hear me?" Despite the heat of the moment, Rachel recognized her own tone immediately: it was the one she used when one of the girls had really crossed the line.

"For the record—not that it matters—I had no idea Jerry had bought a house. That house." Annette started to interrupt, but Rachel barreled ahead. The friend was observing this with a small, impressed smile. "Do I think it's insane, at their age? Yes. Will I try to talk her out of it? You bet. But that's not for tonight. Tonight we are *celebrating*. You are going to fix your face and we are going to get upstairs and smile and clap and pose for the photographer and do nothing but talk about how *wonderful* it all is, the fact that it's possible for two people to find each other this late in life. We're going to say all of the things everyone wants to hear. And we're going to toast my mother and your father—no, not you. You've had enough to drink." Rachel stood and tugged her dress back into place. "But the rest of us are going to raise a glass and I'm finally going to eat some roast beef—and Annette? You are going to *adore* the cake, so perhaps this lovely friend of yours will make sure you sit down to a nice fat slice."

She put a hand on the ladies'-room doorknob and paused, struggling for kinder words. "It's strawberry," she informed the other two women, both silent and staring at her. "With a fondant icing."

Three
AVERY

The food had been so fucking bad he thought it might have been a joke. Seriously. It was hard to comprehend the piece of chicken that had shown up on his plate—poor, poor chicken—stretched out and pounded flat and curled up halfway around a still-frozen shard of butter that had a small piece of red paper stuck to it. As if to compensate for the moisture-less meat, its accompanying puddle of mashed . . . what was it? . . . cauliflower had come ringed with a thin, grayish water—sauce? Dish soap? Sweat from a line cook's greasy forehead? Avery dragged a fork slowly through the mess, amazed. Strange, though, how all these people were chewing and smiling and chatting in ordinary tones over these plates of misery. An urge to burst out laughing bubbled up in him, but Avery contented himself instead with minute examinations of the bleached-out celery salad—what was this herb, for example, tiny flakes of which clung to the wilted vegetable with admirable tenacity even as he tried to scrape some off with a fingernail. Rosemary? No smell whatsoever. An ashy taste, kind of like licking a match head.

But by now at least someone had cleared everything supposedly edible off the table, including the piece of cake that had appeared in front of Avery with one clear thumbprint deeply imprinted on its thick icing. White icing, of course. He realized that the entire meal, from the glass of champagne that sat in front of him, untouched, until its golden showers of bubbles dimmed to a dull stillness, to that entire chicken/dishwater plate to the dessert finale, had been white, or beige, or somewhere in between.

Actually, Avery was glad. Far better for him to encounter all the glorious misery of a truly bad meal, in which he could lose himself, than to suffer through a decent dinner where he would be forced to eat boring bites of unmemorable, unexceptional food with nothing then to distract him from the country-club chatter that swirled all around his grandfather's big night. And the food, its excellent awfulness, kept him parked in this same seat all evening, fascinated—kept him, that is, from walking by the bar. Which wasn't a bar at all, of course, but two long rectangular folding tables set up in a side room just off the dance floor. Earlier, he'd been by just once, just to look—quickly, sidelong—at the rows of square-sided bottles, each slippery now from the harried bartenders' wet hands, lined up casually next to fanned-out stacks of little cocktail napkins and bowls of pimento olives and those snotty little onions that came three on a stick when you asked for it that way. But this wasn't a martini crowd—no, the big draw here was white wine, dozens of bottles bobbing in plastic tubs on the floor behind the long table swathed in starchy cream-and-green polyester cloths. Cheap, thick glasses were set out upside down, the way they never should be, gathering condensation inside their bowls and a musty smell. A few men were asking for rocks drinks, in lowballs that had a nice pebbly bottom. In the first hour of the reception, Avery had allowed himself to skate a thumb across one, furtively. Then he'd snatched his hand back.

He'd agreed to go dry, completely, even though drinking had never been the problem—not the main problem, anyway. But here was the truth: he wasn't sure how long he'd be staying that way. He just hadn't decided that, yet.

Avery loosened his tie one more centimeter, put a foot up on the abandoned chair next to him, and grinned back at his stepfather, Rich, making his way toward him. Across the empty dance floor, Rich pretended to do a little soft-shoe shuffle. At least he seemed to be enjoying himself, although he usually did, even when Annette was nowhere to be found, as had been the case for much of the reception, now that Avery thought about it. It was a running family joke that Avery took after Rich in that way: easygoing, handy with a joke, as opposed to Annette's tightly wound energy, or whatever his long-gone "real" father must be like. So this had created a surprising ally for Avery, in the past year and a half, all through Rehab Stint One and then College Take Two and then Live at Home/Look for a Job and then Rehab Redux: This Time We Mean Business. Rich was cool. He'd never tried to bully Avery, or guilt-trip him, or label himself an enabler, or all those other modes Annette cycled through. In fact, it had been Rich who had finally convinced Annette to allow Avery to make this move, last week, from Chicago to New York.

Actually, maybe he should thank Grandad. Without the old man's crazy, random decision to move here, of all places, Avery knew Rich and Annette would never have considered letting him come to Manhattan.

"Time to blow this joint," Rich said now, emphasizing his own dorkiness. "You need money for the train?"

"No, I'm good." Avery actually could have used some cash for the train, but at the moment he was just so thankful that Rich wasn't bugging him to go back to whatever hotel he and Annette were at, that this alone was worth it. They both paused to watch the band's drummer, his face flat and tired, lug a beaten black case across the empty dance floor, and whack it against a chair nearby. Rich neatly caught the chair before it toppled over, and the drummer banged his way out a side door, not looking back. Although the bride and groom had left at least an hour ago, more than a few of their geezer friends were still lingering at the tables—out later than you'd expect, Avery thought. What was it now, 8 PM?

"Mom in the car or something?"

"Ah. Well, your mom cut out a little early. She's over at the hotel now. She wanted me to see if you've changed your mind about staying the night . . . there's that brunch thing—and we don't fly out until three."

"That's okay."

"Well, consider my duty discharged," Rich said, with a little salute. Avery was so grateful for this, his stepfather's implicit trust. For not pushing it, or grilling him on—*who? where? what next?*—the exact circumstances of his patched-together New York life, which would be one week old tomorrow. It must be a guy thing, Avery thought. Or maybe Rich just knew the truth: that Avery himself didn't know much yet about how it all would go down, this move. Apartment, job, all that.

"So what's the deal with the husband? Cancer, or something?" Avery nodded at Bob Brigham, over by the foyer, talking loudly to a few of those older guys whose wives stood by, holding coats over their arms. Bob had his back to where he and Rich were sitting, and his cue-ball-smooth bald head was almost as wild as that twisting helix of a scar, pink and raised and lumpy, that ran down the back of his head and disappeared under his collar.

"Nope—took a bad fall, is what I heard. Guy's lucky, that's for sure." Rich jingled coins in his pocket but made no move to leave. Avery wondered if he was, in fact, in for a speech about safety and the bottom line.

"Jesus."

"That one daughter he has is a looker, huh?"

"Really?" Avery wrinkled his face. That irritating kid who'd latched on to him earlier, bugging him with questions about the tattoo on the back of his hand? *What was it of?* (Chinese dragon.) *Did it hurt? Did they use a big needle? Was his mom mad?* (No, yes, who knows?)

"You don't think? Well, I don't envy him. Going to be tough once all those boys start coming around."

Then Avery saw who Rich was talking about. Not the younger girl, her older sister. Avery saw both of them, trailing their mom, each with an armful of flower baskets culled from the tabletops. And yes, that taller one—with her waterfall of blonde hair and that skin, golden-tan and smooth as anything. He could see what Rich meant. How old was she? Sixteen? His new—what? Cousin. Stepcousin? Thinking along these lines made Avery feel perverted.

"So, listen. I don't want you to worry about her."

"Who?"

"Your *mother.* She'll get used to this—" Here Rich waved his hand vaguely at the dance floor, the Brigham family, the few remaining white-haired guests. "Stranger things have happened, in families."

"She's flipping out, huh?"

"Well. She has worked up quite a lather, but . . . let's all give it time. Settle into things. There were quite a few folks unhappy when *I* burst on the scene, if you recall."

"Nah," Avery said.

"In any case, I wanted to give you a heads-up about something." *Here it comes*, Avery thought. "This deal you made with your mom in order to move here, all the talks we've had—"

"I *know*, Rich." AA or NA, weekly calls to old shrink, careful transfer to new shrink, constant contact with home. One screwup and it was back to Chicago. Or worse.

"Yeah. So, about your grandfather—"

Avery got real quiet and stayed that way when Rich paused for his response.

"Now that you're both here in New York—I know, I know, it's the suburbs—and you're in the city, fine." Rich hustled to cut off Avery's first objection. "We think it's best if you train out for regular visits with Jerry. Check in on him—you know. And it'll be quality time for you guys. He won't be getting any younger."

"I already said I would. Every once in a while."

Rich shook his head pleasantly. "Regular visits. Meaning once a week."

"Once a *week*?" Avery almost fell off his chair. "So what happens if I can't?" *If I don't*, is what he thought, but he already knew the answer. They had him. He was out of that house, finally, but they still had him—and they knew it.

"Let me put it this way," Rich said, with a wry smile. "It would *behoove* you to follow through on this, for your sake. And your mom's. She'll talk to you more about it."

"Uh-huh." Avery couldn't help it: his inward, unreasonable reaction was a fierce, childish disappointment. Here he was, at last on his own, in New York City, and he was being forced to punch a time card with his *grandfather*.

"Oh, come on. That's not so much, is it? Bud?"

"Grandad's not going to know if I'm using, you know," Avery said flatly. "I mean, I doubt he'd even be able to tell if I was high. So if this is the grand plan to keep tabs on me—well, then you're fucked. And so is Mom."

Rich didn't answer for a minute. "Avery," he said, finally, and shook his head. Then his stepfather stood to go, and briefly rested a hand on the top of Avery's head. "Give a call soon."

New York so far had proved an immense disappointment, if Avery was willing to admit that to anyone. Or himself. He'd spent the past six days riding the subway, all the way up and down the 6 and 2 lines. If a stop looked appealing—Astor Place, for example, with its funky mosaic sign and the packs of skater-punk kids exiting en masse, plugged into iPods and jittering with energy—Avery would get off too, ready to roam. But then up from underground the first thing that he'd see would be some huge Starbucks. Or a Barnes and Noble. Or a Kmart—no shit! Astor Place had all three on one corner, and it all proved too much for Avery, skater kids notwithstanding. He'd turned right around and glumly re-descended. He hadn't come to New York-fucking-City for Kmart.

Central Park was okay. Loaded with hot moms pushing double strollers that were bigger than the crappy Honda he'd sold before coming out here. But the hot moms were too busy with the stroller occupants to pay any attention to Avery, wandering here and there, checking it all out, the passing scene. One afternoon some loud-talking woman stopped dead in her stilettos to size him up, and then went on to ask a series of questions he'd heard before and wasn't particularly interested in. She'd handed him a card—VIP TalentBooking something something—and strode away. Avery flipped the card around for a while and then stuck it, with a handful of change, into a raggedy coffee cup loosely held by the nodded-off bum sitting next to him on the bench. (Last time this happened he'd been waiting on line outside Schuba's Tavern, on Southport, and his friends' reactions had been ferocious and unremitting. They'd howled and yanked away the business card, everyone calling the agent's cell again and again, in between shots of whiskey, over the course of a long night. Poor guy. *Yeah, hi, this is Avery Trevis? I'd like to model your smallest nut huggers? And I'd like to shave my*—Give it back, Smitty! It's still my turn!)

Museums were another way to go, but after an hour or so in the new MoMA, Avery was still thinking about the twenty bucks it had cost to get in.

One afternoon he had joined the long lines to view where the World Trade Center had stood. People stood on a platform and shuffled respectfully past that canyon. There were long lists of names, boards with reprinted photos, flowers and notes twisted through the wire fence. There were vendors with makeshift carts full of merchandise—pins and baseball caps that said, 9/11, ALWAYS IN OUR HEARTS, under logos of flags or eagles. So many men were wearing official-looking NYPD or Fire Department T-shirts that at first Avery was moved, thinking they had all come to mourn lost comrades. But then he realized that these shirts, hats, were also for sale. He hadn't known it was—what?—legitimate to dress like a police officer if you weren't one.

He avoided the indie culture. He stayed clear of Tompkins Square Park, Avenues A through D, Orchard Street—anywhere he'd heard was DIY, was punk, was cool. He couldn't afford cool. He couldn't afford to start longing for that scene, the loners and artists and hackers and freaks that he'd torn himself away from in Wicker Park. He was exiled from cool, an alt-dot fugitive, at twenty years old. Avery knew it was a rehab cliché, and he wasn't even sure how entirely he bought it, that whole "change your friends" rule. But as of now, he was staying clear of the whole scene, just in case.

Only once had he broken this self-imposed restriction, and it had been yesterday afternoon. The memory goosed a shot of pure adrenaline through Avery now, still sitting alone at a table in the Waugatuck Tennis Club.

Thompson Street, below Houston. The screeching music drew his attention first, speakers blaring that Japanese girl group who covered "Freebird" in wild, broken English and thundering bass lines. SILKWORM, read the sign, set askew over the open door in a tiny storefront. Boutique shoe store, was Avery's first guess. But then he saw the Ramones poster, and the retro-style barber chairs, three of them, jammed tight in one line. Three or four pale, skinny dudes clustered inside, talking loudly over the music, ignoring Avery, who was now just inside the door. They all had Mohawks of varying lengths and color, and tattoos up and down each arm. One was sweeping clumps of hair in slow circles around the floor.

"Yeah?" Guy on a stool looked up from a tiny computer he was balancing on one knee.

"How much for a haircut?"

The manager—if that was who he was—looked over Avery's head. "First time here?"

Avery nodded.

"Forty," the guy said, turning back to the screen.

"Any one of these?" Avery looked at the three empty chairs. Not one of the tattooed kids made a move. No sign of whether they worked there or were just hanging out.

"NONA," the manager yelled. Nothing happened. The guy with the broom hoisted it and *whapp*ed the handle against a back door. A woman stuck her head out, angrily.

"I'm on the goddamn *phone*," she said. "You take him, Trevor."

"On break," Trevor said, and brandished a pack of cigarettes for proof.

"Jesus fuck," the woman said, and disappeared. Avery made himself comfortable in the chair closest to the window. The mirror he faced was scratched and cloudy, and covered on all sides with stickers, taped-up photos, and Magic Marker graffiti.

Then she was there, standing behind him. Nona. She finished tying on an apron and pushed at his head, this way and that, roughly.

"Maybe shorter on the sides and—" Avery began. The music changed to that song by the Killers that had been everywhere last summer.

"Yeah, I'll take it from here," Nona said, not meeting his eyes in the mirror. Avery grinned and shut up. He watched her razor up the back of his neck and scissor-snip the top into a wild, spiky tangle. She worked her mouth as she bent to check how even things were on the sides, and muttered something to herself, her warm breath puffing against his earlobe.

Avery checked her style—the beat-up, half-laced work boots, a cheap silver snake thing clamped around her upper arm—and recognized it, of course. She was one of his kind. But there was something else: Nona's face, pale, and faint lines on her forehead. Purple skin under her eyes. Her hair, a mess of twisted black dreadlocks, had streaks of gray growing out from the roots. Why did that set his heart humming? Avery wondered. The way her strong bare arms did, and the heavy softness of her breasts under the apron front.

The whole cut took less than ten minutes. He thanked her, and she nodded, wiping her hands on a small towel after flicking it down his shoulders.

Avery paid the guy on the stool his forty bucks and checked his wallet for a tip. All he had was another twenty. "I don't have any change," the manager said, shrugging. He slipped an earpiece in, unconcerned.

Avery turned to Nona. "Just my luck," she said. "Don't worry about it."

"This you?" he asked, reaching over to touch a battered post-card stuck in one corner of her mirror. He'd been staring at it during the haircut, a grainy black-and-white image of a woman bent forward and howling into a microphone. He pulled it out. Dates and clubs were printed on the back.

Nona looked up into his face as he studied the card. "It's my last one."

He handed her the twenty. "I'll take this as change." One of the Mohawk dudes snorted, a hooting laugh that both Nona and Avery ignored. One half-turning-up of her mouth, that's all Avery allowed himself to savor, standing there, one beat of perfection passing between them. Then he pushed back out onto Thompson with the postcard stuck in his pocket, hands shaking in a powerful kind of jones, grinning at everyone and no one, just like your basic village idiot.

Enough of Hartfield, already. Somewhere in the dark tangle of streets in this little town was the train station that could get him back to Manhattan. But where exactly, and how would he get there? What time did the trains run? Avery had none of the answers, but he wasn't too fazed. He'd figure it out. On his way to the door, though, he was stopped by a commotion in the country-club foyer.

A cluster of people, some kneeling, were gathered around an old woman lying on the floor. *Don't move her*, the people were saying to themselves. *Give her some air.* Avery edged closer and saw a thin line of blood running from the woman's nostril. Her eyes were closed, but she was breathing, hard, through her open mouth. He didn't recognize her, although that didn't mean anything. She must be a guest, maybe a friend of Grandad or his new wife, just one of the many old people in attendance. It was revolting to see an old lady lying like that, he thought, flat on her back on the hard carpet of the entranceway. Why didn't someone cover her legs, at least? They shouldn't be out in the open like that, all bony and ridged with veins. Avery stared at the shiny new sneakers on her feet, unable to look away. He owned the same brand, same style.

"Coming through," someone said, and Avery allowed himself to be pushed aside by the EMS guys and their wheeled stretcher.

Not sure where to go, he wandered slowly outside. The soft suburban night air was filled with crickets or cicadas; a bat looped underneath the awning over the door. A feeling he'd had earlier in the day, at the church, flashed back to him—a horrible feeling, like a nightmare . . . There was everything in place for a wedding: the altar, the minister, the flowers. The bride's white dress, the groom in a suit, everything normal until you looked in the smiling faces of the marrying couple and saw how old they were, how gray and wrinkled and stooped. A warp-speed fast-forwarded life. Twilight Zone stuff.

Now suddenly all the parts of his grandfather's big day curdled inside Avery. He pulled his tie over his head and stuffed it in a pocket. What was the point? Sure, it was great how the old man had found someone again, this close to the end of his life. Everyone was saying so. But now it hit Avery just how insubstantial it all was—love, marriage—compared to the hard physical reality of the world. The old lady on the floor in her neon sneakers; her bloody nose. This was coming soon for Grandad, whether he knew it or not. Wasn't it ridiculous for everyone to get all dressed up and pretend otherwise?

Avery watched as one of the valet attendants tossed a pair of keys high into the dark air and then caught them behind his back, one-handed. Nice. Then he stepped off the porch and walked slowly into the lush night streets of Hartfield. He'd find his way to the train eventually.

Four
WINNIE

How could it be after eleven? Jerry would be back from the clinic any minute, where he twice weekly submitted to the cheerful, horrible ministrations of a physical therapist named Becka. In her kitchen of twenty-two days—big enough to hold her old dining-room table and a desk and chair set, not to mention the two ovens and a gleaming stainless-steel refrigerator whose front door dispensed not only carbon-filtered water but either crushed ice or cubes—Winnie took out a small battered saucepan and set a wood spoon across it on the stove. Then she unpacked the brown paper bag with this morning's shopping load: four different cans of soup. For lunch, soup; Jerry always had soup for lunch—he'd had soup for lunch for decades and wouldn't be stopping soon, despite the month, despite the heat. He wasn't a man you had to fuss over; he ate what she fixed and said little about it. So yesterday afternoon it had surprised her, when she'd caught him peering closely at the bowl, poking the little vegetables this way and that with a spoon.

"Is this the kind with the green label?"

"It's minestrone, if that's what you mean—why?"

"Tastes different."

"Different bad? Let me go check. I can't remember what brand it is." Jerry had waved that away, and then he'd gone on to eat the rest. But before washing up Winnie had fished through the garbage, and then the recycling box, and held up the offending red-labeled can.

So, to the store. Or several, as it were: at the last minute, Winnie had turned into Fresh Market's lot, where she had been buying groceries for at least twenty years, just to double-check, but she didn't even need to walk all the way down the aisle to tell—no green-label soups there. With a fast wave to Donnie, behind the meat counter, she moved on. Winnie tried Associated next, the bigger store in town, and saw red labels, blue labels, large white boxes of chicken and beef stock, and some orange plastic bottles for children called Squeezy Soup. The stock boy was no help at all. Nor was the ditzy old gent at the register in the health-food place (used to be Red's Cleaners, until last year). He seemed to think Winnie was interested in a cup of lentil made fresh that morning, and she didn't care for the way he eyed her up and down. At last, in a Fast-Mart on Route 9, halfway to Mount Morris, she found what she was looking for, a dusty row of pea-colored cans on the bottom shelf. Tasty Harvest was the brand name, which Winnie severely doubted, but she bought one of each kind—minestrone, cream of mushroom, tomato noodle, and hearty beef. At checkout, she made sure to smile at the nervous teenage boy who gave her incorrect change; Winnie had a feeling she might become a regular customer at Fast-Mart.

Tomato noodle thudded into the saucepan in a brick-red congealed cylinder. Winnie filled the can with tap water and poured that in. She mushed at it all with the spoon, lighting a burner underneath, until the soup turned into a bubbling liquid.

The phone rang, and she answered immediately, hoping—and dreading—that it would be Rachel. But it was Grass Is Greener, with estimates for the monthly lawn mowing, and so Winnie dutifully copied these down in their allotted space on a page in her now-bulging notebook, even though there was only one particular landscaping element she was waiting to hear about. She fended off the fellow's sales pitch easily and said she would call back.

She had never been busier, which was a good thing. If it hadn't been for the two different phone lines newly installed, Winnie couldn't imagine how she might keep on top of everything. At times she even found herself actually using two separate phones at once: on hold with a wholesale outdoor furniture outfit in Hoboken, while simultaneously leaving a return message for Greg of LuxPool, Inc. Yes, she supposed it looked silly—a phone to each ear.

The pool project had taken hold of her as nothing had in recent years, other than helping Rachel in the year after Bob's accident. But even that had been someone else's cause, and this was hers alone, although it was the idea of Jerry's pain—that bitten-down grimace, whenever he stood up or bent over—driving her forward.

"Water's the only thing that really helps," he'd admitted once, just after the wedding.

"So what about the pool at your gym? And there's always Waugatuck, of course."

"Too crowded," Jerry had said. "Too many noisy kids."

She'd scoffed lightly at that, until one afternoon when she saw for herself what it was like for him. It had taken all the efforts of a lifeguard and Matty, his driver—who bent over at the side of the pool, still dressed in his black jacket and shiny shoes—to lower Jerry into the water. At one point, jostled by someone in a hurry, Jerry slipped on the sharp plastic ladder and nearly cracked his head on the cement. Winnie couldn't bear any part of it—the shakiness in his arms, the gritted teeth as he tried to smile up at her, the sidelong glances from others.

Soon after, she got to work. Six days after moving in, Winnie followed the first of many pool men around the still-unfamiliar grounds of her new home. They looked in back first, but the short, steep downhill slope, covered in thick brush to where the neighbors' property began, proved impossible. So it would have to be in front—not ideal, but no matter. There was plenty of room and nice, flat ground. She tried to keep up as the man paced off different lengths, kicking at errant twigs, and held up his arms to show where different sizes or shapes of pools could be sunk.

He had been the first to say it out loud, clipboard on hip and squinting up at the sky, though by now she had heard the same general opinion from at least three different pool companies, as well as one landscaping firm, plus a "tree man" that Rachel had personally recommended.

"It would have to come down," the pool man had said, and at first Winnie couldn't grasp what he meant. But she followed his gaze to the wide, sweeping branches and thick, peeling trunk of the sycamore tree in the exact center of the yard. "Kind of a shame. But there's no other way to lay the foundation—not to mention . . ." Here he had gone on about set grades, building inspection rules, and air compressor lines, terms Winnie was now thoroughly acquainted with. The house itself was tucked behind a cluster of conifers, and there was a stately row of maples along the low stone wall that bordered Greenham. Winnie had one linden tree just outside her kitchen window, and she guessed the huge, dark threesome over by Franklin Street were horse chestnuts. But this sycamore was the only one on the property. It was the tallest thing on the whole lot, a massive structure rising high above the house—later, Rachel's tree man estimated it was at least a hundred years old.

"I know for a fact it's the only one in town been around that long. They had one over at the school, but the storm in ninety-eight brought it down."

"Is that so," Winnie had said, politely enough. She'd paid his fee and thanked him for his time. But a tiny new determination bloomed inside her, like a drop of blood in a glass of water.

So far, while she did her pool research, she'd said nothing about the tree to anyone, but Winnie could just imagine what people in town might say. *But—but—you wouldn't* really *cut down that beautiful tree? For a* pool, *of all things?*

Yes, in fact, she would, Winnie would inwardly retort. Not for any old pool—for the one that would take away a measure of Jerry's pain. Her *husband's* pain. The custom-designed heated one that he could step down into, ramps and rails at hand, and float in all morning and all afternoon, if he liked. The absence of the grimace: that alone was worth ten sycamores.

But some of these fast-talking pool salesmen—well, they'd show up and take one look at the imposing size of 50 Greenham, and you could almost see the dollar signs lighting up in their eyes. The combination of her age and the lush, spreading lawns surrounding her new home probably gave most of these pool men the heady sense that they were about to score the commission of a lifetime.

They've got another think coming, Winnie vowed, stirring the tomato soup a little too vigorously. She hadn't grown up the daughter of a railroad man for nothing. Along with a lifelong punctuality, often bothersome even to herself, what Winnie inherited from her father was a scrupulousness that extended itself to almost every area of her life, and usually, her children's lives. She remembered the logbooks her father kept in a glass-front cabinet in their living room, where most folks would display a Collected Shakespeare or an encyclopedia set: their pebbly, dark-green faux leather covers, and the lined pages the color of buttermilk. Winnie used to run her fingers down the paper, across the rigid columns of dates and numbers entered in her father's careful hand. She could feel, even now, the scratchy ridges and depressions of those old pen marks.

Jerry's money had come into her life, there was no denying it. And such a pool was something most people would consider a luxury, she could admit that. Still, Winnie had no plans to become, at nearly eighty years, something she was not. She would spend no more than she had to. In fact, her general plan was to ignore the money, all of it, for as long as she could.

The phone rang again, this time in Jerry's office. She turned the gas to low and went to stand in the foyer, listening. It was that same young lawyer again. Did he think his other two messages this morning hadn't taken?

"—And since we just received another set of papers, I thought you should be aware that things look more serious. At this point, it looks like we'll need to file a response by end-of-day tomorrow. So again, give me a call as soon as you—"

Winnie detoured back through the living room, trying to ignore a slight hum of alarm the call had set off inside her. From here, she'd be able to glimpse the big Oldsmobile pulling up around back, idling a few minutes, while Matty finished whatever story he had been telling. But there was nothing in the wide driveway with its blue and white basketball-court markings. (She'd once suggested painting over them, but in response Jerry had pretended to bounce and shoot an imaginary ball, all in such a lovely, boyish way that Winnie knew she wouldn't mention it again.) Turning away, Winnie saw a doorway she'd never noticed before, in the short hallway leading to the sunroom—a closet? Stairwell?

Together, she and Jerry were exploring the house. Each night after dinner, and after a television program or two, they wandered into a different room and flipped the light switches on and off. They wondered at a strange water stain high up on a wall or tried to guess which child or grandchild might sleep there when visiting. On one of the first nights they did this, Jerry announced that he wanted to furnish the second-largest bedroom, the one that looked out onto the spreading branches of a blue Douglas fir, with twin beds in matching pink. Rachel's girls should share a room, he'd said, because girls that age liked to stay up and talk. He stood in the doorway, Winnie in the middle of the room, both of them assessing the light, the space. After a moment, she noticed that Jerry had stopped talking, and saw how he was looking at her.

"Would you—" he began, and stopped. "Your blouse," her new husband had said, lifting his chin. "Never mind," he said almost as quickly, flashing a smile at what he'd revealed.

Winnie held still, in his gaze, in the empty room. Then in one motion she unhooked her skirt and let it drop. The blouse came off just as easily, a simple pullover. She didn't stop there; underthings soon joined the rest in a soft heap on the bare wood floor. And then Winnie closed her eyes, the better to feel the air cross her bare skin—the better to revel in the heat that built from being loved in this way. She could hear Jerry's breathing. She could hear his footsteps as he walked a slow circle, all the way around her.

Yes, that was a lovely room. Rachel's girls would have some fun picking out curtains, rugs.

"Presuming Rachel ever darkens the doorstep," Winnie said now, reaching out to wipe a smudge on the glass with her cuff. She said it lightly, dramatically. That was the right tone. The rose-bush behind the stone bench was wilted and drooping again already; after lunch she'd drag the hose across the lawn to perk it up. That she and her daughter were barely speaking—were talking only enough to continue a wearying, weeks-long argument about things that were none of Rachel's business—chafed at Winnie, but what could she do? If it was the fact that she hadn't consulted Rachel before buying the house, all right, fine, she'd apologized already. But if it was the fact of the house itself, this shadowy jewel-box, a beehive of rooms within rooms, boxes everywhere, the place where Jerry and she slept and woke and ate their meals—well, what then? There was no going back. Even Rachel didn't seem to know what she was so angry about. When they did speak, her daughter toggled between the two—the not-telling; the house itself. The house itself; the not-telling. Back and forth, back and forth, in increasing agitation, until one of them would end the conversation, in fluster and dismay.

Just as she moved to shut off the heat under the soup, the back door opened, and there was Jerry, a brown-paper package under an arm, his shirt collar cockeyed on one side. Winnie breathed in. She imagined that she could smell him before he was even fully in the room—that harsh yellow soap he liked, the metallic whiff of the car's air conditioner, and the heat coming off his big body.

"I was just starting to worry," Winnie said.

"Went over to the post office. Had to sign a few things, registered mail. Am I late?"

"No, no," Winnie said, taking the package away. "Sit down, now."

Jerry drained a full glass of water while she set up his lunch. "There's something," he said. "I didn't want to get you all worked up, but . . ."

Winnie sat down at once.

"It's all a lot of nonsense. Just a strategy to get some attention. All will get sorted out in the end." Jerry pushed a half slice of bread in his mouth. He seemed embarrassed to be having this conversation.

"Is it Avery? Did he ever call back?"

Jerry, mouth full, shook his head.

Winnie had a new thought. "It's not . . . the other thing, is it? That . . . other sort of trouble?"

Jerry shook his head, swallowed mightily, and drank again. He hadn't touched the soup.

"Would you rather have sweet tea? I can make a pitcher—"

"What about soda water? We have any of those cans left?" Winnie jumped up to get one. She desperately worried he might ask for a sandwich. "You eating, Winifred?"

"Me? No, I had something earlier. Shall I call him again? Avery?

We could have him out to dinner. A barbeque with Rachel and the girls. Or just us, I don't know. Whatever you think would help."

"It's not Avery—it's Annette."

"Yes?"

"She's suing me. Not to put too fine a point on it." Jerry wiped his mouth and finally picked up his spoon.

"What do you mean?"

He made a disgusted *tch* sound. "It's not a matter for the courts, or anything like that. It better not be. Business decision. She wants to force a change in the board—make a play for something she and I disagree over. It's not personal."

"Not *personal*? I don't understand! What does she say to you?"

"Hasn't said anything, because I just heard about it this morning. From Ed Weller."

"But—but—" Winnie didn't know what to ask first. How could he be so calm? A *lawsuit*? Was Annette even allowed to sue her own father? Her father, who built the very company she was in charge of?

Suddenly, something occurred to her. "Jerry. Could she be—I mean, is this about us? Me? I know it's been hard for her to accept."

"Now, this is why I didn't want to say anything," Jerry said, raising his voice. He started to point the spoon at her, then put it down. "And maybe I shouldn't have."

"But I signed the papers. Annette must know that, right? The—" Winnie hated the term, that always-shortened, flip sound of it. "Pre-nup."

"That's different. That's not part of this. What it is, is . . ." Jerry exhaled heavily, and looked around the kitchen. "One of the companies, the original one—TrevisCorp—well, Annette's heading that up. And she's been making noises for a year about wanting to separate from the rest of the corporation, to run it on its own. Then take it public, probably. I don't know what she's all about."

"And you won't let her."

"No I *won't* let her! Frank and I built that shop from the ground up, back when we were just out of the army. I'm not putting my name, or my brother's name, on some foolish IPO, just so Annette can outsource labor to India and run up a quick profit. And anyway, she's not ready."

But why now? Winnie had to wonder if it wasn't a coincidence that Annette would do something so horrible now, less than a month after her father remarried. But it seemed selfish to ask, somehow.

And she was still learning how to talk with this man, her new husband. Their first real conversations had been by phone—Jerry from Chicago, she in Hartfield—and were full of gentle, teasing laughter as well as careful listening. Jerry asked her many questions, all about her life—what her parents had been like, and what she thought about her grandchildren, and how George had treated her. Winnie had treasured these long afternoons in her old apartment, walking back and forth, her ear growing hot from the phone's receiver. She had been flattered by his attention, and perhaps she got caught up in talking about herself. Every once in a while she would try, of course, to turn the subject to his own experience, but she could tell right away that while Jerry didn't mind talking about himself, he wanted to be the one leading the conversation. He much preferred to do the asking of questions. So she let him: it was heaven, the sensation of someone wanting to *know* you.

"Happens all the time," Jerry said. "It's a power play." But he looked tired now, and he still wasn't touching his food.

"Of course," Winnie said, not certain about any part of it. "I'm sure she'll listen to reason. Eventually."

"I only told you because some of the lawyers are coming out tomorrow. And I didn't want you to overhear something and get worried. Just put it out of your head."

Winnie smiled, with difficulty, and said no more.

What would it mean for her own relations with Annette—were they still going to Chicago for Labor Day, for example? How could they possibly? Would there be shouting over the phone, a big fight at Thanksgiving? But the startling news and her fears soon shrank down to nothing but a manageable buzz inside her head, in the moment that Jerry blew noisily on a spoonful of soup, and then ate it. And another, and another. He put away the whole bowl in one swoop, and all Winnie did was sit, and watch, and fill with happiness.

Five

RACHEL

The phone was ringing as Rachel unlocked the door at 10:05 AM. She tossed an armload of folded clothing on the counter and caught up the receiver at the last moment.

"Hand Me Down, children's consignment," she said, out of breath, flipping on the lights. Could she reach the air conditioner, too? The room was sweltering.

"Is this Rachel Brigham?" It was a young woman's voice, both familiar and not, tentative in tone.

"Yes?"

"This is Leanne Draper. From the management office at the pool?"

"Yes? Wait. Is everything all right with Lila?"

"Oh, no, it's nothing like that." A little note of relief came into Leanne's voice. "I was just—well, it's just that your check got returned? I tried to reach your husband first, but . . . anyway, I left a message for him. So this is the other number that we have on file."

"My check . . . really? I didn't think I'd paid August yet. Did

Bob mail it in already?" This was impossible, of course. Bob would no sooner know the fee schedule for Lila's pool membership than she herself would know how to fix a carburetor.

"It's the check for July. The bank just called us."

"Well, I don't see how that could have happened."

"Yeah," Leanne said. "I bounce stuff all the time."

"You guys are just depositing July now?" Rachel did some fast, sloppy calculations in her head. Last she'd looked, there was six hundred something in her checking account. If the July check for $850 had already bounced, would that mean that it was coming back into her account? Or that something else had bounced, too?

"I can take care of this over the phone for you, if you want. We can do pretty much any kind of credit card."

Rachel was trying to think, in the still, hot air of the store. The Visa card would never handle that kind of charge. And American Express would be due by mid-month anyway. She could transfer from savings. Again. That would be the third time this summer. Then again, Vikram's rent check would come in . . . when? Friday.

"I'll drop off a check this weekend. Saturday, since we'll be over for the meet anyway."

"Um, okay," Leanne said. "Maybe you could bring the check for August then, too? I mean, since Saturday's the second."

Pushy little thing! "Thanks for letting me know, Leanne. I'll see you this weekend." *Thanks for letting me know?* Rachel wondered if she should have been apologetic. But she didn't *feel* apologetic. She felt furious. "Fuck," she said quietly, to the yellow sundress in front of her. There was a pair of ducks appliquéd on its front.

She tried Bob, first at home, then on his cell. Melissa answered at home but rushed off the phone when Mrs. Simmonds honked outside, waiting to pick her up.

A customer came in and browsed the Boys Winter section. He picked up a pair of ski boots that they'd had out for over a year and weighed them in one hand, contemplating. Rachel quickly went to the back and turned on the air. She straightened up the counter and then covertly dialed Citibank, but then hung up when the automated menu options proved overwhelming. She marked up three new items, including the duck dress, and arranged them on various racks. All the while, her eyes burned and her throat ached. Leanne worked for Deb Towney, who lived in Butterfield but was close with at least three of Rachel's friends. She supposed she should feel lucky that it hadn't been *Deb* who had called—although—what if Deb had specifically asked Leanne to call? Had said, *Oh, would you? I really can't. It would be so* awkward *for her.* Aghast, Rachel stood at the front window, replaying this imagined moment over and over, unable to stop. Finally, the ski-boot man came to the register and purchased a pair of high-tech mittens in neon green, which she wrote up quickly and in silence. He was mildly startled when Rachel gathered her purse and keys and left the store with him, flipping the sign to CLOSED on the way out.

Until this year, working at Hand Me Down had been a kind of hobby. The owner was a friend of Rachel's, and filling in once or twice a week while the girls were at school hadn't been strenuous—had been fun, even. But the endless medical bills and Bob's leave had gradually increased her hours at the store, until she was now more-or-less working there full-time. Which she should be grateful about, probably. *At least it's not the Gap*, she told herself. For some reason, working at a consignment store—which featured the lightly used outfits of her friends' children—was a world better than selling new retail at some bright-and-shiny chain, in one of the anonymous shopping centers near Mount Morris.

That the new coffee place on Tremont was called The Grind had almost ceased to bother Rachel, although she still felt there was something vaguely inappropriate either about the name or the fact that she went there every day. And why the relentless dim lighting, the throbbing club music? Why, at ten minutes to eleven in the morning? Winnie refused to meet there for their regular coffee or lunch get-togethers—regular until recently, that is. It had been several weeks since Rachel had seen or talked to her mother, though her pain over this was dwarfed by the more immediate humiliation of the bounced check. She ordered a half tea, half lemonade, declined an extra "flavor shot," and obediently stepped over to the pickup counter.

She idly glanced at the three people crowded into the one back booth, their papers scattered across the table.

Then the man said, "Ray?"

She turned, face already arranged in a half smile for whoever it was. But it was Bob, in a Waugatuck Girls Diving baseball cap, sitting there at The Grind with two mother-hen types.

"Your hat," Rachel said stupidly, gesturing vaguely. Without it, his pale, bare head stood out—he'd stuck with shaving himself bald, after all the surgeries, and liked to say he rocked that look—and his scar, of course, was unmistakable. "I didn't recognize you." Meanwhile, Bob had half risen, but effectively pinned into the booth by the table and the unmoving ladies to either side of him, he gave up with a shrug and then sat down and blew her a kiss. This last was so awkward and strange to Rachel, a gesture she'd never once seen him perform, that she flushed hot with distaste.

"You know Maureen, Rachel. And this is Dara Moss—both in my class."

"Hello," Rachel said. Her iced tea arrived. Bob was explaining something interminable about how one might consider this a sub-committee meeting, a micro-version writers' group within a bigger writing class, ha ha, everyone chuckling, Rachel got the point. They were talking about words on paper. Meanwhile, Rachel stood directly in front of their booth and sucked deeply on her iced tea.

How was it that the very traits of Bob's that she once loved the most—his sunny, unflappable nature, his single-minded ability to focus, and that *friend-to-one-and-all* attitude—had become the things about him that annoyed her most?

"Well, I've got to get back to the store," Rachel said, shaking the keys. "But Bob, can I talk to you for a second?"

"Sure," Bob said. He smiled up at her. Everyone waited. "Oh—did you mean?—right. We're at a good break point. Maureen?"

Maureen agreed, but then she pointed to a question mark on her page and asked a question about that and the three of them went on for at least another minute, wrapping it up, and then Rachel lost it. She turned to go.

"Don't worry about it," she said loudly, over their protestations. "No, I don't want to interrupt. We can talk at home. It's just . . . the check to the club bounced, so maybe we should talk about that. Bob. When you get a chance." The ice rattled loudly in the bottom of her plastic cup. Had she drained the whole thing already?

In silent unison, the two women slid out of the booth and left without further delay.

One of them touched Rachel lightly on the arm as she passed. "Don't you just hate when that happens?" she said, in a friendly, conspiratorial whisper.

Left alone, Bob rubbed at a spot above his right eye. "Okay," he said, drawing the syllables out.

She sat down on the extreme outer edge of the banquette. The seat was still warm. "Well, what did you want me to do?"

"I thought we weren't going to pay Discover this month."

"I *didn't* pay Discover," Rachel said hotly. "The windows guy had to have half in cash."

"Wasn't that June?"

"Well, the bill just came for the rest. That's four hundred right there, then the mortgage—I'm assuming you paid the mortgage this month." Rachel made no attempt to strip the sarcasm from her voice.

"You should have told me."

"Told you about what? That Waugatuck is due at the beginning of the month? Or what Lila's diving costs in the summer, with the pool fee and the coach fee and the travel fee? Christ, you're the one wearing the damn hat."

"I mean, we need to talk about this stuff." Bob's voice rose a degree, and Rachel didn't need to see the back of his neck to know how that rope of scar tissue would be standing out white in relief to his reddening skin. "Half the time I have no idea what you've paid, from which account."

This was usually Rachel's claim, and hearing Bob put it forth so reasonably, as if it was a piece of self-evident wisdom, enraged her.

"Oh, what would it matter? We'd just be having this conversation again and again. Better to be in the dark."

"This isn't a conversation."

The roar of the coffee grinder interrupted them. When it stopped, Bob said, "Could be worse. Could have been the cable bill."

"Are you kidding? I'd a million times rather bounce a check to some faceless corporate—"

"Joke. Joke! Come on, Rachel, don't make this bigger than it needs to be. I mean, being short on one's country-club payments doesn't exactly mean the poorhouse."

"What about Con Ed last month? And didn't you say you'd stopped the IRA contributions? Again?" There was an older man at the milk-and-sugar station nearby, but Rachel didn't lower her voice.

Bob blew out a long breath. "I don't think we want to revisit the diving thing."

"*I* don't," Rachel cried. "Do you?"

"No," Bob agreed. It happened this way each time: one or the other would broach the obvious, Lila's diving expenses, and then both would back off, swearing not to change the girls' lives more than they already had been. Rachel worried, though, that hanging on to Waugatuck was starting to look odd, especially as more and more people knew about their circumstances.

"Like those welfare moms with flat-screen TVs," she said to herself.

"What are you talking about?"

She waved it away, because something else occurred to her. "Weren't you supposed to see Nikki today?" The speech thera-pist. His language, in those first few weeks of recovery, had been jumbled—"metal detector," he'd called his IV pole, and "box" for cup—and although it had seemed to right itself almost immediately, those incidents had propelled him into long-standing sessions of rehab work, just in case.

"I canceled," Bob said.

"What?"

"We had a *writer's group*," he explained patiently, gesturing toward the rest of the booth. "And now that I think about it, that's a fifteen-dollar co-pay right there. Not to mention parking. What do you say we blow it all on two cheddar scones? I'll even throw in another iced tea, in honor of . . . well, just because I'm that kind of guy."

"But—" She knew it sounded childish. "I thought I was the one who made the appointments." She'd been calling Nikki for over a year to schedule Bob's visits.

Bob reached over to give her arm a little shake. "Ray. What do you want me to do? Go back in time and turn down the leave? A whole year's leave at half pay? Because sometime over the summer it might cause a little problem for my daughter's *diving lessons*?"

"Well, if you're going back in time, why stop there?" Rachel said, and then stopped, confused. She had started to say this lightly but knew right away she had crossed some kind of line. Bob was quiet, watching her closely as if to track her own response to her remark.

They sat, silent. Hannah Deardon, a past babysitter of the girls, now married and very pregnant, caught Rachel's eye and waved energetically from the window out front. She mouthed something long and complicated, supplemented with much pointing and hand gestures.

Bob waved too. "What's she saying?"

"That she's due . . . next month? And will be coming by the store soon. Which reminds me." Rachel put her hand on the keys, on the table.

"I'll transfer from the savings," Bob said.

"No, I'll do it. Or—well. Maybe our *tenant's* check is in the mail. If not, I'll go bang on his door. Our door, I mean. Ha ha." But Bob ignored this little attempt. Rachel lingered. She had the distinct feeling of being in the wrong. But then again, an apology, a real one, was beyond her.

"Did you see her picture in the newsletter?" The club mailing had arrived with a front-page photo of Lila in full pike position, midair, her forehead nearly touching her calves. The caption read, "Airborne! Fourteen-year-old Lila Brigham takes first place at the Waugatuck Invitational."

"When I showed it to her, all she said was that she wished they'd run a picture of her inward two. She said the front flip was worse." Bob smiled thinly, recognizing the long-standing joke about Lila's perfectionism.

"All right," Rachel said uncertainly. "See you back at the ranch." She wished he wouldn't just sit there, as she pushed through the door back into the hot, patchy sunshine.

She had been in the shower when he collapsed, that morning, March 20. That was the best she could do, piecing together a narrative from the jagged holes of the day. It was a Saturday, damp and overcast. Melissa had been invited to a birthday party at an ice rink in Mamaroneck, and by the time Rachel had gotten back from dropping her off, it was close to noon, and she and Bob were due at Lila's meet by 2 PM.

"What are you doing?"

Bob was in the garage when she pulled in, still wearing his faded corduroys and a stained windbreaker. His hair, thick and unruly, curled down over his collar.

He held up the stick end of a broom, mock-heroically. "Gutter time."

"Oh, my. What have I done to deserve *this*?" Unclogging the mess of leaves and twigs gumming up one corner of the back drainpipe had been something he'd been talking about, off and on, for weeks.

"You haven't asked how much I charge."

"I see."

"I'm wildly expensive. My tools are known as the industry standard." Bob hooked a thumb through a belt loop and gave his pants a tug.

Rachel reached out to gently brush a fluff of dust from his eyebrow. "Is that so."

"Booked solid through the spring. You're lucky I could even find time for you. Ma'am."

"Find time for me, huh?" Rachel moved closer, pushing one of her thighs between Bob's legs.

"Unhand me, Mrs. B! That kind of thing won't get your drains clear!" When she lingered, Bob swept her out of the way with the broom, pushing harder against her ass—swatting, even—as she resisted, laughing. As she left, she could hear him singing some James Taylor handyman song, the one he warbled during all home repair projects.

How many minutes elapsed? That's the way they always asked, the medical team. "Elapsed." As a consequence, Rachel's visual memory of the day always stamps a timer on the bottom of the frame, one that immediately runs up the seconds, the milliseconds, as she watches herself putter around the house, after leaving Bob. There was a phone call, though she can't remember who. She knows she poured a second cup of coffee, for she found it, rimmed with white mold, three days later, sitting on her dresser. Down in the basement, she had folded the girls' clothing into two teetering piles, and she had put in a load of towels, snatching one back out for her own use. Ticking, ticking, upward. Back upstairs, would she have heard the ladder bumping and scraping against the back wall? Only if she'd stopped in Melissa's room, whose window overlooked that side of the yard. And had she? Had she? If Rachel wasn't able to remember, that same afternoon, in the trauma unit of the hospital, weeks and months later she certainly wouldn't be any closer to knowing.

Nor how long she had been in the shower. Several people seemed very intent on this point—the woman driving the ambulance, and that first surgeon. So, how long did a shower take? She definitely hadn't shaved her legs, so there was that. But she did own, that winter, a certain hot-oil type of hair conditioner that needed to be applied for ten minutes before rinsing. Occasionally, Rachel liked to use that time to zone out in the shower, an objective justification—see the instructions, right on the tube!—for a lengthy, luxurious water waste. So, had she used it, March 20? In any reconstruction of her hurry that afternoon, their perpetual fear of missing Lila's first dive, Rachel can't imagine that she did. But it was impossible to know for sure. By now, she was familiar with the way memory worked, its own sly insertions into a long lost sequence of events. Ticking, ticking. In any case, she had blown her hair dry and put on her clothes.

A gust of cold air, the first sign. Confused, she had stopped on the stairs. Why was the front door open? Swinging, banging, wide open. A creeping unease. She shut it and went back down the front hallway when something caught her eye. Bob, in the living room. Flung back on the couch, way back. The clock, still ticking at the bottom of the screen, in those last moments before her awareness. When she had wondered, for a flash, if he was pulling a prank. Before she saw his head, how it was tilted to the side and how it was bulging, along the temple and behind his ear. His eyes, open only to their whites.

Doctors who specialized in head injuries, Rachel was to learn, occasionally spoke about the "first injury"—to them, this meant whatever initial impact, that first blow, the one that set off a chain of dire problems inside the skull. They also spoke about a "second injury," but while Rachel had originally thought this referred to another impact in the accident—another fall, collision, blow—what the doctors meant was the trauma that occurred inside the patient's head, a buildup and overflow of blood, a rapid swelling that broke apart those neatly coiled tubes of brain. She got it, sort of, but the terminology continued to bother her because in Bob's case, they still—years later—didn't know how the two were related. Bob had been in a coma for eight days, and his amnesia, later, blacked out everything after that morning's breakfast. He could remember Melissa dropping an open box of cereal, for example, the corn puffs skidding across linoleum, but he didn't remember the broom, the ladder, or the James Taylor song. Everything about his first injury remained a frustrating mystery. There were a couple of leading theories.

The gutter had been cleaned out. So had he fallen off the ladder, as was first assumed? There was no sign of it—no blood, no dent or disturbance in the grassy dirt along the back corner of the house. Plus, the ladder was neatly replaced in the garage, hanging on its metal hook as usual. Was it possible that he fell, recovered, and then went inside—disoriented, unaware of the damage done—to collapse on the couch? Possible, the neuromedical people conceded. They said that it was more often the second injury that incapacitated people, not the original impact, whose damage many victims underestimated, and hence delayed treatment. But Rachel couldn't believe that Bob would fall off a ladder and then take the time to fold it up and carry it all the way back into the garage, before coming inside. Winnie had to agree.

The doctors ruled out a stroke or a heart attack. They traced the initial impact to a blunt blow along the left side of his face. That first night they spent at the hospital, after Bob's first surgery had begun, Winnie took the girls back to her apartment. She phoned Rachel and Bob's neighbor, Bruce Everwine, to ask him to check that the house was closed and locked. When Bruce arrived, he noticed that their car was backed partially out of the open garage, left at an odd angle, keys in the ignition. No one knew what to make of this. Had Bob driven anywhere, in those minutes Rachel couldn't account for? Had he been in some kind of car accident? No sign of it on the car itself, Bruce reported. One nurse in the trauma unit wondered aloud if the car had rolled backward, had hit Bob in the head, in the garage. Rachel tried to picture this. Had he, for some reason, turned on the motor and then bent down behind the car? Had she, somehow, left it in drive after returning from dropping off Melissa? None of it seemed likely.

"You might just have to live with never knowing," Dr. Richards, who led Bob's team, had said to both of them several months later, once Bob had survived both the major surgeries.

And because they were instantly plunged into the world of rehab and recovery, those endless months of scans and programs and treatments, for a long while there was no time to consider any alternative. Then, as time went on, Bob didn't seem to want to know. Even after he was moved back home, he showed such little interest in parsing out either of their movements on that day that Rachel finally stopped asking or hoping for something to trigger a flood of actual recollection. She burned for answers, still, but because no one else seemed to understand that urgency—everyone talked about "moving on," and "moving forward"—she learned to hide what she really felt.

And then, she simply split into two. Little by little, Rachel realized that in this new world, new life, she would have to be two people, one overt and the other private. There was the concerned and mobilized Rachel, the one who was caught up in all the immediate, mutable crises and daily triumphs of a husband's recovery. The one who sometimes wept fiercely to have him back, alive, and then who was tear-free in the next instant, nailing down every detail of his eight medicines and the rotating shifts of three home-care nurses. This Rachel kept all of them *going*, the four of them, propelled by everything she had to do, buoyed by Winnie, by friends and neighbors, all of Hartfield, who celebrated Bob Brigham's miracle and never let her forget how grateful she should be. But sometimes, deep inside, Rachel heard and saw another version of herself, one who shook off what she knew was *the right way to be*, a Rachel who flew at poor, slow Bob—forgetting what the frightened girls might witness—and gripped his upper arm, and marched him around the living room and garage, forcing him to look, to remember, to explain, shouting at him, shouting for someone, anyone, to tell her exactly *what the fuck had happened to her life?*

As she reached Hand Me Down, Rachel walked slow and slower. She passed Rudy's shoe store, where a sign announced, FALL ARRIVALS SOON: GET READY FOR SCHOOL. In July! Rachel shook her head. She could remember taking the girls on the first warm day of spring to Rudy's to buy each a pair of sandals. And how they would wear the new shoes deliriously home, a balloon string tied securely to each girl's wrist, winter shoes—all of a sudden so heavy and worn—packed away in the sandals' pastel-colored boxes. *Old Hartfield*, she thought of this—a private designation to mark what Rachel remembered about the town, which had changed somehow when she wasn't looking. It couldn't be true, but it felt to Rachel that she had gone underground for those months while Bob was in the hospital, while he was in bed at home, and then when she finally came up for air, everything about where she lived was utterly different. More expensive, more typically suburban.

Rudy's didn't give out balloons anymore. And the staff would smile sadly if you stopped in anytime past February to buy spring shoes, because you'd missed the fashion season when those were in stock. *New Hartfield*.

She passed the bank and crossed the street. Outside Hand Me Down's front window, Rachel came to a stop and stood there, staring blankly through the glass at the racks of outfits as if she were a potential customer. She took out her cell phone and held it tightly, dread rising like nausea. She tapped it against her thigh and strolled next door to look in the Christian Science Reading Room window. Rachel, used to crisp actions, wondered at the roiling fear and doubt inside her. Was this what a panic attack felt like? Ridiculous, after all that she had been through, to fall apart now. Rachel reached out to the window to steady herself. People did this all the time.

While she was dialing, a woman walked up to Hand Me Down, tried the door, and frowned at its CLOSED sign. Rachel smiled at her, mimed a shrug, and listened to the ring on the other end of the line. The woman looked at her watch, shook her head, and walked past.

Winnie answered, cautiously. They spoke a little about the weather and the girls. Winnie was saying something about a pool—or a tree?—but Rachel couldn't follow it.

She leaned her forehead against the Reading Room's glass, next to her forearm. As usual, metal clamps were placed neatly on a page of the open Bible, bracketing off the week's chosen passage. In the contrast of sun glare and the dim gloom of the display, all the words were hard to make out. "For by grace you have been saved through faith; and this is not your own doing . . ." Rachel could delay no further.

"Mommy," she blurted. And stopped, horrified at what had come out of her mouth. The words *Mom* and *money* must have collided, with the result being every bit as humiliating as Rachel had imagined this moment to be. A short, giddy laugh escaped her.

There was a pause, on Winnie's end. "Is everything all right?"

"I was hoping to ask you for a loan. Or Jerry. Not—you know what I mean. I'm not asking *for* Jerry. Ha. Just to borrow some money. From him, from both of you. Whatever." Rachel shut her eyes and held very still, overcome by painful self-consciousness.

"Well . . . of course. Don't be silly. Of course we can do that. As long as you're all right." Winnie's voice was warm but retained an uncertain note. Rachel could feel the sun on the back of her neck. "You are, aren't you? Rachel?"

"I didn't want to bother you," she whispered. Meaning, *I didn't want you to know.*

"I can hardly hear you. Why don't you come over after closing up. That's at five, right? We'll have a glass of wine, and Jerry will be here, and you and he can talk about the . . . about all of it. It's going to be *fine*, sweetheart."

Rachel could hear her mother relieved to be back on firmer terrain: making plans, solving problems. And it felt good to her, too, simply to be on the phone again; these past few weeks of tension between them had unsettled Rachel. Would it really be having to ask for a loan—she shivered with embarrassment, again, at the thought—that would bring things back to normal between her and Winnie?

"I didn't want to bring this up, but as long as I've got you"— now Winnie was fully back in the swing of it—"remember we wondered why we hadn't seen the Donaldsons in ages? How they weren't at the church barbeque, or the other thing? Well, turns out they were out of town, for almost two weeks. At a place called Casa Naturale. I think it's in Mexico."

"So?" Rachel walked over to unlock Hand Me Down. She was smiling, despite herself. They were back, she and her mother. "They went on vacation, so what?"

"Don't you get it? Casa *Naturale*." Winnie was brimming, triumphant. "It's a nudist colony! I thought it sounded funny, so I Googled it. Ian and Sherry Donaldson, naked on a beach. Now tell me *that* didn't just make your day."

Six
AVERY

He stared at the silver tube of lipstick in the toilet water. God*damn* it. It had happened in slow motion, the merest bump of his towel-wrapped hip against the sink, itself an overflowing steamed-up mess of jars, bottles, and strange metal wands. All he'd done was reach for the faucet and there it went, right off the edge and *plunk* into the toilet before he could even stretch out a hand. Now it was lodged in the stained porcelain hollow at the very bottom of the bowl. Of course it was. Avery looked around the tiny bathroom in dismay. What was all this makeup, anyway? It was like a fucking pharmacy in here. Well, there was only one thing to do, and it wasn't going to help to spend a lot of time thinking about it.

He plunged his hand in, almost to the elbow, fishing and fumbling, and then he had it. Now what? His first instinct was to wrap it in a wad of toilet paper and bury it in the trash. How could she miss it, really, with all these other lookalike lipsticks? He'd get her another one! Replace it, later tonight, and she'd never know. The dime-size label on the bottom read only GARBO. What did that mean? And what if it was a favorite? She was so particular about her outfits, not just for performances but planning costumes for herself every day, a shifting thrift-store parade, calibrated to minute changes in mood or plan or the music playing on the stereo. What if, stumbling into the bathroom after him, Nona started to brush her teeth and then thought, *You know what would be perfect for today? Some Garbo lipstick.*

At the thought of her, naked and warm in bed right now, on the other side of the wall, buried under a tangle of pillows and blankets, that soft rumble of her breathing—Avery slowly closed his eyes, still holding the tube in his dripping hand. He was so close to climbing back in there with her, fuck it all, to sleep and fuck and sleep again, until it turned dark outside and then they could go out to that all-night Vietnamese place, for a burning shared bowl of pho, and sticky rice balls wrapped in lettuce, and mango pudding. Except that's pretty much what he had done yesterday. And most of the week before, stints at work the only exception.

"This is *it*, Avery," his mother had said yesterday, when she finally reached him. He had managed to buy himself a few weeks, citing minutiae of job and apartment searches, but the excuses were running out. "I'm not kidding. If I don't hear that you've been out there by—"

"What kind of evidence do you want? Photographs? Sworn statements?"

There was a slight pause, and for a moment Avery wondered if he'd gone too far. "Just go see him, all right?" As usual, as soon as his mom's voice took on that tired, overwhelmed tinge, Avery conceded. He could barely hear her as she went on: "There's a lot going on that I can't even . . . Just go see him."

With the happy thought that the sooner he left Nona, the

sooner he could return, Avery rinsed and soaped the lipstick, drying it on a corner of his towel. Uneasily, he dropped it back into the mess of cosmetics, but not before giving it a quick sniff. Nope. No toilet smell whatsoever.

Nona's bedroom was three unevenly cut pieces of Sheetrock banged together against the apartment's main wall, not much bigger than her double bed. To open the bottom drawer of her overflowing dresser, you had to tug the bed out of the way first, the foot of which served as desk chair, coffee table, and laundry hamper all at once. And then there were the teetering stacks of CDs and records on every surface, everything from 1950s opera to hip-hop demos made in garages. Nona's stereo, wedged underneath a rickety night table on the floor beside her bed, was a shockingly expensive brand from Germany, probably worth more than the entire contents of the rest of the apartment. Her thick-cushioned headphones were invisible, buried under the pillows somewhere, but the sight of the cord trailing down from the bed sent a flash-shiver through him—last night, toward the end, he'd put them on Nona just to watch her face, eyes shut and mouth open. (Avery had to believe it wasn't *just* the music that had made her writhe like that.)

He dropped his towel and climbed on top of her.

"Oof. Already?"

"Don't go anywhere," he whispered. "Don't even get dressed."

Nona raised her head an inch, sniffing dramatically, and then dropped it back down. "My God, you read my mind."

"No. No way."

"It smells divine. I can't wait."

Avery pulled on the same jeans he'd been wearing for a week. "You're dreaming."

"Avery's famous popovers. With some of the clover honey. You're a prince among men."

"Nona, these trains only run on the hour! And getting from here to Grand Central . . . Tomorrow, I promise I'll make them. Every day next week!" But even as he scanned the torn-apart room for his wallet, his shirt, he was whipping through ingredients in his head. What a sucker. "Eggs?" Eggs were fast. "Pepper and onion omelet?"

But Nona just shook her head, burrowing deeper. "I love that popover smell," she said sleepily.

Christ! There was barely enough flour, but only one egg, and the muffin tin was still caked with blackened crust edges. Avery dumped the tray in a sinkful of hot soapy water, pulled on his shoes, and fished around in Nona's bag for the keys. Outside it was oddly cool for late August, and, grateful, he ran two blocks over to the bodega, where he bought mildly suspect eggs and butter and, last minute, a bunch of pale-pink tulips. Into the corner garbage can went the cellophane wrapper and five of the six flowers, and then he took the stairs three at a time back up to Nona's apartment.

Seeing Thomas, Nona's sometime roommate, in the kitchen slowed him, though. They'd met once, but Thomas pointed a finger at him and put on a puzzled face anyway.

"Mm . . . Avery, right? Good. Sorry to . . . interrupt." He smiled, eyebrows raised, at the dishes and the flower. "I'm just dropping my things. Off to Seattle later today."

"No, that's cool. I have to run in a second, anyway." He tried not to be self-conscious, cracking the eggs, whisking in flour, setting the empty buttered pan to smoke away into the blackened, tiny oven. Thomas was sorting through mail, leaning against the counter. He taught cultural studies at NYU, Nona said. They'd been friends forever. Gay, obviously, so that was all good. But why the whole roommate setup, when the two of them were—well, old? Thirty-whatever, at least. They'd lived together for years in a series of apartments across Brooklyn, and once in Queens—*eesh*, Nona had shuddered about this—to end up here, in this reconfigured industrial space in Williamsburg. Thomas traveled, Nona explained. She hardly ever saw him.

Avery wished that was the case this morning.

"Is it part of a tour? For your book, I mean?"

Thomas looked up, polite and perplexed. "Hmm?"

"Going to Seattle . . . to sign books, and all that?" Avery had seen Thomas's book—had flipped through it while on the can, actually. The cover image was a curvy nude dancer, posing while a black bar covered her eyes; the title was *Queering the Show: Gender, Economics, and Burlesque in Turn-of-the-Century New York*. For a book about strippers, though, it was pretty boring.

"What? Oh, right. Yes, wouldn't that be something." Thomas chuckled, although Avery wasn't aware of making a joke. He poured the oily batter into the hot pan in precise dollops. With a pen, he wrote, "STOP! DO NOT OPEN OVEN! TURN DOWN TO 350 DEGREES. TAKE PAN OUT AFTER 22 MINUTES," on the back of one of Nona's flyers, and taped it to the oven's grimy handle. Thomas disappeared into a back room. Working quickly, Avery fiddled with his watch alarm—avoiding the time—washed the bowl and whisk, and wiped out the sink. He set out a plate, the sticky honey container, and the tulip in a jelly jar.

Nona's wrist was tiny and brushed with fine dark hair; he

kissed its inside and buckled his watch on her arm as tight as it would go.

"Listen," he said, waggling her arm back and forth. "Six minutes. When it beeps, get up and go into the kitchen. No kidding. Unless you want the fire department."

Nona pulled her arm away and rolled over. But first, she blew him a kiss, eyes still closed.

He had it so bad. Hard to believe how bad it was, how deep he was in, after—what?—three weeks.

On the train, Avery pushed his knees against the seat back in front of him, feet dangling. He'd been carrying Cormac McCarthy's new paperback around forever, but couldn't seem to get past the first dozen pages. Outside the nicked and clouded plastic of the window, metal bridges rumbled by, and the upper parts of Manhattan, and then the Bronx. They crossed highway after highway and then rolled steadily past high-rise buildings, thick forests of dark brick interspersed with paved plazas, empty green benches, neon-lit liquor stores and dry cleaners. Avery rubbed his thumb across his abraded lips, felt the ache in his groin. He was miserable; he was elated.

He hadn't come to that first show, but he'd tracked her band down the next week. And though he would definitely have said that their first few times together were good—great, even—it took a little while for him to realize what was happening. Standing in the back of the crowd, Avery had fought some initial disappointment while Nona howled and swore and stomped through a set or two of standard-issue indie-grunge rock. Yes, she was hot, even in that crazy 1940s-style getup, a boxy gray suit and pompadour hair—a wig, he found out later—and yes, he liked how she met his eyes from the stage. But the overall scene was blah, and those guys in her band were poseurs. Afterward, he'd milled around during load-out and then he and Nona had ended up at his place, and the next night too: standard, right? Nothing special.

Idiot, Avery on the train mouthed to himself, that old version of himself already gone and unrecognizable.

There were moments, though, where he guessed something was up: her dreadlocks splayed across his naked stomach (*like a tarantula*—a thought that coincided with a sudden, baffling orgasm); the way she set down her glass on the bar and left it there for the rest of the night, having noticed that Avery was drinking only water; the long, patient 2 AM conversation she'd had with this guy on the street, some cracked-out bum, about her own shaky finances and why she had a policy against giving out change on the street, and detailed directions to this one shelter she knew wasn't too insane. She listened seriously to this person. She nodded and asked questions as he went on and on with his crazy spiel, all these Swiss bank-aliens out to get him—she held a hand up to Avery when he tried to interrupt—Avery who'd wanted nothing more than to hand this guy a five and tug Nona away, back to himself.

So, there were moments. Hints. Still, he was caught off guard when it came together, all at once—he was blindsided when the fuse lit and hissed inside him, unmistakable.

Their fourth night together, they were sitting up in her bed, naked, facing each other, eating sliced plaintains he'd sautéed with brown sugar, and chocolate truffles from the bodega, each one wrapped in crinkly blue-and-silver plastic.

"Your mom taught you to cook?" Nona asked, sugar grains dripping down her wide, soft belly.

"No. I mean, she loves food and we always had good stuff around, growing up, but . . . no."

"Who, then? Your grandma?"

"Actually, it was this guy Luther." Nona raised her eyebrows, waited for more. All of a sudden, though, Avery was stuck. He couldn't figure out what it would mean to her, or what it would sound like, out loud—all the drug stuff, and the tired, bad way everything had gone down—here in this naked woman's bed in this strange new city. Was this really the first time he'd told someone who didn't already know? Maybe not, but it felt like that. He waded in carefully. "He was head of the kitchen at this place I was at for a year—"

"This place . . . ?"

"Yeah." Avery smiled helplessly, still stuck.

"This place being—rehab?" Her face was calm, watching him. Avery nodded, and then she did, too.

Nona considered the two chocolates left. She weighed them carefully, one in each hand, and then made her decision. "What kind of food did he cook?"

Avery started to speak, and then stopped. There it was, full and clear, what she'd done for him just now: accepted his story, accepted *him*. "Well, everything. He was in charge of meals for fifty, sixty people at a time, so a lot of it was just volume and turnaround. And timing."

"No individual lemon soufflés. No rack of lamb."

"Right. More like shepherd's pie or spaghetti casserole. And it was in Virginia, this place, so we did all the usual Southern food, everything with ham hocks. But he'd been through a lot, this guy—" Avery remembered the two scars along Luther's thick black neck, the time some whiny backwoods addict snarled some racist shit and the way Luther had so calmly, almost gently, set down a stock pot and pinned the kid against the wall with one huge forearm.

"This was like his kingdom, you know? Being responsible for everything we all ate. He took pride in it. And when it was a good dinner, when all the serving plates would come back empty, Luther would be so pumped. Like, here was this hard-core black guy, usually all impassive and intimidating. But then he'd go around chest-bumping us all when the chili came out perfectly. I don't know. Nobody wanted to be assigned to the kitchen, because it was fucking hot in there, and there was no way to get out of all this shit that had to be done, every day . . . but I really got into it, after a while."

"Chili. Is it wrong to want chili in August?"

"I'll make you the best black-bean chili you've ever had." He reached over to put both hands around one of her thighs. "It's so hot you'll sweat."

"But that's not the kind of the thing you usually make. Right?"

"I don't mind a good bowl of chili."

"No, I mean, where'd you learn all the glammed-up stuff? You know, the wrapped-up figs and all that."

Avery blushed. Yes, that antipasti plate he'd made for her had been overkill, six different fussy preparations, including a half ounce of *culattello* from Mott Street he'd stood in line forty-five minutes to buy.

"Toward the end, Luther let me mess around on my off hours. Obviously, I didn't have much in the way of ingredients. He did let me use his knives, though. That was huge."

"Because of rehab. The rules, and so on."

"Because a chef doesn't let anyone touch his knives!" It occurred to Avery that Luther himself would have scoffed at the term *chef*. "That's sacred shit."

"Boys and their toys," Nona said. She lay back against a pillow. "So what are you going to do with all that?"

Avery leaned over and licked sugar off one of her palms, chasing it between her fingers with his tongue. "What am I going to do with all what?"

She grabbed his jaw and shook his face gently. "With food. With your cooking. What do you want?"

"You mean, do I have a 'life plan' or something?" The words came out harsh and scornful, despite himself.

Nona let go. "Yes, that's what I mean, shithead."

"I don't have that kind of—it's different for you, with your band. I—"

"That *band* is not what I do. That's not my real work." Nona drew herself up, an angry queen.

"Okay, all I meant was—"

"Avery. This is when you say, 'so what is your real work, Nona?'"

"No, definitely. I mean, yeah. Of course I want to know."

Nona hesitated.

"Please," Avery said.

"All right. But you'll want to back up some." Avery, confused at first, scooted himself up against the wall on the far side of the bed. Nona closed both eyes and breathed deeply, humming. "Give me a minute, all right? I hate the way it sounds, when I describe it. I'll just show you."

He waited. Nona seemed to have gone deep inside herself, the way she sometimes did when they were fucking. Was she meditating? Was she getting ready to levitate? The seconds ticked past, and still she sat there, frowning now, with the effort of those long, thrumming breaths. Avery had no idea what was coming, but he understood two important things: first, that he didn't care. At all. Anything she wanted to show him, he was open to. The second was that there were few better ways he could think of to spend a silent moment, than sitting here in this bed, across from this woman, strange and glorious and *naked*.

Then she opened her mouth and a blast of sound hit him. It was hard to understand how she had instantly summoned so much noise, or how it had erupted from her without warning, a low-toned foghorn that shifted into a series of undulating cries, before he had a chance to make sense of it. The sounds ping-ponged off the walls, as if Nona propelled each and then caught it—swallowed it—on the rebound. His heart pounded. While she sang—if that was what she was doing—she put her hands on various parts of her body: the sides of her waist, two fingers flat against the base of her throat, and then a fist pressed deeply into the hollow of her ribs. In their lovemaking, of course Avery had already noticed—had closely, carefully noticed—the tiny tattoos sprinkled in clusters of blue and black across Nona's skin: the whorled fingerprints, the Roman numerals, one silver exclamation point. He hadn't guessed they might have some other purpose than decoration, but now he saw where she beat gently upon them as a prompt, or a counterpoint, to her singing.

Hard to believe the sheer amount of sound that gushed around him, or how she could erase it all in one instant, the way she did when the song was finished, although it wasn't at all clear that what he'd just heard was a song. Avery felt like he'd been schooled. He was chastened, both then and—replaying the moment in his mind—on the train just now pulling into Hartfield. Everything she'd just shown him about desire lit up his own default mode of studied indifference, and now he glimpsed what the opposite looked like.

"Holy shit," he had said, and Nona laughed. "That was . . . wow."

"Wow?"

"Um . . ." He'd wanted to say something smart, something that would match the intensity of her performance. Something that would make him her equal. "I've never heard anything like that."

"I don't doubt it. It's part of this longer piece I haven't finished yet."

Avery wanted to know everything. What was it called? Where did she learn to do that? Who *was* she? But instead of saying a thing, all he'd done was reach for her.

"Do you have any idea how much you stand to inherit?"

Jerry's voice boomed in the study thick with heavy furniture, dark drapes, and whirling dust motes. Avery blinked; suddenly he was very, very tired. He'd hardly been in the house—Jesus, this house was huge—for more than a few minutes. Jerry's wife (he couldn't think of what to call her) had ushered him right upstairs, where his grandfather was waiting behind a desk, like he was there for an interview. And it turned out that maybe he was.

"Ballpark figure, you mean?" Avery tried a smile. "Possibly . . . enough to buy a ballpark?"

"There are two things a man should never joke about, and one of them is money."

Give me a break, Avery thought. He was here, wasn't he? He showed up, did his duty, was here for the chatting and the visiting and this whole forced *getting-to-know-you* scheme, so . . . *Come on, old man. Ease up.* Avery's memories of his grandfather were few and scattered: endless childhood Christmas dinners, getting dragged to some big award presentation, watching Jerry on TV. Then he was in high school, caught up by those first waves of drinking and snorting, and what did grandparents have to do with anything? But now, in the hot study, he suddenly remembered one other night, just after his father had left them, when his grandfather had put his hand on his head—the two of them alone in the foyer—and called Avery's dad a *low-down bastard*. Did that really happen? Avery had been barely seven when his parents split. Still, it lingered like the truth: the weight of that hand on his head, the whispered, confiding tone, man to man. *Low-down bastard.*

Avery snorted, thinking about it.

"What's that?" Jerry said. "Something funny?"

"Nothing."

Through the big windows behind the desk, he could see workers moving around the yard. The *ping* of tools—sledgehammer on a metal stake—and the shouts from the men drifted faintly up into this stuffy room. Avery fidgeted in his high-backed chair. Hard to believe he'd traded Nona's bed for *this*.

"Whatever happened to college? Didn't like hitting the books? Wasn't for you?"

"That's right." Jerry waited, but Avery stuck it out. He saw his grandfather soften a little.

"I'm not much for schooling, myself. When I was your age—what are you now, twenty-three?"

"Twenty."

"By the time I was twenty-two I had been to war. And back, though no real credit to me there. Then, in three more years I had founded my first company."

Avery nodded. He thought there was much more polite interest in his expression than the matter warranted; the fact of Nona—Nona in bed—made him indulgent.

"That was with your great-uncle, my brother. Frank was his name. He was two years older than me, but a lot of folks would have guessed the opposite. He was a joker, Frank. A lot like you, maybe."

"Is that him?" Avery pointed to a small framed black-and-white photograph on the wall, of a stern young man in a bowler hat posed in front of a snowy brick wall. Jerry twisted himself around with effort.

"No, that's my father. Only picture I have of him. Here's Frank." Jerry handed Avery another frame, this one from his desk, and Avery glanced quickly at the image of two brothers, each with one arm around the other's shoulders. The shorter man was clearly Jerry, bullish and thickset. Frank was taller, a bit lanky, and he was grinning at something happening outside the frame, while Jerry stared dead straight at the camera.

"Frank was a college man. For a while. He did two years at Notre Dame, and we got a lot of Chicago contracts out of that. We never said he didn't have the degree. We just never said."

Avery set the photograph carefully back on the desk and turned it to face his grandfather. There was a resemblance in that photo that unnerved him. He scanned the rest of the photographs on the desk and realized, even through the faded, out-of-focus images, that there had been—that there *were*—other men who looked like him. Who were related to him. It sparked a small shock of recognition, these old pictures, one that changed the old man sitting across from him: *there is blood here.*

"Frank liked a good prank," Jerry was saying. "One night in the dining hall, he and two fraternity brothers came in late, banged around loudly, pretending to be drunk. Everyone was shocked. Cleared out of their way. Well, the three of them sit down at a table and start to eat noisily, attracting lots of attention. Now, one fellow had somehow hidden a bag of beef stew inside his shirt, and all of a sudden he pushes away all his dishes and starts moaning, 'I'm sick, I think I'm gonna be sick.'"

Avery nodded, as he seemed expected to do.

"Then—whack!" Jerry thumped at his chest with the flat of his hand. "He spills it all over the table and makes a big show of getting sick. There's a horrified silence. Frank and the other fraternity man call out, 'It's all right! Don't worry, folks, we'll take care of it!' Then they picked up their spoons and ate up every bite of that stew."

"Oh, God," Avery said, and laughed for real. "They were legends, right?"

"Just about," Jerry said. He straightened the photo of Frank, aligning it with all the other frames. "That was one of his favorite stories, for years and years."

But the story, and the awkward silence that followed, brought a new feeling into the room.

Avery said slowly, "So I'll miss out on all that. College hijinks, and stuff." He waited to see what Jerry would say. Was this little tale about drinking more loaded than it seemed? Would he now be subjected to probing questions about his city activities and an old-school lecture about sobriety? Obviously, his grandfather had to know about his stint in rehab, although they'd never directly discussed it. They'd never directly spoken about anything, Avery thought, that he could remember. At least since that childhood moment in the foyer. *Low-down bastard.*

Avery set his face, hard and still, but Jerry was frowning at something else, and didn't answer right away.

"What?" he said. "So, you been talking to your mother about all this?"

"About what?"

"TrevisCorp. What she's up to. She tell you to come by and make nice? She figures you have a better shot now?"

"I don't really know what you're talking about, Grandad."

"You don't." Jerry fixed him with a look. "What did she tell you to say to me?"

Avery was baffled. "Nothing, she just—" Wasn't he *supposed* to be here? Wasn't that the deal?

"Eight hundred, forty-five thousand." Jerry rested his elbows on the chair's arms, and his hands on his stomach.

"What?"

"That's what goes to you, when I die. Doesn't include your shares of stock, the futures, or various other holdings. But that's the picture as it stands right now."

"Okay. But . . . that's a long way off. Right?" Avery wasn't sure if he was supposed to say thank you, or what. "Maybe I should get going."

"This all gives me an idea," Jerry said. "You and I should get to know each other, even if your mother—I mean, especially since your mother . . ."

Avery nodded, half out of his chair. "Sure. That sounds great." He wasn't sure what Grandad was talking about, but his ever-closer exit was buoying his spirits.

"Talking about Frank, to you just now. Well, it's a little . . ." His grandfather paused. Avery sat down again. "It brings me back. I'd forgotten that, about the beef stew."

"Good story." There was a steady drilling noise coming from outside the window, but Avery couldn't see the workers anymore. He felt a surprise surge of empathy and goodwill for this older man. Its driving force was Nona, although in the moment Avery could only half recognize that. Suddenly, he found himself wanting to be a comfort to Jerry. Suddenly, he wanted to be *there for him*. "And that other thing? You know, the two things a man can't joke about?" Jerry was blank. "Women. Right? I mean, it has to be."

"Women," Jerry echoed, agreeing. He let a small grin slip free.

This is good, Avery thought. *I can do this. Yeah: we'll be all close and shit.* Now just get him back to Nona.

Then Jerry thumped the desk. "All right then." Avery realized they had just sealed some kind of deal. "So, we'll get started. Same time next week?"

"Uh—actually I work, and Sundays are usually pretty busy, so . . ."

"Your office is open on weekends?"

"It's a restaurant. Called Pita Pie. On lower Broadway." Each thing he said made Jerry look less pleased. "I'm doing some prep cooking there."

"Well, it doesn't have to be on the weekend. My schedule's wide open now, as you can see." In response, Avery smiled weakly. "You can call me and say what day's best. And bring some kind of re-corder."

"Recorder?"

"Tape recorder, something like that. For a long time, I've been wanting to get some things down on paper. About the company—about my life. It'll be important for you, down the road."

"Oh," Avery said unhappily.

"You can type up whatever we record and we'll just take it week by week. All right, then?" Jerry slapped the desk, both hands.

"I don't have a computer, or anything like that."

"What?"

"It's true." Avery feverishly hoped this would be a big enough obstacle to the whole *you-can-type-it-up* plan, but Jerry was open-ing a desk drawer. He watched his grandfather write out a check and slide it across the desk to him. Twenty-five hundred.

"That should buy one of those small digital recorders, too. Like journalists use. Let me know what day next week." Jerry walked Avery to the door, and nodded him toward the stairs. Avery was still holding the blue piece of paper that said *$2500*. Just to the right of his own name.

Downstairs, Winnie—she insisted, laughing, that he call her that when Avery visibly hesitated over her name—seemed per-plexed when he turned down an offer to drive him to the train station. Standing in the kitchen doorway, Avery had fumbled through his wallet—Grandad's check stuffed in there now—look-ing for that little train brochure; he was sure he'd grabbed one in Grand Central. But Winnie knew the Sunday train schedule off the top of her head, and recited it to him, arms crossed, smiling a little at something Avery couldn't guess. Strange, but whatever. She probably didn't have a lot else going on. No, he didn't want a ride, thanks. Yes, another soda would be great. Avery had to get out of there.

He had to get out of there, but Jesus-fucking-Christ, this kitchen. Six-burner stove, immaculate. Two pristine convection ovens. A soundless freezer the size of his closet. And the island—a prep area set off from the counters, four square feet of two-inch maple butcher block. It had its own tiny fucking faucet and sink. Perfect. He had the heft of an imaginary knife in his hand, and he was aching to dice an onion on that butcher block.

Winnie caught him looking around. "Or how about a snack? You have time. Let me see—" She started opening drawers and cabinets, and Avery saw the bags of salt-free pretzels, the rice cakes, and boxes and boxes of Little Debbie snack cakes.

"No, really. I'm fine. But . . . can I ask you something?"

Something in his voice made Winnie stop completely and turn to him.

"Have you heard of Garbo? I mean, is that a kind of makeup brand, or just the name of a lipstick, or what?"

"Garbo?" Winnie looked so helplessly lost that Avery just said forget it. He was embarrassed.

And soon he was running, lame soccer sneakers slapping against the pavement, swooping in a glorious burst of awkward, breath-heaving movement down a long, winding hill, past all sorts of suburban folk doing their Sunday suburbs thing. They glanced at Avery, but he didn't have time to say much since he was *running*. Literally running, with no hurry and no point, a pointless gorgeous action it seemed he hadn't enjoyed in years, and why was that? Maybe he'd buy some running gear. Maybe he'd join one of those groups and run around Central Park every morning. It felt like laughing, this pell-mell formless pounding; it felt like being a little kid. Avery could smell himself, rank and unwashed, but that heat rising up from his chest and armpits just merged with the way his feet gripped the sidewalk and the swish-sound of cars whipping by. He'd be early at the station. He'd probably have to wait a while for that next train back to the city, back to Brooklyn. To Nona. That didn't matter, though, not one bit, and Avery ran on and on down the hill into town.

Seven

WINNIE

It may have been the first week of October, but Jerry still refused to put on an overcoat. He'd looked at Winnie like she was crazy when she suggested it, and began a litany of winters in Chicago. Now *that* was where you learned to dress warmly, et cetera, et cetera.

The high school was lit up on this evening, and their group joined a modest stream of people on the paved path to the auditorium entrance. Bob was at his writing class, although he said he would leave early in order to catch at least some of Winnie's big night. When she'd protested this—no need, her part was so small—he had said he wouldn't miss it. Rachel had said nothing. And now, although Rachel was hurrying ahead with the girls, Winnie slowed, matching her steps to Jerry's labored ones.

The opening reception for "Hartfield Station Stop: A Photographic History" was being held in the Girls' Gym—the photos themselves were installed along the corridor walls just outside, where two dozen people milled and peered closely at the black-and-white images, plastic drink cups in hand. This left the gym itself strangely empty, its two refreshment tables, podium, and rows of folding chairs all stiffly arranged on the waxed, putty-colored floor.

"It's not really the Girls' Gym anymore," Rachel was saying to Jerry, in the crowded foyer. "What do they call it now, Lila?"

"Everyone still says Girls' Gym," Lila said. Unlike Melissa, who had hurried down the hall to a friend, Winnie's older granddaughter stuck close to her mother.

"Really? What about all the drama, with the name change? What ever happened to that?"

"What's wrong with Girls' Gym?" Jerry asked.

"Well, this is the smaller of the school's two gyms," Rachel said. "So you can see why people got upset." Winnie wasn't at all sure Jerry would see, but he merely took in the information.

"Mom, we're not going to have to stand up or anything, right?" Lila whispered urgently. "Because of Nana?"

"Definitely not," Rachel said. "Nana's going to hog all the spotlight."

Winnie said, "Honey, what about when you do all those somersaults in the air? Everyone's watching you then, and you're always such a cool cucumber."

"That's different."

Winnie knew Lila's shyness was real and painful, and yet she thought it a complete mystery, especially for such a beautiful girl. Good lord, if she herself had had that hair and that figure back in her own school days!

Rachel and Lila wandered into the gym, to lay their coats along a row of seats—"not in the front!" Winnie could hear Lila hissing—and so she stayed in the hallway, smiling now and again at acquaintances, while Jerry strolled ahead, looking closely at the pictures and reading their captions. He wore a suit and tie, though hardly any other man there did. Earlier this afternoon, they had planned carefully for there to be time for Jerry to take a rest before bathing and dressing. When he had appeared in the upstairs hallway, pink faced, in his sharply creased dark blue suit, Winnie had cried out in dismay.

"But you—you're so—" She had motioned at her own slacks and turtleneck sweater, now unforgivably casual.

"And I thank you kindly," Jerry had said. "Now go get ship-shape, lady. I'm squiring you, after all." She had rushed back to her closet, heart full.

It was one of their first public appearances, and though Winnie knew it was a little silly to think that way, she couldn't help it. Nor could she help touching her pearls every once in a while or patting at the hips of her wine-colored long skirt, which had a matching silk shawl she was thinking about discarding. It was growing warm in here, with more people filling up the hallway. The only thing that she wished different was the faint discoloration along her jaw-line. Dr. Reynolds had said that it was merely a shift in pigment, not uncommon at her age, and certainly nothing to worry about—or even treat. But Winnie did worry. She hated the darker area that shadowed her left cheek and shaded down to the side of her neck. She hated that she noticed Rachel's glance skating quickly toward it, and away. She hated thinking that Jerry might find it unattract-ive, might find any part of her unattractive. It was so unfair. For years and years she had been all alone, with a perfect complexion, and now this. And she was hardly vain at all! Nothing about the rapidly multiplying folds of her skin or her knobby knuckles or even the strange new puffiness around her knees bothered Winnie. But this darkening patch of skin—oh, she hated it. In her worst moments recently, Winnie thought that she would easily trade a higher cholesterol reading, or even a return of the horrible vertigo, if her cheek would just go back to the way it used to look.

Meanwhile, she had lost sight of Jerry, so she moved through the crowded hallway, weaving around clumps of people, touching some lightly on the back as she maneuvered her way.

Most of the photographs were older, black-and-white, although she passed one blown-up blurry image from the 1970s. That was when the station building had been refurbished, with money from local businesses and a group of overly dedicated volunteers who combed the town for donors. Winnie glanced at the picture without stopping: a few dozen long-haired jubilant residents crowded onto the south-side platform, holding up a drooping banner: *We Are All Commuters!*

There he was, toward the end of the exhibit, where the photographs stopped and the regular high-school bulletin boards and trophy cases began. Notices for cafeteria times, cross-country meet results, and a large poster warning against drug use had been hastily untacked and dropped in a pile on the floor to make room for the exhibit. Jerry had unknowingly planted a foot right on top of the papers, while he studied one of the last photographs. When she approached, he began talking right away, just as if they'd never parted, a habit Winnie had come to adore.

"There he is," Jerry said. "Looks like he had a hard time of it, your father." He pointed at the image, a grainy black-and-white photograph that had been blown up and mounted against a white cardboard backing. Winnie had to put on her little silver reading glasses. The caption to this one read, "Early winter storm delays Hartfield Station completion by another three months. Harold Easton, foreground." And the photograph showed a front view of the half-formed building, no more than an abandoned skeleton, no roof, girders exposed, and an immense pile of construction materials buried under a thick gray blanket of snow. In the far upper corner of the photograph, behind her father, a few bundled-up men were standing around awkwardly and shyly, as people did for photos back then, when it took forever for the image to be processed. Or maybe they were just cold? One had his arm raised, as if to gesture at all the snow.

"My brothers always said they remembered that snowstorm. It must have brought a somber mood into our house, that's for sure. Sad-looking old thing, isn't it."

Jerry studied the photograph some more. "There's more development in town than I'd thought there'd be. See, there's the bank building."

"Yes. It took forever to get the charter. Do you think they have the punch set up yet?"

"And they'd started paving the crossing right there. Any later and he wouldn't have had the room," Jerry exclaimed, jabbing a thick finger at the photo.

"Well, I think—"

"They'd already reneged on a promise for a bigger lot."

"Who had?"

"The township. Says so, on one of those other plaques. They kept offering leases to storeowners, and when the rail men complained, they were told that shops were the way to build the economy, not a station stop."

"Now that's ridiculous," Winnie said.

Jerry bobbed his head from side to side, indicating that there were points to be made on both sides. "In any case, your father had his work cut out for him."

Winnie laughed. "He was that kind of man," she said. "He relished it, I think."

"I would have liked to have known him," Jerry said.

For a confused moment, Winnie found herself thinking, *well, but you must!* She forgot, in a tumbled way, how and why it wasn't possible for her husband to meet her father, and that she wouldn't ever have the simple, complicated pleasure of observing these two men clasping hands. She was overcome by the sensation that she'd somehow *forgotten* to make such an introduction happen and felt a panicky urge to rectify the oversight immediately. Though which of her fathers should Jerry—now at least ten years older than Harold Easton at his death—meet? Her childhood father, the overcoated man spied in one or two photographs lining the hallways of Hartfield High School; the man who presided at Sunday dinner, chiding Winnie's brothers for their unwashed hands, carving the roast into precise, even slices. He must have had so much on his mind then, but he was always gentle at home, always low-voiced and kind to her mother. Winnie could breathe it, right now, the pomade in his hair, the packet of cigarettes in his breast pocket. But if anything, the man Jerry would have met, if at all (which was not at all, of course), would have been late-stage Harold, Harold in his last years, ill-tempered and lonely, uninterested in the newspaper or the meals she and George brought over weekly. They had never had much to say to each other, her father and George, other than the polite usual. Winnie couldn't help imagining that

Jerry's presence then, while her father lived out his long year of dying, would have brought more . . . what? More discussion, more understanding, more *substance* to all those pointless afternoons in the hospital.

Men needed that, she thought now, watching Jerry study the blurry photo of her father. They didn't admit it, but they needed the company of other like-minded men. Especially as they got older.

"Do you wish Daniel had flown in?" Jerry said now.

"What? Just for this, you mean? No, of course not."

"Still, it's nice," Jerry said, looking around at the crowd, the carefully mounted photographs. (Pestered by the committee, Winnie had provided a number of them, peeled out of her albums in boxes now stacked along one wall in the basement of 50 Greenham.) "The way it's all preserved here. All these men, their work."

Down at the end of the hall, Winnie saw Rachel's head emerge from the gym, and then one of the organizers behind her, Erica Stein, who waved with energy. The presentation would be starting any minute, but Winnie turned her back on them.

"You know, I think it's a grand idea, meeting with Avery. We'll just have to keep after him. And having him write down some things, about you. A boy like that shouldn't be at odds and ends."

"What? Oh. Avery. Yes, I've got a plan for that one." Though Jerry's gaze trailed along the photographs, Winnie knew he wasn't really seeing them.

"Annette will come to her senses," she said quietly. "This can't go on forever."

Jerry snorted. "Annette doesn't give a fig about what it takes to build something. She only wants to turn a buck."

"That's not true."

"Nothing wrong with it, either! But there will be no 'Trevis-Corp: A Photographic History' anytime soon."

"Maybe we should just go to Chicago," Winnie said. "Go out for a nice, civilized dinner. In person, all of this could be sorted out. With the lawyers in the middle of everything, and all this back and forth—it's impossible to settle things like a family needs to!"

"That point passed quite a while ago. I filed countersuit on Tuesday, and the board has moved to freeze all company assets while this thing plays itself out."

"Countersuit against . . . Annette? Oh, Jerry." Winnie could hear Rachel's voice, coming closer. Now she understood all the phone calls of last week, the long hours in his office with the lawyers. Still, he'd never until now mentioned a thing.

"Don't 'oh Jerry' *me*. She wants to play this game, we'll play it."

"I still don't understand how it came to this." He had sued *Annette*? Winnie was unnerved; why hadn't he told her earlier? And why would he tell her now, she couldn't help thinking—just as she was about to go onstage?

"How what came to what?" Rachel had appeared. "Okay, Mom, the natives are getting restless."

"Showtime," Winnie said, and struck a little pose. She tried to smile. Maybe Jerry's being so casual was a good sign. Maybe it was just how things were done, in families with all that money.

"Full house in there," Rachel called over her shoulder. She and Jerry had already started down the hall.

Winnie followed, taking the opportunity to touch the fine-grained bumpy spot near her jaw—yes, still there—while looking over the outfit her daughter had chosen for the evening: those battered clogs she wore everywhere, a baggy sweater and *jeans* (well, they weren't exactly jeans, but corduroy slacks that for all intents and purposes looked just like a pair of jeans). This unhappiness of her daughter's, it was a hard thing to face. And tricky too, to know what to do or say. Rachel never spoke directly about her feelings for Bob, and Winnie—who knew something about the ups and downs of a long marriage—was careful not to suggest anything was wrong. A person's marriage was her own private business, after all. And so Winnie did what she could, as much as she could, as she always had, even after Bob recovered: she kept the girls' school schedules on her own refrigerator; she attended recitals and took Rachel's turn at carpool duty. She brought salads to share at Rachel's lunch break; she lent her car and her time and her tips for easing a child's fever. Still, at times Winnie felt it anew, that same sorrow she'd had when Danny and Rachel were children and tripped or bruised or cut themselves; even as she'd rocked, and bandaged, and soothed, she'd mourned with a queasy guiltiness a mother's knowledge that they would know pain, her babies, over and over again, in the life she had brought them into.

Now Jerry was escorting Rachel—or was it the other way around?—down the hall and into the gym. They were arm in arm, talking about the exhibit. She could see Jerry pointing out different photographs, and Rachel leaning down a little, to listen. A sudden peal of her daughter's raucous laughter surprised Winnie, as did the comfortable way Rachel pushed at Jerry in a mock shove.

In the past month, Jerry had transferred ten thousand dollars, twice, into a new account that Rachel had set up. On one of her first visits to 50 Greenham, on a rainy Sunday afternoon, Rachel had disappeared with Jerry into his office upstairs, while Winnie showed Lila and Melissa the secret dumbwaiter that she herself had only just discovered. They took turns loading laundry into it, and then funny things—a single shoe, a dozen apples—to rappel up and down three flights of stairs to one another. Then, Winnie had found a pack of index cards, and while Melissa made flash cards for French class, she and the girls had switched on the television to catch the end of *Rebecca*. Both Lila and Melissa snorted at Mrs. Danvers, thinking the performance over the top and silly, whereas Winnie always found Judith Anderson truly terrifying in this role, icy, slowly unhinged. She tried not to keep glancing toward the hallway leading to the stairs, and just as Manderley burned to the ground, Rachel slid in next to Lila and gave Winnie a calm nod. So, everything was fine. Why hadn't she expected that? What was the lingering unease she felt, while the credits rolled and a debate about pizza ensued?

Since that Sunday, Rachel and Jerry were in cahoots about all sorts of things. Winnie would stop by Hand Me Down and begin to tell the story of the upstairs fuse blowing twice in one night the week before, for no rhyme or reason—and of course her bedside flashlight batteries were dead—only to have Rachel interrupt, saying that Jerry had mentioned it. And then there was the peculiar way the two of them were about the money, never making light of the loans exactly, but referring to them all the time (except for when the girls were around), the tax issues and investments and debt, all with no awkwardness from either one, as if money was an interesting subject in and of itself, as if Rachel and Jerry were merely puzzling out the best recipe for bread dough . . .

This instant connection between the two of them—well, it delighted Winnie. (Erica Stein ushered her to a folding chair near the podium.) It *did*, she insisted to herself, watching Rachel, in the audience, lean casually in toward Jerry and point something or someone out to him. But it was complicated, in a way she wouldn't have predicted. Rachel was using her hands, those long-fingered, strong hands that reminded Winnie of George, tracing something in the air—a box shape?—that Jerry tried to follow with beetled brows. Winnie guessed that Rachel didn't know she was seated on Jerry's bad side, that much of what she said would be lost to him, because he would be too proud to ask her to repeat herself. But there was delight in seeing her daughter there, and her comfort with this man, neither of them paying any attention to her up here on the stage—delight, and anxiety, and satisfaction, all at once.

Rachel *did* like Jerry, didn't she? Just for who he was? Winnie told herself to avoid what was coming, but the searing question arose anyway: it wasn't just about the *money*, was it?

Stop it, she told herself. She was just rattled by this news about Annette. Winnie looked once more at Jerry and Rachel. She wouldn't be sitting cozily next to *her* new daughter-in-law anytime soon.

As Erica gave the opening remarks, Winnie exchanged greetings with the gentleman at her left. Wizened and practically deaf, he somehow let her know he lived with his son in Mount Morris and his cousin—or his late wife's cousin?—had been the photographer for several of the images displayed. *Lord*, Winnie couldn't help thinking, *they're really dragging everyone out of the woodwork.*

Now a woman was speaking—a different one, from Town Hall—saying something interminable about the rise of the "bedroom suburb" in the tristate area, the social history of rail stations, and notable architectural features of Hartfield's own. Winnie had heard it all before, and couldn't imagine anyone who hadn't, especially among this retiree-heavy crowd.

"Red Janson, Hartfield stop's first-ever station agent, was not only dispatcher and ticket seller: he was a postmaster too, and also the town's locksmith. When you needed those new eyeglasses, Red would tell you if they had arrived. He was known to run card games out of the back office, when things were slow, and would let boys toss pennies onto the tracks—he'd also chase them away if they got in the way. One thing Red never did was hold a train. Not for anyone, not for any reason, big or small. 'God and the Timetables,' read a sign over his desk, as you might have seen in one of the photographs—though perhaps Red would not have considered them quite in this order."

The audience chuckled. Winnie restrained herself from reaching up to touch the darkened patch near her jaw. To distract herself, she read the blue and white cloth banners tacked up to the rafters—STATE FINALISTS, TRACK AND FIELD, 1969. LEAGUE CHAMPIONS, GIRLS' SOCCER, 1976, 1977. Someone, unable or unwilling to locate blue felt, had added 1978 with a marker, the numbers squeezed unevenly into the very corner. Winnie recognized a few names hanging there, above her, from families who had been around Hartfield as long as she had.

Last week, while the man from yet another tree service—four so far, each one eventually declining the job—measured the sycamore's trunk and took some digital photos, Winnie's new neighbor Vi Greenberg strolled across the street and stopped to watch. Winnie had waved her in, and Vi had walked slowly across the long, sloping front yard.

"It's not mealy worms, is it?" she called, as she got closer. Winnie had known Vi and her husband, the retired Judge Greenberg, for years and years. George used to treat the judge for hypertension, and Vi's mother, in fact, had known Winnie's slightly—Vi had once shown her a leather guest book with Delia Easton's name carefully inscribed in her familiar hand. Now Vi's grandson was a chaplain in the army, serving in Afghanistan; at church, they prayed for him weekly. His wife, on a base in Florida, was pregnant with Vi's first great-grandchild. "They were in our boxwood, last summer. You just spray this nasty stuff—he'll know the name of it, I'm sure." Vi nodded at the tree man.

"No, it's not mealy worms," Winnie said. She held her smile steady. "They said Indian summer, but you could have fooled me."

Vi stared up at the branches that arched wide and high above the two women, in their matching tan pants and weekend shoes. "Aphids?" she said. "This early freeze should take care of those critters."

The tree man was walking toward them, with his clipboard. Winnie took a deep breath. "Vi," she began.

"Have to check with my boss," the man said. "We don't usually—"

"That's fine," Winnie said. She nearly ripped the yellow sheet out of his extended hand. "I'll be here."

"It's just that with something this size—"

"Fine, fine," Winnie said, urging the man back to his truck.

When she turned back, Vi Greenberg had fixed her with a cool and level gaze.

"You remember when we got a bit of Hurricane Caroline?" Vi said.

"Of course I do, Vi." That was late summer, in 1986. Lila was a baby, and Winnie had spent the night in the spare room at Rachel's, the window rattling hard against its four silver duct-taped Xs.

"The Harrison's maple went over—" Vi pointed to the house next to hers. "And then electrical wires set off a fire on the top of two pines, down by Mina Sullivan." Winnie dug her hands into her pockets, pushing the crumpled estimate down deep. "All I could think, that night, was please don't let the sycamore go. Any tree on our street but that one. Nobody even lived here then, so maybe I felt I had to stick up for it. In the morning, there were branches everywhere, big ones blown up on our porch, even—"

"I *remember*, Vi."

"But when I looked out and saw it still standing, I felt foolish." Vi let her gaze travel up the tree's broad trunk, deliberately not meeting Winnie's eyes. "I thought, who am I to worry about this old warrior? Why, this tree was around before I was born! What an insult, to even picture it coming down."

Winnie's cheeks burned a little, up onstage, the way they had when she could say nothing, there under the tree with her neighbor. Vi had smiled then, and pretended to shiver in the cold, and then hurried back across the street to her own house. Winnie tried to push it out of her head, tried to pay attention. The little old Mount Morris man had been introduced, and he bowed his head, one hand raised, for the applause.

Now Erica was speaking at the podium, her voice high and excited: "—as part of the high school's *permanent* collection, which I'm very pleased to announce tonight." This drew the appropriate murmurs and applause, while Winnie tried to figure out what she had just announced. That some of the photos would be hanging in these classroom hallways, for good? For generations of young people to ignore or jostle, or splash soda on, as they ran by? Winnie wanted to laugh out loud, but now Erica had turned to her with an expectant smile . . . right. She was supposed to say something, on her father's behalf, and so she took her turn at the podium.

"My father would have been very touched by all of this. Actually, by now he would have been asleep. This is far past a railroad man's bedtime." Winnie paused for the obligatory laughter. She wanted to search out Jerry's glance, but the lights were brighter than she expected and the microphone intimidating.

"My father had just a small part in Hartfield's station, which was the product of a lot of people's hard work and the generous nature of the town's founders. So in his honor, I'd like to thank the organizers of this very flattering exhibition—thank you, Erica— and . . ." Here Winnie faltered, forgetting completely, if she'd ever known them, the names of the other ladies on the committee, but her general wave in their direction was apparently satisfactory, because the audience went right ahead and applauded. Winnie was relieved. Most of the time, she thought, people knew what they were supposed to do.

"A question? Mrs. Trevis? Could I ask a question?"

Winnie was halfway back to her seat when she stopped, confused. She couldn't see who was calling out, from the back, though it was a woman's voice, loud and clear.

"Well, we hadn't exactly planned on any Q and A . . ." Erica said. "But if Winnie wouldn't mind? Just one or two, perhaps?"

So she was back up at the microphone. This time she found Jerry, who gave her a frowning, pleased nod. Rachel, next to him, was whispering to Melissa.

"Mrs. Trevis, hi. Over here." Now she could make out the person that this bright, aggressive voice belonged to—a college student, perhaps? The girl had dark hair, pulled severely back, and a notebook tucked under one arm. She smiled widely and stopped waving when she could tell Winnie saw her. Then the girl's clear voice rang out, loud and confident.

"I was just wondering why you plan to cut down the historic sycamore tree on Greenham and Franklin?"

Before Winnie fully understood, Erica Stein was beside her. "This is a photographic exhibit," she said, shouldering her way toward the microphone.

"It's a public forum, and I have a right to speak! Isn't it true, Mrs. Trevis, that you—"

"If you have a question about the train station—"

"That tree is over a hundred years old! It's a living thing!"

Four or five other protesters, in their twenties and thirties, each in a T-shirt that read TREE TRIBE had stood up next to the first woman, and they were all shouting. Shouting at *her*.

"Shade! Clean air! Homes for animals!"

"Order, please, or we'll have to get security! Order!" Erica was hammering at the podium with the flat of her hand, while Winnie just stood there. In her shock, she almost laughed. Was this actually happening, or had she conjured the whole scene by remembering the awkward encounter with Vi Greenberg? How did anyone know about that old tree? Then she remembered: the permit she'd filed at Town Hall two weeks ago.

The audience, after its initial bewildered silence, flurried with movement—some members craning their necks to get a better view of the shouting protestors, others raising their own voices in dismay or disagreement. A hearty "Boo!" came from the little old Mount Morris man who had been seated next to her.

Now, as if on cue, the protestors quieted. Erica did too, wary and relieved. Now maybe they could get back to business.

"I'm sorry to interrupt," the original woman said primly. Then a gleam came into her eye and Winnie realized it wasn't over. "It's just that she's cutting down one of the biggest and oldest, one of the most beautiful trees in town—to build a *swimming pool*!"

At this, the crowd sucked in its breath, an audible gasp. The woman with the notebook and ponytail glared at Winnie, triumphant. You could hear people in the audience repeating the phrase *swimming pool*, their voices low with disgust, as if the woman had announced that Winnie planned to put a puppy mill in her front yard.

As if to capitalize on the mood in the room, the protestors were once again shouting, "Clean air! Shade! Homes for animals!" She saw Jerry, struggling to his feet. He was having trouble pushing himself up from the flimsy folding chair, and Rachel was doing nothing to help him get steady, because she was staring at the protestors. Bob, who had just arrived, was asking everyone, "*What? What happened?*" Winnie saw Melissa and Lila, frozen. It was the look of terror on Lila's face, though, that made her act.

"Now just a minute, here." She leaned in to the microphone, and ignored Erica, who said she would handle it. "How am I supposed to answer anything if you people won't stop to listen?" Her own voice, amplified across the gymnasium, comforted Winnie—she could hear in it a trace of familiar exasperation, but nothing more. No sign of how rattled she felt inside.

"You've got questions—no. You have something to say. You're unhappy about the tree. I understand that, and maybe we can find a way—"

The standing four paid no attention. They weren't even looking at Winnie anymore, because they were busy shouting, "We speak for the trees! We speak for the trees!" Their voices clashed with hers. Still, one by one the other faces in the audience were turning back to Winnie, and she was the one with the microphone, after all.

"That tree is ninety-four feet high," she said. "And its branches are almost the same width—did you know that? I didn't, that a tree's 'wingspan' can be equal to its height." These facts quieted the audience a little, though Winnie didn't know why she was saying them, other than to speak something into the microphone in front of her. "And I did see purple finches nesting there. And blue jays, of course, though they're not so picky. Isn't that right, Tess?" She had spied an old comrade of George's, one of his early-rising birder group.

"*Now* you take an interest," Tess called back, sassy as ever.

Winnie hurried on, afraid of more comments related to George. All these people in the audience—many had known her for fifty years or more, and now Jerry was sitting in their midst, a total stranger to them. It was hard not to feel on trial. Two of the protestors had stopped shouting, for the moment, as if to hear her out. She cast around for something else to say. "Its trunk is nine, ten feet around—oh! Listen to this. It appears that after two hundred years, a sycamore becomes hollow. But it lives on, hollow or not; did you ever hear that? I read somewhere that pioneer families could even live inside one while they built homes. She caught Lila's eye and smiled. "Packed in like sardines, you have to imagine."

At this, Winnie faltered; she was running out of tree facts, and that last image gave her pause. She'd made a faux pas, a bad one; she knew Rachel had to be thinking of her own living situation. In fact, Rachel was sitting still and calm, looking up at her with an expression that read, *You've made your bed, Mom. Now what?*

"Don't think I haven't done my homework," she said, casting her voice across the small audience, her neighbors and townpeople gathered here. "Due diligence, as my son-in-law might call it." Bob saluted her, his bald head lit and shining, the brightest thing in the room. The protestors, though, were not appeased. They bent their heads together for a quick conference. Winnie didn't mind; she realized it wasn't to them that she was speaking. "These photographs, all this history . . ." She waved an arm vaguely toward the hallway where the exhibit was mounted. Winnie felt tired, all of a sudden; she should have told her daughter about the pool, about the tree. A tree all hollowed out, living on despite that emptiness, that gutting out. Why had that stuck with her? Why was it so disturbing?

By now the one security guard, a gray-haired man, had ambled over to the chanting protestors. He wore a small smile, as if to acknowledge the sudden starring role of his minor part. He began to shepherd the group toward the door, calmly, a bit wearily, and the protestors didn't resist. Their voices grew smaller and smaller as they moved toward the back of the gym.

"Some things are more important than the past," Winnie said into the microphone, but that wasn't what she meant, exactly. She knew she sounded as if she were pleading to the audience. How could anything she said make them understand? All those faces, some filled with doubt, others with confusion.

The first woman, who had ambushed Winnie, was the last to be led out of the room. "How do you *sleep* at night, you rich bitch?" she screamed, just before disappearing.

That energy and fury flew directly to Winnie like a sharp slap. "Oh," she said weakly, backing away from the podium, hand to her jaw, covering the dark patch. Her own distressed exclamation, a low sound, hung in the air, and the unintended push she'd given to the microphone stand touched off a piercing squeal of feedback that hissed around the large room. The speakers whined, drowning out Erica. Most people in the audience had left their seats. Someone was saying something to Winnie, but she shook off the kind hand on her arm, and she ignored Rachel's worried expression, now right in front of her, blocking her way. Winnie worked her way free of them all, and either he had made it to her, or she to him, but at last Jerry's thick hand found hers, and they stood still together.

None of it mattered, then—not any suit or countersuit, not this public comeuppance—as soon as Winnie felt Jerry squeeze her hand, once, hard. She returned the favor, and let the tumult go on around them.

Eight
RACHEL

Rachel stood in front of the girls' shared closet in their shared room. Dresses and skirts were crammed tightly together, packed in so close that to dislodge one item meant several others pulled off their hangers in unison. Piles of clothes were on the floor, too, tangled with shoes and an extra blanket that had fallen off a shelf. Tank tops, bathing suits, and summer dresses were still here, in October, forgotten and flimsy-looking, but Rachel had no energy to weed them out and pack a box for storage. Nor had she any space for storage in this two-bedroom apartment. There was a single crawl space under the stairs, but it was stuffed to bursting with brooms and buckets, two extra dining chairs, and too many unmarked boxes of—what? Books, probably, or pots and pans. Parts of their old life: haphazardly packed up, tucked into corners, and pretty much ignored. Rachel tugged halfheartedly at a few items of Lila's, hoping for inspiration—these flared jeans, for bell-bottoms? But then Melissa might insist on some kind of belly-baring "hippie" top. No way. A pink-and-white turtleneck . . . what about a candy cane? Cute, but in a kind of ironic way. Was that even a possibility?

"You wish," she told herself. Last spring a girl in Melissa's class was suspended for wearing a skintight camouflage T-shirt that read MAJOR FLIRT REPORTING FOR DUTY. AT YOUR SERVICE, SIR!

It had come as a surprise this morning, when Melissa asked about a costume. They were having cereal.

"Seriously?" Rachel had said. "Kids are still dressing up? In the seventh grade?"

"I don't know," Melissa said. "Not, like, officially or anything. Not for class."

"It's just that it's kind of late in the game, sweetie. Today's Thursday."

"I don't have to."

"Mom," Lila said, and it had brought Rachel up short, her older daughter's tone half question, half warning. So much had changed for them. Rachel herself had changed, so much, since the accident, since the move.

The problem was, she used to love Halloween.

There had been the Mother Goose year, when Lila was Little Miss Muffet (in lace-trimmed pantaloons, carrying a stuffed spider and a paper cup of sludgy white paste marked CURDS AND WHEY), and Melissa portrayed Hey Diddle Diddle in a furry gray-and-white cat suit that had taken Rachel three weeks to make, with mascara whiskers drawn on her tiny face. She'd carried Lila's school violin for a fiddle—or Bob had, anyway, during trick-or-treating, to prevent its being dropped or dented or altogether forgotten in the heady rush for doorbells and candy. Then, when Lila was about ten and Melissa seven or so, Rachel had made them both into birds, using the same sheer black fabric with flecks of shimmery green, and each girl had long, swooping wings they delighted in all night, and wild feathered headpieces, and curved plastic beaks stapled to elastic bands that itched and chafed and were promptly discarded. In the photos, taken each Halloween on the front steps, you couldn't tell at all that they were meant to be birds (without the beaks, they looked more like 1920s-era flappers), but they were ebullient, barely contained, standing side by side: Melissa's round little tummy, Lila's bare ankles.

Now Rachel stood in the girls' room—smaller than either of their own rooms had been in the real house—and tried to summon that old energy, that once-powerful interest in batting, industrial adhesive, cardboard tubes. Time was short. She made up the beds without needing to move, pivoting from one side to the other, smoothing sheets, pulling up coverlets. Their desk was wedged between the doorjamb and the closet. Rachel stacked folders and righted a pencil cup. She nudged the computer mouse in doing so, and the monitor whirred to life. A screen-saver picture of Greg Louganis mid-dive was immediately covered by a dozen instant-message boxes and Lila's (ldive4gold) and Melissa's (mel5334) "we're not here" automatic responses. Rachel clicked through a few, reading enough to make sure nothing smacked of forty-something-pervert-pretending-to-be-thirteen. There was a certain way you had to arrange the desk chair; to make enough room to get out, it needed to be pushed backward, toward the beds—not tucked under the desk, as one would think—and Rachel, who'd forgotten this, did an awkward little dance with chair and door before figuring it out.

Across the tiny landing was the bathroom, and next to that was Rachel and Bob's room. Was there anything Melissa might use from her own closet? Rachel mentally scanned her gaudiest

dresses for possibilities. But the thought of entering her own bedroom, and the sight of their oversized carved-wood bed and bulky
matching dressers, everything too big for the space, depressed
her. It was always stuffy in there too, mostly because of the single,
oddly rectangle-shaped window, placed too high for any breeze
to cool the room. Most nights, Rachel woke at least once with her
skin on fire, heart pounding.

(Worse, the joke was on her: once, several years ago, between
tenants, they had considered widening and replacing this window
as part of a few projects to maintain the apartment and *Rachel* had
been the one to successfully argue that it wasn't necessary.)

Her mother probably had the right idea about bedrooms. On
a first visit to 50 Greenham, Rachel had been startled by Winnie
casually inviting her to peek into "Jerry's" room—she glimpsed a
high single bed with a tartan print blanket, and a pair of pants laid
across an armchair—and then, down the hall, to "my" room.

"So you don't . . . ?" Rachel said, pointing at the distance between the two rooms.

"What?" Winnie asked with a twinkle, pretending not to understand. "A person likes her space. You'll understand, down the
road."

"Doesn't it make it hard to—you know? Sleeping apart?"

"Absolutely not!" Winnie laughed. "We visit each other," she
said, scissoring her fingers back and forth in a walking motion,
from one room to another. Rachel couldn't decide if this was practical or utterly romantic.

"But you and Dad always shared the same room."

Winnie snorted. "Oh, that. Well, let's just say that we slept well
together."

"Right. Never mind. I don't want to hear about it."

"I'm talking about *sleep*! We were compatible in that way."

"And you and Jerry aren't?" This was the first Rachel had heard of something not perfect about Winnie's new love.

Her mother had flashed a tiny, inward smile, before moving on to show Rachel how they'd decorated the girls' room. "We're compatible in another way," is all she'd said.

Bob took a potent cocktail of drugs before bed—he was still on anti-seizure medicine, as well as several others—and therefore slept a thick, unmoving eight hours every night. He slept better in the tiny, overheated apartment than he ever had in their airy, real bedroom. Infuriating. At one of Bob's appointments last year, Rachel had once, only half joking, protested the strength of his nighttime drugs. "What if there's a fire?" she said. "How on earth will I be able to rouse him?" One of the doctors had glanced over at Bob's shaved head, and the scars. "Trust your luck more," he'd said. "I would, if I had your kind."

"Sure thing," Rachel said aloud, turning sharply away from her bedroom. "Lucky me."

She was supposed to be at Hand Me Down, but she had switched days as a favor to the other employee, Moira. On any other day, she would have been glad for the surprise day off, a chance to run errands and pick Melissa up from school herself. But now she was stuck with the costume problem. Rachel wandered from the living room to the kitchen and back again, eating an apple. Through the back wall, behind the couch, she could hear the clang and thud of Vikram's mail drop through the front door slot and land noisily in his—her—front hall. A minute later, footsteps on the side path as the mailman wedged their own mail inside the screen door.

Rachel put her apple down on the coffee table and wiped her hand on her jeans. She found the phone number in a drawer in the kitchen and dialed, saying to herself even as she hatched the idea, *He could be home. He could have a day off too.* But of course he wasn't, and the call itself was just for show. Rachel listened to the phone ring, in her handset, and the faint, practically unrelated echo from deep within the house. And then she hung up, and found the keys.

In less than a minute she had gone around front and was letting herself in, trying to look natural to anyone she knew who might be driving past. The heavy pop of the lock was a familiar, lost sound. Rachel busied herself with stepping neatly out of her clogs in the entranceway and pulling the door shut behind her, so that she could delay that first long look around her house. It was the first time she'd been back since they moved out.

He—Vikram—had reversed the dining and living rooms, and that was idiotic. Not that she was biased. Three modern sectional pieces (two white, one black) were arranged on a geometrical-print rug where Bob's mother's antique table used to be. A big framed still of Humphrey Bogart and Ingrid Bergman hung over one couch, and a 3-D sort of sculpture (metal, twisted) took up space just outside the kitchen entrance where Rachel had always had a side table and matching mirror. A rough, dark wood table with benches instead of chairs was in the living room, draped with an elaborate red-and-gold runner and strewn with piles of mail and magazines, folders, empty soda cans, a laptop computer, and a bowl of half-eaten cereal. Where their couch had been, the one on which Bob had collapsed, was nothing now. Just empty space.

A cell phone rang somewhere in the house and Rachel's heart

stopped. Suddenly, the stupidity of this plan came crashing in, even as she wildly thought up unlikely, unnecessary alibis—*just checking the . . . furnace*. She took the stairs two at a time, saw with relief that the master bedroom's door was closed, and hurried up another flight into the hot, musty attic.

There they were, neatly labeled plastic boxes, set amid the furniture Vikram had said it was fine to leave. Rachel tripped in her rush, and fell heavily, tearing her sleeve on the head of a nail protruding from one of the unfinished wood posts. She lurched upright, ignoring the stinging in both palms, and yanked at the boxes until the right one tumbled toward her. It was getting hard to breathe. The crib her babies had slept in, dismantled to dusty pieces leaning against the wall. The lamp they'd bought in Florence on Rachel's thirtieth birthday. Her favorite chair, streaked with dirt.

"I'm fine," she said out loud, teeth gritted. "It's fine." *Jeans shirts skirts dresses no no no no no no no.* Wait! Black shimmery polyester, with long, flappy sleeves. Perfect: Lila had worn it in a school play, and Rachel knew there was a hot-pink wig somewhere in the girls' closet. "Funky witch. Kooky witch. Who gives a shit." She heard herself, sounding crazy, but didn't care. She started to stuff the other clothes back in, and then gave up, left it all a mess and bolted for the stairs in the grip of a panicky, powerful urge to get out.

She might have made it too, if it weren't for the other doors, ajar, on the second floor. What she glimpsed made Rachel falter. It was something wrong, and it slowed her, still clutching the witch dress, and drew her over to the rooms inside—Lila's, on the left. Melissa's, right across the hall. Both were empty, completely empty. As echoing and empty as the day they had moved out. Rachel took a few unsteady steps into Melissa's room and her throat closed. She touched the wallpaper, sobbing, the repeating pattern of pastel elephants holding each other's tails.

"She'll grow out of it so fast," Rachel had protested, pregnant, when they were decorating another nursery. She loved their choice but wanted to be practical. "Or he will."

"So, we'll redo it," Bob had said, swooping Lila up over his head in that way Rachel hated. "When he's a surly teenager. Or *she* is. Maybe we'll paint it black. Right, Ms. Big Sister?"

Because she was crying so completely, a shuddering, whole-body sort of weep, the sound of Vikram's footsteps down the hall, and his sleepy-eyed presence in the doorway behind her, were somehow normal, as was the way he took her elbow and guided her to sit down on the floor, with her back against the wall. He knelt, in a half-crouch, asking without words if she was all right. Rachel signaled that she was, a half smile through the gasps. Then it was just a matter of time, of the sobbing's needing to run itself out in a few more spasms.

Pine tree branches were scraping at the front window, the one that gave out onto Locust, like the sloppy dark-green paw of a huge dog.

"That used to drive Mel crazy," Rachel said, pointing. She wiped her face with the witch dress. "It would wake her up at night."

Vikram watched the needles mash against the panes. "It's like being in a car wash, isn't it? I guess I haven't noticed."

"I'll call the tree guys this week to trim it back. You don't want those branches this long over the winter—they get heavy with ice and then break off against the house."

"Or I can do it."

"What? No, you'd never manage. They've got this ladder on a truck—and these machines, automatic saw things—"

"I meant I could call them, if you'd like."

"Oh."

Rachel gingerly put the back of her head against the wall. Mentioning the tree guys brought it all back: last week's mortifying fiasco at the high-school photo exhibit, and the strained, infuriating conversation she'd tried to have with her mother afterward, denying all the while that the real reason she was opposed to this pool was because she hadn't been told anything about it before the rest of the town, when they were all treated to Winnie being publicly shamed by a bunch of vociferous tree huggers, whom no one even recognized as being from Hartfield, by the way. Why that mattered, Rachel couldn't say, except she knew that it did. And the reason she was opposed to the pool was because it was total madness! You didn't just drop a swimming pool in the front of an old property like that! So, Jerry's back hurt—he could have massages! He could try yoga. Rachel told herself to be more sympathetic; after all, she knew about caring for someone in pain, how easy it was to get caught up in a desperate mission—how even the wackiest New Age cure-all could seem a reasonable, prudent form of treatment.

But—but . . . everyone went to Waugatuck to swim. They just did; they always had. No one had their own pool—it would be so gauche, so ostentatious, so . . . *New* Hartfield. *Mom, you can't just go around doing whatever you want in this town*, Rachel had sputtered. *Why on earth not?* Winnie had demanded.

Rachel winced. Her whole body felt sore and shaky. She considered the various ways to extricate herself from this situation.

Vikram was still squatting, his forearm resting on a knee, balancing with the fingertips of one hand on the floor. He wore shorts and a white Dartmouth T-shirt, and his face was puffy, a little creased.

"I woke you. I'm sorry—I didn't think anyone was home."

"My time zones are all mixed up. I flew in this morning from Jakarta, and I took a sleeping pill, so probably"—Vikram yawned, drowning himself out—"didn't hear the doorbell."

"No, you wouldn't have. Listen, do you mind if I ask you a personal question?"

Vikram stuck his bottom lip out. "All right," he said cautiously. "It's not about my girlfriend, is it?"

"Your—? No. Why would it be about your girlfriend?"

Vikram rubbed his face and gave a boyish smile of relief. "You'd be surprised how many things are," he said. "Am I still asleep? I need to have some tea. Could we, please—"

"Of course," Rachel said, taking his hand and allowing him to help her up. He held Melissa's door, so she went first, out into the hall and down the stairs. "I cannot go into the kitchen," she said. "I just can't."

"I know," Vikram said.

When he emerged with a tray, Rachel was sitting on one of the sectional pieces in her dining room, gazing at the photo of Ingrid Bergman.

"I must be the only person on the planet who hasn't seen *Casablanca*," she said. "We rented it once, years ago, and even then I was so far behind—Bob was always after me to see it, and everyone's always, 'How can you not have seen *Casablanca*?' but it just never seemed like the right time—anyway, so then we finally rented it, and the tape broke about fifteen minutes in. Now I figure it's just my fate not to ever watch it. Thank you," she said, about the mug of tea she'd been handed.

"Yours is herbal," Vikram said, a bit pointedly. This struck Rachel as very funny. "My mother is a film professor," he added.

"Wow," Rachel said. "Back in India?"

"No, at UCLA."

"Christ," she said. "I'm sorry."

"Why are you sorry?"

"I just meant . . . I didn't know you were from California, is all."

"I grew up in Hoboken, and my mother moved to L.A. a few years ago, after my stepfather died. Does this have to do with the personal question?"

Rachel flushed. "Maybe I should go. This is all—pretty strange, for me. To be here."

"You don't have to," Vikram said. "What were you going to ask me?"

"Well, okay. It has to do with money, and I just—you're in business, right? I know Bob must have told me, but I forgot what it is you do, exactly—"

"I own a company that restructures other companies. Are you familiar with the energy industry?" She shook her head. "Right. Well, then that's probably the best way to put it. Our primary market focus is South Asia."

"That's amazing—and you're . . . what, not even thirty yet? No, never mind, just ignore that." The tea was bitter, but its warmth had begun to restore Rachel. The throbbing behind her eyes eased, and the physical sense of being in this room—stupid couches notwithstanding—was seeping into her as a slow, unfolding peace. How many meals had she served in here? How many times had she pushed open that swinging door with one hip, plates in hand, children clamoring at the table? These walls recognized her. They righted her.

"It's just . . . here's the thing. My mother, who lives in Hartfield too, recently remarried. Did you hear about all this? No, of course not. Well, her new husband is being sued by his own daughter. Her name is Annette; she's this Chicago—"

"Suing because . . . she disapproves of the marriage? On what grounds?"

"Well, it started as a business dispute. Her father—that's Jerry, Mom's husband—owns this company and Annette has some executive position. I don't know the specifics, but apparently there was a disagreement that couldn't be sorted out, so now it's become a legal issue."

"Not that uncommon, unfortunately. In family businesses." Vikram leaned back. "It's too bad for everyone involved, of course."

"Well, now it's getting more personal," Rachel said. "Last week, Jerry called and asked if he could tell me something, in confidence. I said, fine. He says that Annette has filed a lien on the house, this house that they really shouldn't have bought at their ages . . . but anyway. The daughter now has the lawyers arguing that this house my mother is living in is company property and actually part of the dispute and could be—"

"Why would it be company property?"

"Because Jerry bought it in cash. That he liquidated from company assets."

"Ah," Vikram said. "And I assume we're not talking about an insignificant . . ."

"Two point four million dollars," Rachel blurted. And that felt good, like cursing.

Vikram let out a low whistle. "I didn't know Hartfield had properties in that range—unless, is it one of those newer developments? By the school?"

"No, no. It's on Greenham Avenue. One of the oldest houses in town. You can barely see it from the road, since there's so much wooded area in front. I mean, on Chicago's North Shore this place wouldn't raise an eyebrow, but here in Hartfield—well, everybody knows about this house."

"It sounds grand. But I don't quite . . . why are you telling me this?"

Rachel set her mug on the sharp-edged glass coffee table. "It's stupid, I guess. My mother doesn't even know I know about this, and now she has this wild idea about putting in a *swimming pool* . . . and everything anyone says only gets her mind more set on it. But now with this lien on the house—doing anything like that would be, just, a bad idea, to say the least. Right?"

Vikram opened his mouth to respond, but Rachel went on. "And if I say anything about it, she'll know I know. She's not thinking clearly. Maybe that's why Jerry called me." She stopped. Actually, why *was* Jerry confiding in her? Maybe he saw her as a substitute for Annette. The idea made Rachel—well aware of her lack of business acumen—nervous. Aside from the matter of her loans, Rachel had thought that she and Jerry were striking up some kind of friendship.

"Anyway, my mother has this ridiculous conviction that all of his money doesn't matter. I mean, I don't even think she *thinks* about it, how much the house actually costs. Not that she's accustomed to it or even feels entitled, really . . . but it's weird, isn't it? To practically ignore the fact that Jerry has this incredible wealth? No one in our family has anything like it. No one we *know* does—Hartfield's just not that kind of place!"

Where was Vikram going? He had wandered away during this, into the foyer and back.

"Is this your mother?" He was holding up a copy of the local paper.

Rachel sighed. "It sure is." The article about the debacle at the photography exhibit had mercifully limited its coverage of the protestors—*Editors know these guys only want attention*, Bob had said—but had included an unflattering photo of Winnie, frowning and in mid-sentence at the podium, with the caption, "Derailed! Local resident and exhibit participant Winifred (Easton) Trevis faces tough questions about historic tree on her property." Winnie herself was laughing about it only the next day and had agreed to be interviewed by Melissa for a social studies paper on the event.

Vikram raised his eyebrows, reading silently. Rachel was surprised he even took the *Bugle*. What could he really care about in our town? she asked herself. Why *did* he choose to live all the way out here, anyway, all by himself? From there, it was only a short, inevitable step to *Who* is *this man, barefoot and proprietary, making me tea in my own house on a Thursday afternoon?*

"Jerry seems to think she should stay out of it, my mother. But don't you think she needs to be clear on what's at stake? I mean, at least she should know what she's getting into. Not just float along with this whole *love-is-all-you-need* attitude."

Vikram looked up quizzically. "Why?"

"Because—because it's not realistic. And because other people are involved."

"What does her husband—what does Jerry think? About this pool? Does he want it badly enough to face the possible consequences?"

Rachel started to speak, and then stopped. "Actually, I have no idea. She says it's for his back pain, but as far as I know, he hasn't spoken a word about this whole pool project, one way or another."

"Well. It sounds as if there's not much your mother could do, in any case, even if she did know about the lien. That's what lawyers are for." Vikram checked his watch—or his bare arm, anyway, rubbing at where his watch would be.

Rachel knew she had to go, but felt that something urgent needed to be clarified. "But how do you think it would *look*? To you, as an outsider. Not an *outsider*, but—you know what I mean. A brand-new pool, two old people—I mean, how much use would it get, anyway? Doesn't it seem strange?"

Vikram waited for a moment before answering. "It's impossible for me to say," he said, not unkindly. And he held the door for her, as she gathered the witch costume for Melissa. She slid her clogs back on.

"Thank you for the tea. I'm sorry I bothered you." Rachel wished she had sunglasses to put on.

"Mrs. Brigham—"

"Rachel, please."

"Rachel. If you need to come in sometimes, just let me know. I am not unaware of the difficulties you must face—with our . . . situation." Vikram waved his hand back and forth between the sides of the house—*yours, mine*. "And that it can be hard for the rest of your family too."

"Why? Have the girls—I'm sorry about Melissa leaving her bike in front. We talked to her about that."

"I'm talking about your husband. He was over, one time, not too long ago."

"Bob? What did he do? What did he want?"

"He didn't do anything, really. He had asked if he could just look around, and he said it had something to do with his writing, but I think what he wanted was simply to be here for a little while. He stood quietly in the room there for a few minutes, and then he just thanked me and left."

Nine
AVERY

"Mondays are brilliant," Nona said.

"I know." Avery took her hand and put it in his pocket. "You're off, I'm off . . . and everyone else is stuck in the office. Writing their little e-mails, reading their little e-mails."

"Everyone else?"

"Suckers. Sad sacks. Soul sellers."

Nona rolled a piece of candy from one side of her mouth to the other. It drove him crazy when she did that. She tucked it in her cheek and asked, "What do you know about working in an office, anyway?"

"I know it fucking blows, that's what. What do *you* know about it?"

"I've done time in all sorts of places. Plus, and this might be news to you—I'm no spring chicken."

"Really? I hadn't noticed." Nona stuck out her tongue. The inside of her mouth was stained dark purple. "So then, where've you worked, Office Girl?"

In response she only stretched, arcing her joined hands high enough behind her head to elicit a series of little pops and cracks from her back. He watched her gaze at a garbage truck rumbling past, and how the truck doubled and mirrored itself in her sunglasses. They were huddled in a doorway, trying to stay out of the wind. "Where *is* that guy?" Nona said, stomping her feet.

Avery immediately shrugged off his jacket.

"No, no."

"Shut up." He bundled her up like a little kid. It sent a thrill through him, the way she was instantly dwarfed inside his coat. Nona pulled her hair free from the collar. Long, ratty dreads and braids splayed across the fleece shoulders, and Avery had to restrain himself from tugging at one. Or biting it.

They were on Myrtle Avenue, standing across the street from the bare, padlocked Blue Apple Diner, in the Fort Greene section of Brooklyn. Although gentrification had worked its way through this historic African-American neighborhood years ago—its brownstones revived and resold, cafés and bars full of monied hipsters (a lot like Avery, he had to admit) pushing out the older, original residents—none of that had made it to this stretch of Myrtle, a few blocks north of Fort Greene Park and the looming brick towers of the Wentworth Housing Project. Avery knew that in their demos, the rapper kids from Wentworth called it "Murder Ave." What had been the Blue Apple Diner was the ninth space he had looked at, and the first one he wanted Nona to see too. They had already tried to peer through the soaped windows, and Avery had gone on and on about how little it would take to pull down the old overhanging sign and tear off that nasty, ancient fake-wood trim running along the front. Stripped down, minimal, clean— that would be his look. (At the last minute, he'd avoided saying the word *vision*.) Nona had listened quietly, eyes roaming the street, the scene.

"Anyway, the foot-traffic thing?" he said now, bouncing up and down a little to distract himself from the cold. "Whatever. It's a destination, a place people go to for a reason. Not some place they're just strolling by and stop in to eat a three-hour dinner."

"Some people are already strolling by," Nona said. Across the street, an older black woman slowly wheeled a shopping cart full of garbage bags. They both watched as she paused to hawk a glob of spit into the entranceway of the Blue Apple Diner and then continue on her way. Avery sighed.

"This is the guy," he said, a minute later. A squat, dusty brown car had double-parked outside the restaurant, and Ricardo got out. He was in his mid-forties, with a black leather jacket and complicated, precisely shaved facial hair. They crossed the street to where he was unlocking the metal grate in front of the diner, cell phone wedged between ear and shoulder. He shook Avery's hand and held the door open for Nona, motioning them inside.

"If it says, 'in person,' then it means *in person*," Ricardo was saying into the phone. "Otherwise, what the fuck?" He crossed the room ahead of them and switched on the lights. Avery half wished he wouldn't.

"How much?" Nona asked. Fluorescent panels above them buzzed and flickered, greenish white. A long orange counter ran the length of the room, though where the stools had been was now a row of broken holes in the dingy tile. But the tables were still here, six or so four-tops with flimsy metal legs. Beat-up chairs were scattered around, some knocked over backward, a few set upside down on the tabletops.

"Sixty-five hundred," Avery admitted, kicking aside a crumpled paper bag. "Plus two months' deposit."

"A bargain, then," Nona said.

"Okay, but you're seeing the worst of it. So, all this comes out. I pull up the tile and redo the floors. That's first. Then, the bar. Knock this out"—Avery tugged on the orange countertop and it came away from its base easily—"which won't be too hard, obviously." He pounded it back into place with a glance toward Ricardo, just outside. "What else? Oh, the bathroom. Yeah, don't go in there."

"Roger that."

"But check this out—here's where it all comes together." He tugged Nona around the back of the bar and into the kitchen. She turned in a slow circle, taking in the stained range, uneven shelving, and the walk-in refrigerator, but Avery could tell she wasn't getting it. *Walk-in fridge!*

"No diner has a kitchen like this, first of all. They have a big goddamn griddle and a couple toasters! Two ovens? You can roast four chickens at once in these! You don't need these for anyone's basic fucking fry-up. This guy told me there was another place here, before the diner. Some kind of soul-food joint, in the eighties. It's all been sitting here since then. Probably untouched."

Nona had wandered over to the six-burner stove and reached out to touch something Avery hadn't noticed—a tiny, dark wood frame nailed directly into the wall, eye level. It displayed a worn dollar bill with 1999 scribbled across the front in black marker.

"Another thing: all this stuff is already *here*."

Nona didn't say anything. Avery felt frustrated, talking to her back.

"Did you hear me?"

"I heard you. Is that unusual?"

"*Yeah*, it's unusual. Any other place, we'd be looking at empty holes in the wall, hookups for gas and electricity. This all comes with. I mean, it's not TV-chef shit or anything, but it's another ten or twelve grand I don't have to lay out."

"So, what happened?"

"Well, Ricardo just said yeah, it's included. And if he doesn't know what it's worth, I'm not going to be the one to tell him."

"No. What happened to this guy"—Nona flicked at the plastic covering the dollar bill—"Mr. Blue Apple."

Avery shrugged. "He got behind on the rent." He waited for her to respond. "I mean, yeah, it's a risk. But the way I see it, the neighborhood's not going to support a local place on a regular basis. It's not really the brunch crowd out here. Coffee and eggs, even at a steady pace—say, forty covers—that's not going to be enough."

Nona turned to him and nodded, but in an annoyingly vague kind of way, Avery thought. "Are you getting hungry?" she said.

"The difference is, with a twenty-dollar entrée, there's less pressure to get people in the door all day long. And like I said, it's a destination thing." Avery knew he sounded neither clear nor convincing, even to himself, but it was distressing to see her just wander out to the front again. He was suddenly exhausted, and just stood there for a while, in the musty back area near the john—whatever that god-awful swampy smell was, he just didn't want to know—watching Nona, back out on the street. She was still wearing his jacket. She was saying something to Ricardo, who now got all attentive and serious, in a way he never had been with Avery.

Men did this around Nona. Never once in his life had Avery cared about other guys checking out his girlfriends—back in Chicago, to be fair, he'd often been so high he probably wouldn't even have noticed—but now he found himself seething at the way men bent to listen to Nona, putting their nasty heads down too close to her face. She drew initial looks, double-takes, because of her style—the mass of dreads, the off-kilter outfits, like today's: baggy brown wool pants and splatter-painted sneakers—and Avery might have been okay with that had it not usually led to the kind of riveted, impressed attention that Ricardo was displaying now, whenever Nona began to speak. (Why did she have to *speak* so much? To anyone other than Avery, that is?)

He shut the lights off, and instantly the details of the broken, squalid room disappeared. "What's up?" Avery said, pushing out the door to join them.

"You got my number, kid," Ricardo said. "But I wouldn't sit on it too long, all right? Couple other guys are interested. And another thing," he said, moving past Nona to yank down the grate. "You call me again, it's to sign the lease. I'm not hauling out here to 'Gangland' again for shits and giggles. Not that the company isn't a pleasure"—this with a grin at Nona. Then he padlocked the chain, slammed into his car, and drove off. They watched him do a sharp U-turn on Myrtle and roar past them, heading south for the exits to the bridges.

"I can't get on the train unless we eat," Nona said, smiling. "I'll pass out. And I told Henri I'd be at the studio by four, so . . ." She zigzagged her body to and fro, east and west. "Which way?"

"So, what were you two talking about?"

"What?"

"With that guy. Ricardo. You guys were pretty chatty out here." Avery heard himself, and hated himself, but couldn't stop. Hearing for the first time that she had plans for later in the day— plans that didn't include him—tipped the scales, and now he slid into helpless, half-pleasurable self-pity.

"'Chatty'? Well, yes, we were *chatting*. Quite a bit, in fact, while you finished your tour. Give me a minute." Nona shut her eyes and put a couple fingers to her forehead. "I'll see if I can reconstruct the exact conversation for you. Line by line."

"Whatever."

"Really? Is this a jealousy thing? Right. Sorry—I'm supposed to be flattered now."

"I just don't get why you'd rather stand around and talk to that douche bag about whatever—"

"Avery. Cut the shit. I hardly think a two-minute discussion about Staten Island merits the third degree." Nona cocked her head and smiled, offering a chance for Avery to get reasonable and call it quits.

"Why the fuck were you talking about Staten Island?" he said flatly. "What, does he have some other overpriced shit-hole out there I should go visit?"

"We were talking about Staten Island because he fucking *lives* in Staten Island. And because I was making polite small talk with your friendly slumlord so that you could have a fuck-ing minute in there alone to figure it out. Jesus." Nona stalked up the street, and Avery followed. He was fairly sure she didn't know where she was going. For a little while, they did nothing but walk fast and furious up Myrtle Avenue, Avery a few feet behind Nona.

"Come on," he called up to her. She didn't stop. "Could you just fucking hold on, for a minute?"

In response, Nona threw a hand backward in a kind of get-lost wave.

"Why are you being such a bitch?"

That did it.

Nona wheeled around, unzipped Avery's jacket, and let it drop to the ground. She laughed a little, not in a good way. "What do you want from me? I'm not your mommy, Avery. I'm not your little trust-fund manager. What, I'm supposed to jump up and down because you suddenly get a whim about wild salmon in the ghetto? Grow up."

"I don't have a trust fund!" Avery exclaimed. And instantly thought, *Do I?*

"What would *you* be risking? What are the stakes? When some of us 'get behind on the rent,' we don't tap some suburban nest egg and merrily go along our way."

"Is that what this is about? That my family has money?"

"See, when you say that, with your face all *I can't believe it*—it's like, oh, what a petty little thing for her to bring up. That's exactly the point."

"I didn't make a face like that."

"My *mother* worked in an office. She was a secretary at a law firm in Pittsburgh for twenty-five years. When her first boss retired, she got a new boss, younger than I was—and the same desk, same paycheck, same hour-and-a-half commute. Okay?"

"Okay," Avery said. Music came thumping faintly inside a

basement-level church nearby. An older man, leaning on a crumbled brick railing, watched them with obvious interest. "Well, you never told me that before."

Nona shook her head. She was standing on his jacket, looking unhappy and cold. "See? You don't even— Forget it."

"But you just stood there and looked at all of it and didn't say anything!" Avery said in a rush. "I don't get it! Are you pissed at me, or something?"

"What did you think I'd say?"

"I thought you'd show some fucking *interest*, for one thing."

The man on the stoop sucked his teeth loudly. "Better watch it, boy."

Nona whirled to face him. "Is there any place to eat around here?"

The man took his time, thinking it over.

"Come on," Avery said. "Can we just—"

"McDonald's over on Willoughby."

"That's—that way, right?"

Avery tried to put his hand on her arm. "Nona, please. You don't want McDonald's."

"*You don't get to say what I eat!*" She took off around the corner.

"Thanks a lot, man," Avery called to the oldster on the stairs, bending down to grab his jacket. A smashed, half-eaten donut was stuck to one arm.

"I ain't said nothing 'bout nothing." The man chuckled as Avery ran past him.

He pounded down the street, and what flashed through his head, randomly, was Winnie and that crazy-ass pool she wanted to plant right smack in their front yard. The stubborn, don't-give-a-shit look he'd seen on her face each time one of the contractors tried to argue with her. Wrong place, bad idea, too close to the house? She didn't care. Axe some mammoth tree standing in her way? Fine. Just get it done. *That* was what he should be like, with the restaurant. It was pretty embarrassing to find himself wishing for the mental attributes of some eighty-year-old lady, but there you have it, Avery thought.

A block or so later, he caught up with Nona.

"Listen. Just listen for a second, all right?" She wasn't looking at him, but then she wasn't racing ahead anymore, either. Avery couldn't remember the last time he'd had a fight with a girlfriend— hell, with anyone—when he wasn't fucked up already, or at least had the promise, the consolation, of getting that way afterward. He took a deep breath. "First of all, I apologize for the thing about office people, if that's where this started. I did not, in any way, mean someone like your mom. Who I would love to meet, by the way. When you want me to, I mean—never mind. But, okay, I can see where that was a really shitty thing to say, and why you'd be pissed off and that it would make you all, you know, distant and stuff at the restaurant—" Nona tried to interrupt, but Avery hurried on. "Doesn't matter, doesn't matter. The point is that I should have thought before I spoke. So that's one part."

Nona was watching his face carefully.

"But I have to ask something. Well, two things. Here's the first one, and I just have to know." They were standing in front of a chain-link fence, freezing. "When we went to Maryland. Are you saying that was weird? I mean, me paying for all of it?"

It was going to kill him if she was now going to turn those two days and two nights, every one a strong candidate for Avery's best ever, into some kind of depressing *I-feel-cheap-when-you-pay-for-me* thing. The day after Avery had cashed the check Jerry had given him to buy a computer and printer, he'd spent an hour online at the coffee shop, rented a car, made some reservations, and told Nona to call in sick at Silkworm. Really sick. They'd driven a straight shot to Baltimore, and spent the next forty-eight hours in a salty, blurry haze: softshell crabs in red plastic baskets, one night at a skanky motel and the next at a fussy bed-and-breakfast where they pounded the rattly bed so hard that the proprietor avoided all eye contact the next day, plus one unforgettable blow-out meal at Le Finestrine, a tucked-away place where Avery ordered enough food to earn a hushed respect from the stiff-necked waiters and cause the chef to come join them at the table with a bottle of 1964 Latour. Avery didn't need anything else in the world, in that moment where Nona raised the glass to her lips and he got to watch her face as she tasted the wine. Everything distilled itself—the food, the miles of highway, her body and what it did to him—into one perfect shimmering fusion, right then.

"'Weird? You want to know if I felt *weird*?" Nona said. Was she making fun of his choice of words? Was she ready to stop being mad? "'Weird' is my middle name."

Something wordless passed between them and whatever it was gave Avery the green light to pull her close. Nona shivered in his arms.

"What's the second question?" she asked, face muffled against his chest.

"You don't really want McDonald's, do you?"

"Hell, no," she said, pulling away. "Now, buy me a real lunch, moneybags."

Well, so what if he wanted her approval? So what if trying to do something—the first thing ever, on his own—came as a direct result of wanting to have her see him in a new light, of wanting her to be proud of him? That was only the initial impulse, the image in his head of a new look of respect on Nona's face, the way she could say to people, *My boyfriend? Yeah, he's a chef. He owns his own place—you should really come by some night. Plus, he's* awesome *in bed.* It wasn't just that, though, the stupid fantasies that would run uncontrolled through his head while he chopped cucumber and fried falafel at Pita Pie. (The worst, the most embarrassing, involved flashbulbs going off at opening night, celebrities turned away at the door, and Nona in this tight red dress, perched at the bar and smiling at him as he sent out plate after plate of fabulousness to the ecstatic foodie crowds packing the tables. Really. Red dress. Flashbulbs!) First of all, Avery would argue to himself, what the fuck was wrong with wanting to make your lover proud of you? Was that, or was that not, something totally understandable and decent? But, just in case it was hugely uncool, he hastened to remind himself that there were several other recent factors that contributed to the idea of opening his own place. The plan.

First, aside from wanting to win Nona's favorable opinion on everything about himself, Avery had to admit that hanging around her friends was good for something other than secret inward competitions he would set up all night long and then, naturally, always win: *MacArthur grant? Good for you, bro. But guess what? She's going home with* me! Nona knew everyone and had plans almost every night: workshops, rehearsals, performances, readings. As for her own kind of music—the art-song stuff—Nona didn't talk about it that much, with Avery at least, although he knew she was working hard on some new series. But she took him to a midnight Beckett production under the Manhattan Bridge; she was a regular in this group of people learning how to play folk songs in Estonian or Peruvian or something; two nights ago he met her at a show where men were miming frenzied sex while someone intoned old radio advertisement jingles into a microphone. A lot of it was laughable, some of it was startling, but all of it reminded Avery that he wasn't doing anything. Back home, he'd had drugs, and the galvanizing fear of getting caught. Out here, though, he didn't have a goal or a dream or an agenda or a drive or a burning desire—other than Nona, of course. Not that he wanted to be in a body stocking up on stage, humping some guy, but after a while it started to get to you, all this art. Plus, he was tired of saying he was a cook at Pita Pie to Nona's friends, after whatever performance, when they would politely ask him what he did. Actually, Avery was even tired of saying the *words* "Pita Pie."

But it hadn't been at some cutting-edge downtown performance that Avery's plan had taken shape. No, that had occurred out in Hartfield, of all places. Avery was dutifully taking the train there every week, or almost, for the hour or so it would take his grandfather to talk himself tired while Avery squirmed and fidgeted and tried to look interested. There was always so little air in that study. Avery found himself yawning compulsively, and desperate to fight off sleep. After he'd blown the $2500 on the weekend in Maryland with Nona, he had shown up for their first session with an eighty-dollar used laptop from a junk electronics store on Forty-second Street. Jerry either hadn't noticed the difference or wasn't saying—and there'd been no further mention of a digital recorder. Mostly, Grandad was content to talk, on and on, while Avery pretended to be getting it all down, hunting and pecking with two middle fingers. What did he talk about? Well, it was hard to say, since the busted laptop had one video game that still worked: cascading colored bricks that had to be arranged just so before they landed. Avery was up to the fourth level.

One day he was drafting what he liked to imagine was a scorching love letter, safe behind the open cover of the computer and the tapping of the keys. Grandad was going on and on; it didn't matter much if Avery listened or not. Not that he didn't sometimes listen! They were up to the year when Jerry and Frank, not content with their little paper packing company in 1950-whatever, mortgaged their houses and took out a loan worth four times the size of their entire business in order to buy a competitor's firm. They had six months to turn a profit, or they would default. It wasn't *completely* uninteresting. It just wasn't where Avery was at in his life, this *on and on and on* about the past. He had things to do now.

"So you won't need to make that mistake," Grandad said, laughing at some memory. "No, I'd say we covered that one for you. But good."

Avery looked up. His fingers hovered over the keyboard. *For me?* What was he talking about?

"I'm not blathering on for my own amusement," Grandad said, serious now. "Not *just* for my own amusement. Don't tell me you want to cook peanut sandwiches for someone else for the rest of your life."

"Pita," Avery corrected, but he was distracted. His grandfather took an envelope out from a desk drawer and slid it toward him. Occasionally this is how he would give Avery a little cash, for the train fare. But when Avery looked at the figure on the check inside the envelope, what he saw there wasn't a train-fare kind of amount.

"Now, I haven't signed it yet," Grandad said, taking the envelope back. "But you saw your name there, didn't you? It's waiting here for you, as soon as you're ready."

"Ready for what?"

Grandad waited a moment before answering, enjoying Avery's confusion. "For your first investor to pony up," he said.

Avery was silent, still stunned. *His own . . . restaurant? Could he really? What kind of place . . . what kind of food?* A thousand new thoughts began to form. Grandad watched him, then put the envelope away and shut the drawer firmly. And then he began to talk again, about business in the old days.

Later on, Avery had come downstairs, his head swimming. Had that just happened, with the money, with the idea of his own place? As usual, Winnie was reading on the couch in the living room. She put aside her library book right away—*The Plot Against America* by Philip Roth. Same book in his backpack.

"Another soda?"

"No, I'm good. I should be heading back. What's the latest out there?"

Winnie sighed and glanced out at the lawn, where several stakes and red plastic tape hung, wet and abandoned, in the downpour. "A big old mess," she said cheerfully. "Rachel's tree man went out of town for three weeks—and you should see all the customer complaints I found on the Web, about that one pool company that I'd been interested in. So it's back to the drawing board. That tree's spared—for the moment, anyway."

From where he stood, Avery had a full view of the doomed

sycamore; it was almost as if it had been planted exactly there in order to be seen from the living room's main window. It *was* a pretty beautiful tree, not that he was a nature freak, or anything. He glanced away guiltily, but Winnie caught him—and she had that mischievous smile, the one that said *I'll do what I want.*

Avery hated to put this into words, even in the privacy of his own head, but at times like this he could see what his grandfather saw in Winnie. And then, inevitably—like now—he would find himself appraising her lithe, trim figure as she moved across the room. Or wondering how much action his grandfather was getting. What did old people actually *do*, when it came time to get it on? Did the same standards and rules apply? Or was there a whole new order of business?

"Avery? What do you think?"

He snapped out of it. "I . . . what were you saying?"

"About these visits. We love them, of course. But . . . are they causing problems between you and your mother?"

His mother? "Why would they? I mean, she's the one who made me swear to come out here. I mean, not that I don't want to, or anything."

Winnie brightened. "Good, good. I'll run you right over to the station—but would you mind doing a little heavy lifting first? Rachel dropped off more boxes. You'd think, working in the kind of store she does, that she wouldn't need to *save* all these old things of the girls', but—"

Avery hoisted up a box and headed down to the basement. He didn't really need to hear all the details, and as usual by the end of a Hartfield visit, he was dying to get out of there. But there was something long-ago familiar about the brown-and-cream color of the children's book he glimpsed inside, and when he pulled apart the box flaps and saw the cover of Maurice Sendak's *In the Night Kitchen*, Avery was hit with such a powerful sense memory that he had to sit down on the cold basement floor. *Exactly like my old copy*, he thought, turning the worn pages of the illustrated paperback with a pleasure so intense and unexpected it was actually painful. Maybe it *was* his old copy? An unreasonable thought, but unshakable, since every single picture—a naked little boy tumbling out of his bed into the starlit world of the night kitchen, those fleshy titan bakers alternately terrifying and pathetic, the city made of flour-can buildings and milk-bottle skyscrapers, all set against an inky blue-black sky—every one, Avery knew by heart. All of a sudden he was eight, lying flat on his back in his bed, in the old house in Evanston. If he held the book high enough overhead, arms straight, and angled it just right, he could catch enough light from the window to see the pictures. Occasionally, the strained sound of his mother's laughter would float up from downstairs. He was supposed to be asleep. His father had left them—*gone for good*, is how he'd overheard his mother put it—the summer before.

"Milk in the batter! Milk in the batter! We bake cake! And nothing's the matter!"

In the shadows of his grandfather's basement, Avery allowed himself another moment, sitting there alone. He already knew he'd steal the book and that this theft would be stupid and unnecessary. Of course Winnie would let him have it, if he asked. But he wasn't going to ask. He was going to slip *In the Night Kitchen* into his pack and carry it onto the train, where he could savor Mickey's triumph—soaring up and up, in his bread-dough plane, to pour the milk and save the day—in private. These extra moments, then, here in his grandfather's basement, weren't so that he could finish reading the book. They were to quell sudden hot tears that had caught him off guard.

"I don't get it," Nona was saying to the guy behind the counter at Kennedy Chicken. She had been studying the plastic overhead menu with the utter concentration of someone determined to crack a code. '"Quarter chicken, comes with bread or salsa'? That doesn't make sense. I mean, because the two things aren't equal. Salsa is more like a sauce, like something that should already be a part of the order, whereas bread—that's kind of like a side."

"You want both? That's extra."

"*Maybe* I want both, but first I want to understand the options. Can you show me the salsa? Does it come with anything?"

"Does the *salsa* come with anything? Girl, it comes with the *chicken*." Now it was the cook who was baffled. Avery just leaned against the counter, happy to be here. He'd steered them back to Myrtle and down to Flatbush, homing in on this place that now seemed like paradise, compared to the ugliness of the Blue Apple and their fight out on the street. At least forty whole chickens were cooking away behind the register, spit-roasting in various shades of dark, oily gold.

Avery savored this moment, with Nona taking forever to or-der—now she was hassling the cook about the different sizes of the salsa containers—before they would sit, alone at the tiny plastic table. Before their food would arrive, and they'd have a few min-utes where he'd have to decide whether or not to go there again, back to the fight that hadn't ended so much as come to a stop (there was a difference, he knew, and yeah, he knew that it was significant). Should he push her to say more? He could feel there was stuff Nona hadn't said, about the money, things she was holding back. Which would feel worse: hearing now what they might be, or guessing at them later? This wary peace lulled him, as did the smoky char smell that filled the room. Probably it was all fine. Avery watched the chickens roast. They looked great: fresh and plump. In a minute, he'd ask this guy for the name of his local supplier.

Later today, he'd call Ricardo and go sign the damn lease.

Part II

Ten

WINNIE

It was mid-morning on Wednesday, in the first week of November. Winnie sat alone in the hushed conference room, waiting for Jerry to make his slow way back from the restroom. She resisted the urge to go into the hall to look for him—he would hate any sign that she thought he needed help, especially here. So instead, she fussed with the glass of water the receptionist had quickly placed in front of her after she'd asked—a polite college-age young man, which surprised Winnie—but why on earth hadn't he set it on a coaster? Tiny beads of water ran down the outside of the chilled glass, pooling onto the smooth wood tabletop, and no matter how often Winnie lifted the glass and swiped at them with her bare hand, the wetness remained. One would think that a law firm as posh as McCann Dunham would know to have a few coasters around.

It had been a long time since Winnie had been on the sixty-fourth floor of any building. It was a shame about these translucent shades, pulled down all the way. What she wanted was to look out the windows, all the way down to Sixth Avenue and Radio City

Music Hall, and the tops of the taxicabs moving around like little yellow toys. Or would it be Fifty-fourth Street? Being up this high had disoriented her. Without moving, Winnie tried to picture the view across town—the ash-colored streets, those Gothic midtown churches, that museum tucked away and practically hidden, the one with the newer pictures. (Winnie much preferred the stately grandeur of the Met. Now *that* was the way a museum should look.) MoMA. The acronym came to her, but not the full name, and while she was puzzling it out, she heard voices outside the door.

Ed Weller and Jerry arrived, deep in conversation, and it was astonishing, the way Ed held the door for Jerry and guided him in, a hand on an elbow—astonishing, the way Jerry accepted the help so easily from his old friend and lawyer, the way he let himself be steered to the table, and his cane and chair arranged for him. All while Winnie was accepting Ed's kiss, and smiling and nodding, she marveled at how it had been accomplished—Jerry's submission. She would never have guessed another man could effect it, but maybe that was the answer in itself. He didn't need to protect other men the way he felt he had to protect *her*: a woman, his wife. They all took seats now, at the table, as well as two junior lawyers who slipped into the room and flanked Ed Weller.

"Not a fun job for me, today," Ed was saying. "But I'm glad you're both here. We'll turn this around. No question. The main thing is not to get downhearted. It's a bad business, but we'll turn it around."

"I told Winnie about this fool motion having to do with the house," Jerry said. "I told her, but I don't like having to. Business is business; there's no need to bring my family into the middle of it all."

Winnie saw the two younger lawyers exchange a look. She shifted imperceptibly closer to Jerry. With a surprising rush of sisterly feeling, she found herself thinking of Beth Ann, Annette's mother, and how good it was that the woman was no longer alive. What a sorrow it would have been to her, this ugly fight between father and daughter—and over what? Nothing. Work, money. Then again, of course with Beth Ann alive, none of this would be happening. It was because of her—because of Winnie—that this had all begun.

"It's a tough situation," Ed agreed. "But everyone involved knowing the facts is an important—"

"I told Winnie because I didn't want her to hear anything from anyone else," Jerry said. "Annette's stepped way over the line, dragging this in. My house is my own concern and nobody else's. Just do what it takes, Ed. Send me the bill and let's be done with it."

"That's the plan," Ed said mildly. "But we need to discuss another matter. The game has changed a bit, and you need to prepare yourselves—both of you." Winnie ran cold at the way kind Ed Weller gave her a look. The look said *This will be hard on him.* "We heard from their lawyers early yesterday. I don't know how much of this is coming from Annette—most likely someone cooked it up for her, so just keep that in mind, first of all."

"What's this now?" Jerry said.

One of the lawyers slid some papers out of a folder and was staring down at them.

"They're filing a competency challenge, related to the property sale," Ed said. "It's going to be in a different court, so we'll have the two matters running at the same time. Dan Wickham—you've spoken on the phone—has run up a list of our options, and we have some strong ones, so I wanted to go over these. Let's talk through what the—"

"Competency?" Jerry said, frowning.

"'Petition to set aside deed based on defendant's mental incompetence prior to and at the time of conveyance—'" Dan Wickham was reading from the papers in front of him, but Jerry's strangled roar stopped him.

"It'll get tossed," Ed said, leaning across the table. "No question. I'll testify myself, if I have to. I filed the sale, and there's nothing about it that was improper."

"Mental incompetence?" Winnie said, trying to laugh. "That can't be what she—"

"Senility claims are pretty common," said the other lawyer. "Mostly you see them in a probate case, but with a business dispute there isn't as much precedent. Actually, it makes for an interesting—"

Winnie cut him off, hating the young man for saying *senility*. "What are the . . . grounds?" She came up with the term at the last moment. "There aren't any grounds, of course. What can she possibly say?"

Ed looked at Jerry, who was silent, and then back at her. "There are various ways people challenge agency in the elderly. Is the person lucid? Acting of his own free will? Understands the terms of the deal? Sometimes, if they can't prove full incompetence, they go for weakness of intellect."

Winnie felt for Jerry's hand, which stiffly clutched the chair arm. "Weakness of intellect," she repeated. Worse by far than the news of this claim was Jerry's stunned silence.

"Boilerplate," one of the younger lawyers said dismissively.

"And we'll knock that all down," Ed said. "But there's a mention in the paperwork of a prior history, so at some point, Jerry, I want to get a full rundown on the results of any tests and medication. And if there was a diagnosis, we'll need—"

"All he takes is blood-pressure medicine," Winnie protested. "How could that matter?"

The four men in the room didn't say anything. Only after a minute did the phrase *prior history* hit her.

"I haven't taken those drugs for a long time," Jerry said, finally. Winnie turned to him, but he stared at the table. "Those other drugs. All that was a long time ago."

"She claims that there were tests for pre-Alzheimer's," the other lawyer said, consulting his notes. "And a brief hospitalization for disorientation?"

Jerry shook his head. The younger man, thinking he was being contradicted, continued to read: "Treatment by at least two Chicago-area specialists, repeated CAT scans, and a past motion to prohibit driving, which the plaintiff—"

"Rob," Ed said, silencing him. Ed, she saw, could tell that Winnie hadn't known. His face was full of concern. "Why don't we take a ten-minute break?"

Jerry said nothing. Ed looked at Winnie. A wild drumbeat of humiliation erupted in her, and she fought to keep her composure. Slowly, however, the shock and anger—*how could he not have told her?*—were eventually overcome by fear—*how bad was it?* Pre-Alzheimer's. And then, though she couldn't even look his way, a surge of wordless connection passed between her and Jerry. She knew, of course, why he hadn't told her. Winnie put her hand briefly up to her face; *for better or worse*, she mouthed against her own palm.

"No," she said, to the waiting lawyers. "No need for a break. So, what's the next step? What strategies have you come up with, and what do you need from us?"

Dan Wickham, with visible relief, turned to the matter of describing the various legal motions by which Jerry's representatives would block Annette's representatives from pursuing the claim. There would be a series of challenges on the method of the suit itself—that the documentation wasn't complete, that the time allotted for response was too short—and then, if necessary, depositions would be taken. Winnie borrowed a pen and jotted down some notes. Almost as an afterthought, the other lawyer mentioned that no major work on the property should be undertaken—no renovations, changes to the structure—until this was all sorted out.

Winnie picked up the wet glass and took a long, angry drink. She stared at the white water ring left on the table. Would it be a relief, to give up the pool? She could drop the whole matter, all the calls and the bills and all the ugliness brewing about that tree. But that would be giving in to Annette's claims. To this idea of incompetence. So, instead, as they talked on and on, Winnie conjured with effort and deliberation the now-familiar image of the pool—not just the pool, but Jerry in it, relaxed and talkative, with none of the pain now radiating from the man who now sat still and silent by her side. It trembled and faltered, but she held that vision steady, a willful touchstone.

"You'll come out to Hartfield," Winnie said. "As much as possible. It's too much effort, our driving into the city."

"Yes," Ed said. "Of course." Then he nodded at the other lawyers, who shook hands with Winnie and Jerry, and quickly left the room. Winnie could hear their voices, jovial and unconcerned, echo down the hall.

"I need to visit the restroom," Jerry said, and she held the door while Ed steadied him.

As soon as Jerry was out of earshot, Winnie turned to Ed. "Tell me," she said. "How bad is this?"

By the way he instantly dropped his voice to respond, she had her answer. "It's not good," he admitted. "The case itself is weak, no question. But it will stir up a lot of unpleasantness—personal information, details about his health, then and now. He'll hate that—anybody would, of course. The other thing is, I imagine the news will get out."

"Because of the house? Nobody could honestly believe that Jerry didn't know what he was doing when he bought our house."

"It's the family-feud aspect. Father vs. daughter. TrevisCorp is a well-known company, and once this comes out, the infighting will be an irresistible angle for the local Chicago papers. Less so here."

Winnie flinched, and Ed switched back into his lighter mode. "At least we can all get a good lunch out of it. You might give me ten minutes, and I'll meet you both in the foyer. L'Auberge fit us in at the last minute—Jerry will get a kick out of it. We ate there once twenty years ago, and he had a field day because they forgot my salad or something. He had the manager out to us, on the double—"

"That's so kind, Ed. I just don't think we're up for it today."

"Are you sure?"

"It's me, really. I tire out so quickly these days. I hope you don't mind."

"Oh, of course, of course. Rain check." They could see Jerry making his slow, stubborn way down the long hall.

"Where is that L'Auberge, though? Nearby? I'm sure it sounds familiar." Distracted, Ed told her—Fifty-third Street—his eyes on Jerry's approach. He moved to shake hands with his old friend, and Winnie observed the smooth return of the lawyer's calm demeanor, a natural pose of carelessness—*this is nothing, don't worry a minute, we'll take care of everything*—that somehow managed to be soothing despite it all.

The funny thing was, she and Jerry had crossed paths—barely—sixty years ago. For about a year and a half, Winnie had attended Mary Edward College, a middling women's school now long folded, in upstate New York. It was the only year of Winnie's life that she had been away from Hartfield. She had studied literature; she hadn't wanted to go. But after her mother had begun the long, slow descent of illness, the house was crowded and uncomfortable, and both parents seemed to want her away. When her roommate Beezie Collins became engaged to Dick Trevis, of the Chicago Trevises, Winnie became caught up, mostly by proximity, in the endless round of parties, dances, and introductions that made up a wedding of that sort back then. (The next year, her own to George—studying medicine at nearby SUNY Buffalo—would be a sober, positively shotgun affair in comparison.) Dick's cousin Jerry had attended several events. Winnie wanted to say that she remembered him vividly, and in an undated photo she dug up of Beezie's wedding-party lineup, there he was, next to his brother Frank—short and unsmiling, in an ill-fitting cutaway suit. She herself was standing at the far end of the bridal party, in a pretty gown she didn't remember the color of, holding a puffy bouquet of hydrangeas.

Jerry maintained a long, detailed recollection about dancing with Winnie at the reception—specifically, of asking her onto the floor twice in a row, a noted faux-pas—but she wouldn't put it past him to embellish the memory. It was enough for Winnie that they shared this odd piece of the past, even if it hadn't produced any lasting connection. She would go on to drop out of college to marry George, and Jerry would meet Beth Ann at a cotillion the year afterward, and as far as Winnie was concerned, the Trevis family faded from all significance (she and Beezie exchanged Christmas letters for some time, and then stopped) until March of this year. Just seven months ago.

Danny and Yi-Lun had pleaded with her to join them for any part of their twice-yearly three-week stay in a time-shared house on a beach near Jacksonville. Why anyone who lived in San Francisco would fly to *Florida* yearly for a vacation was a question that was never sufficiently answered, at least so far as Winnie or Rachel could see—but Yi-Lun had family in the area, and she wanted their son, Matthew, to spend time with them. Fair enough, but Winnie had begged off the two years previous. How could she have gone anywhere? With Bob in the hospital for those many months—and then the long year of rehab—she was on the run, almost every day, picking up the girls or dropping them off, seeing to school matters and doctors' visits and dinner preparation and whatever else Rachel needed her for. This March, though, she had little excuse—even Rachel had urged her to go. *You need a rest*, her daughter had said, and Winnie couldn't disagree. The visit had been lovely: sea breezes blowing through the window of her first-floor room, ruffling the pages of a satisfyingly quiet Anne Tyler novel; hours of Scrabble, Danny's childhood favorite; long walks on the beach with Matthew.

On her last night, they had dinner reservations at Deacon's, a quiet waterside lobster restaurant. Winnie, who was a little tired of grilled steak and corn on the cob, was looking forward to it. At least they *thought* they had reservations—as soon as they pulled into the packed driveway, it became clear that something was awry. CLOSED FOR A PRIVATE PARTY, read a sign just inside the door. Dozens of people were packed around the front bar, and the noise level was deafening. While Danny and Yi-Lun argued with the manager, Winnie touched Matthew on the sleeve and told him she would be just outside. She slipped through the crowd, making her way to a side door, out to where the sun was setting in a perfect orange globe over the gray-green water. Winnie was toggling the features of her digital camera, trying to capture the moment, so at first she didn't notice him sitting there—Jerry Trevis—at a round empty table.

"May I take your photograph?"

"Pardon me?" She turned to the man who spoke. He was smiling at her.

"If you'd like, I can—" Here he gestured to the camera, and then to the view.

"A shot of me, standing alone in front of the sunset?" Winnie laughed. "To tell you the truth, I only came out here to get away from the noise. It's awful in there."

"You said it," Jerry said. He cocked his head and gave her another one-sided grin. There came a burst of noise from the party inside, and she moved a little closer. They held each other's gaze just one moment longer than was necessary. "Or I could take one of you and your family . . . your husband?"

Thinks he's pretty smooth, Winnie thought. But she simply shook her head a little, which to another person her age, she knew, would say everything that needed to be said about George's being gone. And he picked up on it, nodding once. She put the camera on the weathered wood of the empty table and he rose halfway as she took a seat.

Then there they were, together alone, in the quiet of the side porch of a restaurant off the highway in Atlantic Beach, while Jerry's niece's second wedding gathered steam inside and Winnie's son tried uselessly to wrangle a table—ten minutes at most, until their flustered children discovered them and took them away. She hardly remembered what they said, how they found a way to introduce themselves, or what specifically occasioned that first, formal letter that arrived in Hartfield five days later, on rough cream stationery in a never-wavering hand that jolted her stomach even before she completely understood who had sent it. But Winnie remembered Jerry's absolute attention to her, his serious consideration of everything she said, the spotless white of his shirt, and thinking that they were perfectly matched in all things—that they had traveled along similar paths through the wilderness of aging and had separately reached the same place.

She remembered this:

Turning away from him, in an effort to regain some inner calm. There was the sun, now mostly gone, a spectacular fiery sinking that spilled flecks of dark gold across the ocean. She said some inane thing about how beautiful it all was, and how odd it was that the most ordinary event could be so stunning. And when she turned back to him, still going on about the view, she saw that Jerry hadn't bothered to look at the sunset at all. *Not bad*, he said, his voice indifferent. But his eyes were only on her.

At L'Auberge, their corner table was secluded. Jerry took a long first pull from his scotch and soda.

"Firstborn children," he said, raising the glass. "Fuck 'em."

Winnie was just relieved that he had spoken at all, and that they were safely ensconced in the cream-and-white formality of the restaurant. In the cab, she had been the one to speak to the driver, and in the restaurant foyer, she had been the one to step up to the maître d' and explain that yes, they were with the Ed Weller party, and no, Mr. Weller would not be joining them. She had even ordered Jerry's drink, from the boy who put down their menus. But now that they were here, in an oasis of muted luxury, and his color was starting to come back, she felt shakiness overtake her from all that effort. The idea had been to be alone, so they could talk about it. Now Winnie realized she didn't want to talk about it.

"I'll probably have Dover sole," Winnie said, scanning her menu, which was devoid of any prices. "You ought to order the tenderloin."

"Not hungry."

She pretended to further study the heavy card stock. "I suppose you might try the duck."

"I don't know what to say."

"There's nothing to say. We'll have a nice hot lunch and head straight home. Are these wines by the glass? Can you make that out?"

"Ah, Winifred. I've really flubbed it, haven't I?"

Winnie waited until the boy had put down their slices of bread with his silver tongs and then left. She tried to look anywhere but Jerry's face, for she knew whatever she saw there would crumble her. Where on earth was the waiter? There had to be a way to right this, amid the desperate wild heaving all around them. "Have you thought any more about the shape? We should decide by the end of the week. I like the kidney-bean one, but you tell me if that's not right for swimming laps."

Jerry just looked at her.

"Or a plain old rectangle. Why not a rectangle? Everyone always wants to get complicated."

"But he said not to—didn't you hear—?"

"I heard," Winnie said. "If only Rachel—" But here she stopped. No. Bringing up Rachel would veer too close to the subject she was avoiding—would contrast Annette too sharply; she didn't want Jerry to face the difference between the two, their daughters, right now. Underneath this, at a deep level Winnie only barely acknowledged, whispered another fear, inchoate, immediately pushed aside, having to do with all the money Rachel had recently borrowed from Jerry. A tiny blood-pulse of anxiety ran through her—*there is danger in this*—and then was gone.

Luckily, their waitress arrived, a tall and sturdy fortyish woman with her hair pulled severely back. She was so warm and solicitous that Winnie had to blink away tears. She fell silent as the woman simply took over their lunch, deciding straightaway for Winnie which wine and cajoling Jerry into ordering the duck, and even— once—into smiling like his old self. The sense of being taken care of, Winnie decided, was what you were paying for. No wonder so many of the other patrons in this wainscoted and chandeliered room were as white-haired as she and Jerry.

When the food came, Jerry said he had no taste for it, and then promptly set about eating half the meat and all of the mashed ruta-bagas, as well as several forkfuls of her fish. They made small talk about the food, and the weather, the crowds on the sidewalks— each new topic a balm between them.

When their waitress returned, with dessert menus they wouldn't need and nothing but the warmest concern for their overall well-being—*A pot of tea? Not even a plate of the plainest sugar cookies?*— something about her tucked-in smile reminded Winnie of Rachel. And suddenly she was furious. Where *was* her daughter? Where was she when Winnie doubted her own ability to walk much far-ther in these stiff shoes, when exhaustion was building at a rapid pace, and when she needed the restroom but everything about the journey there and back threatened to swamp her? Rachel, with all her own needs and her uncontainable fixation on money.

Where is she? Winnie cried inwardly. *Now that I need to go to the bathroom? Now that I'm old?*

Outside their window, the light had changed to a dull, shadowy gray.

"*Incompetent*," Jerry said bitterly, all of a sudden. She had let the silence go on too long. Their waitress whisked away the check and his credit card. "Annette had no problem when I chartered that boat for her birthday and they all took a good long sail around the Caribbean. Or when I bought that beachfront condo two years ago and let her turn it around for a nice chunk of change. She didn't run after me with lawyers *then*."

"What's done is done," Winnie said. "I guess."

"I should have told you," he said, and she met his eyes for the first time. "I was a fool, and I thought it would never come back to bother us. It was never as bad as they made it sound, but I still should have. Even if—"

"Yes, you should have," she said, letting the words cover over everything else: *Why did you think I couldn't handle this? Don't you know how much I love you?* "You should have," she said again, quietly, and Jerry bowed his head. Winnie began to think she might be able to try for the restroom. In the ladies' lounge, perhaps she should call Matty, too, to pick them up.

"Think my grandson's going to be able to dish up anything as fancy as all this?" Jerry said after a moment, trying to smile. Wordlessly, they had agreed to leave it at that, for now.

And so, arranging her face and voice to match his, Winnie said, "I don't imagine the younger crowd wants Dover sole anymore. They like sushi, and things like that. Don't they?"

Jerry grunted.

"Is he really going to go through with it, I wonder? Last week, he said there was some problem with the building license."

"He sure as heck better go through with it," Jerry said, scowling, his usual force returned. "I put up half."

Eleven
RACHEL

She fiddled with the phone cord, plugging and replugging it into the side of their old laptop. Soon the Internet connection started up, with its buzzing little song, and Rachel felt relief. You never knew if it would work on this computer, and without quite knowing why, she hadn't wanted to use the girls' computer, in their room, for what she was about to do.

The house was quiet; Bob had gone to the store and Lila and Melissa were watching a friend play tennis. She rolled her head twice, once to the left, then to the right, trying to dislodge some of the tension there. Finally, the browser sprang open; she narrowed her attention to the screen.

It hadn't been hard at all, to set up a new bank account in her own name. Jerry had talked her through all of it, and with surprising speed and ease she clicked open the right folder and entered her password, and then there it was: $25,000. For a full moment she held herself still and stared at the sum, a figure shining brightly in computer blue. And then she got to work.

She paid down MasterCard first, slowly typing the unfamiliar account number into the form, and then she paid off Discover entirely, with a muttered curse for that 19 percent interest rate. It took longer to figure out how to access the various medical and insurance companies, but eventually she knocked down just a few of those many outstanding debts. The first couple thousand that Jerry had lent her had gone to the most persistent of the collection agencies, the one whose Tampa-based phone number everyone in the house had learned to recognize on caller ID, and ignore. Rachel had planned to hold on to what was left from this $25,000, to string it out as slowly and as cautiously as she could, but on a whim she stood up, went into the kitchen, called Waugatuck, and prepaid Lila's diving fees through the winter. That brought the MasterCard back up, so she went back to the computer with a bowl of raisin bran and paid it down again.

And then, even as she told herself not to, Rachel began to browse a few of the clothing stores that the girls loved, and before she knew it, she had ordered two Banana Republic tops for Lila, plus a skirt for Melissa from that other brand they craved, the English-sounding preppy one. *For Christmas*, she told herself, *or birthdays*. But then again, who knew? Maybe she would just lay the clothes out on their beds, and wait for them to be surprised. She pictured herself in their room, watching them try on the new things, admiring a new style or color, the three of them together. Yes.

Rachel felt like she could breathe again. There actually seemed to be a millimeter's worth more room down around the bottom of her lungs. The deception she was practicing was a temporary one, she told herself. And maybe it wasn't even a deception. After all, she didn't know *for sure* that Bob wouldn't have agreed to borrow from Jerry—she only suspected it. Rachel had said nothing about it to him, then, and it was the first real secret she could remember keeping from her husband; the whole thing, from idea to planning to execution, had been done without his knowing. But not for long, she told herself. She would just get them out from under some of the worst of it, those endless thin envelopes with their cellophane windows; she would ease the burden a little bit, and then tell Bob—if he hadn't already found out. In any case, whatever would ensue—the arguments, his surprise and hurt—was distant, compared to the immediate relief that the past few minutes had brought.

"I don't really know how to thank you," she had admitted to Jerry last week, embarrassed by the way her voice caught on the words.

"Don't have to," he'd said, shaking his head with finality. "Family's family." But then the phrase hung in the air between them. Rachel had been thinking of Bob, with a small measure of guilt, and Jerry, she realized now, must have been thinking about Annette.

Rachel logged out from the bank's website and closed the windows on the screen. She stretched her hands back behind her, as far as they would go. The real secret, she knew, was that Jerry's money—and his generosity, his no-bullshit way about everything—had given her another idea. A plan that Rachel hadn't exactly articulated to herself or anyone else; it had to do with her house, and it had to do with Jerry. She looked slowly around the living room, her eyes traveling up the back wall, which bordered her other home—her real home.

She was about to close the computer when the words on the screen stopped her. It was a file Bob had left open. She read a bit, and then scrolled down to read more, one hand holding a spoon, the other on the track-pad.

Most of the science books and nearly all the head-trauma movies have this part wrong, he'd written.

What it's like to lose your understanding of language, and then to regain it, is less a sudden or glorious deliverance—common metaphors involve lights going on, or random notes of music instantly falling into the pattern of a symphony—than it is a shameful, embarrassing piece of self-awareness. The sensation wasn't so much that I had lost the ability to do something important but that I had fumbled badly—had forgotten my manners at a crucial social event. Left my fly down, exposed myself. It was like farting in public, over and over, uncontrollably. Grasping at something to say, the most basic things, I sent forth great gusts of human stink instead. And then I was forced to watch as those around me, the ones taking care of me, the ones I loved, politely looked away, afraid to let me see how badly I had messed up.

Rachel stopped. It wasn't just that the writing was better than she had guessed it would be—though it was, more confident and clear than she had any right to expect. (Not that she was any expert. But nothing about Bob's life before this had suggested any talent or interest in writing. No one they knew was a writer, after all—Hartfield just wasn't that kind of place.) So what had shocked her about what she had read? Was it that he hadn't told her any of this before? Was it strange or sad or hard to find out these painful thoughts about what he had been through because she *read* them?

Or was it that Rachel hadn't imagined that the experience was a profound one, to Bob, one worthy of examination and—well, why not say it—art? She knew it was hellish, she'd known it was brutal agony as he recovered, and she certainly knew it did a world's worth of damage to their finances. But that it was something *else*, this injury, this recovery—something else to Bob—she hadn't known.

A muffled thump came from inside the house, and then the sound of the grinding gears of the garage door opening. Rachel shut the computer and walked through the apartment, and outside. The pavement was wet under her bare feet as she stood on the path that led to the front of the house. Vikram backed his car out, saw her standing there, and gave a brief wave, which she returned.

If she could only know what had happened the day of Bob's accident, she could handle the rest—where they lived, the fear she knew the girls still had, what had changed between her and Bob. Why she believed this, Rachel didn't know, but she clung to the idea, anyway: someday, she would know, and then everything else would fall into place. But Bob had moved past the events themselves, she understood now. What he had written, what she had just read, confirmed the divide: they were each struggling, but with different mysteries.

She could hear her phone ring, but Rachel remained in front, long after Vikram had driven away. She looked from the garage to the side of the house, up to the windows, and back again. In her mind, Rachel paced out an imagined version of Bob's steps that day, of her own, counting silently. It was an equation she had to get right, so she kept adding and subtracting, over and over, to figure out what might have been lost.

Twelve

AVERY

If it had been up to Avery—*and why wasn't it, when he was cooking the whole meal?*—turkey wouldn't even be on the table. But when he'd floated that idea past Winnie, she'd looked so aghast that he'd immediately backed off. They weren't ready for wild boar with quenelles in Hartfield, at least on Thanksgiving, or goose livers in Sauterne. So, he'd signed on, reluctantly, for the whole boring usual: they'd get their damn turkey, the driest form of meat known to man, and their sweet potatoes and cranberry salad, and two kinds of pie for dessert. (Yes to rum-spiked pumpkin but an emphatic *no* to apple. Avery had to draw the line somewhere. He would *not* bake a fucking apple pie.) Still, he was working overtime to subvert anything he could, even if no one would notice. The sweet potatoes were whipped with lemon juice and then layered with Canadian bacon, Granny Smith apples, and—here, he knew he was pushing it—tiny nuggets of jellied goose fat. The cranberries were there, tossed with orange peel, but also with minced baby jalapeno peppers, and a few dashes of some Catalan spice blend he'd ordered online. There would be a few other surprises too. It was unlikely, Avery thought, that anyone would have an allergic reaction.

A few weeks ago, on one of his Hartfield outings, just after Winnie had invited him to Thanksgiving, she'd asked his opinion on whether they should all go to the 4:15 buffet at the Waugatuck Club, or whether she should have dinner catered by something called "If You Can't Take the Heat."

"You're kidding, right?" Avery had said, bleary from two hours of listening to Jerry go on about corrugated box technology. "Have you seen your oven? Both of your ovens? I could make a turkey *sub* in here that would be better than anything at that place."

So that's what had started it all, with some *Sure, sure, I'll help out* and then *No, don't buy any produce there* to *I'll take care of it, all of it*. He'd been shopping for the past day and a half, borrowed his roommate's car and packed it full of food, and had driven out here at—he still couldn't believe this—seven in the morning. Avery couldn't help it. When it came to food, food that he would be eating or just in the presence of, he couldn't abide any interference or outside opinions. Plus, Nona was coming, and it was going to be weird enough to have her see all this—the house, this whole suburban scene—for the first time, without his having to choke down rubber turkey meat at the same time. But there was something else. Avery could tell from Winnie's nervous, probing questions about Thanksgiving—*Unless you're planning to go home? For whatever your mother will be planning?*—that she didn't know what he knew.

"Need some help?" Winnie wobbled into the kitchen, this incredible fucking kitchen with every single pro detail in place. Who the hell lived here before Grandad? Mario Batali? Even though it was just noon, Winnie was already in full grandmother-type holiday gear: long swishy skirt, a fine dusting of makeup. Avery wondered if he should mention that he did plan to change out of his flip-flops and cut-off khakis.

"I'm good. I mean, yeah, you can if you want." She took a seat across from him at the little round table and just watched. She had already stopped by several times this morning, and once or twice Avery caught her peering at the ovens. (He suspected she was checking that at least one of them did hold, in fact, a turkey.) He was snapping the ends off haricots verts, with a bucket of them on the floor between his feet—three pounds down, three to go.

"How on earth do you do that so fast? Your hands are a blur."

"Try one," Avery said, nodding at the bowl on the table. Winnie carefully bit the tip off a bean. "Awesome, right? They're much better like this, before they get cooked."

"But . . . you are going to cook these, right? Boil them, or something?"

"Boil? Wait, what's that again?" Avery put on a blank face. He couldn't help teasing Winnie; he knew she wouldn't mind. "Don't worry, don't worry. They'll be gray and mushy, just the way you like them."

Winnie swatted his wrist with the bean. Then she winced. "What did you do to yourself?"

Yeah, that burn on his thumb was getting uglier by the day; it had finally stopped peeling, which was nice, but now it had turned a weird orange color. When he'd still had the dressing on it last week, Avery had woken up one morning to find that Nona had drawn a sad face on the thumb bandage and written next to that, in ballpoint letters so tiny he could barely read them, *get well soon because you belong inside me.*

"I can put on a glove, if you want."

"And all these cuts! My lord, what do they have you doing at that bistro?"

"Actually, I've got a new thing now. Craft services. You know what that is?"

"Movie stars!" Winnie exclaimed. "You feed them? On the set? Have you met anyone—what about Al Pacino? I love him. He looks like he might enjoy a hearty meal."

Avery snorted. "Yeah, nothing that exciting. Right now, it's one of those *Law and Order* shows—"

"*CSI*? *Special Victims Unit*?" Winnie said immediately. "Not the Miami one. Is it with that brunette, or the two men?"

"Jesus," Avery said. "I have no idea. I just make the omelets. Anyway," he said, shaking the bowl of beans, "the food sucks, but there's this guy, he's helping me with some stuff for my place."

"Oh?" Winnie brightened. "Then the city permits all got signed?"

"Well . . . that's still kind of unresolved." Avery really didn't feel like going into details. It was hard not to get dragged down by everything that was going wrong with the Blue Apple. Avery remembered the actual shudder that ran through the building inspector's face when he saw the nest of leaky, rotten pipes under the boiler-room floor. "Nah, it's boring, you don't want to hear about it. But anyway, this guy, he's got all these connections with suppliers and he's going to hook me up. Last week I went up to the fish market with him—oh man, you should have *seen* this crazy shit that goes on behind the scenes."

"I'll pass," Winnie said.

"I took a bite out of a live dorado. It was flipping around in my hands, and I ate part of its underbelly."

"Are you trying to shock me, Avery? It might take more than you'd think."

He stopped snapping beans and wiped his hands. No time like the present. "Actually, if you've got a second . . . is Grandad around?"

"He's resting. What's the matter?"

"Well, I just—" He'd wanted to say this in some kind of a carefully thought out way, but with the way Winnie's face looked right now, tight and closed as if she were bracing for impact, he just spilled ahead. "My mom doesn't know I'm here. She doesn't want me to come over anymore. Because of all the . . . you know."

Winnie sat back. "So she told you."

He stood, antsy. He needed to move around—he needed to whisk something. The beans wouldn't need their vinaigrette for another few hours, but he took out a small saucepan, anyway, and set it with a lovely *clink* on one of the polished stainless-steel burners.

The phone rang, but after a glance at the caller ID, Winnie ignored it.

"You want me to answer?" he said. He knew these repeated calls from the tree-rights people were driving her crazy. Didn't they have anything better to do than hassle some old lady? Calls, letters, the works—all for somebody wanting a pool on their lawn in this tiny town. "I'll tell them off, if you want."

"Don't bother," Winnie said. "I'm sure they'd love the attention."

After a minute, the ringing stopped. Avery poured some olive oil and dropped in a chunk of double-cream butter.

"I hate that you're in the middle of this," he heard Winnie say slowly. "I can't stand what it's doing to your family."

"One sec," he said, thinking, rolling mental tastes through his head. Onion? No, something sweeter. Celery? No—he was chasing a fuller feeling in the mouth, with a fizzy bite that came much later. Then he got it: shallot, with dill. With one eye on the melting lump of butter, he got to work mincing.

"I keep thinking I should call your mother."

"Yeah, I wouldn't do that," Avery said. Two days ago, he had absently answered his phone while picking out sweet potatoes at Fairway on upper Broadway. Annette. Skipping the perfunctory *how-are-you* opening, his mother cut to why she'd called, explaining the basics of her legal drama with Jerry and why she was right on this—Avery focused on the yams, sorting and squeezing them—and why he should stop going out to Hartfield, until everything was sorted out.

"So, you're off the hook now," Annette said, and let out a big exhale. "You're welcome."

"Okay," Avery said. He put a potato into his cart, and then took it out.

"I'm serious," his mother said. "You're done out there. *Finito*. Listen, what do you think about Thanksgiving on the beach? We were just looking at some last-minute flights to the islands, and—"

"This is all between you and Grandad. It doesn't have anything to do with me."

"The lawyers say that any contact could escalate—"

"He's pretty *happy* out here, Mom. You should see him and Winnie, they—"

"This isn't about her! Don't say her name to me! You don't know one thing about it, what that woman has done. Buying that place. Taking over his whole— He—they—this is for his own good and I'm the only one who—"

Avery held the phone away from his head until Annette's sputtering died down.

"—hear me? I said, you *cannot see those people* anymore."

"Yeah," Avery said. He gripped a sweet potato so hard that his fingernails broke through its surface. "Yeah, I heard you. The whole supermarket heard you. God—'go see Grandad, stay away from Grandad.' What am I, some little puppet? This is my life out here. I'm clean and I have a job and I'm *sick of being told what to do!*" Other shoppers edged away from him, but Avery didn't care. He had flung the phone hard into the metal shopping cart and picked up another two yams.

In Winnie's kitchen now, as soon as the butter sank into a golden puddle, he drizzled exactly two circles of honey into the pan. "I think she's out of town, anyway."

"But doesn't it bother you? What she's doing? That she's suing her own father, that she's telling all these people that he's senile, that he stole money from her? Or maybe *you* could talk to her. You could tell her how much it means to him, all those times you've come out to visit. I'm just so scared of what this will do to him! He barely speaks about her anymore—he—oh, how can a daughter be such a *monster?*"

He glanced back over his shoulder at Winnie. She tossed the green bean onto the table and put her hand up to her head. "I shouldn't have said that, Avery. You don't have to say anything."

Well, this sucked. *Please don't cry*, Avery wished desperately. Was he supposed to hug her if she started crying? Nona. Think Nona. Nona would be here soon, eating his food, her hand on his leg under the table, making everything real again. He just had to get to that. "Don't worry about it." He scraped the whisk around the pan until it blurred, emulsifying the butter and making a tiny tornado funnel in the brown-gold liquid, just the size of his pinkie finger. Though he didn't want it to, this particular action would maybe forever send Avery back into the kind of sense-memory he'd really rather not experience right there in his grandfather's kitchen in Hartfield, New York: heating up his shot, stirring quickly while others waited their turn, the sick-sweet smell of the methane burner. At this place in Bucktown where he used to score, Avery remembered, what they used was a blackened metal cup—a regular kitchen measuring cup, like the ones he had stacked up right now on the counter next to the stove.

"I want to ask you something," Winnie was saying, in a wavery, determined voice. "I know it's not going to sound very gracious, but I have to ask anyway. Forgive me."

"*Yes*, I'll make sure you get seconds on dark meat," Avery said. He turned, hoping. "There's always a knockdown over the dark meat."

But this time, it didn't work. Without smiling at all, Winnie looked up at him, full in the face. "Why are you here? You've been a good boy to that man, Avery. Your letting him talk to you about the old days—that has been a good, good deed that you've done. But I know you didn't want to spend all those Sunday afternoons out here. Why did you keep it up? Why did you come today, after what your mother told you?"

"What do you mean? I never said I didn't—"

Winnie swiped her hand in front of her face, as if waving off a swarm of insects. "It's just me now. You can be honest. I won't say anything to him."

Avery stood uncertainly in the space between the oven and the table. "Are you saying I'm out here just because of the money?"

"Are you?"

They faced each other. Outside, a thin snow was just starting to blow, hesitant, every which way. The phone rang again, but neither he nor Winnie moved. Avery got the sense that neither of them knew where to go from here. Did she want to know about the drugs, that he was off them? What kind of reassurance was he supposed to plug in now? And how many times, he thought angrily, how many fucking times would he need to tell that story—there was nothing new or original about it, but he had to carry it around, still—flogging himself in the same old ways so that he could get another pass.

"A restaurant takes everything," Winnie said, pointing at the pot of now-cooling vinaigrette sauce. She hadn't dropped her eyes from his. "Everything. You know what I read once?"

Avery shook his head no, he didn't know, and then nodded yes, go on.

"Something like fifty-four percent of new restaurants, across the country, go under within the first two years."

"I *know*—"

"It was over *seventy* percent for New York City restaurants. New ones. Over seventy percent fail, in the two years after opening."

"Those ones didn't have my *poulet grand-mère*. Or my salt cod mousse."

"Avery," Winnie said. She was shaking her head, and for the first time he could hear something tired in her voice that sounded like Rich used to, when he wanted to—what?—bring Avery down to earth.

"I have to go pick up my girlfriend," he said, and the very words kicked him into action—he poured the vinaigrette into a glass jar and started to soap up the pot and a few others left over in the sink.

"The train won't get in until twelve forty," Winnie said. "Holiday schedule."

Avery nodded, his back to her.

"We're looking forward to meeting her," Winnie said, but still, he didn't turn around. "How do you pronounce it again? Such an *unusual* name."

There was a gleaming, enormous dishwasher just to his left, but Avery ignored it, trusting his own precision work more than some machine. If anything, he'd use it for some extra drying racks.

"Avery, all I meant was—"

"What?" He said, and it came out shorter and harsher than he had planned. "Yeah, the odds generally suck, when you try to do something new. Thanks, though. That helps a lot. Knowing the specifics." The water was stinging hot, and he wasn't wearing rubber gloves, but Avery's hands had become so numb to heat or pain that he barely registered. "I thought you were—" But he just shook his head, embarrassed at how suddenly disappointed he felt. "It's not like Grandad doesn't know the risks, by the way. I didn't ask him for that investment money, either. He offered it—it was his idea."

"I know that!" Winnie exclaimed.

"And it wasn't as much as you probably think," Avery said. "I had these old bonds from my other grandparents, from when I was a kid, and I cashed them all in . . . whatever." He flicked the hand towel across the faucets, and then snapped it into an exact half fold to be hung over the lip of the sink. He was getting heat from *her*? After all the time he'd put in here, after all the hours he'd listened and nodded and said *sure, an Olympic swimming pool was just what this run-down place needed.* Did she have any idea what everyone really thought about that? Hell, what Avery sometimes thought, about a person who wants to axe the biggest tree on the block so that a couple old people could splash around before their afternoon naps.

What did she want him to say? Something half true or almost true but still completely corny, like the fact that the old man was growing on him? That spending time with Grandad would always remind Avery of not having a father, but then instantly ease that sharp pain? Or that the great gift of his life so far had turned out to be a woman who made him want to be more?

Where did he put the keys? God. Okay, there.

"You're misunderstanding me," Winnie said urgently. "I don't care how much money he's giving you—you know I don't care at all about that, not at all. I just wanted to know that you'll come back."

"Of course I'm coming back," Avery said gently, nodding at the oven and stove. "Don't burn the place down," he said lightly but without looking at her.

"All right," Winnie said, just as the phone started ringing again. He went past her quickly, so quickly that he couldn't be sure if the older woman had raised her arm to stop him or just put her hand out to him. He thought maybe she had, but he didn't really know and by the time he was even realizing it, Avery was out in the wispy snow air, a trace of chimney smoke there and gone, hurrying toward the strange car he had borrowed for the day.

He was twenty minutes early for the train, so he sat, fiddling with the dial on the useless radio for a while. And then he shut it off and just sat. A few other cars pulled into the tiny lot and idled nearby, puffing exhaust clouds that drifted up and then faded.

Two nights ago, Nona's loud, upset voice had awakened him some time before dawn. Avery slept so regularly over at her place now that his clothes and things were pretty evenly divided between his apartment and hers. He'd come up on one elbow, eyes barely open, confused to find himself alone in bed. The flooding light from the main room poured into Nona's tiny bedroom cave, where the door was ajar. Avery, who was working until 2 or 3 AM six nights a week, slept in a thick, unmoving haze—he always had. But sleep was different for Nona, he now knew. She thrashed, she twisted, she shoved him around the mattress. It was common for her to get up several times a night, often to work—he'd gotten used to the sleep-dazed sight of her naked back, bluish in the light of the computer screen, curved away from him as she sat on the edge of the bed, headphones on, obsessively looping and splicing pieces of her own voice.

That radio was still on, upstairs. He could hear the fuzz and blare through the ceiling, as if someone had left the tuner halfway between two stations—one of them Spanish talk radio—and then turned it up, full blast. Nona must be going crazy, he thought. She'd already been up there to bang on the door—no one answered—and she had been pacing and agitated in the hour or two before Avery could convince her to come to bed. He'd dropped right off to sleep, of course.

"If you could *just go up there*," she was saying from the other room. "Yes. Fine. I'll file whatever you want me to!"

Avery pushed open the door a little more. Nona was sitting on a rickety wood chair in the kitchen area, bent over so that her head was almost between her knees. She held the phone to an ear, and had her other hand buried in her hair, gripping the back of her head.

She looked so little and unprotected, her bare limbs out in the chilly air. And something about the way she was slumped over, caught in the harsh overhead light—Nona didn't just look tired, she looked old. It scared him.

"Listen," she was saying. "It's not just me, all right? My husband works nights. You know? He just got back and he needs to sleep and this goddamn radio is keeping us all up."

Avery, in the car at the Hartfield train station, was seared again by the pleasure of those words—*my husband*—and instantly mortified by how he kept playing them back to himself, the way they'd sounded in Nona's voice. Of course, she'd only said that to try to win a little extra sympathy from whatever unimpressed police officer had happened to be working the phones at 4 AM. He'd known that in the minute he'd heard her say it, and he knew it now. But he couldn't stop remembering it, either, this stupid throwaway phrase that didn't mean a thing.

Didn't mean a thing to *her*, that is. Avery watched the train rumble in, the doors slide open. He understood it then, full force, that he loved Nona more than she loved him.

So it took him a moment, still absorbing such a realization and turning it over in his head (it didn't feel *bad*, exactly, this imbalance—didn't someone have to love someone more?), to realize that Nona wasn't alone, there on the platform. And also that it wasn't a coincidence—as dopey Avery first imagined it had to be—that Thomas had taken the same train out to the same suburb, on Thanksgiving afternoon.

Thomas stood and squinted around the platform. Thomas flipped sunglasses down, from his balding forehead. Thomas slowly followed Nona to where Avery was standing by the open car door, thunderstruck and not trying to hide it.

"Hey, you!" She called out in a fake, upbeat, non-Nona way. That was for Thomas's benefit, Avery understood. Then she was hugging him hard, whispering, "He got in early this morning. He didn't have anywhere to go, and I tried to call, but did you turn your phone off? I just thought—"

Thomas reached them and stuck out a hand to Avery, which Avery reluctantly shook. "Everyone hates a party crasher," he said. "Hope you don't mind, man."

"Of *course* we don't mind," Nona said, and that *we* went a long way toward making it all right, Avery thought, as did her outfit. Far from her usual getups, this was a positively sedate costume for Nona—not only had she wound all her dreadlocks into some kind of single, thick braid that hung down her back, but her plain wool skirt was a size too big, and her dark gray sweater a size too small. Only her shoes, flat and black but scuffed like crazy, with wild pointed toes, could give her away. He knew he was staring, at her clothes and at her gorgeous, un-madeup face, but for a moment Avery just couldn't even move, because he was so taken in by what the effort implied.

"Well, I wanted fucking flowers," she was saying, pushing something into his hands. "I went to the place, but all they had were these limp, pitiful excuses for what was once plant life, and then we had to race for the train, so . . ."

"Juice," Avery said, turning the lukewarm glass bottle around.

"It's this passion-fruit kind from Oaxaca," Nona said. "You can ditch it, or whatever. The bodega guy swore to me that anyone would love it. I mean, it was either juice or some mass-market crap from Grand Central."

"It's perfect," Avery said, tucking the bottle carefully back in its brown paper bag. He put his hand on the soft part of her throat and slipped a few fingers under the collar of her sweater. He went around to open the door for her. Thomas got his bald self into the backseat, and when Avery was putting it in drive, a hand stuck a bottle of red wine in his face.

"Small barrel producer from the Loire Valley," Thomas said. "1997, which was a decent year, of course. Lot of rain. In my opinion, they could have aged it *one* more year, to soften the tannins and make that flabby pinot pop just a bit more, but what do I know? It's serviceable, at best."

"Yeah, thanks," Avery said. *Dick.* He stuck the bottle on the car floor by his feet, where he could feel it rolling around with a couple of empty, crumpled soda cups. He swung the car out of the parking lot and sped across Main to take the back way, along the road behind the school, to Greenham. The engine surged, and Avery didn't really try to rein in this outward sign of his anger. They climbed the long hill lined with huge oaks and sycamores, past houses that were set farther and farther back from the road.

When they pulled into his grandfather's long driveway, Thomas made a sound, pretending to be shocked. And maybe he was. It had been a while since Avery had really seen what this place looked like—at least on the outside: its sheer size for one thing, its mass of heavy stone walls and handful of pointed roofs, the way it spread out in all directions, with paved little patios all over, each bordered by high, dark hedges. He'd forgotten that the front door looked like something out of a Monty Python medieval spoof, twice as tall as any of them, made of dark wood beams and metal bolts the size of a man's fist. And the lawn—even covered in branches and uneven, wet piles of leaves, it looked like Notre Dame's practice field.

"Oh, my *God*," Thomas said. "Should we go in through the back? Servants' entrance?"

"Shut it," Nona said sweetly. She put her hand on Avery's leg. "I'm starving."

Thomas got out of the car and just stood there, making a show of gaping at the house. "There won't be enough crème brûlées," Avery said, low, to Nona.

"He'll share mine," she said, and opened her door.

"Don't worry about the bird, Chef," Thomas called to Avery. "I'll just eat some of the sides."

"He's vegetarian," Nona said. She was twisting her skirt around, trying to right it.

"Everything has duck fat in it," Avery said, following them, holding tight to the bottle of passion-fruit juice. He'd wanted her to meet Grandad, but now everything about this plan was crumbling. What did Nona think, about this house, about Hartfield? She had to know this wasn't *him*, right? Because Avery was totally separate, totally different, from everything that was here: it was just Thanksgiving, after all. "He can have toast."

Thirteen
WINNIE

By the time drinks had been poured and hors d'oeuvres were circulating through the living room, Winnie felt better. The hors d'oeuvres, at least those that she'd seen so far, were reassuringly normal: cheese puffs, a bowl of roasted nuts. At Bob's urging, Lila had put in a tape of her recent diving meet, and a group had gathered around the silent television to watch a revolving series of young girls, in matching green swimsuits, who stood as still as statues on the board and then launched themselves into the air with gusto. Bob and Melissa and the others—whooping or shaking their heads in unison—seemed to be able to tell the most minute differences between the divers and their dives, so Winnie pretended to also, though she wasn't always sure which one was Lila, even. The fire was coming along nicely, after several false starts and many interventions, and a flickery warmth had filled the room.

In fact, it had become a little too warm in the living room, but of course Winnie was wearing a turtleneck sweater—of close-knit blue silk, but a turtleneck nonetheless. The patch of darker skin near her jaw had not receded or faded. If anything, the pigment had deepened further, and now the affected area seemed to be spreading down the left side of her throat. Rachel insisted you could hardly notice it, and if Dr. Reynolds wasn't worried—and he wasn't, though she'd been back twice to check—then Winnie should really try to forget about it . . . Had she tried some makeup, like foundation or concealer?

Yes, of course she had. With dismal results. Last week, when she had been together with Jerry—in her bed, in the middle of their tender contortions—Winnie had become paralyzed by the fear that he might look down at the spot on her jaw, in the moment, and think it ugly. She was distracted, and then ashamed of her inattention, and then miserable on both accounts. So she had edged a pillow closer to her face, and then closer, and all the while they had continued to make love, until she had the pillow arranged, just so, over most of her cheek and throat.

Jerry had opened his eyes then and flipped the pillow out of the way. "Are you trying to smother yourself?" he'd exclaimed, with the barely restrained exasperation of a man interrupted. She had to laugh. And then they had resumed that slow, sweet work, and Winnie forgot the spot on her skin.

But it was harder to forget it now, and if she wasn't tugging the turtleneck up almost to her lips—a silly, unhelpful gesture, she knew—she had to fight herself from ducking into the tiny powder room under the staircase, each time she passed by, in order to confirm that the spot was still there. It was always still there.

Avery's friends were perfectly pleasant, even if they were keeping mostly to themselves, so far. It had been a real surprise to see how, well, *old* his girlfriend was, though she was trying hard to stave that off, what with those regrettable tattoos and that wild mass of tangled hair. After Avery had proudly introduced her to the others, Rachel had sent Winnie an amused look across the room—eyebrows raised—so Winnie knew she wasn't the only one who had noticed. Still, the woman had a kind face.

And if she was making Jerry's grandson happy, then who cared about anything else? The voices filling her home, the gathering of family, the familiar turkey aroma: all were restoring Winnie, but she was still struggling to come to terms with that earlier encounter with Avery. It had all happened so fast, and then he rushed out of the house—Winnie knew she had hurt him, but she wasn't sure how, exactly. This was a rare, fragile connection growing between Jerry and this young man—she had seen how easily they kidded each other, how invigorated Jerry was after these visits. He would ransack the house for a book he'd promised Avery, trudging slowly up and down all the stairs; once he made Matty take them to a Cuban-Chinese restaurant—in the Bronx!—that Avery had gone on about. Oh, couldn't she have kept her mouth shut?

All she had wanted, Winnie argued with herself while admiring Lila's new sweater, was to make sure it was something *real* that was still bringing Avery out to visit—not just the restaurant or its prospects, shifting things like that—but something true and unchanging. Could Avery tell the difference?

But she had botched it.

Avery was a whirling dervish in the kitchen now, firing up every stove burner, and he had firmly turned them all out, even Winnie, who had ventured in a few minutes ago to bring him a glass of cold soda, meaning to apologize (without apologizing, exactly).

"I've got it from here," he'd said, his face red from the heat. He had a red kerchief tied on his head and suddenly he looked like a real chef, moving easily around the kitchen, shaking something in a pan, dropping handfuls of herbs into another pot. She backed uncertainly away, afraid of the distance now between them.

But then Avery had said something in their old, joking way and then, to her great relief, he had even swatted a tea towel her way. "Get out there and keep an eye on my girl, Winnie. Don't let her pocket the silver."

She had mock-scolded him for impertinence, and left with her heart eased. For now. Even the phone had stopped its endless ringing, so there was that, too. And here was Jerry, holding court, in his favorite high-backed armchair by the fire.

With Waugatuck's pool closed for the season, they had found him an indoor place to swim, but it was all the way out in Edmonton, a good forty-five minutes each way, and Matty had said to Winnie—low-voiced, afraid to be overheard—that the drive itself was so uncomfortable for Jerry that its effects nearly undid any benefit the water might have provided. She had quickly found someone to install a whirlpool fixture in the upstairs bath, and that might help, it seemed, at least a little. Still, the pool project beckoned to Winnie—a kind of promise, a way to hold on to something.

Now Jerry began a favorite story, about the time he'd met Alan Greenspan in the hallway outside the men's room at a function in Chicago and dressed him down for using the word "recession" in a speech, even though the point had been that there wasn't going to be one. Winnie knew it well, and she needed to check the table settings, but she stayed for her favorite part:

"He listened to me, thanked me for my thoughts, and then just as he was leaving, leans in real close"—here Jerry started laughing, and Winnie joined him—"and then he tells me that my fly was down. My once-in-a-lifetime five minutes with the Chairman of the Fed. I guess I made a pretty good impression. Completely unzipped."

Winnie savored the sound of laughter as she went in to survey the dining room. Did the new arrangement of nine settings work, or were the places too crowded together? Should she have Bob or someone bring the table's second middle piece up from the basement? That would mean taking every piece of china off, and the runner and cloth, and the flowers and candles—not to mention *locating* the middle piece, because who knew where it could be . . . Oh, who *were* these people who showed up to dinner unannounced and uninvited? To be fair, Thomas had been more than apologetic, in a smooth and charming way. But Avery's tight smile and silence about the matter told Winnie all she needed to know. Surely, though, Avery couldn't be jealous? Maybe she'd have to find a way to tell him the obvious: Nona's friend Thomas was not interested in women, in the slightest.

"Hey, Nana, guess what?" Melissa had followed her, drumming a loud pattern on the doorway, and then the chair back, and then the table. The child never stopped moving, it seemed.

"Do me a favor. Sit down here." They squeezed next to each other near the end of the table, where Winnie's place would be, to test the spacing. "Will your elbow be in your sister's face all evening? Or is this all right?"

Melissa pretended to cut up her turkey with fierce sideways motions. "We can handle it," she said. "Guess what? Mom said she's going to take me and Lila to California to visit Uncle Dan in January! And the beach is, like, right outside their *house*. Although if Lila has practice over the break she might have to go by herself on the plane the next day. Which is kind of scary to her, but not to me. I would *love* to go on a plane by myself, but Mom says no way, José."

"What about your father?" This was the first Winnie had heard of Rachel's plan. And she immediately squelched the thought that it must be Jerry's money paying for this trip: Really, did that matter at all? Then she carefully amended the question. "Or maybe he can't get away. All this writing. I know he's working hard."

Melissa looked at her in surprise, as if something obvious had been ignored. "He wasn't really invited, I guess," she said in a carefully low voice that pierced Winnie. "She says it's just a girls' trip."

"Those are the best kind," Winnie agreed. "Let's go peek at Avery. Do you think he'll let us in there to get the water pitcher?"

She followed Melissa into the hallway leading to the kitchen, trying to recover from the girl's matter-of-fact response. Winnie supposed she shouldn't be so surprised. They were smart girls, and they had been through a lot. Of course they knew more than either she or Rachel assumed, or wanted to admit, about the rift between their parents. This was something she would have to bring up with Rachel, and this thought stayed with her through the last-minute pre-dinner preparations, the serving spoons and baskets of bread and finding a book of matches for the candles, until the very sight of all of them around the same table, talking and laughing and ignoring her, pushed everything else to the side. Lila and Melissa were just to Winnie's right, Lila's perpetually hunched shoulders within an arm's reach, and Bob and Nona next to them farther down. To her left was Nona's friend Thomas, with Rachel in the middle, and Avery down at the other end. And directly across from her was Jerry, of course. Winnie reached out to push one of the glass candle covers out of the way. There. Now he came into full sight, her husband, in his heathered wool sweater and worn sports coat—the gray of that sweater, she saw, matched his eyes exactly; he rapped the table once, hard, said, "What's everyone waiting for? Let's eat."

Last Friday, she had taken Bob to a late lunch at Mary's Café. It was a date she had arranged carefully, at a time she knew Rachel would be at the dentist with the girls. As they took their seats, though, Winnie said something casual about how it was too bad she couldn't have joined them—and Bob had only met her eyes with a calm nod. He knew, of course, that she'd wanted to meet with him alone.

"Well, it's not as bad as I'd guessed," he said, after several minutes of studying the papers she'd brought. He held half a sandwich in one hand and turned pages with the other. "Everything about the sale of the house looks in order."

"But—you see what she's saying about him. That he—wasn't in his right mind when he, when we—"

"He had a car take him over to the closing, right? That's too bad." Bob took another bite and neatly caught a piece of chicken salad that fell. "Weirdly enough, driving yourself tends to convince the court of competence. You see it in probate challenges all the time—some geezer will have left his entire fortune to his pet Pekingese, but if he drives himself over to Dunkin' Donuts that day . . ."

Winnie tried to smile. "Do you miss this? The legal business?

You must learn an awful lot about people. About their unhappiness, that is."

Bob put his sandwich down and wiped his hands with a paper napkin. The early-afternoon light filled the café's small front room, and caught the lenses of his glasses when he looked down. "Sometimes. It's not always juicy scandals and intra-family disputes. Sorry. You know what I mean. Most of the time, it's the usual paper pushing. Especially for those of us who didn't make partner."

"That was the firm's loss," Winnie said. She knew how much that had crushed Rachel, when it happened a year before Bob's accident, but she had never spoken directly to her son-in-law about his career. Even now, it was hard to tell what he was thinking.

"I'm going to tell you something, Winnie. And it doesn't have to go further than this lunch, but it needs to be said." Bob brought a level gaze up to hers. "Rachel can't keep taking money from you and Jerry."

"I didn't know if you—"

"Aside from my own personal feelings about it, which . . . She just can't. Not while you are involved in this lawsuit. Do you know what they use to determine mental weakness?"

Winnie flinched at the term, but if Bob noticed, he didn't stop—his voice was now hard-edged. "It's not just old age that can constitute grounds for this—it's old age in combination with other factors. Including prior history, fraud, or undue influence. What could be construed as undue influence."

This last phrase hung between them in the quiet restaurant.

"Have you spoken to her about this?" Winnie asked. "The money?"

"Have you?" Bob replied. And for a moment, the two of them just stared at each other. Winnie thought about telling him that she had tried to raise the subject with Jerry, a few days after that unbearable meeting in the lawyers' office. *I'm not stupid*, she wanted to tell her son-in-law. Of course she worried about what those loans would mean to Annette, what dangers they might expose Jerry to. She had suggested he put on hold, temporarily, all that generosity he'd shown Rachel, and even Avery.

"Just until it all gets sorted out," she had said, trying to strike a casual tone.

But Jerry had waited so long to respond that Winnie had been afraid she'd crossed a line. And then she thought he was going to ignore what she'd said.

Finally, he spoke. "Don't worry about any of that," he said. "I'll take care of it." Which was a rebuke, of sorts, even though his voice was level. And Winnie was hurt, though she tried not to be, and so she didn't feel like describing to Bob that particular moment, or the fact that she had failed in what she'd set out to do. Nor could she put into words the look on Jerry's face when he'd said, *I'll* take care of it. He hadn't seemed surprised by her suggestion (nor did he show any sign of considering it) or unsettled by any part of the escalating family feud led by his daughter. No, Winnie realized. He'd looked like he'd been down this road a thousand times before, with someone giving him unasked-for advice, with someone telling him what he *should* do with his money. He'd looked like he was spoiling for a fight.

She and Bob might have said more, but just then the waitress came over to the table, and dropped her pen right into a water glass, and then Renata Harwood spied them from the sidewalk, and tapped on the window to say hello, and then Winnie's phone rang—so in the flurry of paying the check and speaking to other people, the discussion was left unfinished.

At Thanksgiving now, she jumped up to get a tea towel—someone had tipped over the gravy boat, and Nona and Lila were trying desperately to corral the spreading pool of brown sauce before it spilled onto the floor. Bob dropped his napkin on top of the mess, still talking, his voice just a shade louder than anyone else's.

"—didn't know what to do with it, so they kept it a Chinese place, for over a year," she could hear him saying, even from the hallway off the kitchen. The subject was the town, and that jinxed little restaurant on West Meade in particular, the one that had changed hands four times in the past two years. Avery hurried past her, loaded down with two platters and a handful of serving implements. Winnie wished he had let her hire someone to help out.

"Dad, it was the Chinese place *after* it was Sunny Sundae," Melissa corrected.

"You're right, you're right. Then it was an ice-cream place. But after Rachel's friends bought it, there was a fire, and before they could collect all the insurance—"

"Not my friends, actually," Rachel said. She was prodding a piece of food, very gently, with her fork. "Is this . . . what is this, Avery?"

"In the mustard greens?" he said. "Caperberries and bacon. But there are some pieces of horseradish in there too, so keep an eye out."

"No, I mean the . . . meat. The other meat. Not turkey."

"Oh, yeah. This guy let me borrow his fifteen-pound sausage

stuffer. This thing is *awesome*. One's smoked pork belly, and the other's lamb. With fennel." Next to Winnie, Thomas gave a delicate, visible shudder.

"You made sausage?" Rachel said. "Wow." She smiled at him and then shot a warning look over to Lila and Melissa: *Don't eat that, girls.*

"Anyway," Bob said. "They couldn't move on new construction for almost a year, so they kept up the Chinese takeout and tried to sell those organic pizzas they wanted to make, at the same time. You could call up and order either. Sometimes, I used to pick up some of each on my way home from the station."

"I miss Sunny Sundae," Melissa said. "Remember the one with pieces of bubblegum on top?"

"What is it now?" Nona asked. She used her knife to load both turkey and sausage onto her fork, before taking a bite.

"It's a boutique shoe store," Rachel said, rolling her eyes. "We've got four now, in town. Because God knows Hartfield women need their three-hundred-dollar driving shoes."

"Lila got Uggs," Melissa said, looking around, as if providing interesting information from a general perspective. "Mom wouldn't let us, and then somehow she did."

"They were *Bethany's*," Lila countered, from the other end of the table. "They didn't fit her anymore."

"Lucky for you," Melissa mumbled.

"Girls," Rachel said warningly.

"What's an *ugg*?" Avery asked Lila, who shook her hair down in front of her face, mortified. "Did it hurt?"

Nona laughed at him, a full, throaty sound that opened up the room and startled Winnie. There was a sexiness in her laugh, a rich uncaring intimacy that made everyone else at the table sudden witness to the rushing current flowing between her and Avery. They locked eyes and he made a little face at her, and Nona just laughed some more, now at the private, wordless conversation of her lover. Winnie, whose first reaction had been mild disapproval—*a little unseemly*—found herself warming to the sound, for all the love and shamelessness she heard in it. She looked across the table at Jerry, to glimpse their own connection amid the raw happiness of the young.

But he hadn't been listening, or so it seemed. He was absorbed in chewing, and was looking over, with an unseeing expression, to where the four oval portraits of her parents' parents were hung above the sideboard.

"Shoe stores," Nona's friend Thomas said, with a disagreeable snort. "Why is it always the shoe stores? Same thing in the city— first comes Starbucks, then the shoe stores. They push out anything useful or independent-owned and then they convince people they need overpriced *grandé* versions of basic things, like a cup of coffee."

"Well, Solo Soles is independent-owned," Bob said. "I just don't get the name. 'Solo Soles'? What does that even mean? You come out of there with one shoe?"

"But you're missing his point," Rachel said. "That's exactly what is happening in town. It used to be a local kind of place. Now we have people driving up from Westchester, scouting out real estate, shopping for designer bath towels. When we were growing up"—here she looked over to Winnie for confirmation—"the same stores had been around forever. Now everything is always changing."

No one spoke for a moment. "Maybe you should put that in the book," Rachel added, to Bob, as if to make fun of herself. *"Hart-field: Don't Get Too Attached."*

"Except it's about head trauma," Bob said mildly. "Not nostalgia lane. And it's my book."

"Those cultural studies of suburbia always wind up with the same conclusion anyway," Thomas said to Rachel. Avery turned to say something in a low voice to Jerry, who chuckled. "Money moves in, people move out. Blah, blah, blah. As if everyone hasn't read *that* before." No one responded, but to Winnie, it looked like Rachel was oddly satisfied with this remark.

"How did you get the turkey this tender?" Winnie called out firmly, down the table to Avery. She wanted to resettle things back to where they should be. "Not a trade secret, is it?"

"I brined it for about thirty hours," he shouted back, echoing her loud voice. "Like I told you."

"What does *brine it* mean?" Melissa asked.

"You just soak the bird in a big bucket of salt water," Nona answered. "He made me take out all three shelves in my refrigerator."

"Thirty hours?" Rachel said. "Is that safe? With all the bacteria that can grow, I mean?"

"She said it, I didn't," Thomas said, leaning over to reach the bottle of wine.

"So you guys, like, stay over at each other's place and stuff?" Melissa asked Nona, who made a questioning face at Rachel.

"Well, since we're all here together," Jerry said, and his voice startled the room into silence. Deliberately, he set down his knife and fork, plate cleaned.

"May I first toast my Winifred," he said, raising an empty wineglass. "No sappy stuff, except to say you've made an old man happier than anyone has a right to be."

"Ooh," Lila whispered.

As the others raised their glasses, Winnie's heart widened, even though Jerry wouldn't look at her. He was busy making himself look fierce and impatient, embarrassed in the wake of all the murmurs and loving looks surrounding him. *Finally*, Winnie thought. This *is what they were together for—the harmony of the expected.*

"All right, enough," he said. "Next is for the chef. My grandson, who cooks a damn fine dinner."

"Hear, hear," Winnie called. Everyone clapped, and Melissa drummed her spoon a little too hard against her glass of water. Avery held up both hands, and Nona blew him a kiss.

"And now that that's out of the way," Jerry said, waiting for them to be quiet. But what was this? Why did he look so serious? Winnie's chest tightened. Rachel glanced her way, concerned.

"Sometimes in a family . . . it's like business. You need to make some changes. Maybe you've done things a certain way for a long time, but then—well, even if people expect things to continue in the way they've been going, and they rely on that, you're going to need to assess the situation and change course as needed. Not always easy. Not always popular."

"Jerry?" Winnie asked. She tried to catch his eye, tried to ease him with a smile. How could she get back to that lovely balance of a minute ago?

"I may be old, but that doesn't mean I'm out of the game. I know how it's played. And Jerry Trevis isn't any kind of pushover, either. Frank here can tell you." Jerry thumbed angrily toward

Avery, who looked as worried as Winnie felt. Nobody corrected the name mistake.

"Darling," Winnie said. "Of course not. Why don't we—"

"I changed my will, and you might as well know about it now," he said, glaring around the table. "I wrote Annette out, and that's that."

There were audible gasps, from Rachel and Melissa. Lila was wide-eyed.

"Is this for real?" Thomas exclaimed, under his breath, to no one in particular.

All Winnie could do was stare down the table at Jerry. "I'm sorry, Winifred, but it had to be done. I didn't discuss it with you first because I knew you'd just try to argue, change my mind. But my mind is made up." She nodded dumbly. And what came to mind was the letter she had written to Annette, the one she'd torn up and written again and then mailed, anxious but determined, yesterday.

Your father doesn't know I'm writing to you, it began. And then it went on to plead, cajole, and apologize. Winnie had thrown herself on the mercy of this strange woman, she had acknowledged that her new presence in the family—she had even, after much internal debate, characterized her own marriage as "sudden"—was obviously causing problems between father and daughter, and she offered to meet with Annette to discuss whatever grievances there might be and how to resolve them. But, in other paragraphs, she also hadn't been above thinly veiled references to Jerry's advanced age, or hints that such a division in his family could make him ill—could, in fact, serve to bring on a recurrence of what Winnie had called "those problems he had in the past," trusting that her restrained phrase would signal to Annette that now she, Winnie, knew everything there was to know about Jerry's mental health. There was no more advantage to be had in withholding that information.

But now, as Jerry was saying something about voiding the prenuptial agreement she had gladly signed, and that he'd met with Ed Weller two days ago, and the new papers had already been drawn up—Winnie could vaguely hear Bob trying patiently to convince Jerry to reconsider—all she could think was that it was all her fault. In writing that letter, by violating Jerry's trust, by going behind his back to try to win over Annette, she might have made a bad situation worse. Now what would happen? Annette would surely tell Jerry, would throw this attempt right back in his face. And then what would she say? How would he react? What would it do to this nightmare?

With this chaos of thoughts crowding her mind, Winnie barely heard or understood what Jerry said next.

"This house—*our* house—will be Winnie's sole property, to use or dispose of as she wishes. To pass on to whomever she wishes. And god *damn* anyone who says otherwise." Jerry nearly shouted this, as if the entire squadron of Annette's lawyers had suddenly materialized at the dinner table. Winnie was flushed, breathless. How could he make her think about living on here, alone?

"And as for my estate, I've made it over to Frank. I mean *Avery*. He'll be sole inheritor." Jerry glared at them all, as if expecting vigorous dissent, when what he met was a continued silence. Then he faltered a little, unsure now, and spoke more quietly to the young man next to him—who was, Winnie saw, even through her own hazy shock, frozen. "It's a bum rap, what your mother and I have put on you. I'm sorry for my part of that. But it doesn't change what I've done. You're going to inherit it all."

Avery looked up, but not at Jerry, and not at Nona, who put her hand on the table and slid it toward him. He turned only to Winnie, and in his face she read the echo of her own stricken expression.

Fourteen
RACHEL

Now she was hungry. Thanksgiving's central meal had been over for an hour, and she was starving. Rachel leaned against the island in the middle of Winnie's barn-sized kitchen and pulled small pieces off the turkey carcass with her fingers. She couldn't remember when she'd last had a turkey that was this tender and flavorful. Her own, cooked for years in the temperamental oven at 144 Locust—and then just once, disastrously, last November in the "kitchenette" in the apartment on the side of the house—had always served more as vehicles for delivering bites of mashed potatoes, gravy, and (admittedly, canned) cranberry sauce. It was a revelation to enjoy the meat of the bird itself. When Avery dumped the leftover sausages into a plastic container near the platter, Rachel picked up one of those and ate it too.

After a minute, she noticed Avery just standing there, watching her, with his hand on his hip.

"What?" she said, popping the rest of the sausage—must have been lamb—into her mouth. God, this kid was good-looking.

Nona should be thanking her lucky stars. Had Jerry looked like that, back in the day?

"Taste any E. coli?" Avery said. "Salmonella?"

Rachel chewed. "Staphylococcus," she said, finally. "And a dash of mouse droppings." He rolled his eyes and went back to the sink.

"Don't think I haven't seen that, and worse, in the places I've worked."

"Spare me," Rachel said. "I never go out to eat anymore, but I don't want to ruin the possibility for the future."

"Ah, nothing that bad's going to get you out here. These places in town probably turn their tables over twice a night, if they're lucky. You won't get any vindictive busboys or seriously psycho waiters, out here in the boonies."

The boonies. Rachel smiled to herself and used a serving spoon to get at the sweet potatoes. "Yeah, but that's just the sabotage angle." Did Avery think that she was so old, so *suburban*, that even a semi-wild night out in Manhattan was completely off her radar screen? It wasn't so long ago that Rachel had been a regular at dollar draft night at McSorley's on East Seventh. Well, okay: it had been twenty years ago, and it was a stretch to say she'd attained the status of "regular." But still, did artfully bedraggled hipster Avery even know where McSorley's was? "What about all the food safety stuff? Outbreaks come from raw ground beef, not waiters sneezing on things."

"They come," Avery said, "from leaving leftovers out too long." He swooped away the turkey platter and the bowl of potatoes. Rachel snatched a last sausage before he firmly snapped a lid on the container.

The phone rang. Rachel wiped her hand on a dish towel and picked up the receiver.

"Don't answer that!" Avery called, from inside the refrigerator.

"Why?" she said, pressing the button. "Hello?" There was a faint rustling noise coming from the line, but no voice. "Hello? Trevis residence?"

"Told you," Avery said, shutting the fridge door.

"Hello?" Was it music? Yes, a recorded song she could only half hear, interspersed with fumbled thumps, as if the other person on the line was holding the receiver up to a speaker. "What is this?"

"Is it Joan Baez again, or that guy with the banjo?" Avery said. He was standing directly in front of her.

"Joan Baez?" Rachel said. Avery motioned for the phone. "Wait a minute." She listened for a moment to be sure and then pulled the phone away slightly. "It *is* Joan Baez. I love this song." She listened again. "What's going on? How did you—?"

Then she caught on. "Are you kidding me? Does this have to do with—? Are these the tree crazies?" Avery nodded, and tried to take the receiver. "No, I'll— Excuse me. Hello? This is Winifred Trevis's daughter. I have to ask you to stop this. What do you think you're doing, anyway? This is a private number, we're having a family holiday here, and—"

Avery pulled the phone away from her and pressed it to his chest. "That's not how you do it," he said. "Watch and learn." Then he held the phone a good six inches away from his face and roared: "*Listen up, ass-hats!* Call this number again, I'm gonna trace it, then get your loser name and home address, and post it on every frat-boy, web-nerd, Joan-Baez-hating blog in the tristate area. See how you like these kids, who have nothing better to do than stalk your every pathetic hour, and TP your house, and stink-bomb your car. And that's just how they warm up. *Are we clear, tree huggers?*"

Rachel was laughing by "ass-hats," and didn't stop for several minutes after Avery pressed END and tossed the phone back onto the counter. Her arms were weak from hard, whole-body laughing, but every time she pictured his red-faced bellowing into the innocent phone, she lost it again. The physical release, which almost brought her to tears, matched an inner buoyancy that had been building since dinner ended, in a general shambles, with Avery storming out to heat the pies, his friends perplexed and uncomfortable, and Winnie utterly silent. The girls didn't know where to look. And so Rachel, in a master hostess stroke, if she did say so, stepped up and made some general, vaguely calming statements—*this is a lot for everyone to absorb, let's all just enjoy the rest of our dinner*—and led the disgruntled party into a conversation about the new Star Wars movie. Bob, to his credit, had joined in right away and little by little they had carried it off. Jerry, who had retreated to a "Who, me?" expression, heartily ate two slices of pie and then announced he was going for a walk. A minute later Winnie rushed upstairs.

"Mom! What's going on?" This was Lila, hurrying into the kitchen from the den, where she and Melissa were watching a movie. She looked suspiciously at Avery. "Were you yelling at her?"

"Someone has to," he said, and winked at Rachel, who tried to get herself under control.

"I heard cursing," Lila insisted. Her calm eyes followed Avery back over to the sink.

"It's nothing," Rachel said. "What are you guys watching? We'll head home in about an hour, I guess."

"*When Harry Met Sally*," Lila said. "But Mel's just texting with some guy from school, so she's missed half the good parts."

"I'll come in soon," Rachel promised. "I'm just going to check on Nana."

"Is she all upset about the—" Lila paused, glancing at Avery's back. "Everything?"

"She's just resting, I think. I'll just run upstairs, and then be right in to watch with you, okay? Is Dad in there too?"

"No," Lila said. "I thought he was in with you, cleaning up or whatever." She turned to go, but not without a last glance in Avery's direction.

As soon as she had left, Avery said, in a low, different voice, "Do you know who Frank was?" He was scrubbing a saucepan with the intensity and focus of a surgeon. Rachel moved to where she could watch him at work, passing the pan again and again under the hot water. The motions were mesmerizing, and tiny stray bubbles floated away on clouds of steam.

"I'd offer to help, but I don't think my skills are up to your standards."

Avery shook his head. "Frank. Did you hear him call me that?"

"Yeah. Who is that, his son? Your uncle?"

"His brother. I never met him. I think he died a long time before I was born. But Grandad's been talking about him a lot, you know. When he tells stories about the old days. Stuff I'm supposed to write down. And I get the sense—"

"Old people get mixed up. He didn't mean it."

"That's what I'm saying!" Avery exclaimed. He brought the gleaming pan up close to his face, and then plunged it back in the suds. "He didn't mean it, putting me in the will. Something went wrong between them, Grandad and his brother, back when they were just getting the company going. I don't know exact details, but it had to do with a deal Grandad cut behind Frank's back. That went bad, somehow. Or maybe he screwed Frank out of some money, either on purpose or by accident. He never says the whole story, but I'm getting the gist of it."

Rachel squinted, trying to understand. "So you think Jerry believes you're actually Frank, his brother, from fifty years ago. And he made you—Frank—the inheritor of his estate to make up for a business debt he owed Frank—you—from the past."

"I'm not saying he really, like, *believes I'm Frank*. What I'm talking about is more symbolic. Repaying someone in the only way he can think of to do that, now."

"Karma?"

"Yeah, kind of."

Rachel snorted. "I'd say it's payback, Avery—but a whole different kind, for your mother."

There was a silence. Avery rinsed off the pot and pulled a dish towel off his shoulder to dry it.

Shit. "I'm sorry," Rachel said. "That just came out."

"It's okay," he said. "Never mind."

"But, Avery," she went on, a little desperate for him to see the way things were. *He's so young,* she reminded herself. *He's freaked out about what his mom will do.* "Even if that's the case, it'll still be okay. He knows who you are. And it's going to be *your* name on the paperwork. Right?"

He reared back and looked at her like she was crazy. "You think I'm worried about not getting the money? Or the legal shit? You think this is about that?"

She faltered. What, exactly, had she been trying to reassure him of? "Well, I thought you might be worried about . . . how it would all be perceived." Rachel finished her sentence lamely, knowing now she'd been on the wrong track. He had already turned away, was stacking things in a cabinet. The dishes, she saw, were almost done.

"Well, I'd better check on my mother." He nodded without turning.

But just as she passed him, Avery spoke again, in the same low voice as before. "Just don't tell her, okay?"

"Tell her what?"

"That this isn't the first time he's called me Frank."

From the window at the landing at the top of the stairs, Rachel could see that the light snow had stopped. In fact, all traces had vanished, from the brushy dark branches of the pine trees that crowded close to the back of the house, from the steeply pitched gables of a side roof, from the cars parked on Franklin Street. She paused at the window, listening. There was no sign of any movement down the hall. Boxes lined the hallway, stacked in piles at odd intervals. Rachel bent to one at her feet, and pulled open the flaps.

A jumble of items: woven baskets, a dusty glass vase, picture frames with glass cracked or missing, a rolled-up wad of material that turned out to be the runner Rachel remembered Winnie kept on the large dining-room table, under wobbly candlesticks and the wide, white ceramic bowl full of seashells she and Danny had collected as children, on summer trips to Long Island. She hadn't seen most of these things since her father died; when Winnie moved to her small pre-furnished apartment, she hadn't had the need or the room to display them. Rachel dropped the stained lace runner back into the box.

She pressed her middle fingers to the bridge of her nose and breathed a long, slow exhale. Boxes. Boxes up and down this hall and, undoubtedly, in the closed-up rooms throughout this huge, hardly used house. Yes, she knew that scientists said that humans used only a tiny fraction of their brains. But couldn't Winnie see how pointless it was, to live as she and Jerry did, huddled close in three or four pockets of this place, the rest a dusty storage center for boxes full of shards of the past?

That's how I've had to live, Rachel thought wildly. Boxes and boxes and boxes of things forgotten. *Can't it be different now? For all of us?*

Last week at Hand Me Down, her friend Cynthia had stopped by, with three plastic storage boxes, the long flat kind made to be tucked under a bed. She and Rachel had pried open the tops and gently lifted out the baby clothes, pressed flat and tight. There were tiny corduroy overalls with rusted hook-and-eye buckles, and blue and red sweaters in squeaky acrylic wool, and lots of cotton rompers edged in curly piqué, the way they used to be made, even for little boys. Rachel got busy with sorting and stacking, mentally dismissing most of it as out-of-date or just slightly too worn. Though some of the overalls had an old-style charm and were lightly used. She set a short pair aside to hang in the boys, 12-month, summer section.

Then a stifled noise made her look up at the other woman, surprised. Cynthia, a petite, slightly pudgy Greek woman that Rachel had known for years, was suddenly gushing tears, and making no move to stop them. They slid under the tinted lenses of her sunglasses and down her cheeks. She was holding out a rather unremarkable dark green one-piece sleeper, its rubber-bottomed feet dangling, the fabric thinned to nearly nothing on the knees. *Eighteen to 2T*, Rachel thought automatically. *$4.50.*

"Oh, my God," Cynthia said. She laughed, gesturing at herself, her face shining wet. "It's just . . . I'd forgotten this one. And he's driving now, you know?" She tipped the sleeper back so that it was resting lightly on her open hands. "Right now. He took my car to La Guardia, to pick up his aunt—my sister. La Guardia," she repeated quietly, amazed. Eyes raking every inch of the faded sleeper.

"Keep that one," Rachel advised. "Show it to him, tonight."

Cynthia took a deep breath and wiped tears out from the folds of her neck. "You must be used to this," she said shyly, recovering. "But it really took me back."

Now Rachel felt the warmth of her own tears, the ones that had somehow made it past her screwed-shut eyelids, on her fingertips. So she opened her eyes wide and tipped her head back. There. She blinked them back where they came from, and found herself staring straight up at a couch-sized water stain on the ceiling. Numbly, she added it to a catalogue of the house's flaws that she couldn't help tallying: the chipped paint everywhere, peeling wallpaper, the torn carpet in the front hall.

Enough. Rachel pressed down hard on her own bitterness. There had to be a way to tackle all of this openly and practically— Jerry's announcement and what it meant, for all of them.

Striding firmly to Winnie's room, Rachel knocked twice, waited a perfunctory beat, and then let herself inside.

"Mom," she began. She expected Winnie to be lying on her bed with a wrung-out washcloth covering her face. But the bed was empty and carefully made up.

"Shh," Winnie said, from the chair tucked in the corner next to her dresser. Rachel was surprised to see her upright and alert, with a phone receiver held tightly to one ear.

"Who are you talking to?" And what were all these papers and folders, scattered on the floor in front of her? Rachel picked one up. *Isn't it time you listened to your heart? A tropical paradise awaits . . . right in your own backyard.*

"Damn," Winnie said, and pressed a button. "They never make these menus detailed enough."

"'In-ground *gunite*'?" Rachel read. "Is that a typo for granite?"

"Dry mixture of cement and sand," Winnie said, still on the phone. "Then they add water and spray it against the interior walls. Wait, here it is. Holiday hours for the weekend."

Each photograph in the brochures displayed a piercingly blue, crystal-clear swimming pool differing only in variety of shape: kidney-bean, amoeba blob, rectangle. Rachel sat on the edge of the bed and sorted through papers until she found what she was looking for: three typed sheets, stapled. *LuxPool Invoice for 50 Greenham: five consultations (first one* gratis*), preliminary underground utilities assessment, design options. LuxPool Invoice: soil test, depth measurement, project installation outline. LuxPool Invoice: ground and deck materials, equipment insurance, custom stairs, plaster finish, pebble application . . .* The zeros attached to the prices next to each item racked up faster than Rachel could process them. Her head swam; this had gotten much further than she had thought.

Winnie hung up the phone. She made a mark in the notebook on her lap. "Well, they have it in the computer that we're on for next week."

"Mom," Rachel began. Where to start? "Mom, it's almost winter. You can't put in a pool now."

"It just so happens that early winter is the best time to install a pool, because the ground is hard and dry."

"But—"

"And I'm not in the mood to hear any more opinions about what I plan to do with that tree. It's coming down, and that's that." Winnie snapped her notebook shut.

"What about all these phone calls? These people are serious about—"

"So you think I should give in, just because they're serious? Just because I'm getting harassed in my own home, on Thanksgiving? Seems to me that's even more reason to go ahead with it."

"It's not just the crazies, Mom. You saw that piece in the *Bugle*, I know you must have. Don't pretend you didn't read it. The editors of the *newspaper* are writing about this tree, saying you should be ashamed to cut it down—and that means next week in the letters section it'll be a free-for-all."

"They dig up any old story to fill space in that paper. Tempest in a teapot."

Rachel threw up her hands and went over to the window, pulling aside the curtain. There, through the window, was the long, gently sloping lawn in twilight, the grass still green in patches, though mostly wheat-colored, and scattered with wet leaves. Though a long line of maples bordered the front wall along Greenham, and several thin conifers speckled the property's edges here and there, the sycamore might as well have been the only tree around, right smack in the middle of the lawn, a soaring, bare-branched giant. It was so tall and assured it gave off the silent perception that everything else in its wake—lawn, house, street—had been arranged to showcase its own massive growth.

What was that mark, on its trunk, about six or so feet off the ground? Through the fading Thanksgiving afternoon light, she could barely make out two intersecting red lines, crudely slashed across the sycamore's patchy bark: a big, spray-painted *X*.

"Jesus," Rachel muttered. "Joan Baez herself is going to be out there."

Winnie had tucked up her stocking feet underneath her, with a defiant look. As defiant as she could be, that is, with that turtleneck pulled up almost to her nose. Rachel wished her mother would grow to accept the darkened patch of skin, and stop with all the endless accessorizing of scarves, and shawls, and big throaty sweaters. What would she do when spring came? Once, Melissa had nervously asked Rachel if Nana's new rash was catching, or cancer—it wasn't clear which one unnerved her daughter more. Every so often, when she couldn't take it anymore, Winnie would burst out in despair to Rachel—*It looks awful, doesn't it? How can I go out in public?*—and Rachel would resolutely argue her down until her mother was calm again—*You're being crazy, it's hardly noticeable.* It was a carefully choreographed routine that never changed. Rachel suspected each of them knew the truth lay somewhere in the middle, that the stain was indeed noticeable but not entirely awful, and that their scripted questions and replies were a form of mother-daughter catechism that she and Winnie had enacted their entire lives. Their long time habit was to seek a kind of comfort, and pleasure, in the expected.

"Mom," she tried.

"I don't care! Yes, it's a big, beautiful tree, but it's just a tree, and it's going to get cut down in a week or two!" Winnie burst out, looking for all the world like Melissa used to, when she was a belligerent preschooler.

"I'm not going to argue with you about this tree right now," Rachel said, exasperated. "It's just that—putting in a pool is a huge commitment, and I'm not sure you've thought this all through."

"Please. You know how I operate." Winnie gestured at the phone, the notebook, the folders and brochures (each pasted with several sticky notes covered in her handwriting).

"All right, fine. You've thought it through." *Without including me.* "But this house needs a lot of work, Mom. Maybe it would be better to tackle some of the more pressing problems, rather than, you know, the fun stuff. Like a pool."

"Jerry's back is a pressing problem!"

"You two aren't going to enjoy the pool very much if the ceiling falls through in this hallway." Winnie was prepared to counter this, so Rachel moved quickly to her real subject. "Also, a pool right in front of the house isn't what everyone wants in this kind of property. You know most people in town belong to the club."

Winnie sat back, astonished. "Who gives a fig what other people want?"

"Well, I'm just saying that it would be smart to get a clear idea of what the potential value is for this kind of major undertaking."

Her mother was silent, so Rachel went on. "The fact that Jerry is leaving this entire property to you means—"

"I don't want to talk about that."

"You might not want to talk about it, but you need to face it. This is a major development, and we have to carefully consider anything that might—"

Winnie stood up. "I need to use the restroom. I'll meet you downstairs."

"Mom, come on." But she had already disappeared into the powder room and shut the door with a definite *click*. "Mom?"

Rachel heard the squeal of pipes opening, and then the rush of water in the sink. She sighed, and glanced down at the pile of pool brochures scattered on the floor—all those chemical blue spheres, each blindingly sunlit, each blank and empty, as if daring someone to take a running jump in—*cannonball!*—and break the smooth surface of the water.

Downstairs, it was eerily quiet. In the den, images flickered silently on the mute TV screen. Melissa gave a wave and then went back to texting; Lila was asleep on the couch next to her, hair spilling over the pillows in a shining mass. Rachel went through the darkened kitchen and let herself out the side door. It was impossible to see anything in the blinding light over the garage, but a noise in the front of the house led her along a path through high, thick bushes.

Suddenly, she came up on Bob, crouched down in the shadows on Winnie and Jerry's front steps.

"Are you okay?" Her heart was racing. "What's going on?"

"Nothing," he grunted, pushing himself upright. "I'm fine. Just some trash." He held a half-full garbage bag in one hand and nudged his glasses into place with the back of the other. There was a light on above the door, and its harsh orange glow lit up Bob's shiny head and the dead-white skin of his scar, a long, puckered rope that began at a spot above his right temple, trailed down behind the ear, and back behind his neck, to disappear under his shirt collar. At times Rachel thought it made him look like a Secret Service agent or a bodyguard: someone who wore an earpiece with discreet wires.

Something about the freshness of the cold air, and the way the two of them were standing there together, right in front of this huge, impossible, beautiful house brought it back to Rachel, that earlier buoyancy. Happiness.

"Well?" she said. "So what do you think?" Sometimes, it was easy to forget how handsome Bob was—he had always had a professorial air, but in a Clark Kent, hiding-behind-spectacles way. Now the bare head and even the scar made him appear more rakish, a bit dangerous. She should really *look* at him more. As if to underline the idea, a flicker of bodily desire rose within Rachel for the first time in months.

"What do I think about what?"

"About the whole—" Rachel swirled her hand vaguely at the house, the lawn, the tree. "This is good news for us! I'm allowed to say that, right? After all, he's got to leave this place to someone . . . why not Mom?"

But Bob had turned away while she was talking. He was wearing yellow rubber gloves and was stuffing something—paper towels?—into the garbage bag.

"What? Jerry knows the score—he's older and it's much more likely that he would . . . Look, if he can face facts, why can't we all talk about this? About what it means? For Mom—for *us*?"

Still, he went on with the papers and that bag, and the way he was shaking his head started to irritate Rachel.

"*What?* I'm just looking into the future. She won't need this huge place—she couldn't possibly! We could sell it, definitely, or we could just—"

"Move in?" Bob said. "Take over?"

"Well, I don't know," Rachel said, caught off guard by the way it sounded out loud, her half-formed thoughts. "Maybe. Why not?"

"Ray," Bob sighed. "Don't get caught up in some big fantasy. None of this is going to happen."

"Why are you saying that? You heard what Jerry—"

"Jerry is an elderly person who is in the middle of a heated family dispute," Bob explained in an overly patient tone, as if he were speaking to one of the girls. Any desire Rachel had felt for him whooshed away, like air from a pricked balloon. "His daughter has already filed a *lis pendens*—that's like a lien on the property. Even if he dropped dead tonight, every asset would essentially be frozen until it could all be sorted out. And then any ownership would be in jeopardy until the original claim is resolved."

"Frozen for how long?"

"For years. And that's just for starters. That's not even addressing the related matter of this last-minute amendment to his will, which cuts his only biological child out of her birthright . . ." Bob wiped his hands on a towel and let out an obnoxious whistle. "That's going to get very ugly, in court, when she challenges it. For years and years—probate court is notoriously slow. Frankly, I'm surprised he could convince his lawyers to put it through."

"We don't know she's going to challenge it!" But even as she threw this out, Rachel heard how stupid it sounded. Wearily, she had to admire the way he sounded like a lawyer again. In a tiny way, she was reassured, even as frustrated tears stung her eyes.

Bob moved closer to her. "Ray. There's no magic here, for us. We're just going to have to stumble through."

She nodded, suddenly ashamed by her childish hopes and the ugliness that had risen within her so quickly. Had she really been thinking along these lines, about how the house would pass to her? For to follow that to its logical conclusion meant Jerry dead—and then her own mother—

No. Rachel blew her breath out, hard. Bob was still watching her carefully.

She straightened up. "What are you doing out here, anyway?"

He half turned and regarded the garbage bag with a wry smile. "Cleaning up a special delivery. Dog shit in a flaming brown paper bag, tossed up on the stairs."

"Dog shit . . . Are you kidding?"

"Ten minutes with Clorox and a now-contaminated scrub brush says no, I am most definitely not kidding."

"How do you know . . . ? And it's from—them? Those crazy people?"

Bob stripped off the rubber gloves and tossed them into the bag. "I heard the doorbell ring and came out to find . . . this. There was a nice note taped to the bag, something along the lines of 'Tree killer,' et cetera, et cetera."

Rachel couldn't understand how he was so calm. "Shouldn't we call the police? This is insane! What if one of the girls had been out here?"

"I'm going to report it. I just didn't see the use of the police coming out when I knew I was going to clean it up anyway. And your mother doesn't need more drama tonight. I'll call it in tomorrow." He motioned for her to go with him, back into the house, but Rachel stared out at the lawn, whose great size and dark shadows now seemed full of hidden malice. From inside came the faint sounds of music. Still she stood at the top of the stone stairs, rootless and worried.

"I just don't get it," she said.

Bob shrugged. "They want to save that tree. Environmentalists aren't exactly going to see eye to eye with your mother on the need for a pool for Jerry's back." He shifted the garbage bag from hand to hand. "A lot of people don't."

"But—here? It just seems like the kind of thing people would get worked up about in the city, at NYU or something. Not here. Not up in *Hartfield*, for God's sake." She just couldn't fathom that anyone she knew would go to these lengths just for one tree. Yes, it was a big tree. But this was the kind of thing you read about in L.A., or in the redwood forests—protesting the loggers or some hippie girl camped out in a treehouse for weeks at a time, giving interviews, posing for camera crews. Rachel felt the way she often did when they attended a production of *King Lear* or *Macbeth* put on at the high school by the local adult theater troupe—watching their neighbors in robes and makeup, weeping and cursing. That same sense of misplaced drama, of scale gone all out of whack.

Bob smiled, either at what she had said, or what he knew to be her train of thought. "People in Hartfield get angry and impassioned and obsessed, just like anywhere else. Come on. It's late. Let's get the girls." Rachel let him put his hand on her shoulder and guide her in.

There was music inside—a loud cabaret song that Rachel at first assumed must be coming from a stereo. Gathered together again in the living room were all the strewn-out participants of Thanksgiving: Lila, sleepy-eyed, on one side of the den doorway with her sister leaning against the other; Thomas, with his back to them, sitting on the couch, his legs crossed, foot dangling. Avery was perched on the slate bench built into the front of the fireplace, his hands on Nona's waist. Winnie and Jerry were in the center of the room, arms around each other, dancing. And Nona—Nona was the music. She was singing as if possessed by the spirit of some famous 1930s chanteuse. The rich, melancholy song pouring out of her open, red-lipsticked mouth might have been dubbed from an old jazz club performance.

Jerry stopped dancing and interrupted the song. "Now do Annie Ross," he commanded. "Can you do Annie?" Nona, who had stopped mid-phrase, just grinned and put her hands behind her back. Everyone waited. Then she burst out in a completely different, faster, jazzy voice.

Rachel saw Jerry had shut his eyes and was nodding his big head. He was just standing there in the middle of the room, with Winnie close by—they couldn't dance to the strange, fast beat of this song.

Nona sang, and then Jerry joined in, exactly in unison, for the chorus.

The group clapped, breaking up the song. Bob whistled.

"More scat?" Nona asked. "I can try some Ella, the earlier stuff. Decca." She moved her voice up and down, giving him a taste.

"I like the Cole Porter years better," Jerry argued.

"Or what about Peggy Lee?" Nona countered. She hummed

and Avery thumped time on her hip. Everyone looked to see how Jerry would react.

But the old man shook his head stubbornly. He was about to say something else, when a touch on his hand from Winnie made his face soften. He stiffly took up a slow-dancing position with her and said only, "Lena."

Nona saluted. She put a hand on her stomach and tipped her head forward. Soon a rich rushing melody burst forth, with another, twangy accent. Everyone knew this one; it was a standard, with lyrics about love and desire and whether it's just too late.

Winnie took tiny steps, pressed up against her husband. And Jerry held on to her, mouthing the words as Nona gave them her all.

Fifteen
AVERY

It was nearly 1 AM. Avery stood in front of the Blue Apple in the freezing pitch-black of Myrtle Avenue, watching for the cops. He launched into a coughing fit and worked up a thick wad of phlegm; unwilling to either spit it out right in the doorway and unable to move even a few feet, he swallowed it back down. *Perfect.* Typical of this hellish week, in which he'd been fired from his craft-services gig (for sneezing into his hands just as the short guy from *Seinfeld* walked past), found out the fire rating for the Blue Apple was pegged at nine (out of a possible ten, one being the best)—which would triple his premiums—and Nona was still out of town, first for an endless music festival in Rhode Island, and now in Pittsburgh to spend Christmas with her mother.

Rhode Island, he muttered inwardly, and kicked at a piece of broken pavement. *Pittsburgh!*

From behind him, inside the restaurant: loud *whams* and a high-pitched, screeching whine. Two guys Avery barely knew were putting in city code-mandated grease traps, one in the front, one in the kitchen. It was one big hassle, start to finish. No, Avery shouldn't have skipped that dumb-sounding all-day "small business boot camp" only to find out it was mandatory for filing the first set of permit papers. Nor should he have blown off the Health Department inspector—he'd either gotten the days wrong or, more plausibly, just stayed in bed with Nona—whose eventual revenge produced a long list of code violations, several involving the phrase "putrescible solid waste." And he'd screwed up the order of things: he should have had Buildings come first, then Health. Apparently, he needed new grease traps in order to get the next round of permits—but needed those same permits in order to install the grease traps.

Christ. Avery could barely figure it out when he *wasn't* flu-delirious. And he didn't want to think of what he'd had to pay, cash of course, for the new traps themselves or for this off-hours, off-the-books installation. Wind whipped the garbage on the street into dark, swirling cyclones. Two hard-looking black guys slowed as they passed him, SUV lit-up rims spinning backward, offering Avery twin glares of unmistakable displeasure.

He pulled out his cell phone, woozy from the effort of standing upright. Problem was, he couldn't figure out who to call. He started to dial Nona, and then erased the number, one digit at a time. He knew she had been sleeping badly, and she'd had a long drive today—or was it yesterday?—from the festival to Pittsburgh. Also, they had just gotten back to a warily balanced good place after the stupid fight, which mostly consisted of Avery's being pissed that he wasn't invited to spend Christmas with Nona and her mom, but not admitting that was the real reason.

God, he missed her. New York was a huge swarming planet of emptiness, without Nona's face and voice during the day, her body against his at night. He was staying in her room, and Thomas, who had been in town for an unprecedented three weeks straight—*of course*—had taken to calling him "sir," in little yellow notes scattered around the apartment like "your turn to buy toilet paper, sir." This had to be some snickering reference to the insane scene that had gone down in Hartfield at Thanksgiving—which Avery was doing his best to block out entirely—and he refused to dignify it with a response. Actually, he and Thomas had settled into a grudging, not-unfriendly truce; at breakfast together, one would shove the cereal box or milk over to the other, without a word, without looking up from the *Post*. Two grumpy old guys, Avery thought, missing their girl.

It crossed his mind to call Winnie. Ridiculous, at this hour, and of course he wouldn't do it. But the memory of all her recent messages stayed with him—the tone of her voice: at first lively—something about that tree in her yard, how it was headed for the wood-chip pile this week—then concerned, then sad and unsure. "He's been asking about you," she said simply, in the last one. That had been over a week ago. Again Avery felt an inner pull on his conscience, but he was still in the throes of the way he'd been caught off guard, and pretty much humiliated, by Grandad, made to seem like nothing but a little lost rich kid caught in the crossfire of a battle between grown-ups, right in front of everyone at dinner—right in front of Nona. Whose careful, respectful silence on the whole matter showed she understood everything about how it was roiling Avery's mind, which was good—but was worrying too, because it suggested they were both in agreement about how big an obstacle this would be to them. This money. Money that wasn't even his. Money he didn't even want! No, he wouldn't be calling

Winnie back anytime soon. Or going out to Hartfield. Everyone would just have to get over it.

So Avery—chilled and feverish, blood pounding in his eye sockets—called his mother. He let the phone ring, picturing the polished, shadowy foyer of the house in Winnetka, with its sweeping white staircase and the tiny flashing red dot of the burglar alarm. It rang and rang, and the answering machine picked up. He ended the call and hit REDIAL. After two rings this time, he heard Rich's voice, frogged with sleep and aggravation.

"It's me," Avery said. There was a slow-moving wheelchair across the street; he couldn't make out the occupant's gender. "I know it's kind of late, I just—"

"Avery?" Rich said. "What's wrong?" In response, Avery could only sigh. Where to begin? It had been so long since he'd talked to Rich. Or to his mother.

"Let me go into the hall. Are you in trouble?"

"No, it's nothing like that. I just had some free time—"

"You're still at work? What time is it?"

"Sort of. I mean, yeah. I'm at work." Whoever was in the wheelchair was balancing two twelve-packs of soda on his or her lap, scooting forward with little steps, feet on the ground. "Is Mom there?"

Rich exhaled. "She's asleep," he said, after a long pause. "We were going to give you a call tomorrow. Later today, I mean. You got the box I sent, right?"

"How come tomorrow?"

"Just to say Merry Christmas. You're not going to have to work, are you?" Avery's mind whirled. He tried to calculate what day it was. Christmas tomorrow? He guessed that made sense. "Did that jacket fit? I can exchange it if you want—and definitely let me know if you want a different color."

"Oh—uh, yeah. No, I mean, it's fine." His current mail situation was a little sketchy, so Avery couldn't imagine where any kind of box sent to him would end up. "Thanks. I, uh, I have something for you guys. I just have to get to the post office. So, can I talk to Mom?"

"I don't think that would be a good idea," Rich said gently. "Not right now."

"Why not?" The wheelchair occupant got out, went behind to the handles, and pushed the chair carefully over a raised curbside. Fury rushed Avery. "What's she pissed at *me* about? This is really fucked up, you know. I don't have anything to do with it, this thing she's got against Grandad. If you even knew what I—"

"Maybe you could try to see it from her side," Rich said. "For once. Do you even know the strain she's under? We've just finally recovered from all the shit *you* put us through—"

"Hey!"

"And now Jerry's moved to New York and lost his mind. He's bent on jeopardizing everything about your mom's career, the company's reputation . . . and frankly, it doesn't help matters that you're so under his sway."

"Just because I wouldn't promise not to go over there? Not that I even want to go over there now, but—"

"She's on all kinds of medications for the stress. Last night she couldn't sleep until nearly dawn, and even then she was crying, saying over and over, 'She's stolen him from me, she's taken him away.'"

"What?" Avery scoffed, unsteady on his feet. *How did his mother even know about Nona?* "That's stupid. I haven't been *sto*—" The words died away, unspoken. He wiped his nose. Not him. It was *Jerry* that his mother had been talking about, not him. She hadn't been thinking about Avery at all.

Rich had continued speaking. "—best for everyone if there's some distance. We'll call tomorrow. Okay, bud? We all need to take this slow." Avery scrubbed at his face, trying to smooth out its sudden crumples. "Avery? Get some sleep, all right? You don't sound so good."

He slammed shut the phone and started walking, fast. Anywhere, any direction, didn't matter. The bite of the wind was welcome; Avery hoped it would slap his face enough to stop the tears, freeze them, stop this lonely anguish filling him up inside. Half walking, half running, in a demented kind of loping jog, he turned the corner and headed west. Once around the block. That's what he needed. Just a little fresh air, clear his mind, and then he'd get back inside to check the grease-trap progress.

But just as he reached DeKalb, something about the corner building caught his eye. Avery slowed, drawn to the neatly refinished exterior and the classy, unobtrusive sign out front: *snack. bar.*, it read, trendy lower-case script and periods firmly in place. Dark inside, unopened, but a fine, copper-edged bar already installed, at least ten bistro-style tables, and funky artwork on the walls. He studied the menu under the STAY TUNED sign.

"Fuck me," Avery whispered. A surge of illness overtook him.

"Global New American," it said. And divided the different parts of the meal based on distinctions of region and provenance, not the arbitrary first, second, dessert course usual—just like Avery had planned to, in his rapidly filling notebook. He wiped runny snot with the back of his glove and then ran a finger down the listings: Maine diver scallops with saffron potato purée, *check*; confit of Muscovy duck breast with fingerlings and honey-tarragon haricots, *check*; seared loin of lamb with local baby greens in a caramelized bourbon glaze, *check*. And on and on. Each one a version of something he'd imagined serving. He squinted to find the carefully understated, italicized name at the bottom of the menu. Chef Daniel F. Miller. Avery didn't know the guy, and instantly hated him. Even the desserts—even the *pricing* of the desserts, a ten-dollar flat charge for each—echoed his plans. Trio of chocolate beignets with sea salt and a cinnamon-pepper crème fraîche . . .

Shit.

Avery walked back the way he came, his hands jammed way down into his coat pockets. This place was, what, a whole four blocks over from the Blue Apple's deserted mid-block location on an ugly stretch of a busy, ugly throughway. *snack. bar.* Well, *suck. my. dick.*, Avery thought.

As he neared the Blue Apple, it seemed even dirtier, more rundown, more *orange* than he'd remembered from a few minutes ago. He could hear a buzzing roar within, and the guys shouting above the noise. Suddenly, Avery knew who he wanted to call, the one person he wanted to talk to about all of this mess. Grandad. Grandad, with his nine dozen different stories about run-ins with the Feds, and God knows Avery had sat through most of them. He could picture Grandad's narrowed eyes at his description of *snack. bar.*, could hear the old man work up some choice epithets for chef Daniel F. Miller. None of that would help the immediate situation, of course, but it sure would feel good. Avery realized how proud Grandad would be, hearing how he was solving the permit problem tonight, with the illegal plumbers and the black-market grease traps.

It was his grandfather's money behind this, behind all of it. Avery stopped, one shaky hand on the Blue Apple's door. But it was more than that—it was his *backing*. Grandad had backed him. It hit Avery what that meant, and even though fear slivered through— *what if I let him down?*—the overall sensation remained, of having someone believe in him, of having someone in his corner. Avery guessed it had been a while since he'd felt that. Or had he ever?

When he came back inside, there was an instant blast of stench from the broken toilets. One of the plumbers, Hernando, looked up quickly from a table with a wide, guilty smile; there was a woman with him and take-out containers everywhere: *sopa de elote* and fresh tortillas, *chile rellenos* and *carne asada*. They waved Avery over, filled him a plate. Pounding behind the bar: *Blam! Blam!* Avery wobbled a little, feeling like he was crossing the deck of some ship tossing around in a plunging sea. *MMMzzzzzzzzzzz* came the drill saw, and then a series of squealing, high-pitched squeaks. He tried to steady himself near the table where Hernando and his girlfriend sat. Then he saw the woman's head duck down and tilt back fast—a familiar, lost motion that Avery recognized in his very bones.

"This cool with you, boss?" Hernando said, talking about the lines of speed laid out amid crumpled paper towels and half-empty plates of food. "Our vitamins, right? We need 'em when we work late."

Avery took a seat nearby, heavily. His head swam. The drugs were more than an arm's reach away. But not much more.

Blam! Blam! Blam! Angry hammering drowned out whatever

the girlfriend was saying, and Hernando's laughing reply. Avery concentrated on not passing out. He realized that a cab, at this hour, from this location, would be impossible. The thought of the subway—the thought, even, of standing up again—threatened to make him cry. *I'm going to sleep here*, he thought, or maybe even said out loud. *On the floor, next to my brand-new grease traps.* Hernando rubbed some speed around his gums and then dug into a container for another piece of grilled meat. His girlfriend was chattering away at a whining buzz-saw pitch. Or maybe that was the drill again. In his haze, Avery couldn't tell the difference between the thumps behind the bar and the pounding in his head. The talking went on around him, shit and food smells mingled together, and the drugs lay on the table. Why should he be surprised? Avery had figured it out: the drugs would always be on the table.

Sixteen
WINNIE

It was Monday, January 2. It was a new week of a new year, and Winnie was busy telling everyone that today was the day. That tree in her yard was coming down later in the afternoon, so everyone would just have to find something else to be upset about. In town for errands that morning, she even stopped by Hand Me Down to tell Moira, the other saleswoman (Rachel was in San Francisco with the girls until the end of the week). "By three thirty at the latest," she said. "I'm going to document the whole thing. Maybe I'll put it on YouTube!" At the bank, she ran into Don Martin. "That tree had a nice, long tree life," she said. "But when your number's up, it's up." She told the young woman behind the deli counter at Fresh Market, who asked what a sycamore was, and she told the young man who bagged up her groceries and set them in her cart. (Winnie remembered when they used to bring them out to your car.) "By dinnertime that old tree will be *zzzvvvippp*," she said, making the appropriate throat-slitting sound to accompany the gesture.

As it turned out, Gil from Lawn Care—the only tree company who would do the job—was anxious to avoid any more media attention, and had obsessed, in Winnie's view, about finding the right date and time for the cutting and removal process. For a long time, Gil wanted to keep the schedule a secret. And then he had even suggested that they purposely leak a wrong date, in order to throw people off the scent. This struck Winnie as overkill, and then she realized that he must be worried that any bad press would be bad for business. But when she mentioned this, Gil agreed only vaguely. *True, we don't need to be on any front page*, he'd said. And then, uneasily: *Plus, there are a lot of freaks out there.*

But Winnie was less scared of the "freaks"—for this, she substituted "prank callers"—than she was of what it would do to her if she had to give up on this. *This:* holding on to an idea, an ideal, about herself and Jerry; everything she'd been promised by falling in love. And if she could dimly recognize that her own need for the pool had somehow taken priority, above even Jerry's back pain, the thought was brief and shaming, and then quickly buried in plans, phone calls, the undertaking itself.

In deference to Gil, she'd kept today's date a secret, but now that the day was here, she couldn't see the harm in spreading the news, nor could she help it. Most people in town received this news with a polite tolerance or perhaps a slight trace of alarm, possibly from the vehement cheer of its delivery. Winnie didn't imagine that she'd happen to run into one of the prank phone callers and dog-waste throwers, whoever they were, but she almost hoped she would. She was spoiling for a fight. One woman, that second daughter of Becca Kingsley's, balancing a crying toddler on one hip, had earnestly tried to engage her in a discussion about the reasons for such a drastic act. Hadn't Winnie even explored any other options? Building an above-ground pool, for example?

Building an addition onto the house for an infinity pool? And they were doing wonders now with acupuncture. Winnie brushed it all off, remembering now why she could never remember this disagreeable woman's name. *Really*, she said to herself, *does she think I'm made of money?* "Nope," she said. "This afternoon I'm going to settle into my front-row seat and watch the big guy come crashing down. I may make popcorn!" She had to admit it was enjoyable, shocking Becca Kingsley's daughter in this way.

Also, announcing the tree's execution later today with such relish helped to block out all the other things Winnie was trying to avoid. "How's Rachel?" Moira had asked. "Getting tan, I bet." "Oh, fine, fine," Winnie had muttered, hurrying back out the door. How could she say anything about the truth, which was that she and Rachel hadn't spoken before they'd left for California, other than a quick Christmas phone call? How could she say anything about how things had been since Thanksgiving? Her daughter was fixated on 50 Greenham—*my* home, Winnie thought—on the money it represented, on what it would all do for *her*, Rachel, and she didn't give a single thought to what it meant to her mother, or to the fact that some things had nothing to do with money. Yes, Rachel and Bob were having hard times. Well, what family didn't, at one time or another? And everything Winnie had done for them, over the years . . .

No. That was not the way to think. Better to focus on the tree—the pool, and the tree, and what Jerry's face would look like as he eased himself into the water, on the first warm day of the summer. Did they still shout, "*Tim-ber!*" she wondered. She would find out soon enough.

"Where's that handsome new grandson of yours?" Eliza McVeer called out, putting money in her meter. "*He's* a corker."

"Busy," Winnie said, scuttling away toward Rudy's to pick up a pair of resoled shoes. "Too busy for us old folks." She could laugh with Eliza, but a pang struck deep. Jerry had stopped mentioning Avery, and she had stopped phoning him.

Last stop was the library, a redbrick Georgian (Winnie remembered her father fretting that the design clashed entirely with his station, three blocks to the east) where she picked up three books on hold: that new biography of John Adams that everyone was talking about; plus a book about garbage in America, which looked particularly disgusting and interesting; and the newest Sue Grafton mystery novel. The same placid, pasty-faced clerk who had worked the circulation desk for years had to slowly sort through all the titles on the shelf behind him, even as Winnie pointed to the right ones. Then she realized he was muttering, "McClelland, McClelland," as he flipped through the paper slips stuck in the books.

"Trevis," she corrected firmly. And the chance to do so, the very word itself, brought such a swell of delight that Winnie found herself magnanimous, benevolent, able to forgive this slow dolt of a clerk. She chatted with him about the weather—no snow yet, but surely by week's end . . . and then of course launched into a full description of the tree and the pool and the sycamore's last few hours. He didn't have much to say, this sour man, just went about scanning her books with the occasional grunt. Well, no matter, Winnie thought. She waved him a jaunty good-bye.

There was a table set up near the library entrance that featured recent books on military history. She paused here, looking over one on the Korean War. Jerry occasionally liked to read these—he'd even been interviewed and quoted once, by a Chicago historian. Had he already seen this one? She turned it over in her hands, recognizing neither author nor title, but that didn't mean anything. And then, one of the disloyal thoughts. One of the scary ones, the ones she was getting very good at squelching. This one ran along the lines of, *Just get it, if you like—you know he won't remember if he's read it or not.*

She flipped open the front cover, reading hastily: "Our Forgotten War, it is sometimes called. On June 25, 1950, a firestorm from North Korean . . ." Winnie paused. June 25. Their wedding day, last year. How strange that Jerry had never mentioned the coincidence of dates.

And then, it came again, one of those memories that veered toward her in waves, another bombing sortie from which she needed to duck and cover. Weeks ago, gathering up the mail from its scattered pile inside the front door, she had been surprised by the sight of a dozen recognizable green envelopes, Christmas cards, ones she knew Jerry had mailed out a few days ago to old friends and colleagues. She gathered them up; each was stamped RETURN TO SENDER next to the unfriendly image of a pointing forefinger. Her first thought: *Had he forgotten the stamps?* But then she saw what he had done, and her stomach tilted sharply. All the addresses were wrong—not wrong in information, but placed awry, all over the envelopes. On one, he'd put the recipient's name and street to the very top right, where a stamp hid most of it. On another, he'd put his own name, and 50 Greenham, right in the front middle, and the rest of it on the backside, circled helplessly. They were all like this, she found, rapidly flipping through—names and addresses set down haphazardly, in Jerry's unmistakable hand, no two the same, sideways, backward, as if according to an entirely different postal scheme.

Winnie hadn't said anything to anyone; she'd thrown away the envelopes and mailed the cards again, in new ones. But that was just the first instance—the first discovery. One little thing gone topsy-turvy.

Now in the library, Winnie pulled out her cell phone. This book looked fascinating, and Jerry might well enjoy it. He was probably on his way back from physical therapy now—she might catch him in the car. NEW VOICEMAIL MESSAGE, the screen read. She put the book down on the table, on top of her own stack, and moved into the chilly small foyer to listen. A male voice, vaguely familiar:

"Yeah, uh—Mrs. Trevis, this is Gil from Lawn Care. We're going to need to be out at your place earlier today, because of another job. And because—you know. Keep 'em off balance. I think the guys should be there by ten or so. Okay? Just letting you know. Thanksandhaveagoodday."

Ten? Ten o'clock today, meaning this morning? Winnie clicked through the phone features, her mind awhirl. 11:42, the display read. But—but—that meant . . .

She fled. She forgot her checked-out books. Someone called to her, in the parking lot, but Winnie didn't even look over. She dropped her keys on the cold pavement, and scraped her knuckles snatching them back up. And in the car, her heart pounding, she didn't notice that she was speaking aloud. "No," she whispered, gripping the steering wheel. "Move, damn it. Move!" A large white delivery truck was backing out of a driveway, blocking Seminole completely. So Winnie swung onto Alden Lane, even though it was clearly marked NO THROUGH TRAFFIC and she knew Bella Guidry might see and recognize her car. Winnie drove fast, much faster than she was accustomed to, and let out a stifled yelp when she sideswiped a wheeled garbage can—left much too far out into the street—when she veered onto Franklin. There was a wordless panic inside her. Winnie accelerated up the short hill as she came onto her own street, and bumped hard over the curb and back down, before she could control the car.

And then she was home, though for a confused moment it didn't seem so. Something was awry. Something about the corner of Franklin and Greenham Avenue itself. Winnie pulled to a stop in her own driveway, and she had to look again to make sure where she was. It wasn't the half dozen men milling around in the front yard, or the two nondescript trucks—one parked on the street, one in the driveway—or the strange orange tractor-like machine that was lodged on the grass. She got out of the car, leaving the door open—setting off an endless digital beeping—and the keys forgotten in the ignition.

What was different was the quality of the sky, January-white and full of clouds. It loomed low over the house and the lawn, over the crumbled stone fence at the lawn's border, and the crossway of Franklin and Greenham, once secluded, now bathed in openness and light. The sky came down so far it seemed to press everything—house, lawn, street—far, far down, flat against the ground, a hopeless ridge of growth that was mocked in contrast to the pale, windy immensity of the sky.

The tree was down.

Winnie walked slowly across the trampled grass. No one had turned out for a protest. There were no hordes of tree huggers, no chanting or singing or angry shouts from strangers. The only spectators were neighbors at their windows, or in their own front yards, watching her in silence—and Winnie didn't notice them;

she didn't see Vi Greenberg there across the street, standing cold and still, hands jammed into her coat pockets. Winnie stumbled toward the center of her unfamiliar lawn, to the pile of sawed-off trunk sections, collapsed together piece upon piece, a giant-child's heap of toy blocks. The pile rose high above her like a bonfire, ready to be set ablaze. She moved close enough to put the flat of her hand against the woody inside of one piece, and found, with a heartsick *zing*, that it was still warm there. Tiny black ants streamed down in rivulets, streamed down and out, across those bright concentric rings, too many to count, across Winnie's own hand. Escaping.

A man wearing blue headphones and a helmet appeared, shouting something at her, guiding her away from the heavy pieces of tree, the unsteady pile. All sounds were drowned out by the orange machine, which whirred and crunched and splintered, spraying out a fine mist from one end. Winnie allowed herself to be led away. She averted her eyes as she passed, glimpsing a branch fed into the machine's wide opening, and the gurgling crunch of the blades, setting to work.

Back on the safe pavement of the driveway, Winnie tried, for a moment, to see where the trunk was. The remaining trunk, that is—the sheared-off piece, still rooted in the ground, where the sycamore had once stood. She stood there, bare and exposed in the newfound expanse of sky. She faced it head-on, this thing she had done—she forced herself to do that, at least. And yet, when she discovered that the cut-off trunk was temporarily hidden from view by the rising pile, by all the bags and men and the machine on the grass, by the blurring of her own eyes, she granted herself a small measure of reprieve. With no right to be, Winnie was grateful; she wasn't sure, at that moment, she could have borne it.

Seventeen
RACHEL

It was Thursday, January 5. Holiday travel and a burgeoning snow-storm along the East Coast combined to thwart all prior plans for Rachel and the girls to return home. Their flight out of Oakland was delayed almost an hour, so although the three of them ran for it, purses and backpacks bouncing, they missed their connection out of O'Hare by about twenty minutes. Nobody at the gate could redirect them, so they'd had to hike all the way out to the main terminal and stand in a United customer service overflow line to be rebooked, on a flight to Rochester that wouldn't leave for an-other six hours, at 10:30 PM. There was a slight chance of going standby on the 6:30, so they trudged back to the gate. Lila and Melissa were camped out along a row of hard-edged plastic seats, and Rachel waited in line at the Wolfgang Puck Eatery, juggling two panini sandwiches, a melon-and-grapes fruit salad, and three bottles of black-raspberry fizzy water.

Their week in San Francisco with Danny and Yi-Lun—Mat-thew had gone skiing in Utah with a friend from college—had been a great respite from everything at home. Well, at least until the night before last, Rachel thought. It had been mild enough to walk around, so they went to Pier 39 to watch all the sea lions flopping lazily around the docks, and they went to Coit Tower and partway across the Golden Gate Bridge (though that had been a little too cold); they took a day trip to Palo Alto, and they ate burritos in the Mission. Danny had been his usual energetic self, always moving on to the next thing, while Yi-Lun's somewhat spacey calm balanced him out. The two of them liked to take long bike rides together every morning, bundled up in high-tech all-weather gear. Rachel sensed Danny didn't want much more than surface answers to his quick, breezy questions about Mom and Jerry—and she hardly knew what to say, either—so, for the most part, they hardly spoke about it. About Bob, Danny had dispatched the usual questions—how's he feeling, how's the writing—and then carefully avoided any further discussion, about anything related to money, Bob's job at the firm, or the subletting of their house on Locust. Danny had paid for every meal and covered every expense of their trip, brushing off any thanks or acknowledgment, and once, late at night, studiously avoiding eye contact, her brother had offered Rachel a loan. Or rather he had started to, before jumping up to clear away some dishes and dropping the subject entirely. It was clearly awkward for him, speaking this way to his older sister, to whom he was cheerful but not close, and so Rachel—a bit startled herself—hadn't even thanked him.

In line at Wolfgang Puck's, she shifted the slippery-sided sandwich boxes, thinking that Jerry's last loan (or was it a gift?) had been over a month ago, now long gone, the last of it spent on these plane tickets. The problem was, even if Rachel wanted to take Danny up on it—and she might have to, sometime soon—the sum her brother had in mind might not at all be what she needed. And the unclear offer of an unknown amount—had he been thinking hundreds of dollars? A thousand or two, maybe?—had as its most potentially embarrassing result that moment when both of their expectations would be laid bare. It would be a delicate conversation, that time she might call Danny and say, "Remember that time you . . . ?" Would she first name a figure? Would he? Would the two be anywhere close to equivalent, and if not, how would that be managed? "Oh," she could imagine her brother saying, if she asked for more than he'd bargained on lending, that one syllable wrapped in shades of surprise, embarrassment, and recalculation.

It would have to be a nice big check, Rachel thought, craning her neck to see how many people were still ahead of her in line, to make that moment worthwhile, bearable.

And then there had been the scene with Melissa, two nights ago, which had cracked the comfort with which Rachel assumed that the girls had been mostly spared the social tensions and agonies that she herself suffered, in and out of Hartfield, over the past year. Mel hadn't come to dinner, and had locked herself into the guest bedroom she shared with Lila—Rachel could hear her sobbing but couldn't coax her out. Lila eventually told Rachel that Mel had just gotten dumped by a boy she'd had a crush on. "Just dumped how?" Rachel demanded. "He's here in San Francisco?" "He IMed her," Lila had to patiently explain—and that she blamed this on Rachel.

"You never gave me any money for the Holiday Party!" Melissa flung at Rachel, bewildered, when Rachel and Lila had eventually talked their way into the guest room and were sitting together on the bed with Mel, her face a patchy, swollen red. "It was ten dollars to get in, but you forgot to give it to me, and then when I didn't have it at the door, Ben White said he would pay for me, and then all the sodas and cookies were extra—"

"But—that's nice that he paid for you!" Rachel protested. "It means he really likes you. Doesn't it?" Both girls stared at her pityingly, so clueless about the ways of the world.

"Mom," Lila said. "Nobody does that."

"Everyone's been bugging him ever since then!" Melissa yelled. "They're all like, oh, Ben White really *likes her.* He has to pay for *everything.*" She hiccuped herself into another crying fit. "And then he—he—"

"He broke up with her," Lila said gently, to spare her sister from having to say it.

"Ten dollars!" Melissa said. "How could you let me go to the Holiday Party without it? Everyone *saw!* They felt *sorry* for me!"

"I didn't know you needed it," Rachel spluttered. "It didn't say on the sheet—"

"If we're so poor now that I can't even have ten dollars, then how come we flew all the way to San Francisco?" Melissa said. "How come—"

"Mel," Rachel said, stifling a sympathetic smile. "We're not poor! It wasn't that we didn't *have* ten dollars, it was that I didn't know you had to pay to get in. Lila didn't have to pay when it was her year, did you?" Lila shrugged—this was clearly beside the point. "I don't see why they charge, anyway," Rachel argued. "It's a school event, it should be— Anyway, we most definitely have ten dollars. Next time, I'll double-check the sheet. But the main thing is, you don't have to worry about that." Poor thing, Rachel thought. *Ten dollars.* She was glad to be able to reassure them both, truthfully, on such a small matter.

"*God,*" Melissa cried. "I'm not worried about it. It doesn't matter whether I *could* have had ten dollars to go, it was that I *didn't.* And everyone was, like, coming up to me all night and being fake nice. They were all like, It's a good thing Ben White really likes you. And they were all talking about me behind my back, saying, Well, you know she doesn't even live in her own *house.*"

Rachel was stunned.

"Fake nice," Lila had explained, agreeing. "Like how everyone was when Dad was in the hospital."

They had made it better, eventually, Rachel reminded herself. She was almost at the front of the line. Melissa's anger and tears had subsided, little by little. Rachel had stopped trying to reassure her and had just listened. And then she hugged her daughter tight and didn't try to tell her that everything was going to be fine. They had re-emerged from the guest room a tired threesome, to where Yi-Lun—who had probably overheard the whole thing, Rachel realized, but who was tactfully silent—had brownies in the oven and *The Wedding Planner* on rental from Blockbuster.

"There's a problem with your card," the skinny, Latino guy said, when she finally reached the cash register.

Rachel nearly blew a gasket. "No way," she said, suppressing a laugh. "Not with that one, there isn't." She'd given him the American Express.

He shrugged and swiped it again. "See? Card declined. You want to give me another one?"

"NO, I do not want to give you another one. And I couldn't even if I— Listen. That card is fine. It happens to be all paid up—it has to be, you can't carry over the balance—" The guy shifted his eyes to look around, as Rachel's voice grew louder. "As you may or may not know, about this particular card. Which I do. Which is why I gave it to you, instead of the other four in my wallet. Now please try it again." She stacked the paninis, in their clear plastic boxes, on the counter, and ignored the thrum of impatience behind her in the growing line.

"Lady, I tried it, all right? The machine's working fine. Can you give me another card, or cash, or what?"

Rachel's cheeks burned, but she wasn't letting anyone—including herself—off that easily. "Could I speak to the manager, please?" From behind her, an audible *oh-come-*ON*-already.*

"He's—uh—he's over there, I don't . . . Hang on." The checkout guy left his station and returned, an agonizing minute and a half later, with a harried, portly man wearing a "Service With a Smile" button. He wasn't smiling.

"Problem?"

"Yes," Rachel said hastily. "But with your machine, not my card. I know that for a fact because—"

While she was speaking, the man took the green card and ran it through. "Declined," he said, blank-faced. "You can pay cash or use another card." He tapped a sticker listing the logos of the other cards, ones Rachel *knew* would be declined. There was a negative balance in the joint account—last night, on the phone, Bob had received this news all too calmly—and they hadn't paid the others in months.

"But that can't be true," Rachel argued. "I mean, I'm not trying to bullshit you on this. I *know* about cards declined. I have been there. But this one's supposed to work. It's supposed to work!" The manager just stared at her, without an ounce of interest.

"Excuse me," the man behind her in line said, but to the manager, not Rachel. "Can I pay for—"

"Just a fucking minute!" Rachel shrieked wildly, and then tried to laugh, as if that would help. The man in line pulled back, repulsed. "Can you call American Express?" she said to the manager. "Maybe it's trouble on their end."

"Nope," he said. "Sort it out with them on your own time. Next in line!"

"No!" Rachel said. "Wait, please, just—" She had a brainstorm. "Were you going to pay with AmEx?" she demanded, of the man she'd yelled at. He ignored her. "Were you?" She pointed at the two gaping teenage boys behind him. They shook their heads no. "Was anyone planning to use an American Express card here?" Rachel asked, lifting her voice loud enough that people down the hall turned to see what was going on.

"All right," the manager said. "Move aside, or we're going to have security."

"I was," said a tall woman in a flowery dress. She had a structured haircut, a Southern accent, and a bemused smile. "I was going to use my AmEx. Why?"

Rachel seized on her friendly smile. "Could you take my place in line?" she said to the new ally. "Come on, here you go," she urged the woman, helping her up to the counter. "She can go ahead of me."

"That's not fair," the man behind her piped up.

"I'm getting out of line, all right?" Rachel growled. "Look," she said to the manager. "If hers doesn't work, then it's got to be a problem with the machine, right?"

The manager looked from Rachel to the man to the Southern lady. And something about the latter's normality convinced him, or the idea that this would be the most direct route to getting rid of Rachel, so he took the woman's Caesar salad, rang it up, and then swiped her green card. Rachel held her breath. The man squinted at the screen.

"Declined," he said finally. Rachel let out a whoop. The manager scrutinized the credit card. "Must be something wrong with this vendor."

"Oh well," the woman in the flowery dress said. "Cash it is. But do you—" She gestured at Rachel's abandoned panini boxes.

"No," Rachel said, weak with relief. "I told you," she said shakily to the manager, who regarded her blankly. "I told you it wasn't me!" She backed away from the counter, all the covert, disapproving gazes from those in line now palpable. They were veiled, silent, these strangers, but she could see what they saw: a middle-aged woman who looked, at first glance—with her jeans and T-shirt, her clogs and auburn-rinsed hair—like one of them, but who had revealed herself to be "off."

Well, so what? She thought giddily, staring them down. *Maybe I am*. Maybe she was growing into the kind of person who *didn't give a shit*. After all, none of these strangers knew where she was from; probably none of them had ever heard of Hartfield. It was a fleeting sensation, though, this taste of power, and even as she noticed it, Rachel could feel it begin to fade away.

"Thank you," she called, faintly, to the woman with the Caesar salad, who had already turned aside, preoccupied.

There was no line for the ATM it took her three trips around the rotunda to find, where Rachel withdrew twenty dollars (for a $3.75 fee) from the savings account. She quickly crumpled the unwanted receipt, which read *$80 remaining*, and stuffed it in an overflowing garbage can. A similar receipt rested on a corner of the can's sticky lid: *$7,420 remaining*. Rachel swept that in too.

At the newsstand, three bottles of water, two packs of cheese crackers, a bag of trail mix, copies of *Us Weekly* and *Glamour*, and two huge chocolate bars came to eighteen and change. She paid it, handing over the twenty-dollar bill she'd had less than a minute. It was so stupid, all of it, the magazines and the candy and the way that twenty came and went just like everything else—but it was freeing, too. There was something of a tiny, fierce victory in the exchange that came as a bonus to the plastic bag of mindless, glossy sweets she carried back to the girls. Or was that, Rachel wondered, just one way of making herself feel better? What she should have done, of course, was to pack sandwiches for them back at Danny's house.

Back at their gate, Rachel dumped the loot onto the empty seat between Melissa and Lila. Mel was plugged into her music player, curled up, shoes off and asleep.

"They call our name?" Rachel said.

"They said the flight was full, no standbys," Lila said, digging through the plastic bag. "Yick," she said at its contents. Lila hated junk food.

"Try the granola stuff," Rachel said, twisting open a water bottle. "The line at the other place was insane."

Eighteen
AVERY

It was close to midnight on Saturday, January 7; Avery was walking the ice-speckled streets of the Lower East Side, clutching
Nona tightly to his side. His ears were still ringing. *Concatena-
tion*, the program had been called; it was a memorial of sorts, for
an avant-garde composer who had recently died of AIDS. Many,
many people had performed, and after four hours of sitting in the
decrepit storefront church, Avery had had his fill of the mostly
unbeautiful discordant sound. There had been an instrumental
group who played toy whistles and PVC pipes as well as trum-
pet, trombones, and the rest. There had been a vocal group who
spoke-sang a vehement diatribe against the police (which didn't
seem to be relevant, in Avery's opinion, but whatever). And one
older man had simply stood in front of the group and cried, con-
tinuously, for many minutes. No speech, no song—just crying.
People were riveted, their eyes glued to this sad little man as if to
the most energetic of performers. At first, Avery had been moved
by the man's emotion. Then he felt creeped out by all the voyeuris-
tic pleasure going around the room; next, he felt annoyed by the

man's public display of grief. Weren't you supposed to do that on your own time? How was he crying this much, for that long—was it all an act, after all? Finally, he'd become bored. (It was jarring when people clapped heartily as the man returned to his seat.)

The highlight, of course, was Nona's singing. Avery had seen enough of this kind of thing by now—he was a bit of a fucking expert, at this point—to know how truly special, and different, her gifts were. In contrast to the more elaborate shows of the night, Nona simply stood up at the lectern and sang, a wordless aria that rose and fell with her breath, an icy clarity in her tone that caused the crowd to be still, hushed, and appreciative. Avery was bursting inside. *That's right, you fuckers!* He wanted to shout to all these weirdly dressed people, the sedate audience, when he saw them exchanging snooty glances that read, clearly, *Wow.* During the applause after she finished he had to restrain himself, mindful that this was, after all, a memorial service.

Now they skidded across Delancey, and he fumbled for the right words to tell her how incredible she had been.

"It's like there was *air* in the room again, you know?" He steered her away from some sketchy guy leaning against a crosswalk sign. "You did that thing, what's it called—when you are singing a really high note, and then you swoop down to a low note, but there's hardly any space between the two?"

Nona bent her head close to his upper arm. She didn't answer, but he could sense her smiling. "Whatever that's called," Avery said. "It's awesome. You should do that one more. And everyone around was totally hooked, you could tell. Nobody was talking at all . . . Or eating—God, that guy and the sandwich? Did you see that, earlier? Dude, don't bring your fucking Big Mac into a *performance*. Or a memorial," he added, after thinking about it.

They leaped in unison over a slushy pool gathering at the curb-side, but still Nona said nothing. Something was bothering her, or was she just quiet after her performance? She could get like that, Avery had noticed. Maybe he should just shut up already and let her be. Avery struggled with this for the few minutes they were on Orchard. It went against his nature, being comfortable with silence, and anyway he was so happy, now that she was back from Pittsburgh, now that they were through with the stupid fights and being apart. He bubbled inside and couldn't help it—he wanted to talk for hours and hours. He wanted to hear everything she had to say.

But something occurred to him, a possible reason for Nona's quiet. Avery narrowed his eyes as he remembered it. In the drafty foyer, amid the commotion after the service, Avery had held Nona's coat and waited patiently as she said good-bye to about a hundred different people. He could tell she was hurrying to get over to him, but again and again she was stopped by a well-wisher or acquaintance. At one point, getting somewhat closer, she shot Avery a mock-harassed look and mouthed, *"The fans!"*—the back of one hand pressed to her forehead. But then a tall, thick woman approached—it *was* a woman, though he'd had to do a double take to make sure—who made Nona instantly still. He had never seen Nona at all daunted, as she seemed then, while the woman, in a blond buzz cut and an Oriental-type robe, spoke a few words to her and then rapidly left.

In the cold of Orchard Street now, Avery worked out just how he was going to put the question. He was totally fine with the concept—the *theoretical* concept—that Nona had had other lovers before he met her. Avery believed this was generous of him. And he was prepared to accept the idea that some of those past lovers had maybe been women. You never knew. Plus, Nona ran with such an artsy crowd . . . Anyway. The concept, though, and confronting its possible physical reality (even, or especially, if it did come in the form of a giantess wearing a kimono) were two totally different things. And not that he was an expert in decoding the emotional language of lesbian musical ex-girlfriends or anything, but there was something about the charged moment when that short-haired woman spoke quietly to Nona—something that set off an alarm bell in Avery.

"So, um—who was that, in the lobby?" Totally casual. Just asking, no big deal. "That huge woman with the weird robe?"

"Why?" Nona asked, eyeing him from under her big fur hat, the kind with ear flaps. The fact that she said only this gave credence to Avery's fears.

He had to tread carefully here. "Was she—like—an ex?"

Nona stopped entirely in the frozen street. She studied Avery's face as if to determine that this was, in fact, what he really meant to say, that he wasn't joking. And then she pulled him along so they could keep walking.

"That was Lynda Carroll," Nona said.

"Uh-huh," Avery said. It was clear he was supposed to know who that was, but as far as he was concerned, Nona hadn't answered the question. "She's a pretty big deal, or something?"

"Yes," Nona said. "She is a pretty big deal. To me. She's . . ."

"Is she a singer? Musician?"

"She makes food," Nona said, "for your ears." Avery was silent. He could see the lit windows of Kohlmarkt up ahead. "She's very famous," Nona went on, grudgingly admitting this, as if it were beside the point. "Her work is the inspiration for almost everything I do. She did a piece in the mid-seventies called 'It Begins,' where her vocals essentially narrate a car accident without words and—"

Avery, heartened by all signs that pointed to the fact that the giantess was not, in fact, a rival, helpfully made a few screech and bang sound effects, as if to demonstrate. Nona reached up to clap a hand over his mouth. She shuddered. Avery put his tongue out to the warm leather on the palm of her glove. He was so happy he could have done a backflip.

When they got to the front of the restaurant, he said, a little absently, scanning inside for the perfect table, "So, that's excellent—that she came up to you afterward. Yeah? She was blown away, like the rest of them."

"Well, I've met her twice before," Nona said, quietly again, as if talking to herself. Avery didn't notice. "In fact, she was the one who—"

But now the owner, his friend Carl, had spotted them from the bar, and Avery ushered Nona into the warmth and noise of the restaurant's entrance. They stamped the snow off and shrugged out of coats, and his friend came over to welcome them. Avery wasn't really hungry, but Carl had insisted that Kohlmarkt was doing things that no other restaurant in the city could match, so of course they were here. And in the bustle of their arrival—the place was jammed, even this late—Avery dropped the thread of the conversation. He'd already forgotten her name, this woman from the church who had made Nona motionless and reverent.

Three series of small plates later, Avery was duly impressed. Unless this was one of those places that knocked appetizers out of the ballpark and then sent out blah main dishes—there were many such places—he was willing to grant Carl a lot of credit. They'd had toasted circles of dark bread with a piping hot Liptauer spread, an omelet served in small, quivering eggy squares, and schnitzel, of course. This first schnitzel had been the traditional breaded veal; Avery was sure there would be more schnitzel coming up, so he was pacing himself.

Nona, however, wasn't eating much at all. Nor was she wearing a bra, he could tell, a happy discovery made after she had unwrapped the top of her dress (which wound around her like a mummy's shroud, over shoulders and under arms and around her torso) in the heat off the kitchen nearby—Carl had set them up at a prime table just outside its swinging doors, a windowed corner fogged with steam—and let it hang around her in loose folds, revealing a cut-up blue undershirt, and the contours of those heavy, beautiful breasts. He wanted to reach over and hold one, just for a second, just to weigh its complete perfection, as he had so many times before. *Later*, Avery told himself, selflessly.

"When are you going out to Hartfield again?" Nona asked.

He snorted. "That would be . . . never?"

She met this with silence, so that his words hung in the air, childishly.

"I don't know," Avery said. "Why?"

"Just that it's been a while, since you've seen him."

The fact that she said *him*, not "your grandfather," not "Jerry," irritated him, as if there was some great friendship there. Well, what irritated him was knowing that he, Avery, had set up this expectation. He used to talk to Nona all the time about Grandad. He used to recount all the funny things the old man had said. Like the time Grandad went off about the idiocy of book-smart business-school types with no real-world sense. "Yeah, well, I once thought I'd go to Harvard too," he'd drawled. "Harvard didn't see it the same way." Or the time that Avery had mentioned off-hand how stumped he was when the application for the Blue Apple's liquor license had called for a copy of his "business plan." What the fuck was a business plan? A week later, a FedEx envelope from Chicago had arrived at Pita Pie just as he was starting his shift: a ten-page document, with a budget and charts and data, all putting forth the fiscal viability of Blue Apple as owned and operated by Avery Trevis. Grandad had had some office flunky back at TrevisCorp put it all together. All right, so there had been good times, sweet moments, *bonding* . . . whatever you wanted to call it. But that wasn't his real life! That wasn't this, the schnitzel and his girlfriend's breasts and how maybe he could talk Carl into teaching him how to make schnitzel and the way Nona had sung tonight and what he planned to do for her in bed later and was it even feasible to put some schnitzel on the menu at Blue Apple? This was his life. Hartfield, trekking out there all those weeks, had just been a passing kindness he did for a relative. He shouldn't have given Grandad—or Winnie—the idea that it had been anything more. Then there wouldn't have been any of that deluded stuff about the will.

"Try this," Avery said, scraping the last piece of omelet onto Nona's plate. "We gotta make room for what's coming."

"He might not ever mention it again," Nona said. "He'll know he shouldn't have told you like that, in front of everyone. He's probably sorry for how it all came out."

Avery chugged the rest of his water. The Riesling he'd ordered for Nona sat untouched in her glass, a honey yellow. "Yeah, well, he's not the only one." Then he batted away the topic like a buzzing insect at their table. "It's a big ball of crazy over there, and I'm steering clear. I should never have brought you out there, anyway."

Nona looked as if she disagreed, but instead of arguing with him, she said softly, "I have to talk to you about something." Right then, their entrées arrived. The runner put the plates down with ceremony while Carl hovered, explaining something, giving a preview, pointing out the homemade noodles . . . Avery heard none of it. His heart was fluttering—now it all made sense: her preoccupied quiet, the wine left in her glass. Nona was pregnant. He'd made her pregnant! Oh, God. A million thoughts swarmed his head. *Stay cool*, he told himself. *Don't look so excited.* She was probably scared and conflicted, not to mention feeling really pukey (*see, he was already on top of this!*)—so Avery marshaled his most concerned, supportive, *I'm-here-for-you* expression, but it was hard, since he wanted nothing more than to jump up and kiss her.

"—since Lynda's been involved with it, they usually have two composers and two vocalists, and—"

Wait. What? Was she talking about the woman at the church again?

"—no idea I was in the running, even after I applied. Workshops, some performances, but more of a lab to develop new—"

The food cooled on their plates. Avery hadn't even looked at it. A humming sense of dread was rising inside him.

"—funding for a year's fellowship. Didn't really believe it until tonight, until she said congratu—"

"What?" he cried. He'd heard her say *Italy*. Please let him have this wrong.

Nona was startled by how he'd cut her off. She looked miserable, but he caught one sharp gleam of thrill that broke through. "It's a year's grant for a residency in Rome."

They stared at each other. Avery forced himself to ask questions. "A year, like . . . the whole year? In Rome?"

She nodded.

"You have to go to Rome."

She nodded again.

"When?"

"The end of March," Nona said, and she put her hand on the table, sliding it toward him.

Avery pushed a huge piece of tafelspitz in his mouth, and then another. His stomach closed up against the gamy beef, but he crammed it in. "No shit," he said, mouth full. "That's so great. Really fantastic."

"Don't."

The potatoes were a congealed, gluey mess, but if he loaded on enough of the thick gravy, he could choke them down. "Italian guys are suckers for that extended-technique stuff you do, I hear. Seriously. They dig that electronic crap, the microtones, everything. You won't have any problems. They're going to line up to shag you." He swigged water to bury the urge to vomit, and then shoveled in a mouthful of limp, bitter greens. "Huge cocks," he said, stifling a burp. "Uncut, too. You're a lucky girl."

"It's not something I can pass up," Nona said.

"Who's asking you to!" Avery shouted. People looked over, but she didn't take her eyes off him. "Go! Go to fucking Rome. Why the fuck wouldn't you?"

"The chance to work with these people—there's this woman from Japan . . . It's a once-in-a-lifetime thing for someone who does what I do," Nona said, fast and low. "My song cycle is going to be part of a collaboration with some artists that have been touchstones to me—they are giants in the field. Really on the cutting edge of what's happening in the vocal—"

"Why for a whole year? Why Rome?"

"It's actually just outside Rome. There's this place, an artists' colony—you live in a villa with five other people, and other musicians visit—"

Avery held up his hand. "You don't need to read the brochure to me," he said. It was the harshest he had ever spoken to her, this ugly sarcasm, but there was no reason not to.

Nona took a deep breath and went on, determined. "I don't know why it's a year," she said. "It just is. That's how long the grant lasts."

"So you can be back and forth," Avery said, his fork hovering. "A month here, a month there—"

But she was shaking her head. "It doesn't work like that. There's voice class every day, and weekly—"

"Then I'll come," Avery said. He stared at the meat dripping off the tines. "I'm not kidding. I'll come too."

Nona put her head in her hands. "It's shared facilities," she said, nearly whispering. "They don't allow spouses or children to—"

"Well, I'm *not your fucking spouse*, am I?"

One thing he loved about Nona was that she never told him to keep his voice down. If anything, whenever they fought, she was just as loud in public, if not more so. They'd been glared at in restaurants all across the city, roaring at each other, cursing, slamming tabletops so hard the plates rattled. (Nona had once observed a direct relation between the cost of dinner and their likelihood of a big, ugly spat: the pricier the entrée, the louder their voices.) But for once she was quiet. She didn't warn him to calm down, but she didn't raise her voice to his level, either. And that's how Avery understood this was serious. She was really going to leave him. A blast of self-hatred nearly made him swoon. God, he could just kick his own ass, for that fantasy of a few minutes ago—paying for the abortion he couldn't argue her out of, holding her hand at the clinic, comforting her afterward.

Avery forced himself to swallow more food.

"What would you do in Rome?" Nona said gently, trying to make him see reason.

"What am I going to do here?" he said. "Without you?" That last was so hard to say out loud that Avery almost coughed up bile. Carl, headed their way with a big smile, veered sharply in another direction as soon as he caught sight of Avery's face.

"You have your family," Nona said. "Jerry needs you now. You have your friends here, you have the restaurant—"

"The *restaurant*?" Avery laughed. "Are you talking about that run-down money pit I've spent months trying to get off the ground? Yeah, that's a real winner. It's never going to happen."

"Don't say that," Nona said. "It's your work. When you find your real—"

"Do me a favor," Avery snapped. "Spare me the patronizing

bullshit, okay? 'Be a good boy, Avery, now go and cook your little dinners.' Fuck you, all right?"

"All right," Nona said. She put her napkin on the table. "I got it."

"I don't care about the restaurant," Avery said. His voice thinned out. "I could care less about the whole thing. I only started it because you—" He fought the trembling in his throat, near his eyes. "Because I wanted you to—"

Nona gathered the straps of her dress and pulled them haphazardly over her shoulders. "I'm going to the bathroom," she said. "When I get back, I'd like you to take me home." Her eyes were warm, but her voice was hollow and dried out, and when she squeezed past his chair, she didn't touch him at all.

He tossed his credit card on the table, not noticing or caring that it landed on his plate, in a puddle of gravy. When his phone buzzed, he stared at the number dumbly, not recognizing the area code and not caring. Because there was not a single other goddamn thing in the world he could think of to do, Avery answered the call.

"Yeah?"

"Avery? It's . . . I'm sorry to call so late. I thought maybe I'd get your voice mail. This is Rachel Brigham, by the way."

Avery said nothing. The name meant nothing to him. The busboy plucked his card out of the food and wiped it on an apron.

"Your grandfather's been in a car accident. Earlier tonight, with my mom. It was basically a fender bender, but he's in the hospital and I just thought . . . Can you come out? Tomorrow, on the train, I mean? I can pick you up at the station."

Avery sat still. A faint promise of nausea rumbled deep inside his intestines. "Avery?" Rachel said. "He's fine. Physically, he's fine. But there are a lot of—well. Your mom is flying out, either sometime tomorrow or Monday. And I just think it would be a good idea if you got here first. My mom and her, together—well, do you know what I mean?"

"Okay," he said, not knowing what else to do or say.

"You'll come?" There was relief in Rachel's voice. He nodded, stupidly. "Oh, thank God. That's great. Just call me anytime, when you're out of Grand Central, and let me know which train."

Avery pressed END even as she was still speaking, thanking him. He could feel Nona's approach, behind him, without looking, and now he braced himself to turn and face her.

Part III

Nineteen
WINNIE

January 8

Early morning. In the Valley Park emergency room, they were separated by a green curtain hung on metal rings. From the bed, where she was fastened to some sort of monitoring device, Winnie couldn't reach the curtain to pull it aside. She watched the number of pairs of blue-bootied feet in that next space, increasing as the hours passed, sometimes three and four at a time. Barely anyone came to Winnie, once her minor forehead laceration had been stitched. Nor could she hear Jerry, or be heard by him, in the general din. When the wheels of his bed suddenly began to roll, taking him away, she called out in fear, unable to follow. Rachel held her hand, saying, *They're just taking him for some tests. It's all right.*

Over the course of the night, their fortunes had tipped in opposite directions. In the initial hours after the impact, it was Winnie who caused the most concern. That was due to all the blood, of course, but her wound was a surface one, a half-inch gash near her left temple from the good hard smack she'd received from the window. Matty and Jerry had helped her from the car, now spun around and stopped in the middle of the intersection at Ardleigh and Meade. It wasn't until Winnie put a tentative hand up to her head, and brought it instantly down, a wet red glove, that she felt faint. And then she merely floated in and out, while Matty carried her to the grassy knoll by the side of the road, while Jerry crouched on one knee in front of her, while the EMTs—one had a Yankees symbol shaved into his hair—strapped her to a gurney and spoke loudly to her, making little jokes as they fixed her up on the short drive to Valley Park. And wasn't Jerry standing there while they stitched and bandaged her? Or perhaps that had been Matty. White-faced, sweating Matty. *Not your fault*, she tried to tell him. They had been on their way back home from cocktails at Rena Davidson's house; Winnie argued they hardly needed to call Matty for this outing, just on the other side of town, but Jerry had insisted—he never liked her to drive him, anyway. *Came out of nowhere*, Winnie struggled to say, to Matty/Jerry, *that other car*. (Later, she would learn that the other driver was a fifty-year-old woman covering her son's shift for a pizza delivery company in Mount Morris.) It flew through the light and plowed right into them. *Lucky it wasn't worse*, she told Matty—or Jerry. Or tried to; in her shock, the words she intended weren't exactly making it out as speech.

By 10 or 11 PM, though, she was clearheaded enough to be cross at Rachel, who asked only the doctors and nurses about her mother's condition.

"I'm right here," Winnie complained. "I'm not asleep."

"Go right ahead and sleep, Mom," Rachel said, missing the point entirely. "I'll be here."

From her curtained-off section right next to him, Winnie could only glimpse the flurry of activity around Jerry. Rachel was avoiding the truth, or didn't know, either, what was wrong.

At 1 AM, the resident who had been on Jerry's side of the green curtain came to her bedside. He was a kind-faced Japanese man, with bright gray streaks in his hair. "A fair amount of delayed disorientation," he said, asking for details of Jerry's medications and previous conditions.

At Winnie's halting mention of the pre-Alzheimer's tests that she had learned about that day at Ed Weller's office, Rachel snapped her head forward in surprise, and the doctor's eyes flared with new interest. He asked a few probing questions and then seemed to put the matter away.

". . . well, sometimes a typical inflammatory response to injury . . . be admitted, CT scans . . . know more in a few hours."

Winnie became soundless. She was afraid to ask any questions, in case the answers suggested that Jerry could die. And the doctor's compassionate smile as he carefully explained things to her, and to Rachel, at the foot of the bed—that meant that Jerry couldn't die. Didn't it? When a gray-haired Japanese man, with warmth in his tired eyes, delivered news in such a way, when he touched your head gently and bent to examine your stitches, pronouncing them as fine and tight as if he'd sewn them himself, didn't it mean that everything was bound to be all right?

January 10

In the hallway outside Jerry's hospital room, waiting for the doctors to emerge, Winnie recognized the LuxPool number on her phone, and pressed IGNORE for the third time since yesterday. Keeping her distance several meters away, Annette, in a navy blazer and crisp blue jeans, still somehow managed to overhear what Winnie murmured in response to Rachel's question.

"A pool?" she cried, a sharp sound of disbelief in her voice. These were the first words she had spoken to Winnie since arriving from the airport six hours earlier. "You think you're putting in a *pool*. On that property."

Winnie and Rachel just stared. Annette looked away. She dug an electronic device out of a bag and typed away with both thumbs.

A bent-over woman slowly pushed a walker past them, grinning up for approval with each step she took.

Annette let out a short laugh through her nose. "A *pool*," she said again, confiding this idiocy to the electronic device.

Dr. Lee had apparently been briefed on the Trevis family situation; when she came out of Jerry's room, she knew to address both Winnie and Annette (as it turned out, Avery didn't come out until several days later), taking turns with which piece of information she would distribute, like a mother carefully dispensing equal amounts of cookies to fractious children.

"The scans don't show any bleeding internally," she said to Winnie. "But we can't rule out swelling or brain contusion at this point." This was directed to Annette. "I'd like to hold him for observation"—back to Winnie—"but I'm also going to order some more specialized brain MRIs, because of what we know with his prior experiences with dementia"—this last to Annette, who pressed her lips together tightly.

"I have to warn you," Dr. Lee said, and this time she looked at the door to Jerry's room. "Sometimes trauma to the head, in a patient with a previous history of Alzheimer's-type difficulties, can speed up or exacerbate any existing or dormant symptoms."

"What do you mean, speed up?" Rachel asked.

"Let's just wait to see what these scans reveal," Dr. Lee said, retreating to the safety of knowledge delayed.

Both Annette and Rachel launched a volley of questions at Dr. Lee, competing to drown each other out, but Winnie said nothing. She stepped quickly into the room with Jerry, and pulled the door shut behind her. What stayed with her: how much like Jerry Annette had looked just then, jaw thrust out, arguing her case.

January 16

The gift shop in the hospital lobby hadn't gotten the newspapers yet; it was barely 8 AM. When Winnie asked the friendly Indian woman opening up what the date was, she said "Monday," but Winnie didn't press the point. Magazines, candy, coffee mugs and wineglasses etched with *Valley Park*, a chipped red canister used to inflate balloons, T-shirts of all sizes, including the snap kind for small babies, greeting cards with out-of-focus photos of lilies, their insides blank. She moved around the tiny space, picking things up and putting them down. (They were giving him a sponge bath.) Winnie carried a spiral-bound date book to the counter and paid for it. By counting off days, she found what the date was. The Indian woman lent her a pen; Winnie flipped to JAN 16 and put a checkmark there.

"Take a walk, Beth Ann," is what he'd said to her, when she asked if he wanted her to leave the room.

Beth Ann? But Winnie had said nothing.

January 30

It turned out to be a star day, so Winnie stayed home.

In the front lawn of 50 Greenham, there was now a large dirt rectangle, scraped free of grass, dusted with snow and staked on all sides by uneven slats of wood. Unable to explain why or why not, or to think everything through, Winnie had simply said yes to LuxPool.

She had been on her way to Fresh Market for milk and toilet paper, but after she saw Jerry tease the nurse when she fumbled with the buttons on his shirtsleeves, cursing them under her breath—they both liked her, the sassy one with the bleached blonde hair and a smoker's cough—she took off her coat. These hours were not to be missed. But she would have stayed home even if it had been a check day, and so far these things—flirting with the nurse, and a good hour's nap before lunch, and saying, "Ficus," just like that, out of the blue, when she had wondered aloud what was this new plant the boy from Mendell Florists had just dropped off—had proved only that, a check day. A check was not nothing, though, especially this first week back home. She knew enough not to hope for more. But she had only found out that it was a star day when his eyes lit at finding her there, tucked into a quiet corner of his bedroom, watching the ritual of his vitals check, warming to the way he smiled up at the nurse.

"Well, look at the little church mouse," Jerry had barked, delighted. "Who you hiding from, Winnie?"

There. A star day. Then she had hurried to his side when he slapped the mattress next to him.

"We don't object to an audience, do we?" he asked.

"No, sir, we sure don't," the nurse said.

So Winnie had curled there on the bed next to him, in her slacks and sweater and stocking feet. She had held as still as if it were her own temperature, blood pressure, and respiration being assessed. Only her eyes moved, sliding back and forth between the nurse's busy expression—how she muttered so, this one with the nicotine breath, but he didn't seemed to dislike or notice it—and Jerry's reaction to her swift, competent hands. When Nurse Bottle-Blonde slapped him gently on the side, saying "Let's have at your back, big guy," Jerry rolled toward Winnie—eyes snapping with mischief—and they cuddled there, faces not two inches apart, his breath warm and musty. The nurse bent lower to listen as she moved her instruments along his back, mouth working, her lipstick flaking off in frosted pink shavings. Jerry stage-whispered to Winnie, with a lascivious wink: "In my fantasies, as a younger man . . . this wasn't quite the setup." Both women laughed, told him to just hush.

A star day.

That night, Winnie firmly drew one—two intersecting lines in an X, a horizontal line, and then a vertical—next to the date, in the Sierra Club book she'd bought at the hospital, now kept bedside. With great effort, she resisted the urge to page back, past bear cubs and sunsets and snowcapped ridges, to count the number of star days—or notice their absence—since the accident. On a star day, Jerry knew who she was. He said her name. For the other kind, the bad sort—well, she either marked nothing or put down a squiggly kind of blot, the sort of thing you'd use to cross out a mistake or a wrong word.

A merely good day, on the other hand—one marked with a check—meant that there was little pain, no falling down, minor instances of confusion, and that it was likely she would be *Beth Ann*. Beth Ann, when she brought up his soup around noon, his cookies at three, or when she coaxed him out of the same undershirt he'd been wearing for days. "Beth Ann's always making me eat," he'd grouse to whatever nurse happened to be nearby. "Beth Ann says" or "Don't tell Beth Ann, but . . ." The nurses would nod or agree sympathetically; either they didn't care that he was mixing up her name with his first wife, dead now for almost twenty years, or they didn't even know Winnie's first name themselves, rotating in and out of so many different homes as the job required. Or they cared, and they knew, but what was there to do, really? That was fast becoming her own attitude. So Winnie would grit her teeth when he called her that, to others, to her own face—it was worse when he did it so lovingly—and muster strength against everything that shouted within her, *I am not your Beth Ann!*

February 9

Began as a check day, quickly downgraded.

"That boy never cleans the shitter! He oughta be canned, on the spot! That boy—" Roars coming from his room; she had been on the phone; she had thought he was napping. Flew across the room at her, naked legs covered in excrement, the stench like a slap in the face. He had gone to the bathroom in his closet. Batting away her fluttering hands, face red and violent, he smeared his filth across the blue bedspread.

"I'll whup his ass for him! Teach *him* not to do his duty!"

She ran the shower, in a panic from his bellowing. The room fogged, Jerry rushed in and out, calling for men she didn't know. His yelling was brutal and nerve shattering in that close, tiled space.

Finally he sat on the toilet, a naked, shivering bear of a man. She cleaned him with a warm washcloth, terrified he might hit her. He grumbled and spoke nonsense; Winnie agreed with everything he said.

Outside, the pool men clanged their metal on metal; they were happy, almost to lunch.

February 12

"I should bring *them* some tea," Winnie said, more to herself than to Jerry. They were sitting out in hard iron chairs on the front patio, well wrapped, holding mugs of hot tea, for a fifteen-minute fresh-air break. Jerry was watching the workers with great interest, despite the cold, following their every move. He took out a worn, folded red handkerchief and blew his nose loudly, with relish. For some reason, this cheered Winnie up.

"It's fun, isn't it? But I had no idea there would be so much to do before the actual digging."

The men walked back and forth across the bare ground, carrying tools and equipment, speaking to each other in Spanish. Jerry craned his head to get a better view.

A pine needle fell onto the surface of Winnie's tea; she picked it out. "This is still . . . all right with you, isn't it? Going through with it, building the pool? You still want to have it done, don't you?" Winnie spoke in a low voice, almost to her mug. Jerry hated to waste money; was that what she was doing? And why hadn't she really talked this through with him, before? Last year, anytime the pool had come up, all he'd ever said was, *Go ahead, Winifred, knock yourself out.* But she hadn't really taken the time to find out what he thought; she'd imagined that his reticence was about the back pain, not about any reservations he held about the expense, or the location of the pool, or the tree. She'd dismissed what Rachel had argued, that the pool would damage what the house was worth, but now Winnie wondered if this was Jerry's view. Was he able, now, to tell her what he really thought? Had he been able to, back then?

"I'd better see about this," Jerry said now, pulling the blanket off his lap. He stood to go to the men.

"They're fine," she reassured him. "They know what to do." He hesitated, looking back and forth between the men on the lawn and the woman beside him.

"Straighten things out," he said, but uncertainly.

"You have," Winnie said. "You already did. They've got their orders." This last came out of the blue, but it seemed to work. Jerry sat down again, still keeping a sharp eye on the pool men, but content to stay on the patio. It was sunny, and the hedges mostly blocked the wind's chill. The sky was a cloudless, pale blue.

"I like to watch them build it," Jerry said in a confiding tone.

"I do, too," Winnie said. After a moment, she asked—not being able to stop herself from giving the test—"Build what?"

But Jerry didn't answer; he either didn't hear her or wasn't paying attention to anything other than the busy men: doing a job, earning a wage. That, he could understand.

February 16
Check.

The backhoe heaved and halted, tearing skid marks in the lawn. Its driver made no sign of hearing what the other man was yelling from the sidelines. Avery and Winnie stood at the living-room window, a draft of cold air whispering through the lead and the glass. The arm of the yellow machine lifted and stopped, poised above the ground. Avery held up both fists, and Winnie mimicked him. She was trying to snap back into it. Why shouldn't she? They'd been home for more than two weeks. Jerry was responding well to the medicine; everyone said that. To want more than being here together again, his brain unswollen, and Annette back in Chicago (for now) seemed like pushing it. In comparison to all that good, the matter of being called by another name was a small one, even she could see. It had taken every ounce of sheer will the one time Winnie had asked one of the doctors about it, blushing furiously. "Well, yes," the woman had said, looking up briefly from his chart. "But we can't have everything." Nor could Winnie quantify, or even put into words, the things that were missing—Jerry was too tired, now, to wander the house with her after dinner, peeking in little-used rooms and telling stories about them. That night she had stood naked before him. . .

But that wasn't something that could go on a chart or be measured, could it? So she was trying, in the face of a string of check days—and worse—to be upbeat. After all, Avery was here, even if Jerry had gone down for a nap just ten minutes before he'd arrived. And it was clear that he was upset about something beyond his grandfather's illness, with that pinched *don't-ask-me* smile and wounded eyes. So if Avery was trying, couldn't she?

When the arm of the backhoe wavered and turned, she let out a disappointed sigh.

"Fake out," Avery groaned. "This guy's killing me!"

"Maybe they've never used this machine before," Winnie mused.

"Maybe they have frostbite and can't work the controls. Wait, here they go again."

This time, the arm rose and the claw reared back, ready to dig down—but once again pulled away, at the last second.

"Oh, come on," Avery protested. As if the driver could hear him. "You totally had it. That was the one, bro!"

Winnie wandered away, toward the base of the stairs. Did she hear him? In a heap on the kitchen table was a baby monitor setup that Rachel had brought over last week from Hand Me Down. Every time Jerry tottered past it, Winnie hastily covered the speakers and wires with a dish towel or newspaper, though he'd never wonder, of course, what it was for. She still hadn't gotten up the nerve to install it. Was that him? She went halfway up the stairs and held the banister, which rattled now, loose in its sockets.

Several thoughts occurred to her then, in succession, each one sliding inevitably down to another. Jerry might not be waking up now, but he would soon, and there was no telling what kind of mood he would be in—relaxed and alert, sullen and confused. There was no way to know what was coming, this day or the next. That meant either that she had done all of it, the falling in love and getting married, blind to the possibility that Jerry could disappear—even without leaving—from their home, from their life; or that she *had* known pain like this existed, somewhere, and had chosen to press on despite the terror of the uncertain. Had it been a mistake? Opening herself to this kind of grief, so late in the game? Their time together was always going to be short, Winnie knew. But now she realized she had stupidly counted on certainty; she had generously traded *more* time for a higher *quality* of time that they would share, together. Winnie squeezed her eyes shut and hung on to the banister. The sacrifice was supposed to be what they *hadn't* shared, all those years that had gone before! It wasn't supposed to be like this, with her alone again and so uncertain!

She stood waiting on the stairs, feet on different steps, hand on the wobbly railing, intent upon the possible cry of her nap-dazed husband. Avery shouted for her to hurry back, but Winnie was suspended between the changing present and the possible future, and couldn't move. In this way, she missed the claw's committing to a decision: the sudden bite into earth, the grinding gears, the beginning.

Twenty
RACHEL

They were good at this, she and her mother: nursing men. From those first few days of Jerry in the hospital, Rachel recognized the inherent rhythms of a medical crisis, and she and Winnie seemed to pick right back up how they'd been when it was Bob in the adjustable bed, pale-faced and pinned with tubes, the subject of tests, IV drips, and hushed conversations just outside the door. The same woman was working the cash register at the cafeteria, and she even recognized Rachel, gave her a measured nod. Rachel knew the shortcuts between wings, and she remembered which color scrubs designated nurse, resident, attending. She and Winnie had taken turns at Jerry's bedside, and they knew to feel no compunction about watching their own television shows while he slept or helping themselves to the leftovers from his unfinished lunch tray. They knew the west side of the building got better cell phone reception, and they never went into the depressing, shadowy central courtyard for a "breath of fresh air." Rachel filled most of her shifts at Hand Me Down and drove the girls to and from their activities. In between, she called Winnie, and their conversations were direct, full of medical shorthand, instantly meaning-ful. The world had shrunk, once again, to the boundaries of Valley Park, and any minute shift in the hour-to-hour status of Room 341 needed to be reported and thoroughly discussed. By the time Jerry was allowed to go home, Rachel had already spent hours online; she'd arranged for rotating home care from a local provider, and from various other websites she ordered a collapsible cane, seat cushions, incontinence pads, no-rinse bath products, plastic plates with dividers and suction cups, and three different CDs billed as "soothing" or "calming" for Alzheimer's patients.

Yes, she was good at this, Rachel thought, as she turned into the driveway at 50 Greenham. Winnie had a long-overdue hair appointment, and the next nurse shift wasn't until 3 PM. Jerry couldn't be left alone anymore—without saying so outright, ev-eryone agreed that he had passed that point.

And it was good that she was good at it, this nursing of men, for several reasons. Rachel cut the motor and grabbed the plastic bag on the seat next to her. The reasons, in descending order of worthiness, were: because her mother needed help, and Rachel had enough experience with this exact kind of situation to be able to help. Okay, fine. Good enough. But also—less nobly, she knew—because being thrown into the crisis together with Winnie staved off the growing divide between them. It gave them something to talk about, in the same way combing through the details of Hart-field town life—whose stepdaughter got into MIT, which storm in what year had flooded the school's basement—had always raised their spirits. And last—here was the line of thinking that Rachel, hurrying across the driveway, wanted to squelch—because she had other, less generous motives.

Well, all right, so what if she did? Did it matter what was under the surface of all the hours she spent with Winnie, coaxing Jerry back from la-la land with pills and exercises and fruitless one-sided conversation (just like with an infant, you were supposed to talk your way through every activity—"Now we'll put your other arm in, that's right, here's the sleeve")? Did it defeat the care and effort themselves, if while providing them Rachel's heart had a different goal, if the reasons she needed Jerry to come back were not the same as the ones driving Winnie's endlessly patient labors? Rachel wanted his wise counsel again, and his friendship; she also wanted him to offer another loan, without her having to ask. Honesty about such things was overrated, Rachel told herself. Plenty of good could come from her bedside ministrations, even if their hoped-for outcome was—well, let's admit it—not exactly some pure, altruistic ideal.

Her mother's front yard was a wreck. There was that god-awful hole sunk deep in the ground, and filled with all sorts of crazy boards and what looked like chicken wire. And the piles of dirt everywhere! The flattened bushes—that blue Porta-John sitting right there, out by Franklin, for anyone driving by to see! The two workers glanced up at Rachel as she strode past, staring as one foot skidded out and she wobbled sharply—undignified—but she did her best to ignore them, as she continued to ignore the entire pool project with Winnie. Why should she bring it up, when her mother must already feel ridiculous about it, must be regretting every dollar she had thrown away on this folly? And anyway, they had other things to discuss.

"They didn't have jelly," Rachel called, kicking off her boots in the back hall. "I got raspberry jam, though—think he'll mind?"

"You didn't try the Associated?" Winnie said too loudly, her faux-fur earmuffs already on. "Those seeds get between his teeth and I can't for the life of me get them out."

"I didn't have time." It was as drafty as ever in the small sitting room off the kitchen. Rachel zipped up her fleece sweater. Probably no one had caulked the windows in years.

"He's watching the Bears game," Winnie said, keys already in hand, hurrying to the door. "The Namenda will wear off in another hour, so make sure he takes it in the applesauce—you'll see the tray in the fridge, it's all set up." Rachel pulled her mother in for a quick hug. "There was something else, what was it?"

"I'm sure you wrote it down," Rachel said under her breath. Her mother's endless, detailed notes were legendary. They now covered this place—Jerry's food preferences, his medicines, his need for certain orders and routines with everything from newspaper sections to when the doorbell rang to going to the bathroom.

"Oh well, I'm sure I wrote it down," Winnie said, reassuring herself. She hadn't heard Rachel. "I have my cell phone, of course—call at the first sign."

"I will," Rachel said. The first sign of what? She ushered her mother out and shut the door on the blast of cold wind—and the sight of the pool men, and that hole in the yard. On her way upstairs to Jerry, she stopped in the kitchen. Already the house was taking on characteristics of sheltering someone who was sick. Little signs pointed to the fact that, essentially, only one person was living in these rooms—her mother's things were scattered across the den and kitchen table, sweaters, books and eyeglasses set down on surfaces with no thought toward anyone else using them or needing space. The kitchen counters looked just as they had when

Winnie lived alone, in her apartment, messy and cluttered: there was her unrinsed mug of tea, there a notebook, a package of those scented tissues she used to have everywhere, before they must have seemed too feminine, for Jerry's sake. Even the smell here was of Winnie, a touch of her perfume, which lingered on her sweaters, and the cinnamon breath drops she favored. A damp heap of news-papers was on a chair, each still rolled in its blue plastic bag. No sign of Jerry anywhere.

Rachel privately looked forward to these babysitting sessions, a mini-vacation from her own noisy, crowded home, a chance to luxuriate in the big, old grandeur of 50 Greenham. But now she had to avoid the sadness this all presented, the sense of her aging mother struggling to keep up with everything in this huge, empty house. She finished loading the dishwasher and wiped down the sticky table and counters. She took a soda from the fridge and a container of yogurt, and found a spoon. She did not forget to bring her purse upstairs with her, and what it held inside.

"So, any chance we're going to win this game?" she said, knock-ing on the wood of his open doorway.

"Win the game," Jerry agreed, from his bed. He was sitting up, in a blue cotton robe, unshaven and slack-faced. He raised an arm to point at the small television across the room, one finger brush-ing back and forth in midair, as if he wanted to say something else. But he said nothing else, only stared at Rachel. She pulled his bedside chair closer to the bed, talking emphatically about the Bears' chances for the season (about which she knew nothing), and peeled off the top of her yogurt container. There was a TV tray set up next to him, overflowing with empty glasses, celebrity gossip magazines (for the nurses, Rachel assumed), orange pill bottles, and a couple of deadly looking books from the library—immense histories or biographies—untouched.

He tended to go through cycles—she'd read about this on an Alzheimer's website—and she hoped that something she said could trigger a chatty, clear-minded one.

"You feeling okay? How've you been, since Monday?" But this brought nothing. Jerry's eyes were on a commercial for cat food. She took the remote from his lap—he didn't protest—and turned the blaring volume down.

"How can you stand that racket?" She gestured at the window behind him, and the faint voices of the pool men, calling to each other. With the sycamore tree gone—she and Winnie had said nothing to each other about its absence—it was possible to see clear across Greenham and down the hill to the south part of town, where Hartfield shaded into Mount Morris. Rachel shook her head again at how brazen her mother had been in the face of so much disapproval.

"She really did go out on a limb for you. So to speak. Ha." But using the past tense about Winnie and Jerry—she'd spoken it inadvertently, but still—frightened her a little, as did the betrayal she had planned. There was no other word for it, and as stupid and crazy an idea as she knew it must be, Rachel told herself she had no other choice. And no one would know.

She reached into her purse and felt for the tape recorder. The same one Melissa used to interview Winnie for social studies.

"Jerry?" she said, ignoring the high, nervous tone of her own voice. Maybe that could be edited or cut entirely. "What do you want to happen, with this house? Can you tell me about it?"

Two nights ago, she'd attended a cocktail party in her own

house. In Vikram's part of the house, that is. The invitation had come through their mail slot unstamped, with a handwritten note appended: *Please try to come! Sorry in advance for any noise.*

"He's being neighborly," Bob said, chewing his toast. It was morning, Rachel had been on her way to work, and Bob looked exhausted. He had already been up for hours, writing. "He doesn't mean for us to come. It's just good form—you know that."

"Good form is warning us about the noise. An invitation is something else." Rachel slid it under a fridge magnet that said, PIZZA THE WAY ITALIANS DO IT! 555-4200. "I'm going to go."

Bob turned a page of the newspaper. "Suit yourself."

The night of the party, she had to change outfits three times— black silk skirt, too dressy. Jeans, too casual. Finally, she'd settled on wide, swishy gray pants and a short-sleeve green top. As Rachel brushed her hair, she listened to her daughters in their room. They were trying to whisper.

"*You* go with her. I would hate it. I'd stand by myself and look like a freak."

"Why do I have to go? There won't be anyone our age."

"You know why. She shouldn't go by herself. She'll get all . . ."

"I don't want to be over there. With that Indian guy, like, hanging out in my room? No, thanks." Rachel could hear the clicking away of the computer's keyboard.

"He won't be in your *room*. Duh. Parties are, like, in the living room and stuff."

"You go then, if it's so important. And if you want to see what *your* room looks like now."

There was silence.

"See? I didn't think so."

With this exchange stinging in her heart, Rachel walked coat-less into the wet night, around the side of her house, and to its front door. Vikram pulled it open at once, like he'd been waiting for her. He greeted her warmly, politely ignored her edgy bab-ble—*I don't even know why I'm here, I didn't plan on it or anything, but I just thought*—and introduced her to a few people standing just inside the living room (the *dining* room, Rachel said to herself). The next hour was a blur—Vikram's friends and colleagues were friendly and voluble. Rachel drank two glasses of merlot, fast, and ate a handful of pecans even though she detested nuts. She smiled so much her face ached, she made a joke about already knowing where the bathroom was, ha ha, and she milled and laughed and admired the art until her eyes and cheeks were burning.

But it didn't really hurt until she overheard a couple talking about real estate in Hartfield. They rattled off sale prices higher than anything Rachel had heard and were unfazed by them. "Vik's on to something," the woman said, eyeing the bookcases Bob had built into the breakfast nook. She had high black boots on, and long, buttery hair. "I've been giving him shit for moving, but who knows, if I actually get pregnant this year . . ." "God," her husband said, in his rectangle glasses and Pac-Man T-shirt. "You did *not* just talk about moving to the suburbs." "But it doesn't feel like the suburbs," the woman insisted, as they moved past Rachel. "That's the genius of this place! It's like this little town, tucked away—you know?"

Rachel knew. She downed the rest of her wine and set the glass down hard on her kitchen counter. *Look at me*, she thought, wan-dering around, secretly appraising the airy kitchen, just like any other guest with a real-estate gleam in her eye. But Rachel understood the basic difference, though she wasn't sure it made things any better: she wasn't scoping out a good deal or some picture-perfect place worthy of a shelter magazine. What she longed for was her own home.

And since when did rich couples move here from the city, bringing their "green" SUVs and eight-hundred-dollar strollers and high black boots? That hadn't been Hartfield's way, not ever. This wasn't Scarsdale, or Bronxville, or any of those status suburbs closer to the city. For the first time, it hit her—the bitter irony of her own grandfather's role in connecting this small town to Metro-North, and thus to Manhattan. Without that, Hartfield might have remained isolated, obscure, borderline upstate. Is that what she wanted? It used to be that the only people who wanted to settle here were people who grew up here, like herself.

But now she saw that things were changing. Or maybe they had already changed, the terrain irreversibly shifted. That had been herself once, and Bob, on the threshold together and about to begin everything.

In the foyer, Vikram leaned close, closer than he needed to, to say his good-byes. Rachel thought she could taste his breath in her own mouth. It wasn't unpleasant. His hair was rumpled in a way she hadn't seen before.

"I've been thinking about what you said, with your mother?" He had to yell, almost, above the sound level. "The house on Greenham? Has that been settled yet?"

"No," Rachel admitted. She started to say something else, but Vikram cut her off.

"It's too bad her husband didn't make his wishes more clear, for the record—oh, hey!" He turned and swept a younger woman into a one-armed hug, almost lifting her off the ground. Rachel slipped out the door. His words rang in her ears. Had he said *for the record*? Or *on the record*. Or something about recording . . .

An idea took hold, there in what was once her front walkway, a desperate and silly idea, built on merlot and a misheard phrase. But still—and maybe . . .

"Do you want to say anything about . . . anything? Winnie's not here, Jerry—you won't upset her, you can speak freely." Last night, Rachel had scanned dozens of websites, with names like elderlaw.com, or respectmywishes.alz.net. She had quickly realized how in over her head she was, how little she knew—did anyone know?—about Jerry's plans or intentions, before that slight car accident sent him spiraling down. Did he have a durable power of attorney? Was that now Avery? What about a living will? Was that related to a regular will? It was a huge mess. Of course the person Rachel knew she could ask, whom she should ask, but whom she couldn't ask—obviously—was Bob. Well, someone had to find this stuff out—for Jerry's sake, Rachel told herself. And the one thing she had gleaned from the websites was the importance of an "advance directive," when it came to what they unflinchingly called *approaching dementia*. Rachel couldn't find many details, but she gathered this was some kind of document (maybe it could be a tape recording?) that set out a person's wishes about their future care—and possibly the future ownership of their legally contested, family-disputed, five-bedroom beautiful wreck of a house, which came with a half-installed pool right smack in its front yard.

Rachel cleared her throat and tried again. "We can be straight with each other, Jerry. Right? You've been a real friend to me, this year. I'm not just talking about the loans, either, which really—" Her throat caught, and she had to stop. His eyes were pinned to the television, where men in white helmets scattered and regrouped against a green background. "I didn't know how much I needed that, someone who could just . . . say what needed to be said, who could cut through all the bullshit. You know? I can't do that, or when I want to, something stops me." Rachel took a deep breath. "But I want to return the favor, all right? I hope you don't take offense. I don't know what the doctors are telling you, or how much you realize what's going on. But here's the deal: I think this might be toward the end for you—not your *life*, I mean—but of really knowing what's going on around you, being able to say what you mean. If you don't come back from this, I want you to have had the chance to tell us what you want. We'll go by whatever you say, all of us, I mean, Annette and my mom and Avery—about your wishes—about the house."

Nothing; no response.

"You can be frank now, Jerry."

At this, his eyes slid over to hers. "Frank?" he said, his voice thin and flat.

"Yes?" Rachel moved closer. "Do you want to talk? Do you have anything to say?"

Jerry's mouth worked for a while, his jaw pumping up and down, before the words came out. "Likes a good joke," he said finally. "He here? Where is he? Frank. Tell him I'm onto him."

Rachel felt something curdle and die inside her. She gathered her hair and let it drop; she touched a pen on the table next to her, the spoon, lining them up. He was gone. And so was this temporary alliance, the thing that had kept her going. Still, that was nothing compared to what her mother had lost, would lose, and the pure ache of the thought washed over Rachel, renewing her, rinsing her clean.

Does she know? Will I have to tell her? That he's gone.

Jerry was still rambling on about his brother, Frank, over the noise of the television. When he stopped to look at her, for confirmation, Rachel blew her nose, wiped at unshed tears and said, "Definitely; you said it. So, what else? What else about Frank?"

He talked and talked, a sudden fount of energy. Rachel put her hand into her purse to shut off the tape recorder, and then, on second thought, left it on. She wandered away to get his medicine and applesauce; when she came back, he was still telling the same story about Frank—or was it now another one? The football game was forgotten; she switched channels and put her feet up on the bed. He took the pills she handed him; she ate the applesauce. Frank hid the hubcaps from someone's car—he pretended to be Chinese—he was a whiz with numbers. Frank sounded like kind of a pain, Rachel thought, but Jerry didn't agree. He told story after story, mixing up the past and the present, as if Frank was just in the next room and would walk in any minute. After a while, he dozed off.

"Hey," a voice said from the doorway.

Rachel froze, her feet suspended in midair. Her first thought: *Pool guy? In here?* But it was Bob, half smiling, a little out of breath.

"Fuck," she said. "Why do you always—"

"I don't mean to. He's sleeping?" Rachel looked over at Jerry, tucked peacefully on his side, mouth open. She clicked off the TV and went into the hall, tugging Bob with her.

"Very weird," she said. "That was the most I've heard him talk in—"

"I sold the first chapter," Bob said. Facing her directly with a strange, sheepish smile. "To *The Atlantic*. It's a magazine. They're going to run the first chapter of my book in the magazine."

Rachel just looked at him, the mottled red and white of the skin on his head, that yellow and black rugby shirt he'd been wearing for twenty years, and the way he seemed to be nodding slightly. At her. He was waiting for her to say something.

"Is that—how did you—when?"

"I just got an e-mail. Jesus, I almost deleted it! I saw the address and thought it was some subscription deal. God, can you imagine? I was sitting there, reading this from the editor, him saying how much he loves the piece and they want to put it as the first person feature, not the next issue but the one after that."

"You know him? The editor, I mean? How did you—"

"My writing teacher has a friend! At the magazine!" Bob seized both her upper arms; his eyes were wide and sparkling behind smudged glasses. "She mentioned once a while ago that she was going to pass it on to this guy, but I totally forgot! Okay, I didn't really *forget*, but I just assumed nothing would come of it!"

Her mind spun. Was this for real? How could it be, when the writing he was doing was just . . . therapy?

"—and Nona might even be able to meet me there, if she's not already in Italy—"

"Wait. Did you say . . . Nona? That girlfriend of Avery's?"

"Yeah," Bob said, enjoying her confusion. "We've been e-mailing, and she knows this open-mic reading series I may go to. I thought it might be fun to bring the girls."

Rachel didn't know what to say. Nona? And Bob? E-mailing? She couldn't keep up; everything about this news was topsy-turvy. Something occurred to her.

"Where are the girls?"

"Lila's at practice, of course, and Melissa's over at Terry's. Why?"

"Did you need the car, or something? I mean—you walked here?"

"I walked here," Bob said slowly, as if she were dense. "To tell you. In person."

His voice rose, as it always did, but before Rachel could shush him, Bob pulled her down the hallway even farther from Jerry's room. He was talking the whole time, about print runs and proof deadlines and how this would seal the deal for a book contract—he was sure of it. Rachel could hardly get in a word, although it didn't seem expected of her anyway. Bob was busy tugging open door after door in the hallway, still talking.

"What are you doing?" she asked.

"Here," he said, thrusting her ahead of him into one of the rooms—dark, musty, closed-up. She turned back to him—what is this?—and suddenly, his mouth was on hers, muffling her surprised squawk. They grappled together there in the half-lit doorway, Rachel stumbling backward and Bob trying to kiss them both farther into the room. She clutched at him to avoid falling backward over some boxes, and he slid a hand up her shirt.

"Are you"—the shock of his fingers on her skin made her cough—"kidding?"

"I can't believe this is happening," he murmured, elbowing the door shut. "All those years I wasted in the firm, when I should have been *writing*."

Rachel didn't want to hear about that, so she kissed him deeper, more thoroughly. Thoughts collided in her head—*sold the chapter? Had she showered this morning? Was* The Atlantic *the one with the cartoons, or was that*—as she helped Bob pull her sweater over her head. They shuffled in the dark over to a bed, no, not a bed, a bare mattress that sent up a *whoof* of dust when they tumbled down onto it.

"This is amazing," Bob said, his breath hot in her ear. "I never thought I'd be here, like this."

"I know." *Were they talking about his book? Or the sex?* Maybe it didn't matter. She wrapped her leg around his back, amazed at the way it still fit there. This was crazy, she thought, their having sex in this house. Their having sex *period*. She couldn't remember a time they had fucked—yes, that's what this was—in any place other than 144 Locust, and God knows she couldn't remember the last time they had done it there in any case; but this was good, it broke through something inside Rachel—the sudden weight of her husband's body, this strange, musty room—it was like being someone else, or maybe it was like being herself again, which she hadn't been for some time. It was a surprise, to know you could still be surprised like this, in your own marriage.

"It's been so long since—"

"Yes."

"I can't believe it. I'm—you're—"

"I know."

Then there were no words at all, nothing else in Rachel's head, only the scratching, rhythmic heave of the mattress against the wood floor, moving *across* the wood floor, bit by bit, sure and steady on its inevitable way—no other sounds until the footsteps on the stairs and a voice out in the hall—*Miz T? Anybody up here?*—as Jerry's nurse made her way up to his room. But even that was quite a while after the mattress had stopped moving, and Rachel and Bob—asleep for how long?—woke naked together with pounding hearts, and told each other to shut up, not to laugh so loud, lest someone find them like this.

Twenty-one
AVERY

"Okay, I get it," Avery said, as the cab turned south off Court Street onto yet another quiet, picturesque street lined with old trees. "Poncy Brooklyn. A little tour of poncy Brooklyn, to get you primed for *la dolce vita*." Jokes helped. Sometimes.

Nona said nothing, just directed the driver along Henry Street to the corner, and then told him to stop. It was almost 10 PM, but there were still plenty of couples strolling the wide, evenly paved sidewalks or sitting on their brownstone steps waving to passersby. Everyone was so *white* out here, Avery thought with disgust, glaring at anyone who dared glance at him unfolding himself out of the cab. Look at all these happy, clueless, white losers. Even this dumb neighborhood name—Cobble Hill—made him want to vomit. Then again, it could just be his mood. Everything that he cared about would be gone in less than three days, and it turned out that was sort of affecting his perspective.

"Well?" Nona posed herself against the chipped green pole of the street sign. Even though the night was springtime warm, she wore a long, raggedy sweater and black tights, and a pair of high-top basketball sneakers.

"Strong Place," Avery read, above her. "Yeah, so?"

She dropped her arms. "Forget it."

"What? It's a cute name? Is that it?"

"Yeah, that's it. I wanted you to appreciate the cuteness." She linked her arm in his, all too easily. Most of his stupid sarcasm these past few days failed to anger her the way it would have before.

"Just one block long," she said, pointing.

"The whole street?" Avery snorted. "Should've been called *Short* Place."

Nona was checking an address she'd inked on the palm of one hand. "That one," she said.

The crumbling stairs they were climbing led to the same kind of reddish brownstone building as all the rest. Nothing different about this one—Number 42—that he could see. No restaurant sign. But Nona had dragged him to so many venues by this point that Avery figured this was just another off-the-beaten-track spot, somewhere only those in the know could find. Or that's what he *would* have assumed, except this block out here in yuppie Brooklyn was eons away from the places they usually went to, in DUMBO or other parts of Williamsburg, or even the Blue Apple's deserted stretch in north Fort Greene. Nona had insisted, though—she was going to take *him* out to eat, for once, and so tonight was her pick, her treat. Avery had tried to seem psyched about the sweetness of this plan, the way he knew she wanted him to, but it was hard. He wasn't even hungry.

It took several buzzers, but finally Nona pressed the right one.

A young guy came to the glass-fronted door, wiping his hands on a towel. He let them in and kissed Nona on the cheek, put a hand on Avery's shoulder and ushered them into the first-floor apartment, pointing out the two kids' bikes in the hall that they should avoid tripping over. Inside, there were two high-ceilinged rooms separated by painted-over pocket doors, and four tiny tables spread out as far as possible across the uneven wood floors—someone's apartment minus the bed and couches. Couples were at the tables, two younger and one older. *Huh*, Avery thought. So it was a dinner party, of sorts. He was bummed; small talk with strangers was not high on his list at the moment.

The guy—the host?—led them to the empty table, and apologized for the paperback book that was propping up its one wobbly leg. They sat, he left, and Avery braced himself for weirdness; soon there would be performance art, some kind of yelling and/ or nudity, he was sure of it. There was a coffee can full of pencils on the tablecloth and a stack of papers underneath it: proof. Of something.

"What's this music playing?" Avery asked, suspicious.

Nona listened for a moment. "Schubert," she said. "Second piano trio. Um . . . third movement."

"Are you going to sing?"

"You never know."

The guy came back to the table—Wendell, his name was—and engaged Nona in a long discussion about a mutual friend. Avery dismissed him as boring (blue button-down, hair parted on the side, big doofy smile) and gazed instead at the older couple at the table next to them. They were forties, or fifty maybe. All dressed up, both kind of fat, and not talking much. Avery wondered why they were already eating. Were he and Nona late to the party? There was a meaty sauce clinging nicely to the man's pappardelle noodles. Avery felt a flicker of interest in sorting out its components—*not beef, maybe veal?*—which then died out.

"Just water," Nona said, flicking her eyes to Avery, when Wendell was going on about Bordeaux and merlot.

After he left, Avery said, "You never finished *Choke*, did you?" It came out more accusatory than he'd planned, but then again, so what?

"I'm not done," Nona said. "I don't read as fast as you do."

"You hated the other Palahniuk novel too."

Nona took a pencil from the coffee cup and started to write, fast, on one of the slips of paper. He tried to read upside down, but she covered it with her hand, like he was cheating on an exam.

"Take a look, why don't you," Wendell said. "But you're the last seating, so no rush." He dropped the edge of a chalkboard onto their tabletop and held it so they could see. Avery stared at it blankly: *Fiddlehead and goat cheese salad, $9. Pappardelle with veal ragout, $17. Grilled grain-fed spring lamb*, MP.

"MP?" Nona asked.

"Market price," Wendell said. "Let me see what we have left, and I'll let you know." He stood the chalkboard against the wall and hurried away.

Okay, so now Avery got it. A pretend restaurant. A performed "dinner party" as "restaurant" as critique of foodie capitalism . . . something along those lines. He'd done this type of thing before with Nona. Audience-participation art. (One had involved a playground at midnight, with adults dressed in overalls and Underoos, swinging and sliding, digging in sand, dead serious. The animal crackers and juice, though, had been a nice touch.) Well, he would play along, if that's what she wanted.

"What are you going to order?" Avery said, leaning back in his chair, grinning.

Nona was studying the menu. "This place is kind of pricier than I thought. Maybe the pasta?"

"Right. *Pricier.*" He snorted. "Did you bring your Monopoly money?"

She ignored this, though, digging around in her shapeless purse.

Wendell came back. "Sorry. No more lamb. But I can seriously recommend the pappardelle. And we've got just enough for two. Nobody has a veal problem, do they?"

"No veal problem here," Nona said, smiling up at him. "That sounds perfect."

Avery shrugged—why not? "And a goat cheese salad, to start? We'll share it." Wendell nodded, obviously pleased. Why wasn't he writing this all down on a fake order pad, though? And he shouldn't be wearing that excited, nervous smile. People doing these pieces were usually real serious, so you got that it was *art.*

"Did you read this much as a boy?" Nona was looking straight at him, without guile or agenda. She wasn't trying to change the subject. She wanted to *know* him. But what did it matter, now? "I always pictured you as a hell-raiser, not some studious little bookworm."

"You can't be both?"

"Can you? Were you?"

Avery toyed with his fork and knife (mismatched silver patterns). He pictured that scared, angry boy he'd been, with messy blond hair and chewed, bloody cuticles, trapped in his room, listening to his mother shout at someone on the phone down the hall. That boy could flip his desk over, again. Or he could get lost in Middle-earth, somewhere between Rivendell and Gondor. What'll it be?

"The first two days I was in rehab," he said, picking his way through the phrasing. How hateful to have to say it out loud, how dull and meaningless. "On the third floor, where you go when you're coming off the shit, when they still think you might go mental on an aide. They take away all your stuff, and you have to wear these matching pajamas—they look like doctors' scrubs."

The salad arrived, already divided on two plates by Wendell, who put them down gently and then departed.

Nona didn't touch hers. "Go on."

"Well, long story short, it's basically lockdown. The guards call it that, to each other. They're not supposed to say it to you, though. But it doesn't take a genius."

"I would have been terrified. Anyone would."

"I couldn't tell if it was the junk, leaking out of my system, after fucking it up for so long. Or the idea of it, that I couldn't leave. That all the furniture was bolted down, the windows . . . yeah. I was so scared. I was scared of being that scared—I had to fight my panic all the time, count squares on the floor, that kind of thing." He let out a deep breath. This wasn't what he'd meant to talk about—he wanted to answer her, about reading. "You going to try that?"

"Finish telling me first."

Avery took a bite of greens—peppery, warm, expertly dressed. Huh. Not bad, for pretend salad.

"The TV room was too depressing, they had it on all the time, the plastic couches, the volume up full bore. So I found where they had some paperbacks on a shelf. Six or seven, all crap. Except there was this copy of *Rebecca*, you know that novel? Kind of a romance-thriller thing. I think they made a movie—"

"You have that novel! I've seen it on your shelf. So that's where you got it, rehab?"

"Oh," Avery said, rattled, deeply embarrassed. "No, I bought that copy. Later." He had to have one around, all the time, since then.

But even as Nona waited, an expectant smile on her face, he lost the thread. Energy rushed out of him, and with it any urge to tell this story. The silence grew; Avery dropped his eyes to his unfinished plate, which was soon replaced with a dish of pasta.

Why? Why should he tell this to her, when she was as good as gone, when all of it was over? His few attempts at protesting—they could make it work, long-distance, and he would visit—had been met with such hesitancy that Avery had instantly backed off, his pride hurt. Look, if he was going to spill his soul and guts and then she would leave anyway and nothing would be different, wasn't it better to just shut the hell up? They would "keep in touch," she might have e-mail (she might not), and there was a chance she could come back once over the summer—fine, but he wasn't dumb enough to think that meant anything. The time for telling each other heartwarming stories about each other's pasts was over. What good could it do now?

On the third floor that day, standing next to him at the pathetic bookshelf, there had been a woman named Gris. Fellow inmate, total stranger, a heavy Mexican woman who argued and pleaded for him to give her *Rebecca*, said she was sick to death of her romance magazines and needed to put her eyes on something other than those godforsaken soap operas. Or herself, in the bathroom mirror. Who should get it first, this stupid paperback? Should they tear it in half? Let the guards mediate? (*Hell no*, both agreed). So they had ended up together, he and sweaty Gris, for several hours, pressed side to side and leg to leg in their matching scrubs, the book held between them; he was faster, so he read ahead, on the right side—she slowly turned pages on the left, sucking her teeth with interest and occasionally interrupting Avery with a question about the plot or a word's definition. Both of them had to hold their heads tilted uncomfortably to one side; both had to endure snickers from the aides and catcalls from the other junkies. Didn't matter. Avery couldn't speak for Gris, but he found there—in stupid, doomed Manderley, in the effort of turning one page at a time, in Gris's solid flesh—the first glimmerings of calm, an easing of his panic, since they had stuck him in that place twenty hours before. He had been using fast and ugly for weeks by then; it had been a long time since he'd read anything.

He shook his head at Nona's gesture—*and then?*

He could smell Gris right now. She had been unwashed; she reeked of exhaustion and body odor and the metallic tinge of meth. Strangely, that hadn't bothered him—the opposite, actually; her physical presence had grounded him. But he wasn't going to tell Nona about that, not now, not ever. Or that he'd never seen Gris after that, after he'd finished *Rebecca* and ceded the book to her. She had taken it into both hands without even looking at him—she wasn't yet at the halfway mark—and then early the next day they moved him down to the second floor. He had improved.

"Don't put cheese on that," he instructed Nona, aiming in his tone for good humor, for *it doesn't matter*. "Not every pasta sauce needs Parmesan, but everyone always dumps it on it, anyway. And keep that in mind in Italy. Seriously. They'd laugh at the way Americans put cheese on everything."

"You don't have to do this. Make jokes about it, be cheerful."

"No, I'm just saying." Avery took another bite of pappardelle; somewhere along the line, he had joined in the pretense, or he had forgotten the need to—this dinner was *good*, fake restaurant or not. And he was feeling better, from withholding that story. Not because it was a *fuck-you* gesture (although, tell the truth, it sort of was), but because a tiny spark had kindled in him: he would need to build up his reserves, to survive Nona's leaving. He would keep things to himself again. He always had, before her, and now he saw why.

"Another thing," he said, mouth full, back in the comfort of lecturing her about food. "It's not going to be like this—" He gestured with his fork at their big plates. "They do pasta as a first course, not the main. Definitely order it, but you have to save room. The meat course comes next. Are you listening? This is important!"

Nona was watching him carefully. "Meat course," she said.

"I will not be held responsible if you go to live in food heaven and miss out on the whole experience. All right? Don't say I didn't tell you."

"I won't." She was eating now too, very slowly. After a while, at Wendell's suggestion, they shared a mocha pot de crème.

The couple at the table next to them, the older one, had finished their meal some time ago. Avery tuned out while Nona talked to them.

"He has one, I'm sure. Hello?" Nona tapped his wrist with her spoon. The apartment was quieter now, without Wendell rushing from table to table—Avery heard the rustle and clank of dishes in running water, coming from the back.

"Has what?"

The woman at the table was staring at him expectantly. "Train schedule?" she said. "The New Haven line? He thinks we'll make it, but I don't know." Her husband appeared, coats slung over an arm.

Avery thumbed through his wallet and handed her a creased and crumpled paper, with its times printed in blurry red ink. Frankly, he was a little annoyed that he even had this thing. He was riding the train so often these days, to and from Hartfield, that he might as well start buying one of the monthly commuter fares. (A whisper of reality: *if Grandad even had another month.*) The guy at the ticket window was starting to say hi and automatically ring him up. It especially bugged him when Winnie took him to the station right at the reverse rush hour, 5 or 6 PM. He hated to see all those suits disembarking from the trains, with the same briefcases and the same tired smiles for whoever was dutifully waiting in the crowded parking lot. All of it made Avery want to shout, *Wake up, people!* There was so much more than this shuttling back and forth: job/home, job/home. There had to be.

But he couldn't deny the pleasures of regular action, he who could clean and chop vegetables for hours in a haze of physical contentment. And though he tried not to, Avery couldn't help warming to that first sight of Winnie when the train pulled into Hartfield's dinky little station. He liked when her eyes found him, the way it felt to be expected.

The couple at the next table pored over the train schedule, laughing. *Big night for the suburban folks, out for a bit of lame performance art in poncy Brooklyn.* Avery lost interest and turned back to his dessert. Wendell came by with a brown plastic folder, with their bill. Their "bill." Nona, who had cash ready, handed it to Wendell, who smoothly tucked it away without counting. Avery silently took back his schedule from the couple, who thanked him and hurried out to find a cab. Nona and Wendell began to make complicated plans to get together for coffee before she left, and Avery looked down. In his hands, a miniature map, where different-colored train lines snaked up and away from Grand Central, pinned down at intervals by dozens of black dots and town names. If he searched closely, Avery knew, he could find Hartfield among them.

Grandad wasn't speaking anymore. Winnie was pretending that she didn't remember how long it had been since he said something—"he'll be so excited!" she said, snatching the photographs out of Avery's hands, those few he had found of himself and his grandfather, scouring the only boxes of junk he had from home. Winnie lingered for one extra moment, on the one that had his mom (in wool hat and sunglasses) standing next to Grandad, one of her hands gripping the collar of a scowling, snow-covered Avery. But she said nothing, only handed the small stack back to him. "He'll be so excited," she repeated.

But Grandad wasn't awake—he wasn't asleep, either, just somewhere in between. Somewhere out of Avery's reach. He tried for a while, like he figured he should, holding up a photo and talking brightly about whatever Christmas it had been, or trip to the dunes, his own disastrous bowl-shaped haircuts (bad, bad, very bad). But Grandad's eyes were unfocused, and his mouth gapped open wetly, which Avery hated and tried not to look at. He focused instead on the prickly white hairs of his grandfather's whiskers, almost curling now, longer than the brush-cut on his head. Avery tossed the photographs aside. Screw old pictures—this man needed a shave.

So, without asking Winnie—without thinking to—he found a razor in the bathroom (electric, thank God) and went to work. This involved bracing himself, one knee up on the bed next to Grandad, and a hand on the side of his cool, dry face. The cheeks were no problem, of course, and the chin, while not exactly easy, was handled by Avery turning himself around and pressing close to his grandfather's face, so that he could make those downward strokes just as he did on himself. When it came to the mustache, and the tricky area around his lips (which were parted and loose), Avery found himself cooing some kind of weird reassuring song, half comfort, half curses, as he navigated the folds of skin that hung there. It wasn't until he was finished, still kneeling on the bed, that he saw Winnie in the doorway. Avery froze—what was the look on her face? He still had his shoes on—did he get mud on the bedspread, or something? He nervously put the razor on the bedside table and followed her into the hall, and downstairs to the kitchen, where it looked liked she was camping out—it was the only lit room amid the dark, cold rest of the house.

"I didn't think to do that for him," she said, her back still to Avery. "I suppose the nurses have been shaving him when they do his bathing, but maybe someone forgot, this week."

"No big deal," Avery said, uneasy. "It's a guy thing. What's all this?"

Winnie laughed once, flat and mirthless. She saw what he was looking at—the piles and piles of insurance paperwork covering the small table, the two phones, two pairs of eyeglasses, a calculator, and a million yellow sticky notes. "My homework," she said. "This is what I get for opting out of math as a girl."

Avery craned his head, but the first column of numbers, so shockingly high, made him rear back. "Whoa. Do you need—I mean, want some help with all this?"

Winnie waved that off. Neither of them, he noticed, ever spoke about Jerry's will or whatever craziness he'd done to it before he got sick. It was as if all that had never happened, and maybe it hadn't, Avery realized. Maybe everyone—his mom, Winnie, Rachel—had just forgotten all about that, in the chaos of Jerry doing . . . whatever he was doing. (Dying. Was he?)

"Did you deposit the checks?"

"Uh—not yet. Sorry."

"But I thought you were opening this month or next! Didn't you tell him that?"

Well, last week he *had* told Jerry something along those lines, glossing over all the continuing Blue Apple screwups and the problems with vendors and the fact that Nona's leaving had thrown him into an utter tailspin so that he could barely bring himself to go to the restaurant, which was more or less rehabbed and ready to go. But he said a lot of things to Jerry, rambling on and on. You had to, when you were sitting next to someone blanked out in a vegetative state. Didn't she get that?

"What are you waiting for?" Winnie said, pressing it. "You know this is what he wants." Not *what he would have wanted*.

"Have you talked to my mom?" This had its desired effect.

Winnie immediately began fussing with a series of pill bottles, arranging them in height order, shortest to tallest. Avery noticed there was no food in sight.

"We're exchanging messages. And I speak to your stepfather, occasionally. I invite them to come and stay here whenever they want. I do, nearly every time!"

"She's probably not up for that, I'm guessing," Avery said. Winnie shrugged. "She called me," he went on. "She wants me to—"

But Avery couldn't say it. He rubbed his right thumb, red and abraded where he must have buzzed himself with Jerry's razor. *Talk sense into her*, his mother had begged. *He should die at home. I want him to come home. He's so far away, out there, and I'm—I'm*—then she had broken down.

"We should go, if you're going to make the four twenty," Winnie said. "Let me just tell the nurse." She went into the darkened hallway, calling back, "There's money for you on the table." Avery, as usual, left the fifteen dollars untouched. It was either sad or funny, the way she still kept trying to pay for his train tickets.

In sleepy Cobble Hill, it was past midnight. Avery stood and left Nona and Wendell, wandering back through the rest of the apartment. He had to see this kitchen—the "kitchen"—and went past empty tables, wiped clean. How was this all pulled off? What was the trick?

In the cramped galley kitchen, a tall, red-haired woman in black-and-white checked pants and a white jacket—splattered and stained—was squatting on her heels, loading a fridge with plastic containers. She looked up at him without much interest.

Avery scanned the scene, saw the small but well-chosen selection of pots and pans, the ancient range and oven, still giving off palpable heat, the hot-water attachment to the sink, the dishes drying in a rack. It was coming to him, even as the chef—for that was what she was—put a hand on her hip and gave him a *can-I-help-you* stare. "Did you cook . . . all that?" he said stupidly. "You cooked it. For real."

"Well, I didn't use a magic wand, that's for sure." The chef shut the fridge, gave a last wipe to the counter, and stuffed the rag into a garbage bag full of dirty linens. She had to nudge Avery aside to switch the lights off. His mind was whirling. This wasn't a game, it wasn't a performance at all, it was. . .

"What?" The chef laughed a little at his confusion, and pulled her hair out of its tight ponytail. "Did you think no license meant no sweat and tears?" She left, calling good-bye to Wendell. Avery followed her into the middle of the room, where Nona wasn't.

Wendell came up to him, handing him a card. "We'll be moving around for the next month or so. Things got a little dicey over the past week, so I'm scouting a better location. But just call anytime. You won't need the password. Just remind me that you know Nona, okay?" Wendell clapped a hand on Avery's shoulder and walked him to the door. "I usually get back to people in two days, with the time and location. Cool, man. Thanks for coming."

"Thanks," Avery said, still kind of dazed and now out in the hall. The card he held read *Dinners only. Invitation only. (718) 555-1223*

Wendell shut the door between them, calling "Don't tell your friends!" with a chuckle that suggested this joke was an old and favorite one.

Outside, Nona was sitting on the stoop. Avery came up behind her and sat down, putting one leg on either side of her and his chin on top of her head.

"You didn't tell me," he said accusingly.

"Tell you what?"

"That wasn't art."

"It wasn't?"

"I mean—that was real. One of those black-market places, right? I heard about those. I always wanted to check that out. But I didn't think—"

"What?"

Avery said nothing. What he hadn't thought was that you could do that kind of cooking, on the fly, off the books, no site or license, and have it all look so . . . normal. Normal like Wendell seemed normal, with his accountant hairstyle and friendly, regular-guy demeanor. He would have guessed anyone running that kind of operation—which was pretty ballsy, Avery thought—would be, well, more punk. But the chef looked like some woman with a job, like a tired mom . . . she looked a little like Winnie's daughter Rachel.

Nona, who had a way of reading his mind, said, "Do you think they know your grandfather? And Winnie, and her family?"

"Who?"

"That couple trying to make the train." She reached a hand back to smack him gently, for not listening, for not paying attention.

"They were from *Hartfield*?" Avery pulled his head up off her sweet-smelling hair.

Nona twisted around to eye him. Then she handed back a tiny piece of paper, crumpled into a ball, still warm from her fist. He unwrapped it and read what she had written with the pencil on the table:

1.   *I hate me, too.*

2.   *Is there any way to not be unbeautiful about this?*

3.   *Asshole, you're welcome!!!*

Avery pulled her face gently toward him and kissed her forehead, her left eye. He was an asshole. He kissed the side of her mouth, her cheek; he put his hands down her front and kissed her throat. "Thank you," he said. "Thank you for dinner," he whispered, kissing her ear softly, gently folding her ear forward so he could kiss the curve of the bone there. He fingered the dark blue tattoos that were speckled on her throat; he slid her sleeve up so he could follow them down her arm.

In front of them, late-night dog-walkers passed by in silence, and blue TV screens glowed in the first and second floors of the buildings across the way. The trees here were starting to bud, and their sweet smell hung in the night air. Avery kept kissing Nona. He would make love to her tonight, and he would *not* cry afterward. She was leaving; he loved her. He loved her, and she was leaving. At least for now, here on this stoop on Strong Place's tiny block, it was possible to hold those two things in his mind, when usually they bucked and fought each other until he thought he would go crazy. He held her in front of him on the steps and thought about restaurants with no names and people from Hartfield who ate at them, and about Gris and where she might be tonight, and what book he might read next, all while tree branches moved overhead, and the headlights of cars rolled slowly around the street corner and disappeared.

Twenty-two
WINNIE

It was May. There was still plenty of chill in the air, but it was the first day of May nonetheless. The pool was finished; it had been filled (Winnie had imagined a more complex process than her own garden hose, but apparently not) and was tamped down under a thick brown tarp. The bright blue-and-white hand-rail lined the ramp that led carefully down to the unseen water. There was still only dirt in the grounds surrounding the pale stone deck, but plantings could be put in as soon as it grew warm enough.

Winnie slowly walked around the circumference of her pool, stooping every once in a while to pick up an errant scrap of twine or plastic wrap. She stopped to listen; the Meyers twins were home now from the hospital, and every once in a while a baby's squalls reached her, even this far, blown on the wind from three doors down. Without the sycamore tree, she'd noticed that sound carried fast and clear across their corner of this Hartfield neighborhood, which made her wonder whether the Greenbergs or the Meyers ever heard her own choked weeping, which she tried to do outside whenever possible, away from Jerry's room, away from the nurses. But Winnie wasn't weeping now.

She thought about the new babies on their street. Rachel as a newborn had cried and cried, endless hours each evening, and Winnie—who had supposed herself, after Danny's easy babyhood, a fairly competent mother—was rattled, having deployed all her usual soothing and bouncing tricks to no avail. George had been working late then, almost every night, so Winnie was left alone with her sleeping son and her wild, thrashing, new daughter who arched her back and screamed when held, pausing only long enough for another deep, shuddering intake of breath. Winnie remembered how she simply gave up one evening, wrapping Rachel in a blanket and placing her next to her on the couch, crying still, while she herself read *Peyton Place*. Surprisingly enough, she managed to enjoy quite a bit of that trashy book. She would turn a page, and then reach over to pat her daughter. They each had their work to do, it seemed.

Nothing drastic happened to make it stop; there was no new trick she had found that soothed Rachel, and after a few weeks (weeks that lasted an eternity), the crying just phased itself out. It was time that took care of it, the way all the old-hand mothers and aunts had told her then. Winnie shook her head, there on the front lawn. Easy enough for her to say, now—for them to say, then. There were times she'd been in complete despair, walking a baby endless paces through the nighttime rooms. She should tell Rita Meyers this story, she thought, slip it in as a possibly unrelated anecdote, just in case it could help. She would bring some brownies over, later in the afternoon, and tell her about Rachel. Sometimes just a story can help.

Winnie squinted up at her house. She saw missing tiles high up on one of the gabled roofs, near a small, pipe-like chimney, and she saw a spreading stain like a shadow above one of the windows—a bathroom on the second floor, she thought, but couldn't be sure. She noticed windows from rooms that she and Jerry had never used. The house was more closed up than not, Winnie understood for the first time. After another long look around the spring-wet lawn and the covered pool, she walked briskly back to the side door, near the kitchen entrance.

It was now May. There was no pretending otherwise. Though Winnie had long ago stopped marking checks or stars in that old calendar book—because all the days were now the same—she had made her own mental deadline, a date that had now come.

Upstairs, she took off her damp shoes before going in to Jerry. He was in bed as usual, eyes closed and mouth covered by the mask connected to the breathing machine. The nurse looked up from his magazine when she came in, and slipped from the room when she gave a brief nod.

She only needed a moment, to do what needed to be done. Winnie crawled carefully into bed with Jerry and lay there with him, on her side, with her head on his same pillow. The creases of his skin fell in soft folds along his sunken cheeks. She slid a finger under the elastic band holding the mask to his mouth to touch his face gently. She picked up his heavy hand and laced her fingers through his unmoving ones. A puff of fresh air blew in above them, from the open window. Winnie could hear teenagers shouting as they shot skateboards down Franklin's steep hill.

She closed her eyes and breathed him in. She told him what she needed to, there on the bed, without any words at all.

In the hall, her eyes were dry. The nurse had a questioning, concerned look on his wide black face, but she ignored it and told him that she had set aside the Sunday crossword puzzle for him, as she'd noticed he enjoyed those.

Down in the kitchen, she dialed Annette's home number. Following the plan she and Rich had put together over the past few weeks, he answered right away. They spoke little—*I'll get her*, he said quietly.

"Yes?" Annette, suspicious, wary.

"I want to move Jerry back to Chicago. Back to you," Winnie said. It wasn't as hard as she'd thought, saying the words aloud, though they still made her heart pitch.

"What do you mean? What is this about?"

"Rich and I have discussed the particulars. There's a service for this—a medical jet, with everything he will need. And the doctors already know about it, so they can help arrange it all."

There was silence on the other end. Winnie put her hand flat on the kitchen table, clear for once of insurance paperwork, which she had finished organizing into folders, each neatly labeled, late last night. Everything was packed into clear plastic bins. They would go with Jerry.

"Dr. Rosen wants to wait until early next week. There is a little fluid near his lungs, but the new drugs should take care of that soon. And anyway, you'll need some time to get a room set up there. I can tell you about the bed to order, the other things you'll need." Still nothing from Annette. "Do you hear what I'm saying?" Winnie asked, letting loose a shot of impatience.

"I don't understand," Annette said finally. "Why? Why now? Has something happened?"

Winnie chose to answer the last question. "Nothing's happened. There's still no change in his catatonia, only that the longer it lasts . . ." She stopped, changed course. "They don't agree on how long he has. As I told you—or Rich, rather—one resident told me weeks—" Was that a muffled sob from Annette? Winnie went on. "But Dr. Rosen said it could be months, longer even. Maybe through the summer."

Summer. That word hurt. It kicked her hard, in the chest, in the stomach. Winnie put the phone in her lap and weathered the blow. She clamped down on thoughts of last summer, of those hot evenings here in the house, tiptoeing from room to room with Jerry's hand in hers. She wouldn't think about the pool that awaited him, outside in the lawn.

When she picked up the phone again, Annette was sputtering. "—finally come to your senses when he should have been here a long time ago, when he never should have—"

"I don't want to argue with you, Annette. He's coming home. What more do you want?"

There was a short pause. "Well, I could ask you the same thing. What more do *you* want?"

"What?"

"Is this some kind of strategy on your part, this sudden reversal? You're trying to throw me off balance—is that it? I know you're not pretending we're about to go to court—in fact, this should all be discussed through the lawyers."

Winnie looked at the ceiling and shook her head. She bit off the urge to hang up the phone. What stopped her: this was Jerry's own child, his only child. Nor did she point out the contradictions in Annette's behavior—after all, it hadn't been lawyers calling every few days for these many weeks; it had been Annette herself, alternately threatening and pleading. Sometimes Winnie tried to talk to her, but more often she just stood immobilized in the dark hallway, listening to the torrent of words unleashed into their answering machine. It occurred to Winnie that what drove Annette was a recognition of her own ugliness, this cruel lawsuit that had brought Jerry so much pain, and that the note of panic in the other woman's voice meant that she'd realized her own chance of making it up to him was fast slipping away. But that didn't make these rage-filled diatribes any easier to take.

Once, Bob had overheard. He was there at the house, taking out some storm screens, and after a minute or two of Annette's voice into the machine, Winnie lost it—she yanked the cord out of the wall, cutting off the sound altogether. There must have been anger in her face, because after a minute her son-in-law spoke. He said what he had to say quietly but straight out: "She has a right to want her father back, Winnie."

So those calls had done their work, after all; it had tunneled into her, all that pain and anguish. Not that she didn't have her own. But Winnie, alone with a failing husband, got to thinking about Harold Easton, about those long weeks in the hospital at the end of her father's life. She had been with him while he died, and as grim as the experience had been, she understood now in a way she couldn't have then, the natural order of things, a child burying her parent. Maybe it was more Annette's right than her own, to be with Jerry at the end.

Though it wasn't just Annette that had led Winnie here, to the decision to give him up. Annette may have been where it started, but Winnie had traveled a long way in these past weeks, while

Jerry lay still and silent, the only sound from his room a nurse's movement or the hum of his oxygen machine. With so much time, and so little to do, Winnie had spent most of it at his side, thinking about the life of the man she had known for such a short time. His whole life, that is. What did she know of it?

Images of Jerry as a young boy, scrapping with Frank and driving their mother to distraction—Winnie had devised most of these from a few stories he'd told. What had he been like as a schoolboy, as an army recruit, as a new father? She held up bits and pieces of his past, examined them minutely. The oxygen machine whispered; a nurse came in with fresh bedsheets. Sometimes, in those submerged hours, what little she knew would get mixed up with Winnie's own memories. She would doze off, smiling at the time Jerry, as a bachelor, misread the amount of soap flakes required, and flooded the laundry room with inches of foamy lather . . . only to wake up with a start—his IV fluids were being adjusted—and realize that it had been *George* who'd had that washing-machine mishap, in their own house, one weekend she'd been out of town, when the children were young.

It took time, but as winter shaded into early spring, Winnie was able to face without flinching how little she knew about the man she had married. Confined to this small upstairs room, Winnie's line of sight expanded. Her heart widened, painfully so at first, but she got used it. *Our marriage is like a station stop*, she thought once, resting her elbows on the bed and her forehead against his unmoving shoulder. An essential station stop, to be sure, and much loved—her eyes filled at this—but not the final destination, or the train itself, or a rail route's long stretch of miles.

There were things, though, about Jerry that Winnie knew and

no one else could: that the soft white tuft of hair in the middle of his chest was the exact size of her hand. That he regularly dreamed about a pregnant cocktail waitress he'd met once, in a North Carolina bar, the night before he'd shipped out to Korea. The tender, thorough way he kissed; the way he took a hot shower both before and after making love; his surprisingly small bare feet.

She knew this: one night, last fall, when he rose from her bed and got hit with such pain in his back that he couldn't help crying out, he had to sit down again. Eventually, Winnie had to help; it took many tries to get him upright again, unsteady and shaking, face pale.

"Son of a bitch," Jerry had said then, turning to where she was kneeling, naked and worried, on the bed. "But it's all worth it, looking at you."

For days, Winnie held them close: what she knew of Jerry, and what she didn't. What she had of him, what she never would. Something shifted inside her, and Winnie recognized what she could do, what she *wanted* to do: let Jerry go back to his daughter. Let him go.

After that, talking to Rich and making all the plans had been simple. She set her May 1 deadline; if there was still no change, she would tell Annette, and they would go through with it. It didn't hurt as much as she thought it would, either. After all, losing Jerry had already happened. She had suffered that, and it was done.

Very little of this could be explained, though, to Annette. And though she was about to hang up on the woman, what stopped Winnie was an image of Rachel. Brave, loyal, maddening Rachel. Stumbling through her own life and always still in Winnie's, always *there*. The person that Winnie would need to have by her side when her own death came. The thought of Rachel gave her a surge of energy, and an idea came to her.

"Actually, there is something I want," she said in response to Annette. "Not any part of Jerry's estate, though. And your son doesn't, either. He's a good boy—a man, I mean. Jerry never signed the paperwork to change his will. I think his lawyer knows that, but I'll make sure of it. He didn't mean to hurt you. He was just angry. Let that go, now, Annette."

Silence.

Winnie straightened her back. "I want this house. He bought it for us, you know he did. On this, I won't back down." She heard herself—she heard *Jerry*—and smiled a little.

"You don't mean you're actually proposing . . . to *trade* my father for that property?"

"Call it what you want. Those are the terms." Winnie considered her own words, this alien tone, and was grimly pleased. She felt light, free. She had a sudden understanding of business and its appeal—you drew a line in the sand and then waited. And what she was betting on was that the lawsuit over the house meant nothing to Annette anymore, now that Jerry was dying. Now that he was coming back to Chicago.

"I don't understand you at all, Mrs. McClelland."

"*Trevis*," Winnie corrected.

And when the pause that followed grew and lengthened, she knew she had won. No doubt Annette would argue and chastise and bluff. No doubt there would be fuss and bother with the lawyers, but at its heart Winnie knew that the deal being struck was sound and true, and she guessed that even Annette could see it, too. Several weeks ago, Ed Weller had described some paper victory claimed in that nonsense about Jerry's mental competence, and told her that the suit was all but worthless; the house was hers. Hers and Jerry's. In the throes of his decline, Winnie had hardly cared, but she did now. She would honor this house, the one they had lived in and loved in, and she would try her best to help Rachel, whose need and envy were real. They were real, these feelings of her daughter's. Winnie had pushed them to the side, had discounted them in her haste to be with Jerry, but she wouldn't do that anymore.

So she had won. She could hear it in Annette's voice as they moved on to the tiresome discussion of when and where. Suddenly weak, Winnie ended the call as soon as she could.

But then she just sat there at the kitchen table, unable to move to the stove to make tea, unable to go find a more comfortable place to sit or lie down. She was paralyzed by a host of buzzing, needling thoughts, and she felt the roar of a distant panic bearing down on her, alone. The square-sided glass saltshaker in front of her was nearly empty, and she closed her hand around it simply to have something to hold.

It took Winnie a moment to recognize the sound pinging in the front hall—it was the doorbell. She made herself get up and walk slowly through the halls to answer, to receive whatever delivery might have come. Her legs trembled; her body ached in a way that was strange and new, and Winnie lightly touched the walls as she passed them, looking for steadiness.

Vi Greenberg stood there in the doorway, in an oversized cotton sweater with big baggy pockets. She was gripping a glass casserole dish, and her mouth was set firmly. Not once had they spoken since that day last fall, before the tree was cut down. Every time Vi walked past or pulled in and out of her driveway, Winnie could tell that the other woman deliberately adjusted her gaze, pretending not to see her.

"Chicken a la king," Vi said, holding out the dish. "Reheat it at three hundred fifty degrees for an hour. Little less, maybe."

Winnie couldn't help herself: the tears began to come fast. This one act of neighborly kindness was going to undo her. Vi's pleasant but firm smile now wavered.

"I should have been over earlier," she admitted. "We've wanted to, but . . ."

Winnie took the casserole and tried to wipe at her wet face with the back of her other hand. For a long time, she had wondered what she might say to Vi, if given the chance—to all those who stood by while she put that pool in the ground.

"Carbonfund dot org," she said—it just came out. "I donate every month. You can offset your emissions—I looked up what the damage must be, the losses from that tree."

Vi's face was puzzled, but she waited for Winnie to continue.

"It doesn't change things," she said now to her neighbor, a woman near her own age, a grandmother so like herself. "I just wanted you to know—for a long time, I wanted to tell you—"

"Tell me what, Winifred?"

But now nothing came to mind. And the whole of it—Jerry upstairs, the sound of his breathing machine, and Annette's voice on the phone, and Vi here now, after all the shamefulness between them—overwhelmed her, and Winnie could do nothing other than stand weeping in the open doorway with her neighbor, and hold the food she'd been given.

Twenty-three
RACHEL

Vikram was going to be home—it was a Saturday, after all, this chilly first day of May—but he'd said he would stay out of the way. So the camera crew (one man, hardly a crew) followed Bob and the interviewer, a bobble-headed woman wearing more makeup than Hartfield usually saw on a weekend—Cherise was her name— around the driveway and into their open garage. Rachel trailed behind as Cherise pointed at where the car had been, that morning of the accident, and Bob nodded. Then they both bent down, hands on knees, to study the cement floor while the cameraman circled around them—as if pretending to be forensic experts on one of those TV shows, Rachel thought. Actually, she half hoped the two of them would spot a clue—a strand of Bob's hair, a speck of his blood—that would solve everything, all at once.

Melissa and Gwen Torres, from two doors down, were in and out of the Brigham's side entrance, walking past the camera activity many more times than was necessary, looking nonchalant. This Saturday was an off week for the diving team, but Lila had made such a horrified expression when Bob had explained what the local news team wanted to film, for a "miracle recovery" segment, amplified by writing success—a few shots of him at home, describing the accident—that Rachel had quickly granted permission for her to go over to a friend's house.

Her own job, as Rachel saw it, was to stand nearby and look appropriately grave as Bob described that day, and then warm and supportive in turn, when the discussion moved to his recovery. Cherise had said to dress "normally"—"like you would on any other Saturday at home." So Rachel was wearing jeans, but also a rust-colored jacket and shiny black flats. She hoped the jacket was echoing the fading red in her own hair, but it was too dressy, and even too warm, for the day. Melissa had finagled makeup from somewhere—she and Gwen were plastered with lip gloss and a heavy black eyeliner; Rachel shot her daughter a look when she noticed this, but Mel just shrugged and grinned, knowing she'd gotten away with it.

Rachel was still shaken by the conversation earlier today, when Cherise had arrived. Rachel had started to point out the difference between where Vikram lived and her family's side apartment, and that this was obviously just one of the setbacks they'd suffered since Bob had to take the year off from the firm. The cameraman was snapping digital images of the front of the house and squinting at them; Cherise was clipping a microphone to the front of her blouse, frowning.

"Doesn't matter," she said. "We just need a few shots here, and we'll be outside for all of it, probably."

"Right," Rachel said. "But . . . won't that be explained? By us, or you, I mean?" She had envisioned some kind of voice-over, sober and sympathetic.

"Not necessarily. The story is your husband and his recovery and his book. Local man has near-death experience, makes good."

"Well, I know. But—you'll be shooting us here," Rachel said, flustered, gesturing to the front of their home, Vikram's home. "Where it happened. And we don't live here anymore."

Cherise nodded affably. This was all beside the point. "The whole segment is ninety seconds," she said, fluttering her fingers. "We don't have time to get into all the details."

Now Bob was pointing to the back corner of the house where he had presumably used the ladder to clean the blocked gutter. Cherise followed with an intent expression, one she dropped instantly when the shot was over.

"I think we've got enough of the exteriors," she said, and the cameraman lowered his equipment.

Bob was still talking and gesturing. "Usually there are other witnesses, when someone has an accident like that. But if I hadn't known how badly I was hurt, if I was just walking around for several more minutes after it happened—putting the ladder away, or moving around in the yard—any one of our neighbors could have seen me, could have even stopped to talk to me, before I went inside and collapsed."

Cherise smiled, but her eyes were elsewhere.

"I don't know; that kind of bothers me," he went on. Bob was in khakis and a polo shirt; Rachel restrained the urge to fix his collar. "That someone could be so . . ." He trailed off, searching for the words, not noticing that Cherise and the cameraman had walked away. As Rachel watched him, the thought finished itself in her own head: *that someone could be so messed up on the inside and still look perfectly normal.*

Exactly. It was how she felt sometimes. Were they actually in sync? Rachel had gotten used to their being so at odds. But coming at it from opposite directions, maybe she and Bob would somehow arrive at the same place.

Cherise and the cameraman were conferring, close by the front door. Rachel saw Vikram's dark head pass by one of the upstairs windows. She thought of Winnie, wished she was here. Winnie would have promptly washed Melissa's face and found a better top for Rachel to change into. Maybe she would have sweet-talked her way into the interview, delighted by the attention. Maybe the minor excitement of this local news team—Rachel had seen passersby on Locust slow with curiosity when they saw the white W-NEF van in the driveway—would have lifted her mother's spirits, for just a few minutes, away from the slow unending sadness of Jerry and Greenham Avenue. He couldn't have much longer, Rachel thought, and maybe that was a blessing. Though certainly her mother couldn't admit that, wasn't able to face any part of it.

Cherise motioned them up the front steps. "We'll just do a few shots inside, maybe have you two moving around the kitchen."

Rachel was swept with outrage. "That's just—there's no—"

Bob shoved his hands into his pockets. "It's still our house, Ray."

"Everyone will see," she sputtered. "Everyone who watches this, will see us in our old house, and they'll say something about it."

"Say something to whom?"

"To each other! It'll look like a joke, the way we're just merrily pretending to cook an omelet or something, in our old kitchen!"

"You won't need to interview," Cherise called. "We'll do some silent shots of the two of you, so I can put some voice-over in later."

"No," Rachel said in a low voice. She and Bob stood together, set apart from the others, at the front door. Out on the front sidewalk, Melissa was watching them.

A sudden nausea trickled through Rachel. It hit her that it wasn't just their old wonderful kitchen that she was refusing, the idea of being there again, not for real, but to playact a happy home while Cherise eyed the furnishings and Vikram kept tactfully out of the way. It was having to enact her marriage in front of the camera, when she wasn't sure how to play her role anymore. Rachel watched herself and Bob in her head, as she knew it would appear on television—the shock of Bob's bald head and his white scar, his tentative smile, her own frozen, fake responses. No. She couldn't pretend, with him, in that kitchen, that nothing had changed since they had lived together in this part of the house.

His eyes met hers. They were warm, open. Was it only two weeks since that odd, lovely, embarrassing hour in 50 Greenham?

"Okay," Bob said so that only she could hear. "Okay."

What had he written in one of the last chapters? *Harder than the recovery, harder than the memory loss, is what it means to not know the answers to every question: how? And why?*

"We're never going to know," she said to him. "Are we? How it happened. We'll never get closer to it, and we'll never be able to find out."

He waited, but she said nothing more. "Are you okay with that?"

"I don't know," Rachel said. "Do I have to be?" They were almost whispering.

After a moment, Bob called "Let's do something else," to Cherise, keeping his eyes on Rachel.

Cherise began some kind of protest, some argument, but Bob just shook his head. "We're not up for the kitchen today. Got another idea?" His tone was mild but final. As they walked back down the stairs to the interviewer and cameraman, to their daughter and her friend, Rachel felt Bob put a hand on the back of her neck.

Twenty-four
AVERY

Time passed.

He'd read that phrase before and been annoyed—time *passed*? well, no shit, Sherlock—but now Avery got it. In the spring of Nona's leaving, in the twenty days since she had been gone, not much had happened at all. Time passed. He was back at the pita restaurant, no hard feelings with the manager, who just wanted someone who could fry falafel and prep the eighteen different toppings with no questions asked. He was back living with the friend-of-a-friend roommate, sleeping on a futon, in a one-bedroom on Twenty-third Street and Eighth Avenue. Grandad got worse and then better and then worse, in increments so small they hardly mattered, and when he was flown back to Chicago, Avery hadn't even gone out to Hartfield to say good-bye or watch it happen. He hadn't done it not because he couldn't manage the good-bye but because there was no need for a good-bye, not yet, anyway.

Avery was headed home, too.

There were two pork tenderloins baking away, sweating in their sage and applesauce. He had crusty rolls from Zabar's on the counter to slice, and a mustard-apple-horseradish sauce going on the stove. Avery checked the dial on the internal thermometer (his own)—yep, 350 on the dot—and marveled, once again, at the power and precision of this oven.

"God, I'm going to miss this kitchen," he muttered.

"It'll miss you too, no doubt."

Avery whirled around to see Winnie there behind him. Fuck. What was it about little old women, always so quiet and tiptoey? "Quit sneaking up on me. Jesus."

"Did you want any of these?" Winnie had a crazy-looking handkerchief tied on her head like Little Red Riding Hood, and she held out a bunch of ties. "I found them in a drawer. Whoops. Thought I'd packed up everything."

"Um—do you want me to take them?" Avery felt a little bad about that *I'll-miss-the-kitchen* comment. "Take them back to Chicago?"

"Would you wear them?"

"Probably not." Ties were not exactly his look. Jerry's wide old seventies-era ties especially.

Winnie stuffed them all into a plastic bag, and her lack of ceremony took Avery back. "He won't need them" is all she said.

He turned back to the bubbling applesauce and lowered the heat a touch. So, she was organizing and he was cooking. Standard modes of operation for both. But did Winnie feel as dead and empty inside? Avery wasn't going to ask anything about it. When that message had come from Rich, saying that Grandad was going home, his first thought was that some crazy legal victory had finally given his mom her way. But piece by piece, the story came out: how Winnie had arranged it, how she'd decided to let him die there, instead of here. *An incredible act of generosity*, Rich had called it. (No word yet from his mom.) Avery's point of view was mixed: Had Winnie really come to believe she should share Grandad? Had she discussed this with the old man, before he stopped understanding everything? What would he have thought—what would he have wanted? Although maybe, Avery saw, these last didn't matter anymore.

It's true that part of him wished Winnie had put up more of a fight—where was that old lady who took on the town over a tree in her yard?—but . . . whatever. Who was he to talk? Avery could barely muster the energy to get on the train to come out here, and he was hardly doltish enough to compare his loss to hers. In any case, he just couldn't go there. This was lunch and lunch only. He certainly wasn't going to do some big emotional recap, their glory days out here in Hartfield, that kind of thing.

Besides, she looked okay. Tired, and she wouldn't sit down, but okay. At least her friends were coming around now; a couple other little old ladies had been here earlier, but they hustled out as soon as he arrived from the train—he walked, carrying the groceries—smiling twinkly smiles and patting him on the arm. *God, I need some guy friends* is what he had thought, doing the chat thing with these short, wrinkled women.

"I have enough food for everyone," he'd protested to Winnie after they left. "Did I scare them off?"

She sorted mail, reading each piece of junk. "They want us to bond," she said absently.

Last night Avery had walked downtown to NYU and wandered in and out of dorms and class buildings that lined Washington Square Park until he found the right lecture hall. There he sat in the back and listened to speaker after speaker read in a monotone from pages they barely looked up from. He would have been hard-pressed to say what they were discussing, since the topics were obscured by sentences so thick and dense they might as well have been in German, for all Avery could understand. Or Chinese. Man, if this was the kind of shit college led to, he had to pat himself on the back for passing it up. Although the fact that everyone around him seemed to be paying attention, listening carefully to this nonsense put him on edge; he hated feeling that his lack of an education marked him out.

Thomas's presentation was just as garbled and boring as the others, though Avery tried, once or twice, to nod at what he imagined were especially good points. He felt a surge of goodwill for this thin middle-aged man who could be such a pisser. Thomas finished his paper with a flourish, and got slightly red-faced when the polite, scattered applause came. He smoothed his sparse hair down in a self-conscious gesture Avery had seen him perform a hundred times.

At the little wine-and-cheese social afterward, Avery waited until Thomas was free and then came up to him and stuck his hand out.

"Oh my God in heaven," Thomas said, with a bit more shocked surprise than Avery felt was really necessary. "What are *you* doing here?"

"I'm a regular at these things. Can't pass them up. Especially when the subject is—" He glanced at the brochure and read aloud. "'Image Theory, Image Culture: Re(Con)Textualizing the Image.'"

"Is that so."

"That's good shit. And yours was the best of the bunch. You wiped the stage with them, Tom."

"Don't call me Tom."

"Sorry. Dr. Friedelson."

Thomas scanned the crowd, and then popped a cherry tomato in his mouth. "You've heard from our fine Italian lady friend, then," he asked, nonchalant, looking down. The older gay man's carefully casual tone nearly broke Avery's heart. "We've been e-mailing. Apparently there's been quite a bit of rain, but that's to be expected, this time of the season."

"Yeah, well, I wouldn't know."

"Oh, it can be torrential. Hi! One second!" Thomas straightened up, his face bright again, ready to go on with his doctorly schmoozing.

"Listen, I just came by because . . . actually, I'm heading back to Chicago, next week sometime."

"You are?" Thomas scanned his face. "Just for a visit or—"

"No, for real."

"Because of—Nona? Does she know?"

Avery held his smile steady, with effort. "And so I just wanted to say—well. You know. Thanks, and everything. And take care," he added, but as an afterthought because, to his great amazement, Thomas put his arms around him and gave him a real and sudden hug. Avery felt himself hugging him back, and it wasn't nearly as weird as he would have thought it would be—this whole-body embrace of another dude (a *gay* dude, nonetheless)—right there in public, in the stuffy ground-floor conference room by the cheese-and-grapes table.

"This sucks," Thomas said, finally releasing him. He wiped his eyes with the tip of a napkin.

Avery agreed, not even sure what Thomas was referring to. "Yeah, it does," he said, his throat aching.

While the pork was resting on a cutting board, he cooked the apples down until they were a quivering gold mush. He took a couple of containers out of the fridge—peppery jicama slaw and a plain butter-lettuce salad—and set the table. On the counter, where she was ignoring it, was an envelope with three uncashed checks that Winnie had sent him, the last of the funds Jerry had meant for the restaurant. Avery pretended that her disapproval didn't bother him, and all in all, what did it matter, anyway. He was Zen, he was letting go, he was moving on; they both were.

The Blue Apple was now a diner again. Avery had sublet to a guy named Rashid who ran two other identical outfits in Brooklyn—one just under the Brooklyn Bridge and one in Carroll Gardens. They were each called Deli to Go, and when Avery watched that sign being nailed above the door, he thought about arguing the point—*there was nothing* deli *about hamburgers and french fries*—but didn't.

So what if when he told her about giving up on the Blue Apple, Winnie first argued and eventually just shook her head? So what if Rashid's egg sandwiches were rubbery and tasted like old grease? So what if no one back home—not his mother, not Rich, none of his no-longer friends that he wouldn't be calling, anyway—knew how close he had come to running his own restaurant? Out there, Jerry was the only one who cared, who knew, and by now he'd forgotten it all.

Avery stared at the kitchen table, now full of food. Somehow he had sliced the rolls and the tenderloins, topped the sandwiches with the apples, and plated the salads.

"I wish you hadn't gone to the trouble," Winnie said, at his shoulder. "Look at all this food."

"Trouble's my middle name. Ready to eat?"

They sat facing each other, neither hungry, each pretending to be interested in a huge pork sandwich on a hot summer day.

"Do you want me to, you know—call you with updates? About him?"

Winnie took a sip of water. She made a motion with her head, somewhere between a nod and a shake.

"Or I could put you guys on speakerphone. And leave the room, I mean. If you wanted."

Avery didn't know why she wasn't responding to any of this. He thought it was a nice idea.

"It's not about what I want anymore," Winnie said. "This is about your mother. And you," she said, although it seemed like an afterthought.

"But—you're going to come out for the—" He stopped himself, just in time. And took a big bite of his sandwich, to cover the word *funeral*.

"I don't know if I will or not," Winnie said evenly. "I don't think I'd be such a welcome presence. And anyway . . ."

"Okay."

"I don't expect you to understand. You're a young person, and—" She put her hand on the crook of Avery's arm. "Never mind. I hate to hear myself start to explain *what it's really like* to be old, as if I'm some sage elder, dispensing wisdom to all the grateful youngsters."

"That's me: grateful youngster."

"I'm not afraid of it, by the way," Winnie said. She looked more cheerful now, though she still wasn't eating. "Death. That's one thing I will say, one thing I wish my own grandparents had told me. The closer you get to it, the more natural it seems."

"Uh—okay. That's good, I guess?"

"I had a dream once, about dying. I dreamed I was burrowing into the warm dirt, like some kind of animal who lives underground. And my eyes were shut, and I was pushing deeper and deeper into the earth, wiggling myself into a place that was comfortable. It got darker and darker, and I knew that when I stopped, once I was wedged into the most comfortable position I could be in, everything would just . . . stop."

Avery put down his fork. "That's—kind of messed up."

"It was reassuring. I took it to mean that death was like sleep—which makes sense, of course. Anyway, I can't explain it, but it was natural; it seemed like the most natural thing you could do."

"Did you ever tell Grandad about that? What did he say?"

"No, I never did. I had that dream long before I met him. And it just never came up." Winnie smiled to herself. "We had other things to discuss."

Avery had other questions, but he kept them to himself. Did she think that Jerry's death would be like that, the warm earth, the falling asleep? Had she been afraid to watch him die? Is that why she gave him up to Annette? (He guessed this is what his mother thought—*Winnie couldn't hack it, when the chips were down*—but Avery knew enough about his mother to know that she had to think this way, because feeling grateful wasn't in her nature.) Or maybe it was just easier to contemplate your own death—more polite, in a way—than your failing husband's?

"What does Rachel think?" He took a mouthful of pork—a little on the dry side, but it couldn't be helped. No one sold fatty pork anymore.

"About—this? I don't know."

"You didn't tell her about that dream? How come?"

"Well, I guess it never came up. Rachel's hardly one to think deeply about these things. She'd laugh it off, most likely. Say I was being morbid."

"Yeah," Avery said, who thought that thinking or dreaming about death was the definition of morbid. "You guys aren't that close anyway, right?"

"What do you mean?" Winnie said. "We're closer than close! We live in the same one-square-mile town, don't we?"

"Well, yeah, but . . . never mind. It's cool." Now he wolfed down another half of the sandwich, wishing he had just stuck to the weather.

"Avery. What are you talking about?"

"Nothing! I don't know! I just said it. Forget it. It's just that—you know, the way everything got so weird with my mom, when you and Grandad got married . . . it just seemed like maybe that's what happened with you and Rachel, too. Or not." Christ. "Don't listen to me."

"That was completely different, your mother and—" Winnie twisted her napkin around and around a finger. "Rachel has gone through an incredible, difficult time, with Bob's accident and having to raise her daughters. She works hard, she has to manage a thousand things—"

"Sure, sure."

"And we talk all the time! We talk four times a day! She's probably on her way over here as we speak. Really, Avery," Winnie said, pushing her plate an inch away from her. "You're mistaken."

"Got it." It figured that without Nona around, every relationship would turn sour. It felt like trying to play the piano with oven mitts on. He'd rarely seen Winnie look this displeased, this upset. "So, listen to this. The other night I went out to a bar." A funny story. That's what they needed.

"What? You shouldn't be doing that."

"True, but a bar is the only place where this game is played. Trust me. Anyway, I figure, with my girlfriend run out on me"—he said this as quickly as possible, as if it were a necessary part of the joke setup—"I better get back in the action quick, before I lose practice. Anyway, I sat there, drinking flat ginger ale, on a Tuesday night, checking out all the girls." Winnie looked nonplussed—and why on earth had he started this story, which, Avery quickly realized, was as depressing in the telling as it had been in the bar.

"Um—there was baseball on, spring try-outs, so I'm watching something about the Mets. Anyway. Then this girl sat next to me, and we start talking." She had been everything Nona was not: tall, thin, young, blonde. Simple. About as interesting as the pre-season Mets.

"So, I'm working it, just a little—I've got moves, Winnie, don't doubt it." This was forced, but at least she gave a wan smile. "But just as things get going, I realized I've forgotten her name, or maybe I never even knew it in the first place—obviously it's a little late to ask because we've been hanging out for over an hour and . . ."

Avery stopped. He laced his fingers and put his hands on top of his head. This stupid story was making him sweat; he could see himself there, in all his misery, in that place on West Broadway. Why did it feel so disgusting? To make yourself go through with something when you knew your heart isn't into it. After a while, the no-name girl had put her palm on the inner part of his thigh, she had whispered something nasty in his ear, and then taken herself off to the bathroom in the back where, Avery understood, he was supposed to join her and lick a stripe of cocaine off her ass before all the usual bodily proceedings commenced. He'd paid for his two sodas and her many Jack-and-Cokes, and left the bar.

Winnie was looking at her hands; she didn't press him to finish the story, which was a relief. The food lay forgotten on the plates beside them.

"I keep promising myself I won't ask you something," she said. "Those times you and he met, in the office. Did he speak very much about . . . your grandmother?"

"About my—?" A faded mental image of his grandmother, harmless and soft and *old*. What did she have to do with anything?

"Beth Ann. Did he talk much about her? All those years he had with her."

Avery realized it then, in the sound of that name and the way it was spoken (*Beth Ann*—he'd hardly remembered that had been his grandmother's name), what was making Winnie so shy and ashamed. He forced his voice to sound hearty and authoritative.

"Nope. Never, really. Just in passing, I guess. Actually, who he mostly went on about was his brother, Frank."

Winnie flashed a little smile, grateful. She wouldn't push him, he knew, but it was the truth, anyway.

"You're being a fool," she said next.

"What?"

"You, Nona. This is not the same thing," she said. "These are not the same situation, yours and mine."

"I don't know what you're talking about."

"All this bearing up, all your brave let's-put-a-good-face-on-it. What are you thinking? Isn't that what they say, nowadays? Why are you so dense?" Winnie's voice had some real heat in it, and Avery was taken aback. In fact, he was pretty proud of his putting a good face on it. He felt like crap, he was lonely and sadder than he'd ever known it was possible to be, and yet here he was, out in the suburbs to cook lunch for some old lady you could argue he wasn't even *related* to. Why was he getting all this shit, then?

"You don't get it. She's away at this place, for a whole year."

"A whole *year*?" Winnie echoed, mimicking him in an unpleasant way. "So? Is it a nunnery? Is she kept under lock and key?"

"So, she's working on her singing, it's this really big deal . . ." Avery trailed off. It was exhausting, even saying this out loud, something so obvious it sounded fake and unsure.

"Did she tell you not to go there? Not to try?"

"It's not allowed—they don't let—"

"It's not *allowed*?" Winnie said, and Avery caught the faint glimmer of a laugh in her voice. "Are you now a person who has to be *allowed* to do something he wants to do?"

Man. It's not like he could explain it to her, the way Nona's face had looked—careful, uncertain—that one time he'd tried to make a real case for going with her. And you would have thought Winnie, as cool as she was, would be more clued in. It was a disappointment, this whole line from her, the way she was acting like there was some big romantic rescue in the works for him. Swoop into

Rome and just . . . what? Announce to Nona that what they had was different and better than either of them were admitting? Life wasn't like that—Winnie of all people should know, right? You had to be—yes, as lame as it sounded—a *grown-up* about things. Love ended. Or it didn't, but you had to suck it up, stagger through, do your thing even when you were a broken person inside.

He was about to respond—*it's more complicated than that, you don't understand, it's not like I could just*—when the door in the hall outside the kitchen opened and closed. Soon Rachel was there, loud and energetic and tripping over a chair. Bags were spilled; curses were let loose. She didn't act surprised to see Avery there in Winnie's kitchen, nor the two of them sitting quietly and close, all mournful and down. She fixed her attention, instead, on the lunch leftovers.

"Good God," Rachel said, picking up half of Winnie's sand-wich and biting into it. "Is this like a Cuban or something? I'm so hungry I'm about to pass out."

Twenty-five
RACHEL

The living room in Dina Sudler's house was packed. The main event was present unwrapping, and the spectators were just as involved as the young woman at the center, surrounded by boxes and discarded wads of brightly colored paper—they passed packages to her across the room, over heads and from hand to hand, pitching in with good-natured complaining, as if they had performed this ritual many times over, which they had. From bridal showers to baby showers to graduation parties to engagement parties, the guests at this Hartfield home embraced these two hours with a well-worn familiarity. Women in linen sundresses crowded four to a love seat; some perched on the arms of couches, a sandal dangling from a foot, and some squeezed together on the piano bench; others, like Rachel, stood in the doorway leading to the front hall, moving aside each time the caterer's girl passed by with another tray of food.

About half and half, Rachel thought, calculating the percentage of New and Old Hartfield in the room. Dina herself was Old Hartfield—her son Derek, just two years out of Northwestern, used to mow the Brighams' lawn for five dollars an hour—and she had orchestrated this June party for her soon-to-be daughter-in-law according to every unspoken rule in town. The invitations were handwritten and had arrived only a week ago. There were bowls of pretzels set out, and fruity drinks in small plastic cups. *From Our Home to Yours* had done the food, and it had been perfectly fine—chilled pasta salad, chicken salad, fruit salad, little lemon sandwich cookies—but for the first time she could remember, Rachel felt slightly dissatisfied with her lunch. She spooned herself portions of the different gelled salads, and oohed a little in anticipation, just like everyone did, but inwardly she found herself wondering what Avery might have cooked. Something brash and overspiced and completely inappropriate for this event. But still.

Many long-time friends of Dina's and neighbors Rachel knew were there too. Hand Me Down was closed for two weeks, the owner out of town. As a result, she and Bob were spending more time together than they had in a long while. They went to Lila's meets together, instead of rotating their parental attendance. Both of them cooked dinner one night (they were having Winnie regularly), and at Melissa's request the entire family had gone to see *Pirates of the Caribbean* at the local movie theater. In the dark, Bob's laughter rang out louder than anyone else's.

He was starting back at the firm in late August; by then, the book would most likely have sold (or so his agent told them) and as for after that—well, Rachel didn't love it, but she was willing to imagine that there was at least a partly different future in store.

"Writers still have day jobs," she pointed out to Bob, whenever he ventured too far into a vision of himself typing full-time. "They teach, or something. And what about John Grisham? He was a lawyer and a writer. It can be done."

"I doubt he does much practicing anymore. But I like the literary comparison—sales-wise, at least."

"I'm just saying, it's not like people just sit around and *write* all day long. They have to do something for money. Even when they've written books."

Bob had just grinned at her. Maybe he realized it too. They were talking about *how* he would fit writing into his life as a lawyer, not *whether*. "I can't believe it," he said, and for once he spoke so softly she could barely hear him. "I wrote my book."

Rachel craned her neck to see where her mother was; she couldn't find her amid the chattering flurry of women crowded in the room. Winnie had been placed in one of the most comfortable seats, an upholstered armchair near to Dina and the bride-to-be, as befitted one of the eldest guests. But she wasn't there now. *The restroom*, Rachel guessed, and then turned her attention back to the presents. Sure enough, soon the girl was opening an enormous box to discover not one, not two, but *three* heavy enameled pots, the pricey French kind that Rachel coveted, too—Gretchen Marra, who'd moved here less than two years ago, gave a little shrug in response to the group's squeal of delight.

"I myself can't get enough of these," she said. "They're so fun!"

New Hartfield, Rachel thought. Ostentatious, anonymous, over-the-top; wrapped by the store, ordered online, most likely. *I mean, really.* A four-hundred-dollar gift for Dina's son's wife? It was despicable. Maybe some women thought this kind of present upped the ante, but Rachel knew it was the opposite—bland, rich gifts like this only made people feel uncomfortable. She could see it in the way that Dina carefully stacked the pots on the floor beside her.

Soon enough, her own present was handed over. Rachel watched carefully, a tiny smile on her face. First, both Dina and the girl—*what was her name?*—exclaimed over the wrapping paper, a thick, lovely violet sheet she had purchased individually at Gramatan Stationer's for four dollars. Rachel led the room's laughter when her own wrapping job—messy, hasty—was revealed, tape everywhere, corners botched. Things quieted when the bride lifted out the gift: a thick, antique silver frame that soon garnered soft murmurs of approval from the women. Rachel waited, though.

"Oh," Dina gasped, and turned her shining eyes toward Rachel, across the room.

For inside the frame Rachel had placed an old photograph she found—after several hours in the crammed closets of her own apartment, and then a dusty sojourn back up to the attic in Vikram's part of the house. She had pulled the picture from one of her own albums, filled with Christmas shots of the girls in their fuzzy nightgowns and ecstatic summer photos of them at the pool, their skinny limbs golden brown. This one, the one she clearly remembered and had set out to find, was marked, "November snowstorm! 32 inches! 1986," on the back, in her own hand. It was of their front lawn, thickly crusted with snow up to a man's waist—or a boy's, for that was who was in the foreground, Dina's son Derek, sweaty and holding a shovel aloft triumphantly, gesturing to the wavery path he'd made from their driveway to the front door. He couldn't have been more than fourteen. Bob had taken the picture; you could see threads from his gray glove in the upper right-hand corner of the shot.

Dina pulled the frame away from her daughter-in-law and clutched it to her own chest. *Thank you*, she mouthed, and Rachel blew her a kiss.

After a few minutes, though, she slipped into the foyer and checked the bathroom under the stairs, but it was empty. In the kitchen, the caterers were loading small glass dishes into plastic crates; no Winnie. Rachel went halfway up the back stairs, calling, "Mom?" Nothing. She couldn't have gone home; Rachel had driven them both.

Outside, the air was thick with humidity. It was a wet, overcast day with oppressive heat, less like June than late August. Rachel wandered down the driveway and out to the street, where cars were parked up and down the sloping hill along the grassy lawns of Dina's neighbors. No one. She went back to the house, but just as she was about to go inside again, she caught a flash of Winnie's light blue jacket through the bushes that lined the backyard. She went up a short series of stone steps and pushed her way through the damp scratchy hedge.

"Mom?" Winnie was standing with her back to the house, in a corner of the lawn. She looked like she might be sneaking a cigarette, Rachel thought, her low heels sinking into the wet grass. "What's going on? I was about to send out a—" But her light tone died away when her mother turned, her face crumpled and red, streaked with tears.

"You didn't say anything," Winnie said in a low, flat voice. "No one has."

"Said something about what?"

"Do you think it's easy for me to come to a party like this?"

"I didn't know you—I thought you were in a good place, about your decision. About Jerry going back . . . there." Rachel had been about to say *home*.

"A good place?" Winnie said. She looked exhausted. "I never know what that means."

"You were fine last week, when we went out after Lila's meet. Wasn't that fun, all of us being together? And Theresa Mead says you stayed at coffee hour after church for nearly an hour, and that you were laughing. A lot."

"Last week wasn't my one-year wedding anniversary," Winnie said. She reached out to touch a tiny boxwood leaf, and then let her hand fall. "And yesterday was, and my husband's in a coma in another city, and . . ."

"Shit," Rachel said. She'd totally forgotten the date.

"Exactly."

"Mom—I'm sorry. I should have—"

"Oh, I know you're trying to help. Trying to be 'there for me.'" Winnie's sad voice put the quote marks around the expression, as if to emphasize its uselessness.

Rachel was stung. She thought she *was* there for her mother; it's nearly all she did or thought about since Jerry had left. It had been hard to understand Winnie's decision at first, although she well knew the constant barrage of pressure from Chicago; still, it was hard to accept backing down from Annette. Little by little, though, Rachel was coming to see it as not just giving, what her mother had done—Bob said it revealed Winnie's true strength of character—but as a gift to her own self. Until Jerry was gone, Rachel hadn't noticed the full extent of what caring for him had done to her mother, who became worn and fragile in a new way, despite all the nurses and Rachel's own constant help. It had aged her, Jerry's sudden decline. Of course it had; how could it not? Now the fear of what it might have done to her was lifted.

Wet blades of grass clung to Winnie's ankles.

Rachel's heart pounded. The way she had found her mother, here in the garden—that instant sensation of calm, with all the world aligned, as soon as she had spotted her: a barely knowable peace, one so utterly taken for granted. What would it be like, when that was taken away?

A burst of laughter came from the open windows of Dina's living room, across the lawn. "I guess I thought you wanted to keep busy. With us."

"You can't always cover up someone's pain with a lot of words," Winnie said, so quietly that Rachel could barely hear. A swarm of gnats rose from the bushes and swept above both their heads. "But we've gotten good at that, haven't we?"

Rachel didn't know what to say.

"Things are better now, at home. For you. I can tell."

"Bob's essentially back to full strength," Rachel said slowly. "They've dropped down his neuro checks to—"

"I'm not talking about the accident," Winnie said. And she came closer to Rachel, put a damp hand on her wrist, and looked up into her face. "I should have said something, when things were bad for you. When you were so unhappy. I don't know why I didn't. Sometimes I thought it would seem like meddling, but . . . I was also too preoccupied, I had Jerry and I just didn't want—"

"Oh." Rachel filled with a sweet kind of embarrassment, like a child whose mistakes are discovered, and quickly forgiven. "There's always so much going on . . ." she said.

"No. I kept quiet, when I should have asked you to tell me how you were. And I won't make that mistake again."

The party was breaking up. Rachel could hear the scraping of chairs on wood, the women's voices dispersing through the house. "It's okay," she whispered. "I'm okay."

"I know you are," Winnie said, and her voice had a thin cord of steel in it. Rachel heard a faint emphasis on the word *you*. A gnat buzzed, close to her ear. Her mother's light blue skirt was spotted with dampness from the wet leaves pressed against it, and her eyes were still wide and clear, watching Rachel carefully. It would be so easy to deflect this moment, to sketch out the awkward scene when Gretchen Marra's pots were opened, or see what Winnie made of Lynn Berberson's new hairdo. They would laugh, instead; they would link arms and walk back to the house together.

Rachel was about to speak, when something about her mother's face caught her eye. Something missing, that is. The spot along Winnie's jaw; it wasn't there. It was gone. It had faded away and she hadn't even noticed, until now.

Suddenly she thought, *We need to move*. Bob knew it too, she was sure. He must have been waiting for her. They would sell 144 Locust; they could give Vikram plenty of notice before putting it on the market, and—who knew?—maybe he'd even want to buy it. Rachel absorbed this thought, scanned herself for a familiar, accompanying pang of scorn, and found nothing.

Early one morning a few days ago, she had hurried out to the front when she heard Vikram leave the house.

"About the stove," she'd begun, hesitating. The estimate for repairing two broken burners was high, high enough that the serviceman had flatly told her to replace the whole stove instead.

"We're going to take care of that, I promise. Things are a little tight, at the moment." It hurt to say this out loud, but not as much as she would have guessed.

"Okay," Vikram had said, bouncing a set of keys on his palm. His hair was wet and there was a backpack slung over his suit.

"I can reduce the rent," she blurted, and instantly regretted this. "At least until we fix it."

But Vikram waved this off. "Actually," he said, leaning forward as if disclosing a secret, "I'm not much of a cook. More of a microwave man. So don't worry about it too much, all right?"

And then he'd jogged down the front steps, hurrying to make the 7:11. She stood there a little longer, in yoga pants and a T-shirt, in the humid early sun of the day. The way he'd made a joke, the trust in her to make things right—

Old Hartfield, Rachel had thought, watching Vikram go purposefully down Locust Street. Not possible, but somehow true.

They would sell the house, she told herself now, and look for something smaller. Maybe an apartment? There was that courtyard building on Clybourne . . .

It would not be "starting over." Rachel didn't know what to call it, but that didn't matter. Surely, Bob would have some catchy phrase. Or Melissa.

"Tell me," Rachel said to her mother, there in the corner of Dina Sudler's lawn, and let out the deep breath she hadn't known she was holding. "Tell me how you are."

Twenty-six
AVERY

Avery woke with a jolt, an hour into the flight. For a moment, he didn't know where he was and he held still as it slowly came back. It was a night flight; most passengers were either asleep or reading under yellow cones of light from the overhead panel. He raised the putty-colored window shade an inch or two—indigo swamp of clouds and wetness—and lowered it again. His shoulder ached (he was at least a foot taller than whoever they designed these crappy seats for), and his mouth was dry.

"Excuse me," he called to a passing flight attendant, but she didn't hear him and moved briskly up the aisle.

"You need to get out?" The man next to him asked. His wife was on the aisle, asleep with her head lolling forward, chin to chest.

"No," Avery said. "Just some water."

"You want a Coke? I brought it on for her, but she won't need it. It's taking up room here, anyway."

"But if she wakes up?"

The man smiled, his face thickly creased. He was short and

thick, and had one wandering eye. "No, she's good. She takes one of these little white pills and *zzvip*—she's out."

"Well—okay, thanks."

Avery drank the warm soda. It was sticky and sweet, but it cleared some of the fuzziness from his head. He tried to ignore his pounding heart; he told himself it was just air travel—no little white pills for him—but the truth was that he had never been scared of flying. So, why wasn't he happier? What was with these nerves? Where was the exultation in leaving New York, where was the soaring music meant to accompany this transition: the close of one part of his life, the beginning of another? This planeload of snoring seniors wasn't exactly the setting in which Avery had pictured himself making his big move, going through with a decision—the first true one, it felt like—that he'd made all on his own.

He pulled the books he'd brought out of the seat pocket and weighed them. Both were paperbacks, picked up at one of those sidewalk tables set up just outside NYU's hulking terra-cotta library. The books were slim, with torn covers and big print: Jim Kjelgaard novels, ones he had read and loved as a kid—*Big Red* and *Snow Dog*. Wooden stories about boys and dogs, and boys rescuing dogs, and dogs rescuing boys. Tests of courage and friendship. Avery flipped through and read a few pages, here and there. Yep. The writing was as bad as he'd guessed it would be, but he didn't care. The sight of the books themselves—at the NYU table, here on the plane—brought him back to childhood, when a new Jim Kjelgaard title was a reason for real happiness. And now he suddenly remembered a Halloween from years and years ago, when he had dressed as Danny, hero of *Big Red* (in overalls and black watch cap, carrying a stuffed dog that looked nothing like an Irish setter). No one at any of the trick-or-treat houses had known who he was supposed to be, which pissed him off, but Avery remembered something his mother said. She rarely got home from work in time for this most important night of the year, and once she had even forgotten to buy candy to hand out. Nor had she been any great shakes as a costume maker; she had to be badgered into finding the black cap, for example, and she had pinned a dorky sign on his front that read DANNY. But that night—a year or two after his father had left—she had said emphatically, "So what?" to interrupt Avery, who was whining that nobody knew the story of *Big Red*, anyway, and they should have found a rifle for him to carry.

"*You* know who you are, and that's the point."

Avery snorted, on the plane. That was probably the last time Annette had said anything worthy on its surface of motherly wisdom, and it figured that the remark came unintended, as a random aside on Halloween. Still, it came to mind.

He unrolled the magazine he'd brought too—Winnie had insisted he take a copy, since she had a whole box, so he'd just stuck it in his pack. Flipping past a lot of dry-looking articles, at first he even overlooked Bob's.

The first time I drove a car again, seventeen months after the accident, I got lost in my own town. The irony of my own wife's grandfather having founded tiny Hartfield's beloved train station stop, and therefore putting us *on the map*, so to speak, doesn't elude me—although I'm not sure I was aware of it that afternoon, sweating through my jacket, going around in desperate circles, peering through the windshield to read street signs that were obscured by tree branches.

Time was running out. My daughter was waiting for me, and this one simple thing—pick her up—was confounding me utterly. I found myself sobbing at a stoplight, unable to remember directions to and from a close friend's home, in the town in which I had lived for over twenty years. To find yourself unfamiliar in the world, unfamiliar *with* the world, is not a bad description of life after head trauma. At times, particularly when I dwell on all that's happened to me, I think it's not a bad description of life itself. But usually the sweet laughter of my girls can rouse me from such thoughts.

In the same way, it was one of my neighbors who rescued me, that first afternoon in the car: knocking gently on the window, having noticed my distress. She offered directions, said nothing about my tear-stained face, and pointed out that Hartfield's winding streets had confused plenty of residents in its time. Armed with her kindness, I found my way.

Avery stopped. He rolled up the magazine again and wedged it in the seat pocket. It wasn't that he didn't find Bob's story interesting, sort of—though for a busted-head essay, there sure was a lot of random musing about Life—it was just . . .

Well, he was done with all that. With those people, all of them. It's not like they were family, or anything. Without really noticing, Avery was bouncing his right leg up and down, fast.

"You from New York?" The man next to him said, eyeing Avery's leg in a way that suggested he wasn't *entirely* annoyed by the jittery motion, not yet.

"Hartfield." It just came out.

"Yeah? Is that upstate a ways? We're from Roslyn. On the Island."

"It's—yeah. On the New Haven line. You know Metro-North? Right. Anyway, that's the one you take." Avery hoped this would be sufficient. He had no idea where exactly Hartfield was, relative to the city, and he really didn't feel like getting into a whole backing-down discussion about it.

"This your first time going to Italy? My wife went once, back when she was in school, but I've never been. So it's kind of a birthday present, this trip. I'm turning sixty next year." The man shook his head slowly.

"No, I've never been," Avery said, pressing a hand down on his knee to stop its bouncing.

"You're not on the package deal, are you? Apple Travel?" The man pulled a sheaf of folded pages out of his thick paperback *Rome: A Traveler's Guide.* Through the yellow glow of their overhead light, Avery could see the shiny red apple logo, and the header, *Tour Itinerary.*

"No, I'm just . . . doing my own thing."

"Yeah." The man studied the pages. "They've got us on a pretty full program for eight days. Hope we don't miss the forest for the trees, you know?" He held out the jam-packed list of sightseeing trips.

Avery, who was all prepared to pass on browsing through some boring tourist pamphlet, caught sight of the restaurant listed first: *La Graviata.*

"Wait. They have you going to *this* place? On your first full night in Rome? Uh, no. Let me take a look at that." La Graviata was name-checked by nearly every foodie website as the most overpriced, overrated tourist trap in the city. Avery scanned the rest of the itinerary, and then handed it right back. "You don't want to go to these places. Here, give me your book."

"This?" The man held up his *Rome* paperback. He looked at the printed itinerary uncertainly. "I think we're gonna have to go with the group, since . . ."

"All right," Avery said, having found the right section in the tour guide. "You got a pen? Good. I'm going to make some marks here. And no, you don't always have to go with the group. You're in Rome, it's the best restaurant town in the world, and it's your sixtieth birthday. You call the shots. Right?"

"Right," the man echoed. "I call the shots."

"Okay, so if this is a can't-miss place, I'm going to put a star next to it. Do everything in your power to go. Seriously: beg, borrow, or steal. Forget the Coliseum, if you have to. And I'm not saying these are the expensive joints—most of the time, they're going to be pretty cheap. Now, if it's just somewhere really awesome, I'll put a checkmark, and you should get to those too, whenever possible." Avery bent his head over the book, whipping through the pages, looking for restaurant names he recognized or remembered, or for any descriptions that included the words *oxtail*, *grandmother* or *saltimbocca*. "Personally, I recommend skipping breakfast. You do that, you can probably fit in two lunches, and then a late dinner. Okay, when I put this—" He showed the man the squiggly blot he'd just marked. "It means stay away at all costs."

"I thought you said you'd never been," his seat companion said, but he was following Avery's notations intently.

"Trust me," Avery said. And the man just shrugged. *Why not?*

He bent his head to the travel book and fought the big dumb smile that was spreading across his whole face. Nona had no idea he was coming; no one did. He'd switched the ticket yesterday; nothing could have been easier. All the stupid, necessary phone calls—he wouldn't think of his mother's sputtering response when he never showed at O'Hare—would be made from Rome, sometime tomorrow. Or maybe he would just e-mail them, Mom and Rich, and Winnie too? Even better.

Avery had no idea what he was going to say to Nona. He had not an inkling of how she would receive him, or what her face would look like that first time they met. He didn't know if they would kiss right away, or not for a few hours. He didn't know if he'd be humiliated in front of all sorts of smirking Italian guys—he hoped not, but he was willing to take the risk. A phrase from Jerry came back to him—*always like your chances*—and Avery considered this. He did. Sure, he could picture being sent away in disgrace, a big scene, lots of gaping from locals. But he didn't think so. He liked his chances.

And so he worked his way diligently through the long list of Roman restaurants for this nameless man sitting to his left. They talked together quietly for a long time, there on the sleepy plane, and all the while Avery thought of the first moment he and Nona would sit together in a restaurant; he held it close, savoring something that hadn't even happened yet—that might not even happen. He didn't know where they would go or what they would say to each other. But he knew what to order—there would be *ciriola* and *murena fritta*; there would be *osso buco* and *semifreddo*. It would be laid out in front of them, the first dishes of this incredible meal, the aroma swirling around them, and the colors of the walls and

the wine, and he would wait just one moment—he promised himself, there on the plane—before beginning to eat. He would match
that sensation with this one, and see if there was something to be
learned.

And then, with Nona's hand in his, Avery would take that first
bite.

Twenty-seven
WINNIE

It was hard to sit still, even on such a hot day. The air in every room of 50 Greenham was thick and musty, but Winnie pretended not to notice. She moved from the living room upstairs to her bedroom, to get a drugstore magnifying glass, and then to the bathroom to study the tiny print on a prescription bottle of sleep pills (she hadn't argued when Dr. Markson suggested them), which reminded her that a set of sheets needed to be moved from washer to dryer, and so it was down to the laundry room, just off the kitchen near the back door. Along the way, she stopped to pick up a pile of unread magazines, forgot the sheets and went to get the recycle bin. In the garage, she glanced at the small but heavy box packed with all those leftover cans of green-label soup; the cabinet that had held them looked so strange and awful now, empty, that she went out of her way not to open it, even if she needed salt or tea or tuna fish.

Even from the den, where she now stood, Winnie could hear shrieks and splashes coming from the pool outside. She peered out the window but couldn't see anyone above the hedges that grew thick and tall, close to the house—only flickers of water catching sunlight, and the occasional glittering drops thrown up by the wild waves Lila and Melissa must be making. For a moment, she lingered in the echoes of their shouting. And then moved quickly away, farther into the house. Earlier, she had brought out cookies and sweet tea, but to sit idly by a pool was just more than anyone could ask of her; there was too much to do inside.

For example, she hadn't sorted these library books, on the table in the hall, in weeks. How on earth had she let that go? Winnie tried to remember which was due when—this new system, with one receipt-like printout, wasn't helpful at all. Why had they started that, when the cards in the individual pockets worked so well? She flipped through a biography of Zora Neale Hurston—now surely, she had read this, even if the details of the woman's life were slow to come back to her. The new Christopher Hitchens book would go back—she hadn't tried it but never understood his appeal, anyway. Then there was that Jhumpa Lahiri novel that someone's book club had loved, and so Winnie had checked it out, but now she worried that it was one of those two-week-only new-item loans. She carried the book over to the computer desk in the living room. You could do everything online now.

"EVERY MEAL I EAT CONTAINS SOME PART OF A PIG," read the subject line in Avery's e-mail, the one she had left up on the screen. He'd sent no message, just one photo of himself, wearing a spattered apron, grinning hugely next to a piece of meat hanging on a hook and giving the thumb's-up sign. Winnie studied the expression on her—what?—one-time step-grandson, avoiding the sight of that pig dangling next to him. Avery was mugging for the camera, goofing off, but she detected, she hoped, happiness there under the silly pose. He had mentioned nothing about Nona, but he wouldn't still be in Rome, almost three full weeks now, if things hadn't gone well. Would he?

Winnie slowly clicked shut the photo, and both Avery and his pig shrank away and disappeared.

He wouldn't be there, in Chicago, when Jerry died. A pang went through her at the thought of Jerry slipping away without either of them at his side. It could be anytime now, Rich had told her, the last time he phoned. They had brought in hospice care for these last few weeks. But he wasn't in any pain, Rich made a point of saying, twice. Jerry was comfortable; they were doing everything they could to ensure that. Winnie had said little in response to all of this. She thanked Rich for calling, though in part she wished he wouldn't, unless it was to tell her that it was all over.

"I know she's thankful for what you've done," he said, a bit uneasily, before hanging up. He didn't need to specify who or what.

"Wouldn't that be nice," Winnie had answered tartly.

"Mom?" It was Rachel, in the kitchen.

"Out here!" Winnie called. She took up a pair of reading glasses and peered at the screen. What had she—oh, yes. The library.

"What are you doing?"

"Trying to get caught up with everything," Winnie said, clicking through the various menus. She glanced over her shoulder at her daughter in a bathing suit, dripping wet, with a polka-dot beach towel wrapped around her waist. "How's the water?"

"Mom, why are you sitting alone in the gloom here? Come get some fresh air. And you should see Lila—she's really putting on a show."

"The air in here is perfectly fresh, thank you."

"You know what I mean. Come be with us."

"I'll be right out. You go ahead. I'll finish what I'm doing and then—"

"I don't mind waiting."

Winnie swiveled in her chair to look at Rachel, now perched on an arm of the love seat, shivering. Tiny rivulets of water ran off her bare legs onto the patterned carpet.

"That's ridiculous," Winnie said, exasperated, but Rachel only shrugged. She picked up one of the library books and riffled through its pages. Winnie understood that her bluff was being called. She studied her daughter, this tall, auburn-haired woman with such strength in her arms—it seemed Winnie had never noticed the muscles in Rachel's shoulders, her straight back, her long, solid legs. She had always favored her father that way, Winnie thought, watching Rachel pretend to read the collected letters of James Baker. Tall, just like George.

"Bob says he has a title, for the book. Ready for this?" When no answer came from Winnie, Rachel went on. "*My Commute: Head Trauma, Recovery, and Finding My Way Back*."

Winnie clicked through the menus on the library's home page.

"Can you believe it?" Rachel said, but her voice was warm. "I mean, I can barely *get* the man to commute. To his job. Anyway. At first I thought it was a reference to the train station, with your father and all that—but apparently it's *literary*. What do I know."

"Commute," Winnie echoed, eyes on the computer screen. The dictionary impulse was as ingrained as ever. "To change, or exchange. To give one thing in exchange for another."

There was silence. After a moment, Rachel spoke again. "Billie says no word yet, from the lawyers." She was referring to the Realtor who was working with both of them. "It's bogged down again."

The lawyers had at first cautiously agreed to allow Winnie to put the house on the market, and then changed their collective mind. There were ongoing issues in the courts to be dealt with, long-lasting repercussions from Annette's—and Jerry's—lawsuits. So far, Annette hadn't openly challenged Winnie's right to 50 Greenham, but things might change, as Ed Weller had put it delicately, "later."

"Well, looks like I win the steak dinner," Rachel said, flipping pages in *James Baker: A Life in Letters*. It had caused Hartfield no small amount of amusement that both Rachel's and Winnie's homes were up for sale this summer, and Friedland Realty was taking bets in the office, they'd heard. Rachel's reaction to all of it—50 Greenham for sale, not for sale, possibly Winnie's, possibly Annette's—had been strangely equable. Winnie waited. What Winnie had expected was a barrage of pressure, suggestions, and advice, but Rachel only continued to read, damply, on the couch.

"I probably shouldn't have done it," Winnie said, looking down at her hands on the keyboard.

"Done what?"

"Put that pool in. You were right, it'll make the house that much harder to sell."

"Maybe not," Rachel said. "People want different things—you never know. And it's beautiful out there, today, that's for sure. Come see."

Winnie smiled briefly at this attempt to make her feel better. But it couldn't work; everything about that pool reminded her of

Jerry, and of her own folly and willfulness; and of how lonely she was.

"I don't even own a swimsuit." Winnie had meant to say this lightly and was caught off guard by the way her voice shook.

"Mom," Rachel said.

"Just—" Winnie held up both hands, warning her away. "I need to be alone, all right?"

She stared at the blurry screen, unseeing. But by the time she turned around, different words half formed in her mouth, Rachel had gone, having left the book behind and wet patches on the couch cushions.

Damn. After a while, she stood and went upstairs. The door to what had been Jerry's room was closed, and she passed quickly, eyes averted. In her own room, Winnie wandered about, picking things up and putting them down. She started to run a bath, and then abruptly turned the faucet off. She took off her shoes and lay down on top of the bedspread, intending to rest, but rest wouldn't come; around and around, she heard the words she had spoken to Rachel, so harshly. The muted shouts and splashes of her grand-daughters bounced around the room. Winnie lay flat on her back, eyes open. There was the clock on the nightstand, an implacable tick. The walls in here were thick and soft, paint layered over paint, the ceiling moldings now blurry, almost indistinct.

She thought about the small, lovely party the week before; Rachel had organized it, to celebrate Bob's essay now running in *The Atlantic*. They had gathered in the back room of Mary's Café, only ten or so guests, plus Winnie and the girls of course. Every-one invited was cheerfully asked to pay for their own meal; about this, Rachel was lighthearted, practical. There was wine and tea sandwiches and a dense, dark chocolate cake with raspberry sauce. After much urging, Bob had stood to read a short section of his article; Winnie didn't remember which.

Her attention had wandered away from the words, and instead she watched her daughter, from across the table. Rachel's hair was down. It caught the light each time she moved her head, brushing her shoulders. She had an arm slung over the back of Lila's chair, and occasionally she would exchange a look with Melissa—*careful, don't spill that*—or reach up to twist her earring. But all the while she was listening, as Bob read. Winnie saw how her eyes flicked up to him at a certain line, and how she nodded, slowly, almost imperceptibly, as he described something.

Jerry's absence was a physical thing, a raw wound.

Dust motes spun in the air above the table. The guests were still and attentive, her granddaughters were close enough to reach out and touch, and Rachel's smile was slow and real, as Bob's voice filled the room.

Winnie sat up on the edge of her bed. She tied her shoelaces and went carefully downstairs. She held in her mind the image of Rachel that night, hair flowing around her shoulders, the ease about her. A sharp pain broke through when Winnie thought of the rich pleasures of a long marriage, and the inevitable bad patches—*we won't have that*, she thought, meaning Jerry. And then, after considering: *I've had that*. Meaning George.

By now she was at the front door, and when she pulled it open, the welcoming puff of warm air on her cheeks and throat really did surprise her with its freshness. The noise from the girls grew louder as Winnie went down the front steps, closer to the pool. They hadn't seen her yet, the four of them by the water. Rachel was sitting on the edge of a chaise, the towel still wrapped around her waist. She had her sunglasses on, so Winnie couldn't see what expression her face held. Next to her was Bob, in a swimsuit and baseball cap, with his hand on her curved back. Melissa floated in the water, slung over a plastic foam noodle. She was shouting instructions at Lila, who was standing still and straight, and beautiful, on the diving board. The impractical but regulation diving board that Winnie had had installed for just this reason, her diving-star granddaughter.

Winnie gripped the stair railing. Late afternoon sun ignited the water, nearly blinding her. Bob chimed in with a different request for Lila, and Melissa tried to overrule him. They argued over what dive she should perform, and all the while Lila waited patiently, a hand on one hip, her long hair twisted up into a smooth knot.

Past her was the low stone wall that bordered Greenham Avenue, and just past that the Realtor sign staked deep in the soil, a white plastic board that swung gently on two hooks. Across the street, on the corner, the Greenbergs' flat red Federal. As her gaze traveled past the front of the house, Winnie caught a glimpse of Vi through the picture window in the kitchen; her small gray head was bent to some task, although now she moved out of sight, called away. Down the hill that led away from Greenham, only the tops of the trees were visible, their highest branches waving back and forth. Past that, the fading blue of the summer sky, patchy with clouds. From where she stood, Winnie couldn't follow the streets that spread to the edge of Hartfield on the western side, the ones that traveled into Mount Morris, and from there to the highways, and the wide hills of the surrounding county.

She must have said something out loud, although her voice was rusty and hardly carried. Because now they turned to her, one by one, each face turned to her standing there above them on the stairs. Rachel took off her sunglasses and put them on top of her head. The water lapped and sparkled. Wind blew by softly, with a faint trace of chlorine. Her family waited, so Winnie cleared her throat and tried again.

"How about a reverse pike?" she called out, meeting Rachel's eyes. Lila smiled. "That one's my favorite."

Acknowledgments

Thank you to the amazing Alice Tasman, for encouragement and commitment and generosity and good humor. Many, many thanks to Claire Wachtel and Julia Novitch, for shepherding this novel with sharp insight and careful attention.

I was lucky to benefit from the support of the Ragdale Foundation and the Illinois Arts Council during the writing of this book. My friends and teachers at the Sewanee Writers' Conference offered inspiration and guidance; I especially thank Margot Livesey, whose incisive comments were invaluable.

Thank you to my Chicago writers' group, particularly Elizabeth Crane, Gina Frangello, and Thea Goodman, for fellowship and smart suggestions. Liam Callanan and Valerie Laken read early drafts and provided wise counsel and essential friendship. Thank you to Simon Canick, for helping me with elder law research, and to Peter Adams, for advice about the restaurant world; any remaining errors are mine alone. I learned about early American rail stations and agents from George H. Douglas's informative and engaging *All Aboard!: The Railroad in American Life* (Paragon House, NY: 1992).

Thank you to the wonderful Sandmeyer's Bookstore in Chicago, and also to Savories Coffee Shop, where much of this novel was written. I am hugely grateful for Caitlin Carlino, good friend to my family and babysitter *extraordinaire*.

For cheering me on, thank you to Lauryn Gouldin, Bonnie Gunzenhauser, Jenny Mercein, Caroline Hand Romita, and Julie Sanford. For believing in me, lots of gratitude to my much-loved family: Alan and Elizabeth Gray (to whom this novel is dedicated), Lowrey Gray Redmond, Jocelyn Gray, and Malcolm Gray.

Finally, to my daughters, Samantha and Wendy, and to my husband, Courtney: thank you. I love you.

About the author

About the book

Insights,
Interviews
& More . . .

Read on

A Reading Life

I NEVER WANTED TO BE A WRITER. Or what I think I mean is, for a long time I never felt the need to be a writer, despite the fact that books have always been the most important objects in my life, and even though it was clearly a lucky, magical job—to tell stories in words on paper—and anyone who could do it well was instantly a hero to me. Publishing my first novel is quite literally a dream come true, but for me this dream evolved in a roundabout way. I have arranged most of my life so that I could be near books, in one form or another, but I didn't need to have writing in my life because I had something else, something much greater. I had reading.

The public library in the center of our small New York suburb was hands-down my favorite thing about growing up there. The red-brick Georgian building was renowned for its graceful architecture and sumptuous furnishings, but I didn't care about any of that. For years I went two or three times a week, marching straight up the winding stairway to the Children's Room, where I considered myself to be on an informal, self-directed mission to read every book on the shelves. Every *interesting* book, I qualified. After each trip I brought home an armful of new discoveries (anything from Roald Dahl to Cynthia Voigt to Madeleine L'Engle), but always at least one of the wonderful Betsy-Tacy series by Maud Hart Lovelace. These well-worn books became such favorites

66 Publishing my first novel is quite literally a dream come true, but for me this dream evolved in a roundabout way. 99

that I could recognize my own library card number on the slips inside the back cover; the same digits were stamped there, over and over. It makes sense that when I decided to get a part-time job, at age thirteen or fourteen, I came directly to the library and asked to fill out an application. I was promptly hired.

It didn't last long. What were these *other* areas of the library, darker and less friendly than the bright, comfortable Children's Room? There was a lot more nonfiction than I had expected, and a weird numbering system to classify the different sections. Most of all, why was there so little time for me to do any actual reading? My conception of this job had been very clear: there would be long, quiet hours sitting behind a picturesque oak desk, with me absorbed in *Bridge to Terabithia*, occasionally looking up with a pleasant smile to stamp someone's book or point out the location of the restrooms. But apparently, part-time at the library—at least for a teenager with no prior work experience—entailed long hours of pushing a metal cart, reshelving book after book in the metal-shelved basement where the boring grown-up books were all kept.

The experience didn't discourage me from later working in our town's local bookstore, which I did over a summer and then a holiday break from college. Yes, there was plenty of reshelving involved, but I was prepared for that, happy about the increased proximity to fiction and my employee discount, which I put to good use. At work, when it was slow, I would walk up and down the ▶

> " At work, when it was slow, I would walk up and down the fiction section, ostensibly straightening or dusting, secretly planning out my next read. "

fiction section, ostensibly straightening or dusting, secretly planning out my next read: should it be Ann Beattie, Paul Auster, or Cormac McCarthy? I was relentlessly nosy about what other people bought, even though it was too often something from the self-help area or a business book. Still, when a customer brought to the counter a novel or collection of stories I didn't know or hadn't read, I made a mental note and immediately set out to fix that. My boss generously allowed me to take over at the register the afternoon that Don DeLillo came in to pick up some books he'd ordered. Nervous, star-struck, I concentrated on making the correct change and not saying anything stupid and fan-like (for example, that I knew *White Noise* was supposed to be his masterpiece but really I had loved *Great Jones Street* so much more). He paid, thanked me, and left; the whole exchange took less than two minutes. But what I most wanted to know, of course, was which books he had bought, and I hadn't even remembered to look!

After college, I went straight into book publishing as an editorial assistant at Ballantine Books, a division of Random House. In my interview, an editor asked me what I liked to read. By mistake, I began rattling off some recent college syllabus items: William Faulkner, Virginia Woolf, Flannery O'Connor. *Sure, okay*, he said. *But what are you reading right now?* I reached into my bag and

❝ When a customer brought to the counter a novel or collection of stories I didn't know or hadn't read, I made a mental note and immediately set out to fix that. **❞**

4

pulled out the newest Elmore Leonard. *Ah*, he said. We launched into a conversation about crime fiction, and later that day I learned I had the position.

Working in publishing was good for many things. It taught me to be able to clearly and succinctly assess, for myself and for other people, why a particular manuscript did or did not work. Every day, I was surrounded by people who were just as passionate about books; it was exciting to play a small part in the process of creating them. However, what do I remember most about my short time working in publishing? The free books. For all of us underpaid book-loving assistants, the unspoken rule was that anything left in a hallway was fair game. My cubicle overflowed with riches: Julian Barnes, Anne Tyler, Haruki Murakami, Alice Munro, John Updike, Jane Smiley. I became so expert at spotting the distinctive stylized Vintage Contemporaries logo that I could pick one out on a giveaway shelf at twenty paces.

When I left to go to graduate school, it wasn't so that I could eventually acquire a teaching career. I wasn't thinking much about a career at all, in fact. Waitressing was paying my rent, and getting a Ph.D. in English seemed entirely about reading as deeply and thoroughly as I could. And those were wonderful reading years. My official duties involved reading James Joyce and Shakespeare—and the relevant criticism—as closely and carefully as possible; but along with that, and not ▶

> **"**I was surrounded by people who were just as passionate about books; it was exciting to play a small part in the process of creating them.**"**

A Reading Life (*continued*)

for "credit," I was hurtling through as many Philip Roth, Charles Baxter, and Lorrie Moore books as I could find used copies at the Strand, Mercer Street Books, and Housing Works. It all went together; each genre enriched the other.

By the time I finished my degree, I had a husband and a newborn daughter. I also was aware that a tenure-track job in English lit wasn't the right path for me. I did love reading the classic works of critical theory, and I liked applying them as lenses in order to interpret literature; when I wrote academic articles in this line, I felt clever, like a puzzle-maker. But it was difficult, within this intricate, arcane form of reading, to just be in love with a book; doing so or saying so seemed a little embarrassing, beside the point. And I missed books themselves. There were plenty of texts and works and editions in academic study, but not as many *books* as one would have hoped. Plus, something else had taken hold during graduate school and afterward: the writing of stories of my own. They were small, they were secret, and I barely acknowledged their existence, even after a few were published in literary magazines.

It was hard to think of myself as a writer. To me, that meant someone who'd set out to be one from the start, single-minded. Writing and revising my stories during the rare moments my daughter napped . . . that didn't seem *real*, somehow. And I was scared, not just of the act of writing itself, which thrilled

> **66** Something else had taken hold during graduate school and afterward: the writing of stories of my own. They were small, they were secret, and I barely acknowledged their existence. **99**

and absorbed and humbled me daily (as it still does). I was scared to admit to myself that this was what I really wanted, to try to write the kind of fiction I loved—to throw my hat into the only ring that mattered. Wasn't it unseemly? A little late in the game? I would think about all those years I had spent around books—selling or reshelving them, editing or deconstructing them—and tell myself that it was just too late to suddenly decide to write one.

But perhaps I had been becoming a writer that whole time, without knowing it. I have never read a book because I thought it might help me with writing; reading is essential to my life, in and of itself. There is no timeline when it comes to art, no practical career path, not just one way to find one's life work. When I think about who I am as a writer, I often picture myself in my childhood's public library: curled up in a chair, completely oblivious to anything outside the covers of the book on my lap. There's a stack on the floor nearby, waiting. That girl wasn't reading because of a job or a career or even an art that would be in her future. She read for love. She still does. ❧

> "I was scared to admit to myself that this was what I really wanted, to try to write the kind of fiction I loved—to throw my hat into the only ring that mattered."

Eavesdropping

WHEN I THINK ABOUT the origin of *Commuters*, I can remember exactly where I was, and what I was doing, when the main story and each of the three characters—Winnie, Rachel, and Avery—appeared as an idea for a novel, all at once. It was mid-April in Chicago, and I was pushing my brand-new daughter around the block in her stroller. Again. We were both sleep-deprived; one of us was refusing to nap, and the other hadn't quite gotten the hang of motherhood yet. Although the crying and confusion could be overwhelming inside our apartment, I'd quickly learned that if we got outside and walked around the neighborhood, everyone's mood improved. On that particular afternoon, I was thinking about my grandmother since it was her birthday. I was missing her (she'd died several years before), and I wished more than anything I could watch her hold my daughter.

When I was about fifteen, I went with my mother to visit my grandmother (whom we called Mimi) in Atlanta. The big news for her was the upcoming wedding of a very close friend, whom I'll call Delia. Delia was in her late seventies, as was Mimi, as were the rest of their close-knit group of female friends. Every time we visited Atlanta, my sisters and brother and I were taken to the ballet or for hotdogs at the Varsity by one or another of these women, who loved us as if we were their own grandchildren. On this visit, I was fascinated by the plans that Delia was making to get married again to an elderly widower. My mother spent hours discussing the wedding with her mother, Mimi, as I hung around eavesdropping, hoping to hear more about this unusual event. What would it be like, I wondered, to get married at the end of your life? Wasn't that kind of sad, as well as happy? What did their families think about all this? What did they say to each other in private? Would Delia and this old man actually, you know . . . have sex? At fifteen, I could hardly picture marriage itself, but I could tell that there were complexities and undercurrents to Delia's wedding, apart from the excitement about the reception, and her dress, and—as my grandmother and her friends debated—whether or not she needed a new trousseau.

I knew not to ask these questions out loud. My grandmother was a Southern lady to her core, happily married for more than fifty years to my grandfather. She was a kind and gentle person who loved dancing and the Atlanta Braves. I adored her. But I wondered what it was like for Mimi, and her circle, with Delia so newly in love. Did it make these women confront their own lives, their longings and losses, how much time they had left and how best to spend it? I've always been curious about what runs underneath the surface of the way we speak to each other, the things that aren't said. There was genuine happiness, and delight, in the way Mimi and her friends celebrated Delia's upcoming marriage. There might have even been the occasional sly comment about sex, ▸

> 66 What would it be like, I wondered, to get married at the end of your life? Wasn't that kind of sad, as well as happy? 99

when they thought I wasn't listening. But what *else* there was, for Delia and her husband-to-be, and their families, and their friends: that's what I couldn't stop thinking about.

As the stroller bumped over the pavement and up and down curbs, my daughter was lulled to sleep. Now would be a good time for me to push her into our apartment and take a quick shower before she woke up and needed to be fed or changed. But I walked on, into the park near our building. An idea for a story had taken hold, about a woman who marries late in life and has to confront the negative implications of her happiness: disapproval from family, trouble with money. It wouldn't be about Delia exactly, since in truth I hadn't known her all that well. It would be my way of investigating a situation that had fascinated me since I was fifteen. Other essential characters—the older woman's struggling, sarcastic middle-aged daughter; her cocky new grandson— immediately came to mind. Even the structure, how I could interweave each character's perspective on the marriage, also became clear. Suddenly I realized, still strolling my sleeping baby, that what I was dreaming up wasn't a short story. It was a novel.

I didn't, however, wheel us immediately inside, sit down at my computer, and begin writing. In fact, I put this idea away for several more years, telling myself that it was too complex, too challenging, for a new

> **❝ I put this idea away for several more years, telling myself that it was too complex, too challenging, for a new writer—not to mention a new mother— to take on. ❞**

writer—not to mention a new mother—to take on. Maybe I wasn't ready. During that time, I wrote short stories and even attempted another novel, one that I deemed "easier" (maybe because it was less interesting to me?) and which was predictably a failure. All the while, my idea for *Commuters* held strong and steady—it continued to intrigue me, the way the story of my grandmother's friend Delia had when I was fifteen. By the time I began to work on it, I'd been dreaming about this book for several years; in the meantime, I'd started a new job, and had another daughter, and moved from one Chicago neighborhood to another.

During the time it took to write this novel, several things about it grew and changed over the course of several drafts and revisions. But the main characters, and the structure, and the heart of the story are all there as I imagined them on that April day when my daughter and I strolled on and on. Was that a gift from the writer's muse, who decided to take pity on a sleepless, frazzled new mother? Or was it the different perspective I had gained by having a child, and my new awareness of family relationships and the chain of generations? All I know is that I'm grateful for having had such a close friendship with my grandmother, which allowed me to see into her world and glimpse some of the intricate emotions of experiencing life as an elderly person. I hope she would recognize all the love and respect I had for her, and her friends, in the story I've told here. ⌁

> " By the time I began to work on it, I'd been dreaming about this book for several years. "

A Dozen Books I Love
(in no particular order)

Unless, by Carol Shields

I love this novel so much, and press it on so many people, that I've inadvertently given it to my sister for Christmas two years in a row. Written during the last years of Carol Shields's too-short life, *Unless* is about motherhood, and love, and feminism, and art. It's tough-minded and heart-piercing and funny. If you haven't read it yet, I envy you; run, don't walk.

Patrimony, by Philip Roth

Roth's memoir of his relationship with his father, who at eighty-six underwent brain surgery, is raw, emotional, and painfully comic. Reading it gave me new insights into the tender, devoted-son aspect of one of my favorite writers, without diminishing my admiration for Roth's unflinching portrayal of the brutalities of the aging human body.

Emma, by Jane Austen

I go back to *Emma*, again and again, in order to relive my favorite parts—Emma's picnic humiliation of Miss Bates, the moment she comprehends Knightley's love "with all the wonderful velocity of thought." So it was with delight that I realized, after finishing *Commuters*, that the name I had unconsciously chosen for my fictional small town—Hartfield—is the same as that of the Woodhouse estate in *Emma*. As a writer, I'm in awe of Jane Austen's psychological acuity, sparkling dialogue,

> " It was with delight that I realized, after finishing *Commuters*, that the name I had unconsciously chosen for my fictional small town—Hartfield—is the same as that of the Woodhouse estate in *Emma*. "

and intricate plotting; as a reader, I'm deeply grateful.

The Lay of the Land, by Richard Ford

This is a big, rich novel full of rewards: a wise-cracking narrator, moments of pitch-perfect everyday family strife and renewal, an ending that manages to be both surprising and necessary. But what I love most about *The Lay of the Land* is the unique way Richard Ford has his main character, Frank Bascombe, survey the terrain of the "Permanent Period" of his own life, with all its moments of grace, despair, common decency, and missed opportunities. It's an unforgettable inner monologue.

Digging to America, by Anne Tyler

Each time I read this funny and touching novel, about the intertwining of two different Baltimore families who adopt infants from Korea, I find myself thinking, *Exactly.* Anne Tyler just nails it, in practically every scene, whether she is writing about becoming a grandparent, or throwing a neighborhood party, or culture clashes between Iranians, Americans, and Iranian-Americans. If someone were to ask me what life is like in America today, I might hand them a copy of this book.

Phone Rings, by Stephen Dixon

By repeating the same event—the phone rings—over and over, within altered versions of what happens next, Stephen Dixon writes a completely original novel about the complex love between two adult brothers in New York City. I sometimes approach books or writers ▶

" If someone were to ask me what life is like in America today, I might hand them a copy of [*Digging to America,* by Anne Tyler]. "

known as "experimental" with both caution and skepticism, but if I hadn't read this novel, I would have missed out on a powerful, off-beat, warmly human story. And there is nothing experimental about how hard I cried while reading its final scenes.

Seek My Face, by John Updike

On a morning in January 2009, I was at my desk writing when my husband called. "I have some bad news," he said carefully, concerned for me; my hands went cold. "John Updike just died." After my initial relief—*thank God, no one we know*—and a laughing reprimand to my husband for scaring me, I was overcome by sadness. Here I choose *Seek My Face*, a sharply detailed novel about the life of postwar American artist Hope Chafetz, but I could just as easily name several other Updike books that I love as much; his work has been incredibly important to me. (In fact, it might have been easier to make this list itself into "A Dozen Updike Novels I Love.")

The Figure in the Carpet and Other Stories, by Henry James; edited by Frank Kermode

These are tales of artists that demonstrate James's utter devotion to the craft of fiction; in them, he explores the meaning of privacy versus fame, the agony of having only one lifetime in which to do one's best work, and the difference between the writer's inner world and his outer, public self. Many of them are set

> 66 Here I choose *Seek My Face* . . . but I could just as easily name several other Updike books that I love as much; his work has been incredibly important to me. 99

up as elaborate, ghost-story games in which we are led to guess what's real and what's not. Oddly enough, these intricate puzzles tell me more about Henry James and his world than some of his more straightforward works.

Charlotte's Web, by E. B. White

As a girl, I loved this sad, beautiful novel. As an adult, I was truly surprised to see how much I loved it still. The descriptions of how seasons change throughout a year on a farm, the cycle of birth and death within a community, the kinship between children and animals—all of this was renewed for me recently when my oldest daughter and I read *Charlotte's Web* together, savoring it, a few pages a night. Enjoying this story with her has been a highlight for me, in parenting as well as reading.

A Ship Made of Paper, by Scott Spencer

In a small upstate New York town, Daniel (who is white and in a relationship) falls in love with Iris (who is black and married); the repercussions of their affair are tragic, but somehow also hilarious and achingly true to real life. I love a novel where the characters make mistakes, screw up their lives, do stupid things that unintentionally hurt the people they care about . . . that is, act like the rest of us. And I love this novel, where sexual attraction explodes into daily life and changes everything. ▶

66 My oldest daughter and I read *Charlotte's Web* together, savoring it, a few pages a night. Enjoying this story with her has been a highlight for me, in parenting as well as reading. 99

A Dozen Books I Love (*continued*)

A Quiet Life, by Kenzaburo Oe; translated by Kunioki Yanagishita and William Wetherall

This book is a fascinating hybrid of fact and fiction, memoir and imagination. Kenzaburo Oe tells the story of a year in a Japanese family's life from the point of view of a daughter, Ma-chan, who is left in charge of her adult, mentally challenged older brother, nicknamed Eeyore, while their parents travel to America. Oe, who has written often about his own brain-damaged son, depicts family life as both fraught and affectionate; he has an unsparing view of the toll writing takes on his loved ones.

Swann's Way, by Marcel Proust; translated by Lydia Davis

It took several tries over a few years before I was able to make it all the way through the first volume of Proust's masterpiece. I think what made the difference when I succeeded was the involvement of Lydia Davis, whose short stories I adore. Finally, I came to understand what so many people already know—the singular genius of Proust when it comes to layering memory, experience, and perception. However, what I fell in love with in *Swann's Way* is the gradual portrayal of the narrator's family; each member of his household comes alive through the minute observation of habit, idiosyncrasy, and character trait. I can't wait to read the second volume. ❧